NOT SO TRULY YOURS

JULIA WOLF

This one goes out to all the grumpy girls.

CHAPTER ONE

Daisy

My smile was crooked. Undeniably lopsided. I pressed up on the downward side, forming an abomination of a grin more like baring teeth than an expression of happiness.

Dropping my hand, I blew out a breath. The back of my head connected with my headrest. Sitting in my car in a bar parking lot, dreading the thought of going inside when it used to be fun, I came to the conclusion I'd been spending too much time frowning. Not that I was a ray of sunshine on a normal basis, but my current situation had crossed a line even *I* wasn't comfortable with.

I sat up straight, thinking happy things.

Camping in the rain.

Beating my genius younger brother at *Final Jeopardy*.

Finally breaking in my new Docs and healing my mangled feet.

Creating the perfect icing rose.

Piping its twin right beside it.

German words like *Backpfeifengesicht* and *Kummerspeck*. Grief bacon was my way of life.

I checked my reflection again in the rearview mirror. The lazy side of my mouth had decided to come out to play. My smile was small but even. Hopefully in the face of making tips, I could dredge up a little more enthusiasm from deep in my stores. After all, it had been a month since I'd been to my second job at High Bar. Fortunately, I had history with the owner, Nick, so he was letting me come back after my sabbatical.

That was what I was calling the last month of doing nothing but what was absolutely necessary. It sounded a lot better than *"breaking up with the man I thought I'd marry and taking to my bed to reevaluate every decision that had led me here."*

Nodding to myself, I zipped my hoodie up to my chin and hopped out of my van, circling to the trunk. My method of packing everything I'd need tonight was an art form. As few bags as possible were involved since making more than one trip was out of the question.

Bags, tray, and box in hand, I breezed up to the entrance.

Duke, the bouncer, unfolded himself from his long-suffering wooden stool the second he laid eyes on me. Duke had once played professional football. I wasn't certain what position since I'd never understood the point of sports, but I had to assume he'd been the guy who tackled everyone. Duke was a big, big boy, the shape of a brick wall gone a little soft in the middle.

"Be still my fucking heart, Daisy's back," he boomed from his barrel chest.

"I'm back."

A grin swept across my face, and I instantly kicked myself. How had Duke not been on my list of happy things? Nice guy Duke who could crush skulls just by looking at them but would never hurt a fly. The protector of High Bar and unofficial mascot. Since I'd started my little business here last year, he'd become the highlight of my night.

He clapped me gently on the shoulder. "Things are looking up?"

"Sure." That dimmed my sunshine a smidge. Duke knew. Everyone probably knew. "How are tricks here? Do the rabble rousers keep you busy?"

He pressed his massive fist into his palm, eyeballing the group waiting their turn for entry. "They know better than to mess with me." Then he winked, just for me. "Get inside, girl."

"I will. Have a good night, Duke."

"Save a cupcake for me," he called.

I grinned as I pushed through the bar entrance. "You don't even have to ask."

This was what I'd missed while rotting on my mattress: the beginning of the night, when anything could still happen. Big tips or obnoxious drunks—who knew? Experience said it was most likely a whole heap of the second, but obnoxious drunks were more entertaining than my four walls.

I passed Bea on my way to the back. She stopped in her tracks, a tray of drinks held above her shoulder, one sardonic brow raised. As always, her pale blue victory rolls were on point, her nails were a perfect glossy red, and her attitude filled the room.

"Hey, Daze. I heard you died."

I gave her a nod since my hands were too full to wave. "The reports of my death have been greatly exaggerated."

"You're funny," she deadpanned. "Now, if you're over yourself, can you please get your cute ass in your costume and work the floor with me? People have been nagging me for your treats. I can't take it a second longer."

I glanced around the modern speakeasy. More tables were full than empty, and the bar was buzzing with customers. Two other waitresses weaved around the floor, but no one worked as hard as Bea.

"Stop talking to me and I'll get to it."

She managed to flip me off while holding her tray, and I let out a noise strongly resembling a laugh. It had been so long since I'd heard myself make that sound, I startled. Bea shot me a dirty look that wasn't quite joking, spurring me to get going.

I beelined it to the back and set my things on the table Nick had declared mine. It pleased me he hadn't found another use for my table in the month I'd been absent. Then again, my ingenious business idea brought him an extra stream of revenue without any effort, so it benefited him to keep my space available.

I rushed through setting up so Bea didn't kill me. Placing cupcakes and charcuterie cups on my tray, I made them look as orderly and appetizing as I could in as little time possible. Once done, I sprinted into the bathroom to whip off my hoodie and sweats and swipe a layer of crimson on my lips.

Despite my month of bed rotting and grief bacon, I didn't look half bad. Red lips and fishnets worked wonders. My little flippy skirt and platform heels didn't hurt either. Twisting back and forth, I studied myself in the mirror, recognition lighting in my belly.

This is me.

Duke might've been able to crush skulls, but I looked like I could stomp the hearts of unsuspecting men.

I couldn't—I *wouldn't*—but projecting that kind of attitude made me feel good.

Plopping the little pillbox hat on top of my head, I now looked like I belonged in Nick's speakeasy.

I scurried out of the back, stashed a box of cupcakes under the bar—easy access to refills was a necessity since my cupcakes sold the fastest—then slipped the strap that held my tray over my head and went to work.

I hoped the crowd was hungry tonight.

CHAPTER TWO

Miles

Tending bar was like riding a bike. My muscles remembered the movements, dodging the other bartender, shaking up cocktails, swiping credit cards with one hand, and tucking away a phone number with the other. I hadn't done this since college, but some things didn't change.

Sorta made me wistful, but not enough to go back to that era. I shouldn't have been here tonight. If not for a favor, I wouldn't have been. I had no problem finding trouble if I wanted to—bar or not.

I was mixing a drink when movement caught my eye. Lloyd was on the other end of the bar, so I knew it wasn't him without looking. Not that there was a chance of mistaking the small, brunette woman with a funny hat perched on the side of her head for my pale, bald, six-and-a-half-foot barkeep.

Before I could ask her why she was back here, she rushed away, leaving a pink box tucked beneath the lip of the bar.

Call me George, because I was a curious little guy. I finished up the drink I was making, then I was on it, flipping the lid to the box to check out the contents.

Tiny. Pretty. Cupcakes.

A few dozen, from the look of it.

Strange of her to stash them behind the bar, but okay. Maybe they were a treat Nick had delivered to Lloyd and me for holding down the fort in his absence. If she were a delivery girl, the funny hat made sense, I guessed. Though, she could have worked on her people skills.

Not a guy to let things go to waste, I picked a cupcake drizzled with caramel, peeled the paper, and popped the whole thing in my mouth.

Oh shit.

Baby Buddha on a bicycle.

I am now a convert to whatever religion these cupcakes belong to.

It had to be a fluke. There was no way all the cupcakes were as good.

I selected another, one with pink frosting and a sliver of strawberry on top. This one, I bit into, fucking delighted to find strawberry compote inside. I'd never considered myself a big fan of sweets, but in these cupcakes I trusted.

Unfortunately, I was pulled away by impatient customers and had to take a break. The good thing? Lloyd was unaware of the existence of the pink box so I could hoard them to myself for a while longer.

Or maybe forever.

I hadn't decided how big of a dick I wanted to be yet.

⋅•◆•⋅

The woman with the silly hat slipped behind the bar as I was pouring a beer with a thick, foamy head that was making my mouth water. Swallowing hard, I turned my attention to the small trespasser.

Her hat had this black netting that draped over her heavy, dark brown bangs, and she had a tray hanging from a velvet strap around her neck.

Interesting. Confusing, but definitely interesting.

She went straight for the pink box, sweeping open the lid. Had she dropped it off in the wrong place? In that case, the rightful recipient was going to be a few cupcakes shy of a full delivery.

"What the fuck?" she muttered.

I sidled closer as her head jerked up. Her eyes narrowed beneath her veil then quickly landed on me with a flare before dropping back to suspicious slits.

"Did you eat cupcakes from this box?"

For such a small person, she loaded a lot of threat into one question.

I crossed my arms over my chest. "I'm not normally a stickler for rules, but in this case, I'm going to have to be. If you need something, hang out on the other side of the bar, and I'll be more than happy to serve you."

Her red lips formed an *O* as she blinked at me. A girl who looked like she did, even in her funny hat, probably wasn't used to being put in her place. To be fair, if this were my bar, I'd let her fuck around back here all she wanted just because she was nice to look at and I liked her cupcakes. But this was Nick's place. Rules were rules unless he said otherwise.

"Where's Nick?" she asked.

"Not here tonight." I made a sweeping gesture. "Move a couple feet and park yourself on the opposite side of the bar and we can talk about whatever you need."

She rolled her eyes with a huff. "Okay, new guy. Obviously, you don't know how things work. Call Nick. He'll explain." Propping her tray on the bar, she started loading cupcakes onto half, next to cups with...meat in them?

"Excuse me. I don't have time to argue right now. I have cupcakes and charcuterie cups to sell."

"Sell?" I spluttered. "What makes you think you can come in here and sell cupcakes?"

"Call Nick and ask him." She didn't stop moving, efficiently filling her tray. My stomach protested with a growl as she emptied the box. "Or Lloyd or Bea or Duke."

"I'm asking you," I bit out more sharply than intended.

She had me on my back foot. My defenses were raised. I really didn't like the feeling of not being in on something everyone else was, and this woman, with her tray of treats, was not telling me what was going on.

Finally, her eyes raised to mine. "Nice power trip. Did they teach you that in bartending school?"

She made an about face and flounced away from me, her short, pleated leather skirt bouncing with each step. I swallowed hard again. Tearing my eyes from this brand of temptation wasn't as easy.

Stopping at the first table to flag her down, she plastered on a smile for a group of guys I could read as fake from here. They laughed at something she said, and she shimmied her shoulders to show off her goods.

That was when I got it.

She was like a cigarette girl from the old days, only instead of tobacco, her tray held treats. Nick, the fuck, hadn't told me about this addition to his business. I'd helped him open this place. We'd planned it from soups to nuts. And he'd never uttered a word about hiring a cigarette girl. I observed her flitting from table to table, selling her meat cups and cupcakes. Nick might've been onto something. I didn't know what she was charging, but customers were paying.

Fingers snapped in front of my face, bringing me back to the present—to the job I'd volunteered for and had been neglecting to watch a woman in a silly hat.

The surly, blue-haired waitress, Bea, was frowning at me. I'd noted she frowned at everyone, so I didn't take it personally.

"Wake up, Preppy. I have orders for you."

I got started on her orders while she tapped her long nails on the bar top.

Cocking my head, I said, "Preppy, huh?"

"If the deck shoe fits."

I almost got offended at the implication of having ever worn deck shoes, but then I remembered that time in the Hamptons. And sailing on Lake Cuomo in high school. And...yeah, there had been more instances. Several of them.

Bea snapped again. "My tips are dwindling every second I stand here while you wallow in your feels."

"I'm not wallowing." More like *ruminating*. "Hey, you know the girl with the cupcakes?"

"Yep."

"She's allowed to be here?"

"Yep."

"Nick didn't mention it."

"Nick's an asshole."

I slid the first round of drinks to her. She waited for the rest.

"You know he's my friend, right?"

She shrugged. "I've called him an asshole to his face. Why would I have a problem calling him one behind his back?"

"Fair point, I guess."

She lifted a finger, jabbing it toward me. "Leave Daisy alone."

"I would if I knew who Daisy was."

Bea didn't care to enlighten me. Grabbing the rest of her drinks, she loaded them onto her tray and marched away, leaving me with even more questions.

Duke was chasing out a few stragglers, and Lloyd and I were cleaning up the bar. The end of the night got me down. Seeing chairs stacked on tables and the lights on high brought a melancholy that was hard to shake.

"Excuse me."

I looked up from the glass I was polishing to find the cupcake girl holding a piece of paper out to me. Setting the glass down, I sauntered to her end of the bar and snagged it.

"What's this?"

"Your bill. By my count, you ate six of my cupcakes."

I rubbed my stomach, trying to think back to the exact number I'd consumed. "That can't be right. I ate three, maybe four."

"Six," she stated. "I keep track of my inventory."

"All right. I guess I'll have to take your word." I glanced at the total. "Nine dollars? For six cupcakes?"

She crossed her pale arms under her breasts, pushing her modest cleavage up and out.

"If you can't afford it, you shouldn't have eaten them."

I almost burst out laughing. There had never been a time in my life when I couldn't afford something I wanted. This probably explained a lot about the person I had grown into, but it wasn't like I could go back and yank the silver spoon out of my baby mouth.

Fortunately, I didn't act like a jackhole and kept my amusement to myself. I was working the bar as a favor for a friend. The rest of the employees were here because this was their job. And hell, nine dollars might've been too much for their budgets.

Taking my wallet out of my back pocket, I pulled out a twenty. "Here. Keep the change."

She grabbed the bill and tucked it in her bodice. "Thanks." Her mouth opened then closed before she said anything else.

I wasn't as smart. "You should charge more, you know. A buck fifty for a cupcake isn't enough."

Her chin shot out, defensive and proud. "They're mini."

"They're delicious. People would pay more."

"I know my business better than some random bartender." She re-folded her arms under her tits. "My charcuterie cups are eight-fifty. No one wants to deal with quarters, so they inevitably buy a cupcake to even out the cost."

"Hmmm. Smart, but have you thought about offering a discount for adding a cupcake to the meat cup while charging more individually? Two bucks a piece surely won't alienate your clientele."

I hadn't thought it possible, but her chin jutted out more, and it was cute as hell. "I'm good. Thanks for the unsolicited and unneeded advice."

"That didn't sound very sincere, and I kinda think you did need it. You're missing out on money in your pocket."

Her upper lip curled into a snarl. "There's a German word for people like you."

"Cool, it's German lesson time." I patted my chest. "Hit me with it."

"*Backpfeifengesicht.*"

I cocked my head. "I can't say I'm familiar with the term."

She shrugged. "I didn't expect you would be."

I laughed as she walked away again, her skirt bouncing with each step.

I Googled the term, using the best spelling I could manage, and laughed even harder. Dear fucking god, I was never telling my brother this. He would undoubtedly agree I indeed had a face badly in need of a fist.

CHAPTER THREE

Daisy

One night of de-rotting myself had done good things. I'd woken without an anvil on my chest, and climbing out of bed hadn't been the daunting task it had been for weeks.

When I returned to High Bar the next evening, I found myself looking for *him*. But not because I wanted to see him. No, avoidance was my main priority. He would not be seeing my new price list. We'd met once, and I didn't know his name, but I could already picture his smug expression.

Nope.

Wasn't happening.

He could take his good advice and handsome, punchable face and shove it.

The problem was, my mood had lifted so much, I'd gotten in early enough to bring my favorite people small boxes of cupcakes. I'd given Duke his on my way in and had received the bear hug to end all bear hugs.

Bea stopped in front of me, just like she had last night, giving a long once over. "Still not dead, I see."

"Alive, and so well, I made you your favorite Funfetti cupcakes." I dropped a small, pink box on her half-filled tray.

"Pffft. I don't like Funfetti," she grumbled, even though we both knew very well she did. "I guess I'll eat them anyway. Thanks."

"I won't tell anyone if you enjoy them."

Lloyd was behind the bar mixing a drink when I propped myself on a stool in front of him.

"Cupcakes for my cupcake," I said wryly.

His brow slowly lifted. "Red velvet?"

"Of course. Have I ever given you anything else?"

"Nope." He finished his drink and opened the box, his dark eyes lighting. "Someone might get the idea you're in love with me."

"Well, someone might be wrong." I poked my chest. "This thing is a raisin. All dried out and shriveled up."

"Raisins are still sweet," he countered.

I wrinkled my nose. "Devil's candy." Then I knocked on the bar top. "See you later, old man."

I wasn't a flirt. Had Lloyd not been one-hundred-percent gay and happily committed to Duke, I wouldn't have danced in that territory with him. But he was easy to tease since we both knew that was all it was. I was much more taciturn with people I wasn't certain about.

I swiveled away from Lloyd to go get my tray ready and stopped short. Standing at the end of the bar was the new guy. One brow winged, his arms crossed, he was watching me.

Stupidly punchable face.

This guy wasn't even my type, but looking at him made my cheeks burn. I had never seen anyone with such a symmetrical face. Thick, dark brows hovered over twinkling hazel eyes. His full, dusky lips were pursed into a mirthful smirk. His ebony hair was artfully disheveled, like he'd just rolled out of bed or a beautiful woman had shoved her fingers through it while he'd ravished her—

Nope, nope. Not thinking those thoughts about a guy I have no interest in.

He blocked the doorway to the back, thwarting my plan to ignore him.

"Hey." He rocked back on the heels of his scuffed leather boots.

"Hi." I nodded toward the door. "I need to get set up."

"Sure, sure. Quick question: did you charge them for those cupcakes?"

"No. Why would I?"

"You wouldn't, because they're your friends." His grin was bright. The pull of it raised his shoulders, giving his entire body a spring. He stuck his hand out. "I failed to introduce myself to you last night. I'm Miles."

Wary, but not rude, I slipped my hand in his. His palm was warm against mine, and he squeezed with the right amount of pressure—not too hard, but not so soft it was insulting.

"I'm Daisy."

His eyes widened. "Ah, so you're the Daisy I'm supposed to leave alone." He let go of my hand and scratched the back of his head. "I would have never guessed that was your name."

This was neither the first nor the hundredth time someone had said this to me.

"No? What would you have guessed?"

His brows drew together as he raked his eyes over me. I was still in my sweats, so there wasn't much to see, but he took his time.

"Lydia," he stated with all the assurance in the world.

"Lydia?" I let out a small laugh. "Why that name?"

"The all-black clothes, prickly temperament, bangs—Lydia suits you."

Something niggled in the back of my brain. A pop culture reference from my childhood. *Who* was Lydia? I couldn't figure it out. I had things I needed to be doing anyway.

"It might suit me, but it's not my name. Sorry to disappoint you, but I'm just Daisy."

He held both hands up and chuckled. "I'm not disappointed at all, Daisy. You surprised me, but I love surprises."

"That makes one of us." I nodded toward the door he was blocking. "Now that we've introduced ourselves, how about you let me by?"

"Sure. One sec." Reaching into his pocket, he pulled out a twenty. "I need some more cupcakes."

"Oh. Well...okay." I plucked the bill from his hand. Money was money, no matter who it was from, even the suspiciously cheerful new guy. *Miles.* "Any flavors you'd like?"

He stepped aside with a wide grin, giving me room to pass. "You know me, Daisy. I like surprises."

⸺◦⸺

The only time men blatantly flirted with me was when I was in my cigarette girl get-up. I'd chosen my outfit with the male gaze in mind, but men looking at my boobs and legs with desire remained disconcerting.

As long as all they did was look, though, I could deal—especially when that meant better tips and selling lots of treats.

Miles was hanging at my end of the bar when I returned for a refill of cupcakes.

"You're good at that." He leaned a hip against the bar, settling in to watch me.

Mid-reach into the pink box, I stopped and turned to him. "At lining up cupcakes?"

He chuckled. "No. Well…yeah, that too, but I was referring to you flirting your ass off. You're good at it."

"Why shouldn't I be?"

I'd just been thinking I wasn't used to the male attention I received at work. Miles was correct to be surprised by my switch in persona.

And I hated it.

He didn't know me well enough to be surprised. Then again, maybe he did. Maybe all it took was one look to surmise exactly the type of person I was.

He uncrossed his arms to hold up his hands. "I never said you shouldn't. I only complimented you on getting your flirt on. I bet you're making bank." His eyes flicked to my updated price list, and a wide grin spread across his face. I couldn't even say it was smug. He appeared delighted. "You took my advice, Daisy-daze. How's it working out?"

I resumed lining up cupcakes on my tray so he couldn't see the powerful blush blazing on my cheeks.

"So far, so good, actually," I muttered.

"You wish I'd been wrong so you could shove it in my face?"

"No." I glanced up at him and then back to my task. "I'm spiteful, but not so much I'd cut off my own nose to prove you wrong."

"Don't think that's how the phrase goes, but I get you. And you're welcome."

Huffing, I closed the lid and straightened my tray. "I'll thank you when my sales remain up for several days."

"I won't be here, so you'd better thank me now."

My brow knitted. "Are you quitting already?"

"I'm not a bartender in real life. I told you I was doing Nick a favor. Tonight's my last shift. If you want to thank me next week, you'll need to give me your phone number."

It was on the tip of my tongue to politely decline. I had a boyfriend and—wait, scratch that. How had I completely forgotten for five seconds I was no longer beholden to anyone? Andy and I had been over for a month. It was just hard to suddenly be single again after seven years.

"I'll think about it," I hedged, though I wouldn't think too hard. Miles was cute—a gross understatement, but I refused to acknowledge how breathtakingly handsome the man in front of me was—but I was in no place to enter into...anything.

"Don't think too hard."

The corner of my mouth hitched. A crooked smile. I wasn't worried about it. "Is that your life motto?"

"Wow, that hurt." He pressed the center of his chest. "Go back to flirting with strangers in exchange for money."

"You're awfully judgmental for someone who just asked for my number."

He winked, and dear god, it was charming instead of cheesy. Before this moment, I hadn't known that possible. "I can't say I won't also be flirting with strangers for money. The homes for the unhoused charity I'm donating my tips to need it."

"Very impressive," I deadpanned. "I'll be using my income to plant trees in the rainforest."

Before he could reply, Bea appeared from nowhere, slapping her tray on the bar. "I have orders, Preppy."

Miles' eyes slid over my face for a lingering moment, then he shook his head and gave Bea his full attention.

"Sock it to me, Bea."

As I walked away with my laden tray, I could have sworn I heard Bea telling Miles he needed to leave me alone.

CHAPTER FOUR

Miles

THERE WERE ONLY A few stragglers left when Daisy returned with a small pink box balanced on the palm of her hand.

I cocked my head, aiming for casual, but probably sorely missing the mark. "My cupcakes?"

She held them out to me. "Just for you."

Forget casual. I whipped that box out of her hand and flipped the top. Six pretty mini cupcakes awaited me.

"Oh, hell yes." I closed my eyes to choose the best one and ended up with a finger covered in frosting. Fuck it. My finger had just become a frosting conveyer. I stuck it in my mouth, groaning when the salted caramel hit my tongue. I'd eaten at a lot of fine dining restaurants with Michelin stars. Sampled rich, decadent pastries from renowned pâtisseries in Paris. It had all been good. Memorable. But nothing in those places had made my knees nearly buckle.

I stuffed the rest of the cupcake in my mouth, groaning the entire time I chewed. Granted, it wasn't long since it was tiny, but a prolonged groan was a prolonged groan.

"I feel like I should throw dollar bills at you."

I opened my eyes. Daisy was watching me, one brow disappearing beneath her bangs. In the seconds I'd been sucking on my own fingers like a hungry baby, I'd forgotten she was there and could see me.

"Feel free. Like I said, my favorite charity can use more tip money." I pointed at the five remaining cupcakes. "I'm going to save these for later—to eat in privacy. I've never had anything as good and need the freedom to groan pornographically."

Daisy's eyes were a little too big for her petite face, which made them striking. It didn't seem like they should've been able to narrow into such tiny slits, but there she went, proving me wrong.

"Don't make fun of me," she bit out, stomping her foot to punctuate her demand.

I jerked back at the harshness of her tone. "I'm not. I wouldn't. You already know I'll resort to theft to eat your cupcakes. Why would I make fun of you and dry up my source?"

She glared at me warily, chewing on her bottom lip. It was cute as hell. I didn't know if I had a type. If I did, it wasn't her, but I couldn't deny I'd spent the last two nights looking at her. If I were in a different place in my life, I might've flirted with her with intent. For now, it was just to get a rise out of her.

Stomping her tiny foot like an angry elf was too adorable to leave alone.

She huffed, her hands fisted at her hips. "I don't know how seriously to take you, and it's bothering me."

"Fifty-fifty," I suggested. "Right now, I'm dead serious. You're going to have to give me your phone number so I can buy more cupcakes from you in the future."

"You don't need my number. You can just ask me."

I shook my head. "Haven't you been listening to me, Daisy? I'm only here as a favor for Nick. Tonight's my last night. If I walk out the door now, you may never see me again."

Something flashed in her expression, and it was impossible to tell if it was relief or disappointment. My ego wanted it to be disappointment, but the realist in me assumed this girl couldn't wait to be done with me forever.

"Wait, really?" She blinked a few times. "I was beginning to get used to you. You're telling me I adjusted for no reason?"

I chuckled. "Sure, I guess that's what I'm telling you. Though, I gotta say, I failed to witness any major adjustments. You've been a prickly little pear both nights."

Shoulders straightening, she looked down her nose at me. Considering she was a solid foot shorter than me, I had no idea how, but she managed.

"And you've been annoying both nights, so I suppose we're even."

I stopped myself from laughing, my mouth hanging open in mock-offense. "I've been friendly, Daisy. You probably don't experience that often with the 'touch me and die, MF-er' vibe you give off, but that's all it is. Friendliness."

"Motherfucker," she muttered.

This time, my mouth really did fall open. What the hell? All I'd done was compliment her cupcakes and banter with her a little, and I get cussed out? *Jesus*. This girl needed—

Stepping closer to me, she pressed her finger to the underside of my chin, closing my mouth. "I never abbreviate my curses. If I'm going to call someone a motherfucker, I go all the way. In this case,

I *wasn't* calling you one—I don't know you well enough to cuss at you. Even if I did, that's not my curse of choice."

I removed her finger from my chin and gave it a squeeze. "That's good to know. You had me spiraling there for a minute."

She snorted a dry laugh. "There are several people I would like to tell off. You're not one of them."

I sensed the silent "yet" at the end of her sentence.

"It's a good thing I'm out of here then. I'd hate to get on your bad side." I shivered. "Seems scary. Probably entertaining, though. By the way, if provoked properly, how would you cuss me out? I'd like to picture it."

She rolled her eyes. "I bet you pulled girls' ponytails on the playground to get their attention, didn't you?"

I'd done worse. Much worse. But she didn't need to know my sordid backstory. If this was to be my last impression on her, I'd rather she remember me as the over-enthusiastic bartender than the guy who'd once decided to crush dreams and ruin years just because he'd wanted to.

So, I put on my best show, bouncing on my toes and grinning. "Come on. Ponytails are just hanging there, asking to be yanked. You can't tell me you've never ever been tempted to tug on one."

"I have—had two sisters. Of course I've pulled a ponytail or two." She pushed up the bottom of her short hair. "Fortunately, I'm no longer in danger of that happening to me."

"It's a good thing you have the face to pull off short hair."

Her eyes swept over me, pausing on mine before moving on. "It's a good thing you do too, though your ears stick out a little."

My hands flew to my ears, which, until this moment, had been perfectly average. "What? No, I—"

Her smile was like the first ray of light shining through a crack of storm clouds. Full and radiant, chances were, it would disappear as quickly as it had broken free. But those seconds had brought me to a standstill and knocked me in the gut.

"I'm kidding, Miles. Your ears are unremarkable in every way."

Plop. That radiant curve of her mouth flatlined, falling off into a puddle, death by drowning.

Dropping my hands from my ears, I dug my phone from my pocket. "Give me your number. I want to text you whenever my ego gets out of control so you can put me in my place."

She dragged her silly hat off her head and ran her fingers through her sleek, mahogany hair. The look she gave me was...pitying? Could I have been reading her right?

She licked her lips, her eyes darting to the side. "Look, I'm sorry if I came off as flirtatious, but I'm not dating right now."

I wasn't either, but I couldn't say her rejection didn't sting. I had been thinking, maybe in a few months or another life, I would have liked to take this girl to dinner and then make out with her grouchy little mouth.

"Whoa, whoa, slow down on the proposals. I'm only after your cupcakes and insults."

She did that magic eye-narrowing thing again. Whatever she saw must have helped her make a decision because she stuck her hand out. I placed my phone on her palm, and she tapped on the screen before giving it back to me. I wasted no time texting her then changing her name to "Lydia-Daisy-Cupcake."

"Now you have my number too. If you ever want to hang out, strictly as friends, I'm up for it." I stuffed my phone back in my pocket, surprised at how sincere I was. "If you happen to be handy,

I'm remodeling my house on the weekends and could use some help."

She palmed her forehead. "Oh my god, was this all some elaborate ruse for free labor?"

I nodded toward her delicate wrist. "Gotta tell you, if that were my goal, I'd aim slightly beefier, like Duke or Lloyd."

She tucked her hands behind her back, the force of her frown renewed. "Maybe you need someone who can fit in small places."

I tapped the side of my head. "I'll keep in mind you're willing to do that. There are definitely some crawl spaces you'd fit into. By any chance, are you scared of bugs?"

With a huff, she swiveled on her toes and marched into the back, leaving me smiling all by myself. I didn't mind, though. I had her number now. I could call her up for cupcakes anytime I wanted.

CHAPTER FIVE

Miles

"Idle hands are the devil's workshop." I was the poster child for the idiom. If I didn't have something constructive to keep me busy, I inevitably found myself making trouble or getting into it.

Since I had been working on turning my life around the last couple of years, I'd discovered I enjoyed working on houses in need of renovation. After two years of indecision, procrastination, and occasional work, I'd recently sold my first home.

So, yeah, while I enjoyed doing it, I wasn't any good at it. If I'd been out to flip houses to make a profit, I would have been bankrupt a while ago. Fortunately, I had the trust fund and big boy job that allowed me to think of buying and fixing up half-million-dollar houses as a hobby and the cushion to catch me if I screwed up.

After selling my last place, I immediately bought a new one, which was more aesthetically displeasing than I'd believed possible. But, as my realtor kept telling me, it had good bones. If it took me another two years to scrape away the layers of wallpaper covering those bones, I wouldn't be shocked...or disappointed.

Nick Garcia walked into my living room while I was doing just that. The layer I'd just uncovered had yellow rubber ducks printed on it. I wondered what the people who'd made the decision to not only purchase but painstakingly hang this wallpaper had been smoking.

And if they were willing to share.

Nope, nope. None of that, asshole.

I paused scraping to wipe the sweat from my forehead and look up at Nick. "Nice of you to knock."

He gestured toward the front door leaning beside the doorway. "I thought knocking would be superfluous, but I can go back and try again."

"For someone I just did a pretty fucking big favor for, you're being awfully sassy."

He bent down to pat me on the shoulder. "I appreciate you, man. That's why I swung by to see if I could lend a hand for a couple hours."

I didn't usually accept help. It defeated the purpose of the project. But I'd bitten off more than I could chew for the day. I was supposed to be sanding the front door—hence why it was off the frame—but my squirrel brain had decided it imperative to target the rubber ducks instead.

"You know how to sand?" I asked.

He cocked his head at the hand sander beside the door. "Yeah, I think I can figure it out."

"Cool. The goal is to go slow and get down to the wood."

He nodded. "I'll be careful." He rapped his knuckles on the door. "Solid piece."

"That's why I want to keep it. Just need it not to be orange."

He snorted a laugh. "I feel that."

Nick got to work with the sander, and I went back to scraping wallpaper, headphones on, music playing to drown out all the noise he was making.

I'd known Nick since high school. We'd been in the same friend group. I hadn't really stayed in contact with many people from school. In the ten years since graduation, I'd seen him here and there, but we hadn't been buddies who'd work on houses together, that was for sure.

Last year, after hearing about Peak Strategies, the business firm I'd opened with my friend, Saoirse Rossi, he'd gotten in touch and hired me to draw out a business plan for High Bar, from the logo down to his hours of operation. Spending that amount of time together had renewed something like a friendship.

Not high school level, but was anything ever as intense as it was when you were a teen about to burst into adulthood with fever dreams and an idealized vision for the future?

A couple hours passed quickly. Nick had gotten the paint off one side of the door and rehung it for me. Knowing myself, I would've forgotten to and woken up with wildlife roaming my living room.

To thank him for keeping me safe from raccoons and mountain lions, I ordered a pizza. We ate it on the back deck, looking over a fenced-in backyard that would be some family's dream one day. It was the one part of the house that didn't need to be stripped down and rebuilt. I just had to make the inside as nice to lure them in.

"Nice back here," Nick remarked.

"Yep. The primary selling point."

"Not the good bones?" He chuckled, tipping a bottle of water to his mouth.

"I have no vision when it comes to my own projects. I need something pretty to catch my eye. The deck and yard did that. I'm pretty sure my realtor would have claimed a cinder block prison had good bones if I'd seemed interested."

"Hey, cinder blocks are sturdy building material."

"I'll let you know next time I see a prison for sale on Zillow."

Reaching over, he backhanded my bicep. "Shut up, Aldrich, and tell me about my bar. How did everyone behave in my absence?"

I lifted a shoulder. "Not sure how they behave when you're there, but I didn't notice anything hinky." My brow crinkled. "Would have been good to be warned about the cupcake girl, though. I almost had her thrown out for hanging behind the bar, then she billed me for eating her cupcakes."

Nick burst out laughing, pressing his hands together beneath his chin. "I'm sorry, dude. I completely forgot Daisy was coming back this week or I would have told you to keep a lookout. You pissed her off?"

"Momentarily, then I paid the bill, making us square. But yeah, you told me to watch out for Bea's spikes but failed to mention the other prickly princess you employ."

"Daisy?" He shook his head. "She's nice to me. I don't know what you did to her."

"Did you hear the part about trying to throw her out of the bar?"

He ran his hand down his face, still grinning. "Man, I really should have warned you about her." He brought a slice of pizza to his mouth. "She's not my employee, though. The cupcake thing is her business. She's like a contractor."

"Huh." I grabbed another slice from the box sitting on the table between us. "Do you take a cut of her profits?"

"No, she pays me a flat fee. I don't ask for much. The customers like her vibe, and it fits with the speakeasy theme, so it's a win-win, for me having her there and her to rake in the dough."

"It's a good idea. Her cupcakes are the shit."

He swiped his mouth with a napkin and balled it in his fist. "They are. People go crazy over her charcuterie cups too. Nothing like sipping a whiskey and eating some nice cheese and cured meat."

I laughed at his tepid description. "Good thing you're not selling her meat cups. I think you'd drive customers away."

He gestured to the front of him. "I'm also not a cute girl in a skimpy outfit."

"Don't tell me you picked that out for her."

"You met her. Do you think she'd wear that if I'd told her to?"

I didn't even have to consider it. "Nope. She'd get Duke to shove your balls into your throat."

"Yep." He chuckled as he took another bite. "I should've asked—you do okay in the bar with the whole no drinking thing?"

My spine went rigid. I had next to no shame and would divulge my deepest secrets to a stranger without blinking, but this was one topic I wasn't comfortable discussing. The only reason Nick knew was because he'd noticed my lack of alcohol in the house a few months back—a massive change for me.

I'd told him I was taking a break from alcohol, which had been true, but I was banking on it being permanent. I needed it to be.

"I can't say my mouth didn't water for an ice-cold beer, but I was fine," I replied. "I distracted myself with cupcakes."

He gave me a sidelong glance. "You won't drop that, huh? You that into her cupcakes—or is it the girl?"

I shrugged. "The girl made an impression. I was thinking about texting her to acquire more of her treats."

Turning fully in his chair, he pinned me with a serious gaze. "Look, I'm going to give it to you straight. Daisy just got dicked over by her ex. They were together for six or seven years, and she's absolutely not over him. If he were to show up at her door tonight, she'd take him back in a heartbeat. That's not a girl you want to pursue right now, you get me?"

I thought back to the grouchy girl in the silly hat, picturing her with this new knowledge. Had she seemed sad? I hadn't met her before the breakup, so I had nothing to compare her to. Maybe she'd been a ray of sunshine before having her heart shattered. I couldn't imagine her like that. Being slightly mean suited her.

Not that I knew her.

Those cupcakes, though...

"I wasn't planning on it."

This was honest and true. But I also wasn't a guy who planned things, which was ironic since my business was making plans for other people. I guessed I was also the poster child for *"Do as I say, not as I do."*

Nick nodded. "Good. I know how you are with women. The last thing Daisy needs is to be used and discarded."

"I've never used anyone, dude. That's uncalled for."

He crushed his empty water bottle, returning his gaze to the yard. "I'm just saying, Daisy isn't like the girls you go for. She's the relationship type. A family girl. Maybe let this one go. Find your cupcakes elsewhere and leave her be."

Not long after that, Nick left. There hadn't been much to say once he'd accused me of using and discarding women. Well...I could've told him to fuck off, but that wouldn't have changed his opinion of me. Plus, it wasn't my style.

I'd agreed not to pursue her, but that was because I wasn't pursuing anyone right now. I hadn't, however, agreed not to text her for cupcakes. That was more than I could promise.

Returning to my living room, I got back to work. These fucking ducks were going down, even if they took me down with them.

CHAPTER SIX

Daisy

THE KNOCK ON MY door startled me. No one ever knocked. If my family was coming over, they'd text first then barge in when they arrived. It was how we rolled.

I peeked out the window beside my door, and Nick waved at me. *Huh.*

He'd never been to my place before. Well, not while I'd been living here. He'd probably hung here a lot when my oldest brother, Beau, lived here, but that had been years ago. Beau was married with a kid now, his days of living in the apartment above our parents' garage long gone.

"Nick." I leaned my shoulder against the half-open door. "What brings you here?"

"I was in the area. Thought I'd check in on you."

My natural instinct was to tell him I wasn't up for company. I hoarded my private time like a dragon with gold. But I had to go help my mother in half an hour. I could be hospitable when I had an escape hatch.

Stepping back, I opened the door wider. "Come in, but I have to warn you, I'm due next door soon."

His steps hesitated a beat before he closed the door behind him. "That's okay. I know you're not one for social calls."

"Nope." I poked my thumb toward the main house. "You want sweet tea and cookies, go see Whitney Mae next door. She'll even serve them on a cute tray and the glasses will have lemons printed on them."

He chuckled. "You think I forget the kind of treatment I always get from your mom? I still crave those little cookies with the raspberry jam in the middle."

"Thumbprint cookies are a Whitney Mae classic."

"Yes." He swiped his hands together. "If you get the chance, put in a good word for me and let her know I've been missing those things."

I shook my head. "Boys and their sugar."

"Yep." He zeroed in on my hair. "You cut it."

I touched the blunt edge that now ended at my jaw. "I did. I needed a change."

"Hmmm. It's different."

Before the breakup from hell, my hair had flowed to the center of my back. Andy had loved my hair. *I'd* loved my hair. About a week after ending things, I hadn't been able to stand it touching me. I'd cut it myself, and my mother had forced me to her salon to get it evened out.

Now, it was short. A "French bob," the stylist had called it. All I knew was I looked like a different person in the mirror, and that was what I'd needed.

"Different is good," I replied.

"It can be." He eyed my hair again. "You can always grow it back out."

"Yeah," I whispered.

He strolled around my tiny living room, which was also my kitchen and dining room. There wasn't much to see. Pale gray walls and crisp white trim. Two comfortable, worn brown leather couches—hand-me-downs from Beau. A couple stools at the narrow kitchen island. A desk with two monitors in lieu of a TV. When I was being a productive member of society, I spent most of my time doing freelance web design there.

"You've got a different aesthetic than Beau," he remarked. "No beer bottles lining the windowsills."

"I'm not much of a drinker, and clutter makes me twitchy." I perched on one of my two stools. "Plus, Beau had never rinsed out those bottles. I don't think you want to know what was living in them."

Nick shuddered. "I'll pass." He perched on the stool next to mine, his hands loose between his knees. "You're doing okay? After...you know..."

"You can mention his name. I won't fall apart."

He waved me off. "Personally, I'm cool with never saying his name again. I doubt we'll cross paths."

"Denver can be a small town like that."

The last few weeks, every time I'd left the house—which hadn't been often—I'd been on edge. High alert. Up until very recently, Andy and I had shared all the same haunts. We had the same habits, favorite coffee shop, grocery store. I didn't know where he was living or if he had a new favorite coffee shop. Thus, the knot in my stomach and feeling exposed whenever I was out.

"Right." He nodded. "So, things went well at the bar? You sold a lot?"

Releasing a sigh of relief, I nodded. "It was good to be back and doing things around other humans."

He snickered, and I wondered again why he was here. Nick was Beau's friend. They'd played in the same soccer league as kids and had remained friends, despite going to different schools. He was four years older, and I couldn't say we'd ever gotten close. Even when I worked at High Bar, I was always too busy to chat with him. If pressed, I would have called us acquaintances.

We had never been stop-in-and-check-on-you level friends. Nor tender looks and careful questions.

Nick plowed ahead like his presence here made sense. "I heard you met Miles."

"I did. You forgot to tell him about me."

He winced slightly. "Yeah, my bad. He told me he almost tossed you out."

I snorted. "It wasn't quite that dramatic, but he did eat a lot of my cupcakes."

"Heard that too." Nick tried to give me a long, meaningful look. I pretended not to notice and checked the time on my phone.

Shit.

I still had twenty minutes.

"Miles mentioned you exchanged numbers."

I shrugged. "He wants more cupcakes."

"Okay, maybe that's all he wants." Nick sighed, and it was loaded with sadness, which made no sense. What did he have to be sad about? "Look, Miles and I go way back, but as Beau's best friend, I feel obligated to tell you the kind of guy he is."

I started to tell him there was no need, that I probably wouldn't hear from him again since it had been days and he'd kept quiet, but Nick was on a roll, so I let him have the floor.

"First off, I don't know if he told you, but he's an Aldrich."

My mouth fell open before I could stop myself. Aldrich was a well-known name in this town. First, as the old-money family whose name was all over hospital wings and concert halls, but in the past decade, the oldest son, Weston Aldrich, had become the one everyone talked about. His outdoor apparel company, Andes, employed thousands of people all over the world. The US team wore Andes clothes in the Winter Olympics. Even *I* had an Andes coat hanging in my closet.

"Miles...is related to Weston Aldrich?" I squeaked.

"Weston is Miles' older brother. They're not close, but Miles still has the Aldrich family money at his fingertips. Kid drove a Porsche in high school."

I wrinkled my nose. "Gross."

He opened his hands on his knees. "Miles is all right now, but back in high school, he was a mean, angry kid. We were friends, but I didn't agree with how he treated others."

"What do you mean?"

"He was a prick and a bully. He picked on anyone he thought was beneath him if he thought it'd make people laugh. And it did, you know? The people who weren't being picked on thought he was the shit."

"Of course," I grumbled. "I bet they thought he was hilarious."

I was all too familiar with bullies. Just hearing about Miles was bringing back the shit I'd had to put up with in school. That was a long time ago, but those had been formative years. It wasn't something I'd forget.

"I just thought you should know." Nick patted my knee. "In case you were actually thinking about texting him, better have all the information now, right?"

"I wasn't going to text him." I puffed up my cheeks and slowly exhaled. I might've *replied* if he'd contacted me first, though. "Thanks for looking out for me."

He gave my knee a lingering squeeze and stood. "Of course. I'm always here for you, Daze. Don't forget it."

My stomach churned after Nick left. Picking up my phone, I stared at Miles' contact. My thumb hovered over it for less than a second before I pressed down and deleted it. I had absolutely no need for his number. It wasn't like I'd ever planned on contacting him anyway.

⟡

After throwing on a pair of black trousers and a matching button-down, I crossed the back courtyard to the main house.

The home I grew up in wasn't just mine. The basement and first floor made up the Dunham Family Funeral Home, while our family lived on the top floor. Whenever I told anyone that, they automatically thought of ghosts. They might've pretended it wasn't the first thought that popped into their heads, but it was.

Unfortunately, nothing supernatural had happened growing up above a funeral home. The dead stayed dead and didn't reveal any profound wisdom to me from beyond the veil. That would have been far more interesting.

Living above a funeral home was just...normal. It was all I knew.

I found my mother in one of the visiting rooms, bustling around. She always bustled. Her hands were busy, and her steps were short and swift, no matter what she was doing.

"Hey, Mama," I greeted as I entered.

"Afternoon, Daze." She stopped wiping a table for a moment and pointed to a stack of programs. "Can you lay those out for me?"

"Here and there?" I asked.

"Just like always," she chirped.

Like the lack of ghosts, Whitney Mae Dunham also threw new people for a loop. When they met me and heard where I'd grown up, they expected my mother to look like Morticia Addams. She was the exact opposite.

Alabama raised, a southern belle to her core, my mom had big, blonde curls and a smile that was bright and sincere. She favored skirts over pants, in somber, neutral tones at work and colorful, cheery prints in her off time.

She doted on her children and loved her husband something fierce. And she gave of herself to everyone who walked into our funeral home in the throes of horrible grief. For someone so small, she gave the most comforting, warm hugs, and she wasn't stingy with them. Anyone who needed and wanted one got one. I'd seen her cradle sobbing grown men and embrace stiff, broken widows. They always melted into her, and she held them steady.

She helped people through one of the darkest days of their lives, and once they left, most hoped to never see her again.

Yet, she remained bright and happy. Loving and unfailingly kind. I had no idea how she could be so open to people who disdained her existence once they no longer needed our services, but she didn't seem to have any trouble with it.

I, on the other hand, had slowly built a resentment toward people who used, took, and discarded. Most of them wealthy, like the Aldrichs.

My mother followed me, straightening the programs I'd laid out. I waited for her by the sliding doors leading to the lobby.

"This is the last viewing today?" I asked.

"Yes. We had one this morning too, but it was small. We're expecting quite a crowd for this one."

"Who died?"

"His name is Frank. He was on the board for Rossi Motors and ran several businesses in town." She clucked her tongue. "The poor man was only fifty-eight. Much too young."

My mother probably knew a lot more about him than that. She always memorized the details of those who passed through here. It was part of what made her so good at this job.

We finished in the visiting room, and I trailed after her to her office. I wasn't an official employee, but I helped out when asked. My mother didn't ask nearly as often as she should have. She had this idea I needed time and freedom to pursue my goals—which had nothing to do with running a funeral home.

"All right, now that we've got everything ready to go, let's chat." She settled in the chair beside mine. "Tell me what you've accomplished this week."

"I got out of bed every single day."

She clapped. "Good job, babe. Your skin is glowin', so I suspect you got some sun."

"I went for a hike yesterday."

"Brilliant. My baby girl is doing this thing." Her eyes twinkled with pride. All I had to do was get some sunshine and drag my corpse out of bed to make my mama proud. "Now that you have more time on your hands not carryin' that albatross around with you anymore, have you made any inroads on your business plans?"

My mother had loved Andy—or so I'd thought—but as soon as we broke up, she'd begun to refer to him as "that albatross." Whatever her feelings had been, if any, were long gone, and she seemed pleased he was too.

"I hate to let you down, but I haven't done anything. I've thought about it, but I've been frantically trying to catch up with work I'd set aside last month and truly haven't had the time."

She nodded. "Sure, babe. That excuse works this month. What's it going to be next month?"

My brows dropped. It wasn't like her to be so...blunt. That was my thing. "Is this what they call tough love?"

She tilted her head and tapped her cheek. "You know, I think it is. You've had this business idea for a long time, and it's just wasting away. What's stoppin' you now that your primary naysayer is out of the picture?"

"Don't mince your words, Mama."

She rolled her eyes. "I bit my tongue for a long time because you loved that boy and I love you, but I don't have to do that anymore. He held you back from living as big as you deserve. Now, you get to do what you want. Start your business. There's no reason not to."

I threw my hands out. "This is bigger than a little web design or what I do at Nick's. I don't even know where to start. I'm assuming I need a commercial kitchen, but maybe I don't. And that's just the logistics. There's also all the marketing material, the graphics, making contacts...I have no idea what the first step is."

One of her dark blonde brows winged. "That sounds like a pile of excuses."

"It might be, but it's also the truth."

Shuffling came from outside the open office door. A moment later, two women dressed in black appeared. My mother popped out of her seat, her professional mask on in an instant.

"Mrs. Goldman, I'm sorry I wasn't out front to greet you." My mother clasped hands with the woman who couldn't have been older than thirty, her eyes red-rimmed and glassy. This must have been Frank Goldman's daughter.

The woman's chin quivered, but she waved my mother's concerns away. "No, it's not a problem. We're early. And please, call me Shira. Mrs. Goldman makes me sound like my mother-in-law." Her sad eyes fell on me. "I'm sorry. We heard voices in here and—"

The other woman placed her hand on Shira's shoulder. She wore a no-nonsense suit, and her hair was cut into a shoulder-length bob with edges as sharp as glass. "To be blunt, we were eavesdropping."

My mom let out a soft giggle. "Well, it's a good thing we weren't discussing state secrets. This is my daughter, Daisy."

I stood, giving them both a solemn wave. I'd learned long ago never to say "nice to meet you" to someone here for a funeral. There was nothing nice about being here for them.

"Is there anything I can get for you?" I asked.

The no-nonsense woman spoke first. "Actually, we were thinking there's something we could do for you." She pressed her hand to her chest. "I'm Clara Rossi, by the way. My sister-in-law, Saoirse, owns a business strategy firm. She does exactly what you need."

I blinked at this woman I'd never seen before but whose last name I immediately recognized. Rossi Motors was the largest manufacturer of motorcycles in the United States. There was no doubt Clara Rossi was part of that dynasty.

At my obvious confusion, Shira softly clarified. "What Clara means is, Saoirse and her partner help new businesses form plans from scratch. Everything you said you need, they will either do for you or find the answers."

"Oh." I shook my head. "I'm just thinking of starting something small. They probably work with much larger clients."

"They work with clients of all sizes." Clara pulled a business card from her wallet. "Call Saoirse. Tell her Clara sent you. She'll hook you up, I promise."

Peak Strategies

I'd never heard of them, but that didn't mean anything. It wasn't like I had my finger on the pulse of the business world. I liked their card. It looked like a piece of wood with the silhouette of Denver's skyline "burned" into the grain. My mind started whirring with the type of business card I would have. Reality struck before I could get lost in my fantasies, though. I had to have a business before I could have a cool card.

Shira took a step forward and reached out but didn't quite touch me. "Frank and I had this game. We'd ask each other to name the bright side of a tricky or shitty situation. I—well, without him, I can't seem to find the bright side in anything."

She broke off to dab the welling tears in her eyes, and I inwardly kicked myself for wrongly guessing Frank Goldman had been her dad. Shira was here to lay her husband to rest.

Shira took a deep breath. "But I think this must be the bright side. I'm not one to eavesdrop, but something compelled me to listen to your conversation. You can't deny serendipity, can you?"

I sucked in a shaky breath. "Helping me out would be your bright side?"

She nodded. I glanced at my mother. Her hands were tucked under her chin, and she looked like she was about to burst, but she didn't say a thing, letting me decide.

Was there any other choice? It wasn't like I could say no to a grieving woman who saw giving this card to me as the bright side of her husband's funeral.

I tapped the card on my palm. "Thank you. I'll call Saoirse tomorrow."

Maybe this would turn out to be exactly what I needed to truly move on with my life.

CHAPTER SEVEN

Miles

THERE WAS A SOFT knock on my office door followed by my business partner, Saoirse, strolling in. Her gaze dropped to my lap, and she pursed her lips, unimpressed.

"You stole my cat."

I stroked Clementine's back and grinned. There was no denying the big ball of orange fluff parked in my lap. "Is it stealing when your cat walked into my office, climbed onto my lap, and fell asleep? I didn't choose this life, this life chose me."

Saoirse perched her ass in the chair in front of my desk, all attitude. "I know about the treats you keep in your drawer. This is bribery."

"You don't have to bring your cat to work, you know. Most cats stay home and nap all day."

"You try leaving her when she's pouting. Not possible." She jutted her chin. "But...I guess you can keep her in here for a while longer, if you really want."

I leaned forward, instantly on alert, which Clementine did not like. She let me know by digging her claws into my thigh and meowing like I was murdering her instead of slightly shifting her.

"What do you need me to do for you?" I asked.

Saoirse's mouth formed an *O*. "I don't know what you mean."

"You would never voluntarily give me your cat. Tell me what you want in exchange."

Saoirse had married my brother Weston's best friend Luca a couple years ago. Us going into business together had started with a casual conversation over drinks. Saoirse had needed funding, and I'd had it in spades. I'd needed a change and new direction, and Saoirse had provided that in our partnership. She'd always been good at helping people set up their businesses, and as it'd turned out, I had something of a knack for it too. Graphics and visual marketing were my main areas of expertise, but I did a lot of everything for my clients. It made the work interesting. No two days were the same.

"Okay, there might be one thing."

I cocked my head. "Give it to me. I'm ready."

"Clara sent me a lovely woman who wants to start a small catering business. We can help her, but I am stretched to the max and can't take her on as a client right now. I looked at your schedule, though, and you can for sure."

I picked up my pen, wobbling it between my fingers. "A catering business? Aren't there enough of those in Denver?"

"It's not quite catering, but I don't know what else to call it. You'll have to hear her explain it."

"So, it's a foregone conclusion I'll say yes, huh? Did you schedule her an appointment with me?"

She rubbed her lips together. "Even better. She's in my office. You can talk to her right now."

I groaned, further disturbing the princess napping on me. "You want me to walk in there blind?"

She dismissed my concern with a wave. "This is an informal meeting, so don't worry about it. Besides, I told her I'm springing her on you. She won't expect you to have a PowerPoint presentation prepared."

"Holy alliteration, Batman," I said, earning an eyeroll.

"If you're reducing me to a comic book character, I'd like to be Catwoman—the Michelle Pfeiffer version."

"Fine, Catwoman, come get your feline friend so I can meet this—what's her name? Or am I not allowed to have any information about her?"

Laughing, she scooped her cat off my lap and started for the door. "Her name is Daisy Dunham. Isn't that the cutest?"

Daisy? There was no way…

Denver was small, but not that small. The chances of this being the same Daisy I'd met at High Bar were low, but I found myself hurrying after Saoirse, brushing cat hair off my trousers as I went.

When Saoirse finally moved her big, blonde head out of my way as we entered her office, my suspicions were confirmed. Sitting there like a little ink splotch in Saoirse's pink haven was grouchy-mouthed Lydia-Daisy-Cupcake.

"Miles, come meet Daisy." Saoirse placed Clementine in her fluffy pink bed and stood behind her glass desk with a wide smile.

"Actually, I believe we've met before." I walked around the chairs in front of Saoirse's desk and propped my ass on the edge. Daisy raked her eyes up the length of me, the full-on frown on her face a sharp contrast to Saoirse's expression. It made me sort of giddy.

"Oh. I had no idea you were Saoirse's partner." The look she gave me was more than her previous wariness. It was almost…scathing. "I'm not so sure this is a good idea."

"You two know each other?" Saoirse asked. "How did you cross paths?"

"We don't know each other," Daisy rushed. "We've only met briefly, when Miles was at the bar where I work."

Saoirse's gaze narrowed on me. "You were at a bar?"

"*Working*," I clarified. "I filled in for Nick for two nights, that's all."

Granted, a recovering alcoholic spending any time in a bar wasn't the wisest decision, and Saoirse's icy glare was all I needed to know about her opinion on the matter. I'd certainly be hearing words about it later.

Saoirse recovered quickly, plastering on her professional smile. "What a coincidence." Then she snapped her fingers. "You have to be the baker of the cupcakes Miles keeps whining about."

I scowled at her. The betrayal in this room ran deep. "I didn't whine." I turned back to Daisy. "I didn't whine. I might have mentioned I was jonesing for one, but there was no whining."

Daisy looked down, and I followed her gaze to the canvas tote at her feet. "Well..." her eyes flicked back to mine, "I may have brought some samples."

I sank into the chair beside her. "For me?"

"They were for Saoirse, but if she wants to share, she can."

"Nah, Sersh doesn't like sugar. You can give them to me."

Saoirse scoffed. "That's a bald-faced lie. Excuse Miles, he gets feral in the face of sweets, and I'm not exaggerating when I tell you I've heard about your cupcakes multiple times over the last week."

This was making me sound really fucking uncool. Like I had nothing going for me besides this woman's cupcakes—nothing else to think or talk about.

"I mentioned them once. Possibly twice. But that's not why Daisy is here, is it?" I leaned forward, elbows on my knees. "You're thinking of starting a business?"

She shifted in her seat. If I'd been a more sensitive fellow, I would have said she was putting distance between us. Since I was aware I smelled good and looked decent, I couldn't think of a reason she would want to get away from me.

"I've been thinking about it for a long time, but that's all it's been—thoughts. Then I met Clara and Shira, and they encouraged me to make an appointment with Saoirse, so here I am. I guess...I want to start a business."

I cocked my head. "You guess?"

She nodded. "Yes."

I exhaled, tapping my index fingers together. I did not like her ho-hum attitude, mostly because I recognized it from myself. I knew what a recipe for disaster not being one-hundred percent committed to my goals was. I couldn't allow Daisy to follow that same path. Even more, I would not go down that path with her.

"Let me be frank, Daisy-daze. If you're all in, I will go balls to the wall with you. I'll work tirelessly to make a plan and bring it to fruition. But you need to be all in or it's not going to work. Saoirse and I can attest, running your own business isn't for the faint of heart. I tried to half-ass it for the first year and ended up with a partner who wanted to murder me. *You* don't have a partner, so it's going to all be on your shoulders. This is where you have to decide: are you in or out?"

Saoirse wound around her desk, perching on the edge I'd vacated. "Daisy's here because she wants this, right?"

Daisy nodded, though there was nothing in her expression or body language I could interpret as hungry.

Saoirse went on, using a much softer approach. "I understand what it's like to shift from having this ephemeral idea you've tossed around and around your head for a long time to making it real. It involves changing your entire mindset. Why don't you and Miles sit down, really lay out what you want to do, then decide if you are ready."

Daisy glanced at me then back to Saoirse. "I'm sorry, I just assumed I'd be working with you."

"I would take you on in a heartbeat if I could move anything around, but I can't at the moment." Saoirse nodded toward me. "Miles and I are a team, and I know he'll do right by you. Wait until he designs a logo for you and tell me you have doubts. You won't, I promise."

"What do you say, Daisy? Want to bring your cupcakes to my office and have a chat?"

Her big brown eyes slid to mine, eyebrows disappearing beneath her bangs. Her jaw was as rigid as her spine. I thought she was going to turn me down, but she nodded once.

"All right. We can talk." Leaning down, she pulled a pink box from her bag and handed it to Saoirse. "These are for you. Thank you for seeing me on such short notice."

"Of course. Anything for Clara and Shira."

Saoirse gave Daisy a hug on her way out, which was really fucking cute since Saoirse was a foot taller and had to bend in half. When Saoirse let Daisy go, her cheeks were red. Even cuter.

"Come on, Daisy-daze. We have plans to make."

And cupcakes to eat.

CHAPTER EIGHT

Daisy

I WAS IN SHOCK. It was my only explanation for following Miles Aldrich into his office. If I'd had my wits about me, I would have thanked Saoirse Rossi for her time and excused myself. After what Nick had told me about Miles, I had no interest in working with him.

But it was really hard to reconcile this friendly, excitable man who baby-talked a fluffy, orange cat and worked with one of the nicest women I had ever met with the person Miles had once been.

People had the capacity for change. That, I accepted. But I couldn't imagine Nick warning me about Miles if he'd truly changed *that* much. Besides that, he was an Aldrich. Richer than god. There was no way he was anyone I'd want to know.

Yet, here I was, sitting across from him at a small, round table, watching him dig into the cupcakes I'd brought.

Saoirse's office had been a cotton candy daydream while Miles' was more rustic. His desk looked like reclaimed wood, and the table we were sitting at appeared to be a repurposed spool.

It dawned on me that Miles must have designed their beautiful business cards. Despite myself, I was excited to see what kind of business card he would make for me.

Miles groaned as he sucked frosting off his thumb. "I've missed you. It's been too long."

"There's something gory about telling the thing you're consuming you missed it."

His mouth hitched into a half-grin. "You may have a point, Daisy-daze." Lifting the last mini cupcake, he whispered, "Thank you for your sacrifice," and tossed it in his mouth, eating the whole thing in one bite.

He swallowed, took a drink from his water bottle, and cleared his throat. "All right. Now that we got the formalities out of the way, let's talk about you. What's your plan, your dream, your idea? How can I help you make it happen?"

I had rehearsed this part since making the appointment with Saoirse, and I'd already laid it all out for her in her office, so the words should have flowed easily. But I hadn't been counting on sitting through the Miles Aldrich show followed by him turning his full, mega-wattage attention on me.

"I—"

My mouth clamped shut. Miles sighed and leaned back in his chair. It was a ridiculously good look. Confident, slightly cocky, he ran his hand down the buttons of his shirt and flattened his palm on his abdomen. Then he flashed me a wide, toothy smile.

"Contrary to what you just saw, I'm not going to bite...unless you turn yourself into a cupcake, then all bets are off."

I huffed a laugh. "I can guarantee that won't happen." I waved off my cobwebs and nerves. "I haven't put my best foot forward with you today. You being here has thrown me for a loop, but I'm ready now."

He held his hand out. "You have the floor, Ms. Dunham."

I sat up straight, my hands on the table. "I would like to start a charcuterie business. You saw my...meat cups, which are only a small part of my plan. I would offer full grazing tables, individual cups, small trays. These would be ideal for bridal and baby showers, weddings, game days, formal and informal get togethers. My cups and small trays would work at business meetings and conferences. I have experience making these for my own family events, and while it's not the most original idea, no one in Denver is doing it. If I can strike while the iron is hot, I think I can find my niche in this town."

Miles didn't say anything. Taking out his phone, he tapped on it, a line forming between his brows. He must have found what he was looking for because his eyes lit, he nodded, then he put his phone down on the table.

"Sorry, Daisy-daze. I was looking up what exactly charcuterie is. Do you know it means 'cooked flesh'?"

I wrinkled my nose. "I did know that, and I try to forget it. Besides cooked flesh, there's cheese, nuts, fruit...the definition has expanded over the years. You can put anything, really."

He cocked his head. "Cupcakes?"

"God, Miles, has anyone ever told you you're obsessive?"

He rubbed the line between his eyes, his smiling lowering but hanging on. "I can't say they have, but I'll take it." Shifting in his seat, he leaned his forearms on the table. "Now, tell me what you have planned for this cooked flesh business."

I threw my hands up. "Nothing. I do these for family events. They're always telling me I should go legit, so I started to believe them." I sighed, pissed at myself for not being more prepared. "I'm wasting your time, aren't I? I'm sorry, I should have written something down. It's just…when I start thinking about this, I get over-whelmed."

Andy and I had talked about my idea a lot over the last year we were together. He'd ask me questions—questions he knew I wouldn't have the answers to, like *who* would hire me—and my motivation always died along with our conversation.

"No. None of that," Miles replied with a cutting edge that made me sit up straighter. "I think you have more than you're giving yourself credit for. That ends now. You're not to come into my office and get down on yourself. Leave that at the door. In here, every idea is a building block for the next one. Nothing you say is stupid or useless. That isn't how I do things, and when you work with me, you'll get with the program. Got it?"

I found myself nodding without thought, as if Miles Aldrich held my strings with the force of his authoritative tone. The grin he gave me coated me in warmth.

Reaching across the table, he tapped my knuckles with his finger-tips. "Good job, Daisy-daze. Now that we have that settled, I need to know more about these charcuterie tables. I want to wrap my head around what you do. How can we make that happen?"

"I'm actually doing one for my sister's birthday party this week-end. I can—"

Miles snapped. "Perfect. I'll come to that. I can be your assistant."

"I was going to say I'll take pictures and videos."

"No." He shook his head. "No, that won't cut it. I'll be there in person."

"It's a family party at my parents' house."

"That's fine. I don't mind meeting your family."

"Miles…"

My mother would love this man. She'd be absolutely thrilled he was going to be helping me start my business. But she wouldn't be the only one there on Saturday. It would be all of us, and we were…a *lot*. Then again, if I threw Miles into the deep end—a party above the funeral home with my very effusive and opinionated family—he might realize how impossible the situation was and cut me loose. That would be best for us both.

"You're not going to talk me out of it," he said.

"Fine. I won't try."

He tapped my knuckles again. "All right. I'm glad one thing wasn't difficult for us to agree on. Text me your address and the details."

"I—" Panic flared in my belly, and my eyes went wide.

Miles' brow crinkled. "Why do you look like that?"

"You can't ask someone why they look like they do. That's rude."

He poked a finger at me. "Don't try to distract me, Cupcake. You're freaking out." He leaned in, peering at me with suspicion. "Text me."

I tried my best to seem easy-breezy. "I will. Later. My phone's low on battery and—"

"Did you delete my number?"

I bit down on my bottom lip, and Miles guffawed.

"You did, didn't you?"

I nodded once.

"Huh. Well, this is awkward."

"It isn't personal."

"Did you delete anyone else's number?"

"No, but—"

He held up a hand. "That's all right. I'm going to text you so you have my number again. Unless you blocked me too…?"

"I didn't block you." I almost had, and, man, this would have been even more mortifying.

"I never know with you." He tapped on his phone, and a second later, mine vibrated. He'd sent me a cupcake emoji. Despite myself, I let out a laugh.

"Obsessed," I whispered as I input my home address and the time of the party. "There. I sent you the details. If you can't make it, I understand."

"Oh, I'm showing up." He flipped his phone face down. "When we're done with our working relationship, feel free to delete my number again. I would hate to clutter up your contacts."

"I'm—okay." I had no words to defend myself, and I certainly wasn't about to dive into why I had half-heartedly severed our connection. "I guess I'll see you this weekend."

"Hold on. Before you go, I have homework for you." He paused, making sure I was listening. I nodded, and he went on. "I want you to write down all the questions you have about how to start—what are you calling it?"

"I haven't decided." I had an idea, though. I hadn't told Andy because I hadn't wanted him to tell me it wasn't any good. He might've loved it, but I hadn't trusted how he would have handled it if he didn't. But I couldn't get out of this without telling Miles, so I braced myself for him to laugh. "But I was thinking I might call it Grazing by Daisy."

Miles pinned me with a long stare. So long, I couldn't sit still under the weight of it. I shuffled my feet and moved my ass in my seat, nearly jumping out of my skin when he slammed a hand down on the table.

"Yes. I like it. It works." Picking up his tablet, he tapped on it, saying nothing else.

I didn't know what to do. Was the meeting over? It seemed like it was...though, it hadn't been much of an ending. I squirmed a little more. Miles was lost in whatever was happening on his screen, so I mentally called it.

Grabbing my bag, I rose to my feet. "I'll see you this weekend."

He glanced up, the corner of his mouth quirking. "I'll be there, Daisy. Don't forget to do your homework."

"I won't."

I left Peak Strategies feeling...well, I didn't know. Optimism wasn't really my thing, but there was a lightness in my chest that hadn't been there before I'd walked in. To be honest, I'd been dreading this meeting, assuming it would only punctuate how far I was from achieving anything.

That hadn't happened at all.

Between Saoirse, the cat, and Miles, it was like I'd just gotten off a tilt-a-whirl.

My mind was whirring, but I knew this was a step. A small one, but before today, I'd been too stymied by self-doubt to even shuffle my feet.

I plunked myself in my car, thinking about my homework assignment, when a text vibrated my phone. I lifted the screen, and blood drained from my face.

Andy: *Hey. How are you, Daisy? I thought I would have heard from you by now. Just because we're not together doesn't mean we* *can't be friends. Let's be grownups. We have too much history to just disappear from each other's lives. Talk to me.*

A bucket of dread dumped on the sliver of optimism that had been breaking through my cracks. Andy must have had some sixth sense that I was moving on, doing something for myself.

My thumb hovered over his contact. I had no need for it. We weren't going to be friends. Not after...everything.

Heaving a sigh, I let my head fall against the steering wheel.

I couldn't do it. I wasn't ready.

I would. I had to.

But not today.

CHAPTER NINE

Daisy

MILES SHOWED UP RIGHT on time. I hadn't pegged him for the punctual sort. I watched him climb out of his SUV from my kitchen window, check his phone, then peer at the funeral home.

I hadn't warned him about where I lived. I should have, but I'd wanted to see how he would react. I'd been through this plenty with new friends and dates. I'd seen a spectrum of responses, but I truly couldn't predict what Miles's would be.

A minute passed. He was still standing by his SUV, looking doubtful, so I went outside to the landing at the top of my stairs.

"Miles," I called.

His head whipped in my direction. "Daisy-daze!" He closed his door and started toward me. "I thought I was in the wrong place."

"Right place, right on time." I leaned against the wood railing, waiting for him as he climbed the steps. "I should've told you I live above a garage."

"That would've been helpful." He grinned, his gaze sweeping over me. "You might've mentioned the funeral home too. It's a pretty big landmark."

"Have you been here before?"

He cupped the back of his neck. "To the funeral home? Yeah, a few times. It's been years, though, and I can't say I'm sorry for it."

"I don't blame you. No one's eager to come back here."

Miles stood in front of me on the landing, his arms crossed over his chest. "Daisy Dunham. That's your family's place."

He wasn't asking, but I confirmed anyway. "It is. That's where I grew up."

"Must've been interesting."

I shrugged. "It was just life. I've never known anything else."

I showed him into my little apartment, bracing for his judgment or intrusive questions. I'd heard plenty over the years, from the time I was little into adulthood. People didn't like to think about death, but once they knew what my family did and where we lived, most found it impossible not to think about it, and it made them uncomfortable.

"How long have you lived in this apartment?" Miles asked, taking me by surprise. That was not the first question I'd expected to come from him.

"Not long. Just over a month. My older brother lived here before me, and my sister before that."

He nodded. "It was your turn."

"I guess."

His gaze swept over me, lingering on my bare feet. "You're not wearing black today. Only on your toes."

I wiggled my polished toes and tucked my hands in my jeans. I wasn't wearing anything special. Just old jeans and a slightly cropped red T-shirt. "Sometimes I like to acknowledge there are other colors."

"Red looks good on you. But I liked gothed-out Lydia-Daisy-Cupcake too."

"Lydia again?" I pressed my hand to my forehead.

"Suits you."

Then he was on the move again, checking out the kitchen, looking at pictures hanging on the wall, even peeking into my tiny bedroom. It didn't feel intrusive. This apartment wasn't really home yet. It was a way station until I figured out my next move. I was lucky to have had this after the implosion of my relationship, but the flip side was this place had become a reminder of that failure.

Miles swept his palm over the postage-stamp-sized island in my barely-there kitchen. "You moved here after your breakup."

"Yes." I wrapped my arms around my middle. "How did you know that?"

"Nick likes to talk, which is why I never tell him anything I don't mind being spread around."

"That was tragically uncool of him."

"Yeah, but in this case, I'm glad I know so I don't make any off-color jokes about spinsters or cat ladies..." He flashed me a wide grin before spinning away to continue his tour of my apartment even though he'd already studied every surface.

"I'm relieved you aren't joking about me dying alone, my face eaten by my pack of cats."

And more than relieved he wasn't giving me pitying looks and using that soft tone so many people spoke to me in the days and weeks following the breakup.

He finally completed his tour and took a seat in the big squishy armchair—my favorite place to park myself at the end of the day. "Tell me everyone I'm about to meet, then put me to work."

"Work?"

"Aren't I your assistant?"

"You're more of an observer."

"Daisy…" He shook his head as if he were ashamed of me. "Never turn down free labor. If that's not rule number one, it should be."

I perched on the arm of the couch. "Even if that free labor will just get in the way?"

"I'm a quick learner. If I get in your way, you can kick my ass. By the way, grazing-by-Daisy-dot-com is available. You should jump on that if you're sure about that name."

I blinked hard at him. "You checked if the domain was available?"

"Of course. I told you I'd be all in with you, Daisy. Are you still all in?"

I was all in a tizzy, flustered beyond words. "I—I'm all in, I just didn't know we were already starting."

"What do you think I'm doing here? Hanging out with you for fun?" He scratched his chin. "To be fair, I would have come to your sister's party for the hell of it, but I don't think you would have invited me."

"Considering you don't even know my sister's name, no, I wouldn't have."

He chuckled. "I should have asked. That made writing her card difficult, but I pulled through in the end."

"You got her a card?"

"Of course I did. I'm not going to show up empty-handed."

A breath whooshed out of my lungs. I was beginning to think I had no idea what kind of man Miles was. Everything I came to know about him contradicted my previous knowledge. I was always on my back foot, trying to catch up.

"Her name is Landry, and she's turning thirty. She's married to Tom. They have two kids named Edie and Hazel. I have an older brother, Beau, but he's in Laramie and couldn't break away from work to be here. We'll probably FaceTime him at some point. My mom's name is Whitney Mae, my dad is Seth. My youngest brother is Reed. He probably won't talk to you because he's fourteen and pretty much hates the world—us included. It bums me out, but I don't blame him. Being a teenager is the pits."

Miles had a line between his eyebrows by the time I finished listing everyone. I hadn't expected him to remember anyone beyond Landry but had wanted to give him the rundown anyway.

He tapped his temple. "All right, we've got Landry, Tom, kids Edie and Hazel, Beau in Laramie, Whitney and Seth are Mom and Dad, and emo teen Reed. Did I get it right?"

"Uh, yeah. You're good at that."

"Thank you. It's a skill I picked up from years of meeting my parents' friends and business associates. Paying attention to those kinds of details was drilled into me."

"Smart." I sucked in a breath, trying to cover how deep and husky my voice had sounded. "Now that we have that covered, let's put those big arms to use."

Miles carried almost all my ingredients and supplies next door. My parents were still working, and Landry's family hadn't arrived yet, so we had my family's home to ourselves for the time being. I directed him into the kitchen to set everything down, and he took instruction well. I hoped that continued if he insisted on helping me set up.

"This is nice," he remarked on my parents' recently remodeled kitchen. "Can I see your childhood bedroom?"

A laugh burst out of me. "What? No, you can't. Why would you even want to?"

"Why can't I?"

"Because it isn't anything like how I left it. Now, it's just a room. I took most of my things with me when I moved out and packed the rest away in storage."

"Your mother didn't want to keep a shrine to you?"

"No, she doesn't need a shrine. I'm here all the time. She can worship me whenever she likes." I put my hands on my hips. "Let's get started. We have two hours and a lot to do before everyone gets here."

"Put me to work. I'm ready."

I might have been mistaken, but I swore he flexed his biceps.

The even crazier thing was, I didn't mind at all.

CHAPTER TEN

Miles

A FEW DAYS AGO, I'd left our strategy meeting dubious about Daisy's commitment to this idea of hers. Our clients always came to us raring to go. Often, Saoirse or I had to rein them in and bring them back down to earth. With Daisy, I felt like I'd practically had to twist her arm to get her to even consider going through with this. It had not inspired a lot of confidence. Watching her meticulous preparation now convinced me she took this seriously.

Flitting around the rustic wood kitchen table, she chewed her bottom lip, deciding where things went. Since I kept getting in her way, she'd given me busywork of opening wrappers and packages. In the end, she created a dessert platter—giving me a cupcake before I filched one—and a table covered in carefully arranged cheese, cured meat, crackers and bread, nuts, dips, and dried fruit.

"Stand over there and look like you're arranging things. I'll film you, and you can put it on your social media when you're ready," I directed. The house would make a nice backdrop. The eight-foot windows drew a lot of light into the open living room and kitchen combo, making the place even more inviting than it already was.

Daisy shot me a glare that said, *Are you actually dumb?* At least, that was how I interpreted it.

"I've been doing family and friends' parties for years, Miles. I have more footage than I know what to do with."

"No, you know what to do with it. You were using your big brain and thinking ahead. You're going to have a backlog of posts you can make once we get your social media fired up."

"Yeah…" She waved what I was saying away. "I can't think about that right now. Everyone's going to be here soon—"

A sweet southern voice called Daisy's name from the entry, cutting her off. Next thing I knew, a parade of Dunhams filled the kitchen, led by a small woman with big, bouncy blonde-mixed-with-silver curls. She went straight to Daisy and hugged the life out of her then turned her attention to me.

"You have to be Miles." With her accent, my name became "Mals," and I never wanted to hear it another way.

"I am. Miles Aldrich." I stuck out my hand, and she immediately batted it away to envelop me in a hug just as tight as the one she'd given her daughter. She smelled like flowers, and her arms and chest were softly cushioned. I couldn't remember ever having a hug as good as this one.

She pulled back, keeping her hands on my arms. "Whitney Mae Dunham." She gave my arms a squeeze. "My, my, someone keeps up with the gym. You'll have to show me some moves. My doctor says I need to lift weights to help strengthen my bones. Isn't that a doozy? Thinking about my bones makes me feel old."

"Mama," Daisy tugged her mother away from me, "let him breathe. I might need him later."

Standing next to each other, their resemblance was obvious. It was in their big brown eyes, the heart shape of their faces, their petite stature. But where Daisy was lithe, her mother was plump. Daisy was cool, and her mom was warm cookies. Daisy was dark and wary, and her mom was bright and open.

I beamed at her. "I could show you around the gym, Whitney. It's where I get my best thinking done."

"You didn't tell me how cute he is," Whitney admonished.

Daisy closed her eyes. "I didn't notice."

Whitney hmphed. "Sure you didn't."

A tall, wiry man in a black suit came to stand between them, spreading his arms around their shoulders. "Is my wife hitting on you?"

I grinned. "No, she's simply stating a fact."

Daisy groaned, and her parents laughed. Her dad stuck his hand out, and we shook. His hands were large and smooth. For a split second, it occurred to me he'd probably handled dead bodies, then logic kicked in. If he *had* handled them, he'd undoubtedly worn gloves. Besides that, I'd shaken hands with plenty of people, and how many hadn't washed their hands after using the bathroom? The percentage was probably staggering. That should have given me pause.

"Seth Dunham. Welcome, welcome. Have a drink, grab a seat, I'm going to go change out of my suit." He loosened his tie and held it up like a noose. "Can't stand these things."

This must've been who Daisy had gotten her dark side from. I liked it.

And I hated wearing ties too.

After that, I met Landry, a leaner, more outdoorsy version of her mother, her husband Tom—bland, but seemed decent—five-year-old Edie, and three-year-old Hazel. Edie and Hazel were two sides of the same coin. The older had a little brown bob, and the younger had the blonde version. They both stared at me with the big brown eyes that carried through all the Dunham women.

Landry was all praise for Daisy's efforts. She and Hazel examined the grazing table while Edie climbed on a stool to get eye-to-eye with the dessert platter on the kitchen island.

I leaned on the cool marble beside her. "Those cupcakes are mine."

She turned sharply in my direction, her eyes narrowing. "No, they're not."

"They are. Your aunt Daisy made them for me. You can eat the brownies."

"You can't hog all the cupcakes," she hissed.

"It's not hogging if they're mine to begin with."

Her eyes were slits. Her tiny mouth pulled into a deep pout. "Why are you here?"

"To help Aunt Daisy and celebrate your mom's birthday."

"Do you even know my mommy?" She pushed up on her knees and brought her fists to her hips. "I've never seen you before."

"I know, kid. We just met a few minutes ago. I'm Miles." I shook my head. "Geesh, you might want to get your memory checked."

She scrunched her button nose. "How do I check my memory?"

"It's easy." I put one hand on top of my head and the other flat on my stomach. "If you can pat your head while rubbing circles on your tummy, your memory's just fine. If you can't...well, I don't want to talk about that."

I demonstrated, and damn, it wasn't as easy as I remembered. Once I got going, she started too. Kid was rubbing her head and patting her tummy then rubbing both.

"You almost have it," I said.

Her tongue peeked out as she concentrated. "I can do it. I know I can."

The longer she worked at it, the more family gathered around us. Daisy had edged in beside me, shooting me a warning look. I didn't know what she was warning me about. I was on my best behavior.

"What are you doing?" she muttered.

"The kid thinks she's entitled to cupcakes. I'm setting her straight."

"She's five."

"Never too young to learn life skills. Look at her, she's getting it."

Sure enough, little Edie was rubbing circles on her middle and giving the top of her head pats. Her dad let out a whoop, and her mom clapped for her, which threw her off her game, but it didn't matter. She'd had it for a while there, and that was what counted.

I gave her a thumbs up. "You passed the test, kid. For that, you can have one cupcake."

She puffed up her chest. "Three."

I groaned like she was hurting me. "Fine. Three, but that's my limit."

Edie turned to Daisy. "Miles isn't very good at sharing. I don't think he should come back to Grandma and Grandpa's house until he can share better." Then she flickered her bright eyes to me. "They taught me to share in preschool, when I was three. Did you forget to go to preschool?"

"All right, girlie." Her mom scooped her off the stool. "Let's leave Miles alone. If we get in his face too much this time, he'll be too scared to come back."

Daisy folded her arms. "Miles is just here to see what I do. He's not coming back."

Landry rolled her eyes. "When has Mama met someone who isn't her new best friend? Before you know it, Miles will be over for Thanksgiving."

"Is that an invitation?" I winged a brow, teasing Daisy. "If it is, I accept."

"Thanksgiving is months away," she intoned.

"I'm completely free that day."

My last Thanksgiving with my parents had ended in my father throwing the turkey against the wall, leaving a streak of grease and my mother in huge, sobbing tears. She'd gotten wasted and went on an online shopping binge. He'd left for his "club"—more likely code for one of his mistresses' houses. I'd spent the following day lining up a painter who could come out on short notice, and by Saturday afternoon, it had been like it had never happened.

That was two years ago. Last year, I hung out on my own and watched the parade and dog show. Turned out, being by myself had been far more preferable than with parents who couldn't possibly care less for me or each other, quite fucking frankly.

"You're not coming here for Thanksgiving," Daisy argued as her mother approached.

Whitney Mae gasped. "Miles, do you need a place to go for Thanksgiving? You're more than welcome here. In fact, give me your phone number so we can arrange it."

"Mama, it's April."

Whitney flipped her curls. "So what? It's never too early to start plannin', Miss Daisy."

I grinned at them both. They were quite a pair. Sunshine and storm clouds. "Yeah, Miss Daisy. You know how much I like plans."

We were talking shit. I knew this wasn't actually going to happen. But, man, the idea of being with this family on a day all about families made me kind of wish it would. I'd even share the cupcakes.

Somewhere around the third time Tom sank my battleship, I got up from the family room floor to stretch my legs. It turned out all Landry had wanted for her thirtieth birthday was to hang out with her family playing board games and eating her sister's food.

I was waiting for all of them to peel off their skin and unveil their true demonic selves. No one was actually this wholesome. This had to be some supernatural quest to harvest souls or something equally nefarious.

Either way, I was having fun.

I raised my arms over my head to stretch out my stiff spine and twisted left and right. The person standing by the kitchen island had me doing a double take. No one else seemed to have noticed or cared he was there, but I ventured over, focusing on the wrapper in one of his hands.

Casually approaching the dessert tray, which had been picked over but still had plenty left, I plucked up a brownie. Daisy was getting me hooked on all her baked goods. She'd also made a sick baklava and delectable cinnamon and walnut rugelach.

The guy looked up, his shoulders jumping when his gaze landed on me. This had to be Reed, the youngest Dunham. From Daisy's description, he was fourteen, not an easy age.

"Hey," I greeted. "I'm Miles, Daisy's friend."

The kid wore wire-framed glasses, and his mop of curls hung down his forehead, dipping behind his glasses to half cover his eyes. He peered at me for a second before looking away.

"You're not her friend. She's paying you," he muttered.

"That's not strictly true. No money has passed hands, but you might be right about the first part. We're more like acquaintances, but I have a good feeling about her."

He sniffed. "She doesn't need a boyfriend."

"Cool. Are we sharing things our siblings don't need? Is it that time again? My brother, West? He doesn't need another pair of hiking boots. He has an entire closet dedicated to outdoor wear. Granted, he owns a company that manufactures it, but I still say he doesn't need it."

Reed had the Dunham squint down. His eyes were narrow slits, but his glare was like an x-ray, seeing right through me.

"Why are you talking to me?"

"It would be kind of weird to stand here while you're standing there and not speak."

He shrugged. "Would've been better than listening to you talk about your rich brother."

"That's what you got out of that story? I was aiming for sharing Westie's overconsumption of hiking accessories, but I see what you mean."

I wasn't going to let this kid get to me. I recognized an angry teen. It was like looking in a time machine, though I hadn't been quite as spindly.

"Why are you even here?" he asked.

"Why are any of us here, really?" I drummed my fingers on the counter. "Are you going to come hang out with your family?"

Another heavy shrug. "I'd been considering it before...this."

I went to poke at him some more, but Daisy appeared next to her brother. She was older by a decade at least, but he towered over her.

"Hey, Reed." She rubbed his arm and gave him a gentle smile. "Landry would die for you to play a game with her. Your choice, even though it's *her* birthday."

Reed hesitated, flicking his eyes from Daisy to me. "All right." Then he ducked around us, his head down, curling into himself.

When I turned back to Daisy, she was examining me with her usual wariness.

"What did you say to him?"

"Not much. I introduced myself, he told me you don't need a boyfriend, so I told him about my brother's hiking boot collection. I think we were bonding, but you interrupted before we could fully cement it."

"He's shy."

I nodded. "Yeah, I got that. Got that he's pissed off at the world too."

"He used to talk to me." She shoved her hair behind her ear. "He doesn't anymore."

"Well, you're a girl."

"No kidding."

I chuffed. She didn't get it. "Think about it. Try to remember being that age." I squeezed her shoulder and dipped down, speaking low. "I'm going to head out. Thanks for having me here and giving me a glimpse of something nice. I had a really good time."

"You don't have to go."

"That's nice of you to say, but I'm going to leave on a high note and let you do your family thing." I picked up a cupcake and a brownie. "Monday, Daisy. Come to your appointment ready to dig in."

"Okay," she murmured. "I'll be there."

Whitney didn't let me leave before I took her phone number, then she hugged me even tighter than the first time. Two hugs in one day was a world record for me. And they were so high quality, they'd keep me full for a year at least.

They'd probably have to.

CHAPTER ELEVEN

MILES HAD DONE A lot of work for me. My stomach churned looking at his beautiful logo ideas and well thought out spreadsheets. They were beautiful and meticulous, but deep down, I knew this was all for naught.

I shouldn't have let myself be optimistic. For a moment, I forgot who I was, but this town was always here to remind me.

Miles stopped in the middle of a sentence, cocking his head left then right.

"You're not in," he surmised.

I sighed. "I'm sorry. I should have texted you to let you know this wasn't going to happen. You did all this, and it was for nothing."

He drummed his fingers on the round wooden table we were sitting at again, his jaw rippling.

"What changed? The last time I saw you, you were in."

I leaned back in my chair, folding my arms around my middle. "I had some time to think about it and realized what I'd already known all along: this isn't going to work. Not in this town, not for me."

"What do you mean? Why not here? Why not you?"

"You won't let me get away with saying 'no thank you,' will you?"

His brow dropped. "Not a chance. Get with the talking, Daisy-daze. My patience is finite. I'm almost to the stage where I flip you over, hang you by your ankle, and shake it out of you."

My upper lip curled. "I'll cut you."

He rocked back in his chair, laughing. "Don't be cute. It's not going to work to distract me. Talk."

Cute? I'd meant it. It was annoying how nonthreatening I looked. If only I could broadcast how dark my mind could be. There were chainsaws and...cupcakes. Dammit, even my mind wasn't intimidating.

"There was always a reason I dragged my feet to start this." I chuffed, blowing my bangs up in frustration. "My mom, Reed, and I went to brunch yesterday. Reed was in a good mood for once, we had bacon and pancakes, all was well. Then a group of expensively dressed ladies were seated at the table beside ours. One of them recognized my mom, or maybe me, and she yelped. It was like there was a spring in her chair, she was out of it so fast."

"She...yelped?"

"Like a kicked puppy."

"Why?"

He would never get this. Then again, he knew what it was like to have a name people recognized...

"When people hear your last name is Aldrich, they react, right?"

He rubbed his bottom lip and nodded once. "They often do, yes."

"Does it open doors to places? Lend you respect you haven't earned?"

"Put hearts in women's eyes who wouldn't have given me a second look without it—make it so I can never be sure if someone wants to know me for me or what I can do for them? Sure. All those things."

"Poor little rich boy," I deadpanned.

He dropped his hand to the table, flipping it over. "You asked. Don't be pissy it's not all sunshine and roses being an Aldrich. Now, tell me what this line of questioning has to do with the lady who yelped."

"I'm not pissy."

He didn't bother to hold back his laugh at my expense. "Okay, Cupcake. You're a ray of sunshine, if that's what it takes to get you talking."

"Fine. The yelping lady asked to be seated elsewhere because she didn't want to sit beside our family. I know this because she wasn't quiet when she made the request."

"*What*? Why would she do that?"

"People do not like to be reminded of death. They don't want to have brunch next to the family who took care of them during the worst times of their lives. Then they would have to think about the fact that one day they'll be in the ground. It's worse with the wealthy—who happen to be the majority of our clientele. Their money insulates them from the painful and mundane, but not death. They look at us, hear the Dunham name, and remember they're just human—mortal like everyone else. It makes them uncomfortable."

"I don't buy that. It doesn't bother me."

I shot him a dubious look. "Really? There was nothing about being at my house and meeting my family that gave you pause? Tell the truth."

His fingers curled into his palm. "For a fraction of a second, sure. A few thoughts ran through my mind, but I got over it without yelping."

"But you paused. Just like you might before hiring a Dunham to create a grazing table at your event."

"That's what you think will happen? That's why you don't want to go forward with this?"

"I know it'll happen. As much as I hate it, people with expendable income would be my main target audience, and they won't want to have anything to do with me."

He opened his mouth, and I held up my hand before he could deny it.

"Look, I've lived with this legacy my whole life. I was called Dead Girl through school. In elementary school, kids said I had the death touch and ran away from me. Not everyone thinks that way, but enough people do to make a difference. It means I won't get hired, and in the off-chance I do, they won't pass my name along to their friends for fear they'll be judged. Let's just cut our losses now. I'm sorry I didn't tell you sooner and wasted your time—"

"Stop, Daisy." He pressed the air with both hands. "I refuse to believe there isn't a solution. It's my job to figure out things like this. Let me think."

He got up and roamed his office, pausing at the windows for a solid minute or two. I sat there, patiently waiting. It was the least I could do after all he'd tried to do for me.

After several minutes, Miles turned toward me. "My initial plan was to bring you with me to several functions I've been invited to attend this spring and summer to introduce you to potential clients."

My stomach plummeted with regret. That was a really good idea. If I were anyone else, it would have been the perfect opportunity to network.

Miles strode back to the table and sat across from me. "We'll still do that, but I'll give you my name, which, like you said, lends me respect I haven't earned."

"What do you mean? How can you give me your name?"

"Not literally, but if I tell everyone you're mine, you'll go from Daisy Dunham to Daisy, Miles Aldrich's girlfriend."

I burst out laughing. He'd almost had me. I was so eager for there to be a solution, I'd been on the edge of my seat, and here he was jerking my chain.

"Okay, sure. I'll just be your fake girlfriend, and everyone will like me."

He peered at me through narrowed eyes. "I sense sarcasm, but I don't know why. You might not see it, but I'm well known for my charm. Those circles you want to break into? They love me. It's why my parents send me to all the functions for the charities they support."

My eyes darted back and forth between his, searching for the punchline to this insane idea. Miles wasn't laughing. In fact, his sincerity was pinned to his sleeve. He really meant this.

"Why not introduce me as your friend?"

"I thought of that. It's what I had intended to do before the story you just told me. But I don't think being friends will be quite enough. Saying you're my girlfriend implies a deeper commitment. Having you with me at these events will show I'm willingly connecting my name to yours."

I didn't know what to say. This was ridiculous, and it infuriated me that he might actually be right—that posing as his girlfriend could truly convince his crowd I was worthy of their business and a modicum of respect.

"I don't know, Miles. This seems so far-fetched. Why would you even want to do this?"

He slowly exhaled. "Before you got here, I was looking at my calendar and saw an event I'm obligated to go to coming up. Do you know what I felt? Dread. Most of the conversations I hold are drier than toast. They're boring, fake, tedious, but how can I say no when it's for charity? So, I go every year and hate every moment. But if you come with me...I think we could have fun pulling one over on everyone. Besides, there's nothing that gets me off more than seeing one of my clients succeed."

I sniffed. "You probably shouldn't talk to your clients about what gets you off."

He shot me a crooked grin. "Yeah, but we're friends too."

"Are we?"

"We are."

"I don't think we're friends who talk about getting off."

His grin expanded. "We should be. Social norms are boring, Daisy-daze." He smacked a hand on the tabletop. "Now, are you in or are you in? Don't let all the work I did for you be in vain."

I shook my head. "No one would ever believe you and I are a couple."

"Why not?"

"Because we're not...you are...we're just different."

"Yeah?" He folded his arms over his chest. "What'd your ex look like?"

"That doesn't matter, and it's not all about looks."

His brow crinkled. "That ugly, huh? Don't worry, Cupcake, you're good looking enough to date me. Objectively, I'd say we're on the same level of attractiveness."

"What? No, I wasn't saying that," I sputtered. "Andy isn't ugly, and I definitely wasn't saying I'm not attractive enough for you. You have an astounding ego. Wow."

He shrugged. "It's not like I did anything to earn this face. It's not an accomplishment. My ego isn't attached to my outsides. If you said I was ugly, I'd say you must have unconventional tastes *or* you're a liar, but I wouldn't cry in my pillow. But that's not the point. I want to know why you don't think we would make a convincing couple."

This man might as well have been holding me upside down and giving me a shake with how rattled I was. I'd walked in today prepared to turn him down, and now I was trying to explain how we didn't suit each other. How had we even gotten here?

Miles.

It was all Miles Aldrich and his mind that moved a mile a minute. He'd bounced from failure to a path to success without taking a breath, leaving me to catch up, and I hadn't quite gotten there yet.

"Our aesthetics are opposite. We're nothing alike. You're you, and I'm...me."

"You know," he leaned forward, bracing his forearms on the table, "I'm disappointed in how shortsighted you are. Just because you have a little emo heart and a penchant for all black doesn't mean we have nothing in common. As for our aesthetic, that's easily addressed with a shopping trip. I'll expense it."

"How do you have an answer to every one of my objections when you only just came up with this idea?"

"I'm fast on my feet," he replied. "I don't understand why you're objecting. Are you afraid to take a chance and actually succeed? Is that what's happening?"

"I—" I swallowed hard, my denial going down like a ball of railroad spikes. He'd figured me out in one guess, before I could even figure myself out. "Maybe."

He nodded. "I get it. I see it every day. Clients excited until the day comes to put everything in motion. Then comes the backpedaling, bargaining, request for delays. I'm extremely familiar with self-sabotage, and I don't allow it in my office. Tell me you're in, Daisy Dunham, and we'll do this. I won't let you fail, but you have to be all in, no backing out."

Miles Aldrich was not who I'd expected him to be.

He was far more insightful and deliberate than he presented at first glance. I hadn't thought it possible for me to trust someone new this quickly, but I was beginning to trust him. It was a fragile, wavering trust, especially after what Nick had told me, but it was there. I might have been uncertain of Miles as a person, but he took his role at Peak Strategies seriously—of that, I *was* certain.

That was most important to me.

I held my hand out. "I'm dubious this will work, but I'm all in on trying."

His warm palm slid against mine, and he gave my hand a firm shake. "It's a deal. I'm going to text you my address. Come over tomorrow night and help me remove some wallpaper while we cement the details of our fake relationship."

"Remove wallpaper?"

"Yes." He grinned. "I can't exactly bill you for being your fake boyfriend, now can I? You're going to pay me by helping me with my house renos. Still in?"

I gaped at him. "Oh my god, you did it. You found a way of tricking free labor out of me."

That made him laugh. "I told you, if that were my plan, I'd aim for someone with more muscle mass. Besides, it isn't free. We bartered this deal. You get something, and so do I."

I knew nothing about house renovations, but this was good. If this was strictly a transaction, no lines would get blurred. I helped him, he helped me, that was all.

"Okay, I'll be there."

"With bells on, I hope."

"Now you're going too far."

When he grinned at me, the muscles in my face easily responded. I grinned back. Maybe this wouldn't be so bad.

"By the way, how's Reed?" he asked.

"Reed?"

"Reed. After the rich bitch at brunch asked to be moved, how was he?"

My chest twinged. My brother...he was having a rough go of it. Being fourteen wasn't easy. Add in slightly different, kind of scrawny, and having the last name Dunham, freshman year of high school hadn't been kind. I'd been watching him disappear into himself for months and didn't know what to do.

"He didn't want to talk about it, but I could see how angry and defeated it made him feel. He just wanted to go home and disappear into his room, and that's what he did."

"Sucks." Miles' chin fell heavy on his fist. "He gets a lot of flak?"

I nodded. "He won't talk about that either, but I know he does. He's having a pretty miserable school year, and when he's home, he locks himself in his room making music."

"What kind of music?"

"He makes DJ mixes, I think. That's what I hear through the door since he won't let me listen."

"Hmmm. At least he has something he's into. Did you ever consider he plays it loud enough for you to hear without having to invite you in?"

"No, I never considered that." I rubbed the tightness away from my chest. "It's a nice thought. Thank you."

We said goodbye after Miles assigned me the homework of learning how to remove wallpaper so he didn't have to waste time teaching me.

It wasn't until I was in my car that what I'd agreed to really sank in.

I was officially Miles Aldrich's fake girlfriend.

Miles was now my fake boyfriend.

I waited for panic to take over, but it didn't come. Instead, I experienced a half-manic kind of giddiness. This whole idea was crazy, outlandish, completely off the wall.

But what if it worked?

CHAPTER TWELVE

Miles

"Die, duck, die."

I'd gotten off track. The rubber ducks were still living in my house because the downstairs bathroom had called my name. Now that it had been demolished, I was back at the ducks.

This was why it took me years to finish a house. Undoubtedly, a squirrel or broken tile would distract me again.

The doorbell rang as I was preparing to launch a full-scale attack on the duck that had been giving me the side-eye for a solid week. I tossed down my scraper and wiped my hands on my athletic shorts on my way to let Daisy in.

Swinging the door open, I found my helper standing there, her hands crammed in the pockets of an oversized black hoodie.

"Hello, Cupcake."

"Cupcake?" she repeated drolly. "I can handle Daisy-daze, but Cupcake?"

"I know for a fact I've called you that multiple times and you haven't complained. Now that we're exclusive, you're trying to change me?"

She stomped her little booted foot. "You can't nickname me after my job. It would be like if I called you...I don't know, Spreadsheet. That would be weird."

Reaching out, I grabbed the front of her hoodie and tugged her into my house. She stumbled over the door jamb and caught herself on my chest. Taking her by the shoulders, I steadied her until she shook me off.

"You can't start complaining before you've even left my front porch."

"Is that the rule?"

"It is in this house. There's no complaining inside either." I smiled down at her, pleased she'd shown up. Once she'd left my office yesterday, I had begun to doubt she'd go along with my plan after she put some thought into it, but here she was.

Without warning, she jabbed me in the sternum with her cute little finger. "Landry told me what you did."

"What did I do?"

She poked me again. "That card you gave her had a voucher for a weekend getaway at a bed and breakfast. That was..."

"Kind? Thoughtful? Generous?"

She growled through gritted teeth. "Yes, *Miles*. All those things. Why did you do that?"

"She didn't like it?"

I was rewarded with an epic eye roll. "Of course she liked it. It was kind, thoughtful, and generous. She and Tom really needed an excuse to take time with each other." One more poke. "My whole family loves you, by the way."

"Cool. I didn't do it to buy their love, you know."

"Then why did you? That's an over-the-top present for someone you hadn't even met at that point."

Something ugly crawled across my brain. An age-old neediness reared its ugly head. Had I given Landry that gift to get her to like me? It wouldn't have been the first time.

"If she doesn't want it, tell her to toss it or give it away." I pinched the bridge of my nose and turned away. "It's fine. I get it."

Crossing the room, I picked up my scraper and pointed out the supplies to Daisy without looking at her. "There's another scraper for you. You can work on that side of the room."

Her footsteps were careful yet audible on the old, creaking boards. She stopped next to me, her hands on her hips.

"Hey, Miles?"

I cast her a glance. "Hey, Daisy."

"Remember me telling you about the shitty way my family has been treated?"

"Of course."

She situated herself between me and the wall, putting us as face-to-face as our height difference allowed.

"That's what we're used to—what *I'm* used to. When someone does something nice for no discernable reason, it makes me suspicious." Her toe tapped mine. "You didn't deserve that. Sorry for being a dick. Landry and Tom *love* your gift. I happen to know she already has a thank you note in the mail on the way to you. You did a good job."

"I go overboard."

"I can't accept nice things, even when they're not given to me. We're quite a pair." She kicked my shoe again. "I bet you're rethinking the whole fake dating thing, huh?"

"Not for a second." I held up the scraper between us. "You're not getting out of your job."

Grabbing the scraper from me, she spun to face the wall and gasped. "What the hell is this? There are ducks on your wall."

"I know, and you're going to help me kill them all." I had to stop myself from smacking her ass. She deserved it, but I didn't think she'd take too kindly to me doing it. "Get to work, Cupcake."

Glancing at me over her shoulder, she saluted me with the scraper. "Ay, ay, Spreadsheet."

Daisy turned on music while we worked on my walls. We sang to Tracy Chapman and Sheryl Crow, then I taunted her about her taste in music, so she turned on Liz Phair to drown me out. For a while, it was like a nineties Lilith Fair in my living room.

Then we got hungry. I ordered subs for us, and when they arrived, we kicked back on the deck. I picked the music—my "chill vibe" playlist—and lowered it so we could talk and hear the night sounds while we ate.

I nodded at her bottle of water. "Sorry I don't have anything stronger to offer."

She raised it to her lips. "No worries. I wouldn't have turned down a pink lemonade, but that's as strong as I drink."

"Pink lemonade? That's specific."

"I know what I like."

"You don't drink alcohol? At all?"

"No." She wiped her mouth with her napkin and slid her gaze my way. "This is between us."

"Anything you say is between us. You don't have to ask."

"My dad is an alcoholic. He hasn't had a drop to drink in almost twenty years, but I can still remember him stumbling around our family room when I was little." She turned her water bottle in a half circle on her knee. "Once he got sober, we never had alcohol in the house. I tried it a few times in college, but I hate being hungover, and being drunk isn't really my thing either."

Something thick coated my throat. I had to clear it a couple times before I could respond.

"I don't drink either."

She looked up from her water, her eyes darting back and forth between mine. "You're sober?"

I nodded once. "Nine months ago."

Her lips parted, and out of nowhere, she reached over and slapped my leg. "What the hell were you doing working at High Bar?"

"Nick needed a favor."

She tried to slap me again, but I caught her hand and squeezed it. That earned me a scowl, little lines pulling her mouth down.

"That was so dumb, Miles."

"Yeah. Not my finest moment or best thinking."

Wiggling her hand free, she picked up her water bottle and crumpled it in her tight grip. "Nick would have still been your friend if you'd turned him down."

I shrugged. "I wasn't thinking whether he would be or not when I said yes."

She looked me directly in the eye. "You go overboard, right?"

"Yeah." I shoved my fingers through my hair. I liked Nick, but he wasn't someone I'd lay down my life for. Yet, when he'd asked, I'd only considered how he would've felt if I'd said no, *not* what saying yes could have cost me.

"If I see you at High Bar again, I'll have Duke bodily remove you."

"Got it, Cupcake. No more risking my sobriety. Thanks for caring."

Nodding once, she rolled her lips over her teeth. After a moment or two, she reached over again, but I didn't get a slap this time. Grabbing my hand, she gave it a firm squeeze.

"Congratulations on nine months. What an accomplishment."

I almost downplayed it, but her intense expression stopped me. There wasn't an ounce of sarcasm in her congratulations, and when I let it settle, it felt pretty damn great to have my nine months acknowledged. Not many people in my life knew about it. I was glad Daisy was now one of them.

"Thanks, Daisy-daze. Cool of you to say so."

"I'm sending my dad your way if I see you being stupid," she threatened, and it warmed lonely parts of my heart.

If we didn't change the topic, I was going to do something more embarrassing than admitting the depths of my failures as a human to the woman I was supposed to be guiding.

"Got it." I nodded toward the food in her lap. "Eat your sandwich."

She put down her water and took a big bite of her turkey sub. It was fascinating how much she could fit in her mouth.

"Did you just unhinge your jaw?" I asked, making her sputter and choke. I quickly held out her water, but she waved me off while pounding on her chest, getting ahold of herself.

"Miles," she gasped.

"You opened it *so* wide."

She covered her eyes and laughed. "Can't I eat in peace?"

"Go ahead. I'm not going to risk you choking again."

Peeking at me from between her fingers, her mouth curved in a small smile. "I take big bites."

I chuckled. "I noticed. Sorry for shaming you, it was just shocking. I'm glad you're comfortable enough around me to go to town on your sub that way."

"Since this is a fake relationship, I figured I didn't have to impress you. Besides, I don't have the mental energy to be anything other than myself right now."

"Why would you want to be?"

"I just mean, if you and I were really dating, we'd be in the honeymoon phase where I'd only want you to see my attractive qualities."

My forehead crinkled from how high I raised my brows. "You think being able to unhinge your jaw *isn't* an attractive quality?"

A laugh burst out of her, taking me off guard. I hadn't known Daisy Dunham capable of such effusive laughter. All the weight she carried rolled off her shoulders as they shook with her giggles.

I mentally added a new goal to my objective with Daisy: make her laugh like that as many times as I could before the end of our agreement.

CHAPTER THIRTEEN

Daisy

I SHOVED A CUP of coffee at Miles when he opened his front door. He took it without a word and let me into his house. I plodded into the living room, my sunglasses firmly in place. He closed the door and strolled after me, casually sipping his coffee.

It was eight in the morning. Saturday morning. Being awake and functional on this day, at this time, didn't make sense.

"You should know, I'm not a morning person," I intoned.

He grinned—big surprise. And he was bouncing on his toes, all vim and vigor. "You could have come over later but..."

"I know. I'm helping at the funeral home." I puffed out a breath. "We could have done this through email."

"But then how would you have helped me remove the backsplash in my kitchen?"

I shoved my free hand in the pocket of my hoodie. "I'm surprised you haven't done that yet. Smashing tile seems like something you would have done right away."

"Oh yeah, I did. And I hung some marble and glass subway tile a couple weeks ago. Thing is, I hate it, so I'm going to rip it out."

"You hate it?"

"Yeah. It's dated. I should have gone more simple."

"Shouldn't you have thought that through before going through the trouble of hanging the tile the first time?"

He sipped his coffee and rocked back on his heels. "This house is my hobby. One day, I'll get it right and sell it. I'm in no rush."

I squeezed my eyes shut behind my sunglasses. "But the waste…"

"I'm thinking we can remove the backsplash without destroying it. The thing about me is I do shoddy work. Chances are, it'll come off easily."

I couldn't stop the giggle that bubbled out of me. God, Miles just said anything on his mind. To be honest, it was an ability I was jealous of.

He circled his arm around my shoulders and spun us toward the kitchen. "Like that, Daisy-daze."

"What?"

He squeezed my shoulder. "When I can make you laugh and all your troubles fall away. It's nice."

I didn't know what to say to that, but he didn't wait for me to come up with a response. We entered the kitchen, and he showed me the backsplash, then went on to point out all he wanted to do. To be fair, the kitchen looked like it hadn't been touched in at least thirty years. It needed a lot of work I wasn't sure Miles could provide, but I would reserve judgment. Plus, he had enough money to hire someone to come in and redo everything he messed up, so the stakes were low.

Over the next hour, we carefully pried the backsplash off the wall, only breaking a few pieces. Miles was going to donate them to a friend's charity that built houses for the unhoused. That certainly softened my feelings about his casual, easy-come-easy-go attitude.

Once that was done, we ended up back on the deck. Miles ran inside to get drinks, returning with a big jug of pink lemonade and two glasses.

He poured it without a hint of smugness and handed me a glass before pouring one for himself and sitting beside me.

"You remembered."

He kicked his feet up on the deck rail and took a long pull of his lemonade. "Of course. I just saw you a couple days ago. Unlike Edie, I don't have issues with my memory."

I groaned. "Landry said Edie's been nonstop patting her head and rubbing her tummy."

His mouth hitched. "Smart kid. As long as she keeps up the exercises, she'll be good to go. Now," he set his glass down on the table between us, "we have our first event the weekend after next, and at this point, I'm not sure we're going to be able to sell this relationship."

I tucked my hair behind my ear. "Okay...how do we make ourselves more believable?"

"Let's play a game. Two truths and a lie. You know it?"

"Of course. How is this going to help?"

"We'll learn things about each other in a non-boring way."

"Talking is boring?"

He rubbed his chin in contemplation. "Not to you, it isn't. But why not spice it up even more? You go first."

"This was your idea. You should go first."

"All right. Here goes: I didn't finish college, I'm allergic to shellfish, and I crashed my first car the day I got it." He raised a brow in challenge. "Which one's the lie?"

I leaned over in my chair to peer closely at him. This wasn't as easy as I'd expected it to be.

"You crashing your car feels on brand," I said.

"Okay. What do you think is my other truth, and what's the lie?"

I tapped my cheek, mulling it over. "The lie is shellfish. I don't think you're allergic."

"Errr." He made the sound of a buzzer. "Wrong. Give me a shrimp and give me death."

"Wow. I guess it's a good thing I didn't put any shellfish in the food I've given you. I was experimenting with clam cupcakes..."

He pressed a finger to my lips, shushing me. "No, no, Daisy. Never mention that again."

Batting his hand away, I laughed. "All right, so you didn't graduate from college. Weren't your parents mad?"

"Nah. To be honest, I'm not sure they even realize I didn't graduate. They just stopped getting bills for my tuition my junior year and never asked why."

"Did you flunk out?"

He chuffed at my question. "I dropped out voluntarily. The social part of college was the only thing I enjoyed. Classes were torture. It might take you by surprise, but I have ADHD."

"*No...*" My mouth curved into a smirk. I wasn't surprised at all. Earlier, I'd noticed his medicine bottles lined up next to the kitchen sink. Even on good meds, Miles was still heavy on the *H*, moving, fidgeting, bouncing on his toes.

"You little shit," he muttered. "Ten years ago, I had no idea how to regulate myself. I was all over the place. I've figured out I need to be busy with a variety of work. Hence, the house, the job. No two days are the same, so I stay interested and focused."

"Good for you. College isn't for everyone. Beau didn't go at all, and he's doing well for himself in Wyoming. I went, got an English degree, and now I make my living building websites and making—"

"Meat cups." He beamed at me, clearly amused with himself. "Your turn. Let's see if I do better than you."

Meat cups. If he didn't stop saying that, I was bound to slip up and call them that myself.

I took a deep breath. "Okay, here we go: I've never touched a dead body, I was in a sorority, I don't eat cupcakes."

His eyes flared. "Wow. You want this game to be impossible for me, huh?"

"Did you need me to go easier on you?"

"Never." He got up from his seat and leaned his back against the deck railing. "Now that I think of it, I've never seen you eat a cupcake, so as much as it pains me, I'm going to say that one's true. The other two, shit, Daisy-daze, I'm stumped. On the one hand, there's no way you would have willingly joined a sorority, but how could you have never touched a dead body? I've touched a couple, and I didn't grow up in a funeral home."

"*Above* a funeral home," I corrected.

"Sure, sure." He dipped to squint at me. "Were you in a fucking sorority?"

"Is that your final answer?"

"Yes. No. Fuck, I don't know." He yanked at the side of his hair. "Fine. Yes, that's my final answer."

"Errr." I made the same obnoxious buzzing sound he had. "I wasn't in a fucking sorority, Miles. Come on."

"I could almost picture you in a sweater set with a ribbon in your hair." He threw out his arms. "How have you never touched a dead body?"

"I just...haven't. I've seen plenty, strangers and loved ones, but I've never felt the urge to touch one."

My sister's still form flashed in a memory that never went too far from the front of my mind, but I tucked it away for now. This wasn't the time to think about Quinn.

"Huh." He took his seat again. "See how this is more fun than a regular conversation?"

I laughed at that. "Sure. Should we go another round?"

"Absolutely. I'm going to win this time." He rubbed his hands together. "I had a crush on my brother's fiancée in high school, my favorite vegetable is green beans, I want to live in Denver forever."

"Hmmm..." I tapped my chin. "Green beans is true. I'm not sure about the other two. Denver is nice and all, but I don't know anyone passionate enough about this city to want to live here forever. Now, if you'd said Colorado as a whole, I might believe you. On the other hand, having a crush on your brother's fiancée...that's outrageous enough to be true."

"You're getting better at this. She wasn't his fiancée in high school, by the way."

I snorted. "I should hope not. Do you still...?"

He wrinkled his nose. "No. She's like my sister now. That would be gross."

"Is it my turn?"

"Yep. Go for it, Cupcake."

"Okay, here we go. My mother grew up in a commune of traveling musicians slash grifters called the Traveling Roses, my middle name is Edna, and I've always wanted to try living in another state."

"Whoa." His eyes flared. "The last one is truth. But the first two? This is tough. On the one hand, if your middle name is Edna, that means your initials are DED, and I would hope your parents are smart enough not to lay that on you, given...you know, their profession. On the other, I can't picture Whitney Mae as a grifter. She's too proper."

I stacked my hands in my lap, smug. "The middle name is the lie."

He clapped his hands. "I knew it."

"My middle name is actually Ethel."

That took the wind from his sails. "So, your initials are DED?"

"Yep. It never occurred to my parents that would pose a problem."

"Kids were assholes?"

"Of course they were."

He expelled a puff of breath and muttered, "Of course they were." Then he cocked his head. "All right. The Traveling Roses? For real?"

"For real. That's how my parents met, actually. My mama was performing at the Colorado State Fair with some of her cousins. My dad took one look at her and asked her to stay. She'd been looking for an excuse to get off the circuit, so she agreed. One of her other cousins is sort of a famous rock star."

He clicked his fingers. "I *knew* I'd heard of them before. I read an article...okay, a headline. Callum Rose from The Seasons Change is your relative?"

"Very distant, and it's not like I've ever met him."

He shook his head. "You keep getting more interesting, Daisy-daze."

"It's your turn." I nudged his leg with my toe. "Go on."

"I was a state champion wrestler in high school," he pointed to a scar in his brow, "got this from a wineglass my mom threw, intending to hit my dad, and I have another scar from a bullet."

I gaped at him, really hoping he'd forgotten the rules and had given two lies. "Jesus, Miles. I don't know which one I want to be the lie more." I puffed up my cheeks and slowly let the air out. "I'm going to guess the bullet is the lie. Right?"

He shook his head. "Nope. I was shot about a year ago."

"No you weren't. I don't believe you."

"I was. Want to see?"

"The scar you made up? Sure, show me."

He hopped up and turned away from me. Then he hooked his fingers into the waistband of his athletic shorts and lowered one side, exposing most of his ass cheek. There, right in the middle of his smooth, golden skin, was a round, puckered dent.

My mouth went dry, my head fuzzy. I said the first thing that popped into my mind. "How is your ass so tan?"

Chuckling, he pulled up his shorts and turned to rest his elbows on the railing behind him.

"That's my natural glow, Cupcake."

"You can't just show me your bullet wound and expect a sensical reaction." I rubbed the throb between my eyebrows. "I mean...are you okay?"

"Yeah, I'm all good now. I'll have a gnarly scar for the rest of my life, but no other lasting side effects."

I dropped my hand to glare at him. I couldn't explain it, but I was suddenly incredibly pissed off at him.

"How in the hell did you get shot, Miles Aldrich?" He opened his mouth, but I waved him off. "Wait, let me guess. Were you caught running out of some rich, married lady's bedroom by her angry husband?"

His eyelids lowered over sparkling hazel eyes. He was amused while I was all out of sorts.

"Not quite so harrowing. There was an incident last year at the grand opening of my friend Elliot's building. A crazy old man was waving his gun around, and I put myself between him and my friends to distract him. It had worked. The guy got tackled by security, and I thought it was over, so I turned around."

He clucked his tongue. "Old man got a shot off before they got the gun away from him. Hit me right in the ass."

My throat was tight. I did not like this game anymore. "Did it hurt?"

"It didn't feel like angel kisses, that's for damn sure."

I couldn't explain my urge to strangle this man. My fingers curled around the wooden arms of my Adirondack chair, wishing it were his neck. This wasn't something you just dropped on someone during a game.

Miles took a step closer, worry furrowing his brow. "You doing okay?"

"I'm—" I focused on the rip in the knee of my jeans. "You're just so...casual about being shot. It's hard for me to wrap my head around."

"It's been over a year for me. I didn't feel great about it when it happened. I had to sit on a donut for a solid month after I got out of the hospital." He huffed a laugh. "But I'd go through it again, no question. If I hadn't been there to take the bullet, it would have hit

Elliot, or his wife, Kit. Might've hit my brother or his girl. Much better it was me."

I lifted my chin, pissed at the people he'd named for no discernible reason. "I hope they'd take a bullet for you too."

"Eh." He shrugged. "Doesn't matter what they'd do in the same situation. I did what I thought was right."

"Of course it matters." I climbed to my feet to pace. If I didn't walk some of this fizzing anger off, I'd scream. "Surely your brother would have taken a bullet for you…?"

"It doesn't matter," he said softly. "No one can say what they'd do in a situation like that."

"Except you." I tugged on my hoodie strings. "You can."

"And I'm kind of banking on never having to go through that again." He nodded at my glass. "Drink some pink lemonade and chill, Daisy-daze. Everything's fine. My ass isn't as perfect as it once was, but I'm told women are into scars, so…"

Groaning, I whirled around and guzzled my lemonade. I was annoyed with Miles for being so nonchalant, but more annoyed with myself for reacting this way. We barely knew each other, yet my gut was churning at the possibilities of what could have happened to him. Add the fact he wasn't sure his friends, let alone his brother, would have done the same for him, and I was feeling like a crazy person.

"What do you think about hikes?" Miles asked out of nowhere.

I glanced at him over my shoulder. He was back to relaxing against the deck rail. "I go for a hike at least once a week."

"Want to go on one tomorrow?"

I turned fully to face him. I knew what this was. He was trying to distract me, and I was going to let him.

"With you?"

"Yeah. I invited myself along with Weston and his fiancée, Elise. If you come too, I won't be the dreaded third wheel and we can practice."

"Practice what?"

His eyes rounded. "Being boyfriend and girlfriend, obviously. We have to make sure our relationship is convincing."

"You want to fake it with your brother?"

"I do. Chances are, he'll be at some of the same events we go to. I can't have Westie blowing our cover."

"I suppose I could go for a hike tomorrow. If it's awkward or obvious they don't want me there, I'm going to slap you on your gunshot wound."

A wide grin spread across his too-attractive face. "Wow, you went from concerned to malicious at the drop of a hat. My mercurial little Cupcake."

I stopped my eyes from rolling, but just barely. "Do you think we could spend some time talking about Grazing? You know, the reason we're doing this in the first place?"

"Absolutely." He straightened, going from relaxed to business in an instant. "Tell me what you've been working on."

For the next hour or so, I showed Miles the website I'd been building, along with new branded socials. He had suggestions for elements to add, and created rough drafts of graphics he thought I needed on the fly. We bounced ideas off each other as easily as old coworkers. His enthusiasm bled onto me. My usual pessimism was brightened by his relentless positivity. We might've been faking our relationship, but this was real. I didn't think it had truly hit me until that moment. Grazing was actually happening.

I was terrified. If not for Miles, I might have cut and run, but he never would have let me. He would've lassoed me by the ankles and done that dangling thing he'd threatened.

We worked for a while longer, then Miles tried to rope me into more renovation, and I packed up my computer as quickly as I could.

It wasn't until Miles had shown me out, the door clicking behind me, that something else hit me.

Miles never told me what the lie was.

CHAPTER FOURTEEN

Miles

Weston was annoyed with me.

Nothing new about that.

"What were you thinking?" Weston shoveled his overgrown flop of hair off his forehead. "You can't believe either of us want to spend the next four hours with a random woman you met when you hired her for a lap dance or wherever you're finding them these days."

The thing about me was I liked to ask for forgiveness rather than permission. I'd sprung Daisy on Weston and Elise when I'd pulled into the parking lot at the base of our hike. I'd been so thoughtful, I'd told Daisy to come fifteen minutes later than the real meeting time so I could get the conversation out of the way before she arrived.

If she'd heard Weston calling her a random stripper, I might not have let it roll off my back so easily.

My brother was almost four years older, and while I'd always looked up to him, he could be a gigantic, stubborn dick. It was his way or the highway. The only person he bent for was his fiancée, Elise, and that was because he'd lose her if he didn't. He almost had once, and I'd been there to tell him how stupid he was.

"Say whatever you want about me, but Daisy is off-limits. If you'd paused a fucking second, I would have told you I'd met her at work. She's starting a business I'm helping her with, and we hit it off." I stepped into his space. "You'll be nice to her, or I'll hire some of those strippers for your bachelor party and tell Lisie it was your idea."

Weston raised his hands and backed up. "All right. I'm prepared to be wrong, but it's still a dick move not to forewarn us."

Elise laid a hand on my brother's arm. "It's unexpected, but certainly not unwanted." She flashed a dimple at Weston, and he instantly relaxed.

"Thanks, Lisie. I can always count on you to be on my side."

Weston growled and tugged her close. "She's always on *my* side."

Elise patted his puffed-up chest. "Is it possible we're all on the same side? I'd love it if we were." She pointed at something. "Oh, look. That has to be her pulling in."

"Be nice," I warned Weston.

He gave me a long, assessing look. My brother was smart. At twenty, he'd invented a thin, lightweight, environmentally-sound insulation for outerwear and started his company, Andes. He'd build it into something more massive than any of us could have foreseen, even him. So, when he looked at me the way he was, he was using that big, fancy brain of his to find the things I wasn't saying.

I'd never warned him about a girl before.

Had never invited one along on a hike.

Had never met one at work or talked her up the way I had Daisy.

He was seeing there was something different at play here. This wasn't casual.

That was true. This thing with Daisy was serious. I didn't fool around when it came to my business, and this relationship had become the focus of my work.

Daisy made her way across the parking lot toward our trio. Her head was covered by an army green hat, and she wore a plaid shirt tucked into slim, dark brown cargo pants. On her feet were a fine pair of hiking boots—boots that told me she really was a hiker.

I went to her, stopping ten or fifteen feet from Weston and Elise. "Hey, Daisy-daze."

"Hey, Spreadsheet."

I tugged on the bill of her hat. "I'm going to give you a great big hug now. Act like you like it, okay?"

She wrinkled her nose. "Oh, all right. I'll try."

With a grin, I swooped her into my arms and lifted her right off her feet. She was too short for me to waste time bending over and trying to get in there. Her arms circled my neck, holding me tight in the same way her mom had. For a second, I found myself wishing she'd wrap her legs around me too.

"You've got that Dunham hugging gene," I said as I buried my face in the side of her neck.

"Why hug if you're not going to go all in?" She played with the hair at my nape and sighed. "You can kiss my cheek, but then you have to put me down."

"What if I want you to kiss *my* cheek?"

Without a word of argument, she turned her head, catching her lips on the hinge of my jaw. A soft press of warmth and it was over as quickly as it had started. "There," she whispered. "Put me down now. I'm dangling."

"I didn't get my kiss yet." I pulled my face out of her neck and slid my cheek along hers, touching my lips to her chin. "There."

I set her on her feet, holding her elbows until she was steady. "Ready to meet my asshole brother and his sweet fiancée?"

"I heard that," Weston called.

I grinned at him. "Why do you think I said it so loudly?"

Daisy went ahead of me, greeting Elise then Weston. She shook their hands, the little business lady. Of course, Weston approved. Probably because the last woman he'd seen on my arm had been at Elise's birthday party almost two years ago. She hadn't really even known where she was, much less whose birthday she was celebrating.

Daisy and I were an arrangement, but if one of the effects of faking it with her was building me up in my brother's esteem, I would take it. Weston didn't give a shit about names or pedigree. He judged based on work ethic and loyalty. I already knew Daisy had plenty of the first, and I was banking she wasn't short on the latter.

"Do you do a lot of hiking, Daisy?" Weston asked.

"I make sure I get out at least once a week." She hooked her thumbs around the straps of her backpack. "I don't know if that constitutes a lot."

Weston stared down his nose at her. "By yourself?"

She shrugged, not seeing the danger she was about to step in. "Sometimes. It depends if I can find someone to go with me. But I'm always on populated trails, so I've never felt unsafe."

He whipped his head toward Elise. "Tell her about the mountain lion."

The four of us naturally fell into a group, Weston and me behind Elise and Daisy. I listened to Elise tell the story of the time she thought she was hiking on her own. Little had she known, Weston had been following her. She'd fallen asleep by a stream, and when she woke, Weston was there, telling her to be quiet.

"Oh my god. I would have screamed if Miles had appeared out of nowhere," Daisy said.

"I might have screamed, but he told me to look maybe fifteen feet away, and then I couldn't even talk," Elise replied.

Daisy gasped. "Was a mountain lion watching you?"

"Mmmhmm. If Weston hadn't been there, I probably would have walked right into it and wouldn't be here to talk about it."

Weston tensed beside me, his hands balling into fists. I'd heard this story a couple times, and he never failed to look like he wanted to hunt down that mountain lion and wrestle it. It had been nearly two years, and West almost always walked slightly behind Elise when they hiked. I'd asked Elise about it once, and she'd explained mountain lions attacked from behind.

My brother.

Total dick at times, but there was no question he loved his woman.

Elise reached behind me to twine her fingers with West's. They walked like that for a minute or two before he let her have her hand back. When he did, she looked at him over her shoulder, her dimple popping, and mouthed, "Love you." He told her he loved her at full volume.

Elise and Daisy had an easy conversation going, discussing their favorite haunts in Denver, the best hiking spots, their jobs, people they both knew. Elise and I were a couple years older than Daisy, but growing up in the same town, friendships and acquaintances were bound to overlap.

"You'll have to come to High Bar when I'm working," Daisy said. "It's a fun place to hang out, and once a month, the owner brings in some kind of act, like knife swallowers or acrobats."

"You work in a bar, Daisy?" Weston asked.

"Only two nights a week now," she answered, seeming ready to leave it at that. But my girl did more than wait tables. If she wasn't going to toot her own horn, I would.

"Daisy is a contractor there. She has a sweet little business as a cigarette girl, only she sells her homemade cupcakes and charcuterie cups," I explained. "You should see how feral the customers get for her treats."

Elise turned to her. "Oh, do you wear one of those trays strapped around your neck?"

Daisy nodded, her cheeks slightly flushed. It might have been from physical exertion, but I hadn't noticed them this red before. No, I swore my little Daisy was embarrassed.

"She wears a silly little hat on the side of her head too," I added.

"A pillbox hat," Daisy explained. "I play fast and loose with the time period of my costume, but none of my customers really question how accurate I am. They like the treats and short skirt."

"Okay, I'm definitely making a point of visiting on a night you're working. I'll bring Saoirse. She'll love it." Elise bumped her shoulder into Daisy's. "Don't let me forget to grab your number before we head home."

This was apparently what it was like to be dating a functional person who got along with my brother and future sister-in-law. In no time, Daisy and Elise were friends, and Weston wasn't poised to vault between them to keep Elise safe.

I was nine months sober—nowhere near ready to date for real. When I was...I'd look for a girl just like Daisy. One free and clear of feelings for anyone else. She'd be a little grumpy, with enough pessimism to balance me out. Someone who was good with meeting new people and gave hugs tight enough to squeeze the juice out of me. There probably weren't many out there like her, but she was setting the standard.

◆

There was a stream at the turning point—not the one where the mountain lion had appeared. It was lucky Weston hadn't razed the ground there back then. If Elise had tried to go back to that spot, he undoubtedly would have.

Elise and Weston took their shoes off to wade. Daisy plopped down on a flat rock, turning her face up to the sun. Since she was all good, I wandered around the area, stooping to pick a few wildflowers—one bunch for Elise, the other bigger one for Daisy.

When I got back, Daisy had lost her flannel, leaving her in a white, ribbed tank top that hugged her tits and stomach. Weston and Elise were a short way down the stream, so I took a moment to appreciate the hotness of my fake girlfriend.

I'd done well for myself, that was for sure.

Whoever had dumped her was an absolute idiot. If circumstances were different, I might've tried to win her over. Might've said something stupid, hoping she liked my sense of humor. If that hadn't impressed, I probably would have flexed my arms to show her I was strong enough to toss her around if she wanted.

Christ.

It was a wonder I'd ever gotten laid. Then again, I couldn't remember the last time I'd picked someone up while either of us were sober. I was a lot funnier to drunk people.

Sitting down on the rock beside her, I thrust the wildflowers at her. "For you."

She stared at them then her eyes flickered up to mine. "You...picked flowers for me?"

"Yeah. Probably dumb. I should have left them in the ground, but I saw them and pictured them in a jar on your desk. I thought you'd like to look at them while you're working."

Her hand covered the top of mine. "It's not dumb at all. You surprised me. I haven't gotten flowers in ages, and I didn't expect you to go out of your way to pick me some." She prodded my fingers open enough for her to slip the flowers from my grip and held them up to her face. I couldn't name a single one, but they were yellow, blue, white, and purple. "I love them, Miles. I bet you picked that other bouquet for Elise, didn't you?"

Something in the roughness to her voice alarmed me. I dipped down to get a good look at her face. She had her bottom lip pinned between her teeth, and her dark eyes were glassy.

"Hey." I took her chin between my fingers to raise her head, bringing her eyes to mine. "What's this about, Cupcake?"

She gave her head a shake, but it was halfhearted. No effort into breaking free from my hold.

"I told you, I'm not used to this type of kindness. I don't know how to handle it."

"Daisy—" I had a thousand questions, and my biggest was about her ex-boyfriend. If he hadn't treated her with kindness, how in the hell had he treated her?

Before I could bombard her—what I would have done—Elise and Weston made their way back to us. Daisy popped off the rock and waved her bouquet at Elise.

"Look what Miles found. Aren't they so sweet?"

Elise's gaze bounced to me, and her brow lifted in a way that signaled her approval. That did something to me. Meant more than I could explain. Elise and I were friends now, but we hadn't always been. Our history was steeped in mutual trauma and a flurry of mixed feelings. Slowly but surely, we'd been working our way out the other side. This felt like it could have been the final step to putting it all behind us.

Too bad it was all pretend.

I waved the second bouquet. "Got you one too, Lisie."

She claimed it from me, giving me a half hug. From the pure annoyance in his gaze, if Weston could have lit the flowers on fire, he would have.

On the way back, Weston ended up beside Daisy, while Elise and I took the lead. I kept an ear open, just in case, but mostly trusted Weston not to mistreat her.

Elise leaned into me, keeping her voice low. "Saoirse didn't tell me you were dating anyone."

"She doesn't exactly know."

Her brow crinkled. "Do you think she'll have a problem with you dating a client?"

"Hope not." I took off my hat, shoved my hair off my forehead, then replaced it. "I have no intention of making a habit of it. There's just something about Daisy..."

"Yeah, there is," she agreed. "Are you going to bring her to the wedding?"

"I—uh..."

This was where being impulsive got me into sticky situations. In six weeks, I was going to be the best man at West and Elise's wedding. If Daisy were my real girlfriend, she would be there as my plus one. Since it hadn't really crossed my mind—*yeah, terrible best man, I know*—I hadn't discussed it with her.

When I didn't respond quickly enough, Elise took the job out of my hands.

Twisting around, she said, "Hey, Daisy—are you free the evening of June seventh?"

Daisy shot me a wide-eyed look before shifting her focus back to Elise. "If it's a Saturday, I normally work, but I can take the night off since I'm technically my own boss. Why? What's happening June seventh?"

Weston chuckled. "You just got invited to our wedding."

Her mouth fell open. "What? I mean, wow. Thank you. I'd love to come." Her quick recovery was impressive. It was almost as fast as the threatening look she shot me.

I imagined we'd be discussing this later.

"Good. We'd love to have you." Elise elbowed my arm. "See how easy that was?"

"Thanks, Lisie." I almost threw my arm around her to drive Weston crazy but stopped myself, not wanting Daisy to feel weird.

"You're not going to say you can't wait to share the first dance with me?" she asked.

I barked a laugh. That sounded like me. "Nah. I'll let Weston have that. I'm going to be busy dancing with my own girl."

Surprisingly, I was really looking forward to it too.

CHAPTER FIFTEEN

Daisy

I HAD NO CLUE how Miles and Weston came from the same parents. If I didn't know they were brothers, I never would've guessed. Weston was a couple inches taller, and his build was on the leaner side. Miles was more broad, with heavier muscles. Weston had light brown hair with some blond highlights, while Miles' was chestnut brown. Their hazel eyes and sharp jawline were the only similarities I could find between them.

It wasn't just in their looks where they differed.

Miles was a bright ball of energy, while Weston kept himself tightly locked down. I had a feeling he was similar to me—slow to trust, wary of intentions, but once someone was in with them, they were in for life.

For that reason, I didn't find his reticence off-putting, but I did wonder how he and Miles had turned out so differently.

Weston cleared his throat. "Your family owns the Dunham funeral home?"

"Yes." I braced myself for what came next.

He nodded tightly. "I've been there several times. It's nice for what it is."

"Thanks. My parents take a lot of pride in it."

"You don't want to go into the family business?"

"I don't. My brother-in-law works with my dad on his end of things, and my sister assists our mom part-time. They'll take it over when the time comes. I help out when they need me, and I keep their website running, but I don't want to die in the same place I grew up."

"That makes sense. I never had an interest in joining my father in his business ventures. Then again, he had a tendency to run his investments into the ground."

Ahead of us, Elise and Miles were having an animated discussion. With how at ease they were, I wondered how long they had known each other.

"You're not the type of woman Miles has brought around in the past," Weston stated.

"No? We haven't done a lot of talking about our past partners—"

"Forgive me, but I wouldn't call anyone I've seen Miles with a partner. They were...distractions. Acts of rebellion. Definitely not a partner."

"Distractions from what?"

Weston rubbed his scruff and peered at his brother's back, an enigmatic smile curling the corners of his mouth. "That's something I have yet to uncover. The root is probably our shit upbringing, but my brother doesn't talk to me, so I wouldn't know the rest."

"He doesn't talk to you?" I found that hard to believe. From what I'd seen, Miles had never met a stranger. He could talk to a brick wall and be happy.

"Not about anything real. We're doing better, though. Getting there," he gruffed. "Having Elise around helps. He likes her a lot more than me."

I huffed a laugh, doubting that. "Have they known each other long?"

"He didn't tell you?"

"He's shared a lot, but not those kinds of details."

"Ah...well, I've been friends with Elise and her brother Elliot since early childhood. Miles and Elise got to know each other in high school. He was a major dick to her, but he's managed to win her forgiveness in the last couple years."

"I hope she made him work his ass off."

He chuckled. "She didn't make it easy."

"Good."

My stomach twinged, thinking back to Nick's warning. This must've been what he'd been talking about. Chances were, Weston was underplaying just how big of a dick Miles had been. But if Elise was willing to forgive him, it wasn't on me to hold a grudge on her behalf.

Miles threw his arm around Elise's shoulders, drawing a growl from Weston, which made me laugh. He shot a dark gaze in my direction.

"That doesn't bother you?"

"No. I come from a tight as hell family. Someone's always touching up on someone else. That's what that looks like to me. Family."

He peered at the two of them again and nodded. "Family. You're right. That's what they are."

I chuckled at his tight jaw. "It still bothers you."

"I have a solid possessive streak I struggle to deal with," he muttered.

"I bet Miles knows that, doesn't he? Might he be egging you on?"

Weston's jaw rippled. "He might be. Kid was born to antagonize me."

"That's what little bothers are for."

"Little bothers?" He huffed a laugh. "Sounds about right."

"I have one of my own. Right now, he's going through a sullen teen phase, but he spent his first thirteen years laughing at me whenever he could."

Weston hummed, looking ahead on the path then turning to check behind us. Had Weston not been so alert, I might not have believed the mountain lion story. They hadn't been pulling my leg.

"By the way," Weston started.

"Yeah?"

"I noticed you're not wearing anything Andes."

"Oh." I ran my hands over my no-name cargos, suddenly self-conscious. This man had freaking *invented* the filler for his company's coats, and they made so much more. We'd been receiving Andes' catalogs for a few years, and I never failed to drool over the gear. That price tag, though? "No, I'm not."

"Do you own anything Andes?"

"I have an old winter coat in my closet." Purchased for a song at Goodwill. Not that I would tell him that.

"Hmmm." He tucked his shaggy hair behind his ear. "Forgive me for using you as market research, but may I ask why? You seem like an avid hiker and lover of the outdoors."

"I am, but Andes is beyond my budget. I buy dupes—oh, I probably shouldn't say that."

He let out a short, dry chuckle. "It's fine. I won't have you arrested." He hummed again. "I think our prices are fair for what we offer, but it's always bothered me that we're not more accessible."

We volleyed ideas back and forth about accessibility and luxury brands. Once Weston got on the topic of his company, he became another person. More like Miles, enthusiastic and practically bouncing on his toes.

I decided I might like Weston Aldrich. I definitely liked his fiancée, Elise.

When we reached the parking lot, Elise and I hugged, and Weston gave my shoulder a pat before he tugged Elise to his side. Miles mimicked his brother, gripping my hip possessively.

I would have liked it if it were real.

Miles walked me to my car and backed me into my door. "Play along. They haven't left yet. If you were my girl for real, I'd be making out with you right now."

I pressed my hand to his chest. "I'm not making out with you."

"I didn't expect you would." He dipped down, shoving his face in my neck like he had at the beginning of the day. Only now, I had been outside for hours and done a decent amount of sweating. When Miles inhaled, I cringed.

"God*damn*, Daisy. You smell delicious."

"I'm sweaty."

His nose dragged along the side of my neck. Something wet poked against my skin for the barest second, followed by a low groan. If I hadn't known better, I would have said he'd licked me, but that couldn't have been right. It must have been his lips.

"Like I said, delicious," he uttered.

My stomach swooped and crash-landed at my feet. Maybe I hadn't been wrong.

He broke away from my neck to peer down at me, one arm braced beside my head, the other still holding onto my hip. His fingers dug into my flesh, kneading me.

"You made friends with my brother," he stated.

"'Friends might be an exaggeration. We had a pretty good conversation once he relaxed, though."

"That's what I mean. Weston doesn't relax."

I shot him a small smile. "Well...he relaxed in that he didn't see me as a threat to Elise or you." My fingers curled into his T-shirt. "Were you and Elise friends in high school?"

He scoffed. "No. I wanted to be, but I didn't know how to get her attention in a constructive way. I was a dick to her."

"Those were Weston's exact words."

"I'm surprised he didn't say worse." The hand resting beside my head moved to my hair, stroking the fine strands. "We both worked at Andes a couple years ago, and I forced my friendship on her."

"Seems to have stuck."

"Yeah."

I felt the need to poke at him a little. "You didn't get jealous when she went out with Weston?"

He let his forehead fall against mine. "You're treading on a really complicated bevy of emotions right now and don't even know it. The bare bones answer is no, I'm not jealous Elise and Weston are together. Them ending up together was always inevitable. I'm just happy to be along for the ride."

I cupped his cheeks, coaxing his face away from mine so I could look at him. "There's so much you're not saying."

"Too much for a parking lot." Wrapping his fingers around my wrist, he lifted my hand, turned his head, and placed a kiss on my palm. "Thanks for coming out today. You really raised my brother's opinion of me."

"I didn't do anything special, Miles. I think he already likes you."

He straightened, his hand sliding down my arm. "We did a good job convincing them this is real. I'm giving you the credit for going along with whatever was thrown at you. I didn't think you'd be so flexible."

I snorted. "Big family. Grew up above a funeral home. I am used to chaos and every day being different. Today was easy-peasy."

He squeezed my bicep. "God, you're cute, Lydia-Daisy-Cupcake."

I rolled my eyes. "I still seem like a Lydia?"

"Yep, but Daisy is growing on me."

Miles was growing on me.

He was like the wildflowers he'd picked for me, splashes of bright beauty that seemed to come from nowhere.

We said our goodbyes with promises to meet next week to talk about my progress with Grazing. My social battery was almost on empty by the time I started driving home. When I arrived, all I wanted to do was shower, curl up on my couch, and veg for a solid two hours.

As I trudged up the stairs to my apartment, I remembered the flowers nestled in my backpack. I found a jar in my kitchen, filled it with water, dunked my sweet little bouquet inside, and put it on my desk—exactly where Miles had envisioned.

Then I took a picture and sent it to him.

Me: *You're right, they look perfect here. Thank you again.*

Miles: *Look at you, taking my vision and bringing it to fruition, just like you're going to do with Grazing. You're very welcome, Daisy. I'm honored you kept them and put them where you'll look at them. xx*

The next day, Reed showed up at my door. It was enough to knock my socks off. Reed rarely left the house. I could have counted the times he'd visited my apartment on one hand. What almost put me on my ass, though? The big box he was carrying, stamped with the Andes, Inc. logo.

"This was just delivered for you." His flat intonation caught my attention. Reed had never been a flat sort of guy, and lately, getting *any* reaction out of him was a challenge.

"Come in and help me open it." He followed me inside, placing the box on my coffee table. I gave him a pair of shears, letting him do the honors of slicing it open.

He picked up an envelope. "There's a note. See who it's from."

"I'm pretty sure I know who."

"You have a hookup at Andes?"

"Um. Let me read the note first."

Daisy,

Elise helped me pick out what she deemed "essentials" for you. If the sizes are wrong, you can exchange them at any Andes store. Included is a voucher for hiking boots.

I'd love to discuss ways to make Andes more accessible to a greater population. Maybe next hike?

Elise says hi, and she'll be texting soon.

Best,

Weston Aldrich

"Holy shit." Reed was standing behind me, reading over my shoulder. "That's the CEO of Andes."

"Yeah." I slapped the card against my palm. "You know my friend, Miles? Weston is his brother. I met him and his fiancée Elise yesterday when I hiked with Miles. Weston was miffed about my lack of Andes gear."

"You landed some rich friends, D."

"Not on purpose." I elbowed his side. "Would you believe none of them asked me about ghosts?"

"No. I don't believe it." He nodded toward the box. "Open it."

"All right already."

I ripped open the tissue paper, my stomach a bundle of nerves and excitement. This was a *big* freaking box, and it was filled all the way to the top.

There were several tops, long sleeve and short, all made of material to wick sweat, two vests, socks, hats, gloves. Three pairs of pants that looked like they'd fit just right, and a dark plum windbreaker with fleece lining I wanted to slip on. On the bottom, there were two thin puffer coats.

Reed eyed my piles of clothing and outdoor wear with envy, while I was overwhelmed by the sheer amount.

"I don't need all this," I stated. "It's way too much."

He picked up the black puffer coat, running his finger down the front. "You're lucky. I've always wanted one of these."

It struck me that Reed was...well, excited would have been too strong of a descriptor, but he was emoting. There was light on in his beautiful brown eyes, and he seemed interested enough not to be jonesing to get back to his room.

"Well, I have two—one more than I need. What about if we go to the Andes store and exchange that one for one in your size?"

His brow dipped. "But these are for you. I don't have rich friends."

"No, but you have a sister with rich *acquaintances*. Besides, I happen to know Weston Aldrich is all about sustainability. He would hate to see the clothing he gifted me going to waste. You'd be doing him a favor by taking that jacket." I picked up a couple T-shirts and the boots voucher. "These too. I just got new boots. Since you're growing at the speed of light, I'm sure you could use a new pair. Let's go on a shopping spree, courtesy of Weston Aldrich."

Reed rubbed the back of his neck, his gaze sliding to the side, no doubt searching for a reason to say no. As of late, my brother went to school and came home. He'd dropped his hobbies, and I hadn't seen many friends around. It worried me. Worried all of us. Getting him to do this with me wouldn't cure what ailed him, but we could have a nice afternoon together, and that was something.

"All right, but only if you're sure you don't need that stuff," he mumbled in his sullen, put-upon teen way.

"I'm completely sure."

Our day out together ended up being short, but no less sweet. Reed even agreed to take a selfie with me in our brand-new, matching Andes vests. It might've been wishful thinking, but I swore he stood a little taller in his new gear.

I sent Miles the picture of us together.

Me: *Send this to Weston and tell him thank you from me and Reed.*

Miles: *Cute pic, Dunham siblings. Why am I thanking Weston?*

Me: *He sent me a huge box of Andes gear. Reed and I took a trip to an Andes store and exchanged some of it for his size. Now we look like rich outdoorsmen.*

It took so long for him to reply, I thought he was going to leave me on read. Then a text finally came through.

Miles: *Sorry. Had to get some screams out. I gave you weeds, and Westie gave you a new wardrobe. Honestly, fuck him. I mean, I'm happy for you, but fuck him.*

I snorted a laugh. I could picture Miles pacing in his rubber duckie living room, cursing his brother's name.

Me: *Reed hasn't left the house with just me in months, but sure, make this about you.*

Miles: *Okay, honestly, could you make me look like more of an asshole?*

Miles: *I looked at the picture again. Is he...almost smiling?*

Me: *Almost! He was feeling himself in his new vest.*

Miles: *That's awesome. I forgive Weston for attempting to usurp my place as #1 in your heart.*

Me: *He did say Elise picked everything out. If anyone in this scenario is going to be #1, it's her.*

Miles: *Sounds like her. You guys had a good day, huh?*

Me: *Yeah. I've missed my brother. It was exactly what I needed.*

Miles: *So, what you're saying is you're in a good enough mood to come help me peel wallpaper?*

Me: *Not on your life.*

After a few more minutes of texting, I found myself driving over to his house, eager for another uncomplicated, easy hangout with Miles. It had been a long time since I'd looked forward to anything, but in the short time I'd known Miles Aldrich, he had given me a lot to look forward to, both big and small. I had a feeling, if I stuck around him, this was only the beginning.

CHAPTER SIXTEEN

Miles

THE WEEK AFTER THE hike, Daisy and I worked on my house together twice, and she came to Peak for a strategy meeting. Since then, it had been a week since we'd seen each other. I'd gotten so busy with other clients, almost everything else had fallen by the wayside.

Tonight, though, I was hers. In a professional capacity. It was our first event of the season. I had my cards in one pocket of my jacket, and hers in the other.

I was early. When I'd arrived, she'd yelled at me to let myself in, so I was sitting in her cozy little living room, waiting for her while she finished getting ready.

There was a pink box on the coffee table in front of me, and it felt like one of those tests behavioral scientists gave little kids.

Watch the man with next to no self-control to see how long it takes him to open the box.

I was forcing myself to wait, but given it had been a solid ten days since I'd eaten one of Daisy's creations, it wasn't easy. It was good for me, though. It built character. I couldn't always have immediate gratification. The best things were worth waiting for.

"I'm coming," Daisy called. "Sorry for running late. I put on a dress and realized how long it had been since I'd shaved my legs."

"Don't give in to society's beauty standards, Cupcake. Let your hair flow."

She emerged from her bathroom, rolling her eyes. "You don't understand. My leg hair isn't fine and wispy."

"Was this a Sasquatch situation?"

My mouth was moving, saying words, but all my brain could register was the woman walking toward me. Her dress was black and off-the-shoulder. It skimmed her body, ending right below her knees. A wide leather belt with heavy, silver buckles cinched her middle, and straps went over her shoulders like suspenders.

Her lips were midnight red. Thick lashes curtained her eyes. The skin of her exposed shoulders had a sheen to it. Not glitter. Never glitter. Something subtle and sexy.

She plunked down beside me on the couch, a tube of lotion in her grip. "You haven't eaten your cupcakes yet?"

"What?"

She pointed her bare toe at the box. "Is it empty, or have you really not dug in?"

"I haven't dug in." I caught her foot on its way down and slid my thumb over the dark gray polish on her big toe. "I like this color."

Her feet were powder white and soft as a petal. I allowed myself one stroke of her arch before gently releasing her.

She softly gasped. "Miles Aldrich, are you a foot man?"

"I'm an admirer of the female form in general, but yes, I like a pretty foot." I grabbed the box off the coffee table and blindly stuffed a cupcake in my mouth, hoping to distract from the fact that I basically just felt her up.

Daisy wasn't as kind. Propping her foot on the coffee table, she snapped open her lotion, drizzled a dollop on her calf, and wiggled her toes as she lathered the cream into her skin.

"Tell me about the event we're going to again."

I stared at her, wondering how the hell she expected me to have a coherent conversation with most of my blood firmly lodged in my dick.

Instead of responding, I ate another cupcake, and she laughed.

"My Mama let me and my sisters be who we wanted. She never vetoed our clothes or hairstyles. But she wouldn't budge on taking care of our skin. From a young age, she drilled into us the need to lotion every inch of our bodies and wash our makeup off before bed. She'd always tell us, 'That includes your feet, ladies. They carry you where you want to go, so you need to treat them nicely.' I've been getting biweekly pedicures since high school. What color do you think I should get next?"

I blinked at her. "What'd I do to deserve this?"

She dropped her foot and leaned forward, tapping her chin. "It's fun to see you flustered, Miles Aldrich. I didn't think you could get embarrassed, but your cheeks are cherry red right now. It's adorable."

"Christ, Daisy. This isn't embarrassment. You made my dick hard, and your little speech about how you take care of your feet isn't helping. It would be helpful if you could walk your pretty ass back to your bedroom and not come back until you have shoes on."

Her mouth fell open. "You're serious, aren't you?" Then her gaze drifted to my dick, which was doing a convincing impression of a tent pole. "Oh my god, Miles."

She leaped up and scurried back, her eyes bugging, cheeks as flushed as mine. Then she spun and disappeared into her bedroom, the door flying shut behind her.

Damn.

It had been a long, long time since I'd gotten laid. Even longer since a woman had turned me on without trying. Obviously, I needed to spend more time with my hand before hanging out with Daisy. That interaction hadn't been professional at all. Hopefully I hadn't freaked her out and ruined our working relationship—or what felt like a budding friendship.

A minute or two later, she reemerged, much more composed. In the time she'd been absent, I'd reminded my dick of a few world atrocities, shaming it for its behavior.

"Okay, I'm almost ready. Just one more thing." Daisy circled the coffee table to stand in front of me. "Which do you think I should wear? Heels or booties?"

The shiny boots balanced on one hand and strappy heels dangling from the other made my chest tighten and blood leech from my head.

"You're a menace," I gritted. "Put the fucking boots on before this gets any more awkward."

She collapsed on the armchair, her shoulders jiggling with laughter. I sprung up and crossed the room, putting the kitchen island between us.

"I'm sorry. I really am, but I couldn't resist." She waved the boots at me. "Don't worry, the heels don't match my outfit. I'm wearing the booties."

Once she had her feet safely tucked away, we were in my car and on the way to our event.

"Art gallery grand opening," I reminded her. "Pet project for Louisa Maddox. She and her friends are known to throw events in constant rotation. If you can get in with them, you'll be golden. But everyone you meet tonight will be an important connection."

She fiddled with the clasp of her clutch, opening and closing it. "Got it. Don't make a fool of myself and be personable."

"I'll do the personable thing, Cupcake. You look trustworthy and tell stories about the cheese guy from France who proposed to you last year."

"He didn't propose—he asked me to spend the month with him."

I shook my head. "Shoulda taken him up on it."

"I had the whole live-in boyfriend at the time."

"And look where that got you."

Her sharp intake of breath was clear indication I'd gone too far.

"Sorry. I shouldn't have said that."

She smoothed her hands over her skirt before folding them in her lap. "No, you shouldn't have. He's the last thing I need to be reminded of at the moment."

I probably shouldn't have reminded her of him anyway, since she wasn't over him. She wasn't dating or looking. Whenever I broached the subject of *Andy*, she'd get this lost look about her and promptly shut me down.

Reaching across the console, I patted her hand. To my surprise, she flipped hers over and clutched mine.

"If you do a good job tonight, I'll take you for a burger after."

Another hitch of her breath. This time, with excitement. "Really?"

"Really."

"I'm starving. I was too nervous to eat before you came, and these things never have anything good to eat. I could go for a burger for sure."

"It's a deal."

Whether she forgot or it was purposeful, Daisy held my hand in her lap the rest of the trip, and I saw no reason to point it out.

I was only sorry when she let go.

CHAPTER SEVENTEEN

Daisy

RICH WOMEN ADORED MILES Aldrich.

As soon as we walked into the gallery, they fawned over him. And the wild thing was, his gold plating flowed onto me. Because I was with him, as his girlfriend, they were interested in finding out my name. No one asked if I was part of *that* Dunham family, and if it had occurred to them, they hadn't found it necessary to confirm since I had Miles' approval.

He was *good* at schmoozing without making it feel like schmoozing. I'd felt his charisma more than once, but watching him work his magic from the outside was fascinating.

When I wasn't watching Miles, I was checking out the space. With polished concrete floors and crisp, white walls, the gallery was chic and surprisingly expansive. There were a lot of people here tonight, but the wide-open spaces allowed everyone to spread out, pretending to check out the art while checking out each other.

"I call them meat cups," Miles explained to a woman dripping in diamonds.

The woman giggled then addressed me. "Oh, I'm sure you adore when he does that, don't you, darling?"

I hugged Miles' arm and made a show of giving him a pinch. "Let's just say he's lucky he's so cute."

She winked at me. "I think we're all lucky for that."

After a moment or two and Miles slipping her my business card, we wandered away, trying to catch a waiter carrying canapes. All the trays had been cleaned out. The bar on the far side of the spacious room was my only hope.

"Okay, if I can't eat, I'm getting a drink. Think they have pink lemonade?"

His hand slid down my back, resting just above the curve of my ass. "Let's go find out."

"Are you sure? I can get drinks for both of us."

He cupped my elbows and pinned me with a hard stare. "I'm not going to vault over the bar and guzzle a liter of vodka. To be honest, I'm pretty solid in my sobriety tonight, and having you with me certainly helps that." He stepped into me, his hand leaving my elbow to return to the small of my back. "You don't worry about me when we're at these things. It's my job to worry about you, Daisy...what's your middle name again?"

"Wha—?" I lifted my eyes to his. He wasn't getting me to say it. Once had been enough. "I don't have one."

"Lies." His eyes narrowed. "You do have one. You told me it once. Daisy Eth—"

"Don't say it," I warned.

"It's either I say it or I commit light torture."

I shimmied my shoulders to distract him. "And what if I like a little light torture?"

He groaned. "Daisy Devil. That suits you better than Ethel."

"Okay, sure. We'll go with that." I nodded toward the bar, still partially hidden by several layers of people. "Weren't we grabbing a drink?"

"Were we?"

I slipped my arm through his. "Come on, Spreadsheet. I'm parched."

We wove through the crowd, finally making it to the bar, and stopped short.

My girl Bea was tending bar in a white button-down and bowtie. I almost hadn't recognized her with her thick, chestnut hair pulled back in a low ponytail.

"Bea! You're a brunette."

She tugged a clump of strands. 'It's a wig."

I leaned my elbows on the bar. "It looks good on you."

"I prefer the blue, but this job doesn't let me have unnaturally dyed hair, so here we are." Her gaze flicked to Miles then back to me. "You hanging out with Preppy?"

"Miles knows where all the free food and drinks are," I hedged. I didn't want anyone to know about my near-future plans, so there was no need to explain *why* I'd begun hanging out with him. "So, this is your second job?"

"Or my first, depending on how you look at it. I'm on call with the catering company whenever they need me."

"Good money?"

"Better than retail, but not as good as Nick's. That's why I like these events during the week. I can still take my Friday and Saturday night waitressing shifts."

"Hope you make bank tonight." I drummed my nails on the glass countertop. "By any chance do you have pink lemonade back there?"

"Hmmm..." She tapped her chin. "Will you settle for yellow?"

I huffed. "If I have to, but I won't be happy about it."

"Complaint department closed," she deadpanned.

Miles snickered as he wound his arm around my waist from behind. He was good at this fake boyfriend thing. I couldn't say what I'd expected from him when I'd agreed to this idea, but I didn't think it was this. That might have been because I'd spent the last seven years with a man deathly allergic to even mild public displays of affection. Andy might have held my hand on Valentine's Day and my birthday, but that was a stretch. Miles hadn't stopped touching some part of me all evening, and I had found myself joining in on the action.

It was nice being able to lean on the man I was with, assured I wasn't bothering him or making him uncomfortable.

We took our drinks from Bea with a thank you. It didn't get past me that Miles had slipped a fifty in her tip jar, nor did I miss her grabbing it and stuffing it in her bra.

"Come, let's actually look at the art." Miles pressed my back with his palm, guiding me to the edges of the room.

We stopped in front of a mural that reminded me of the spinny art I used to do as a kid. There was a red dot next to the nametag, indicating someone had actually purchased it. I would have never claimed to be an expert on art, but I couldn't see any possible reason this thing was worth the hefty price attached to it.

Miles brushed my hair aside and dipped to put his lips next to my lobe. "This looks like it was made with a spin art kit."

I tried to hold my laugh in. I'd hate for the artist to overhear, not to mention all the people we were trying to impress tonight.

"Shut up, Miles."

"Tell me you weren't thinking it."

I heaved a sigh and twisted so my front was brushing his. "Of course I was. I loved making spin art. Though…I don't think a canvas this size would have fit in my little machine."

"Chances are, you're right. I bet this guy built his own."

"His own machine?"

"Mmmhmm. For that, I add two points."

Miles carried on discussing his rating system, and I listened as we walked from piece to piece. When my glass was empty, he plucked it from my hand and set it down on a table with other discarded dishes.

I scanned the space, catching sight of a familiar head of chocolate brown hair above the crowd. Andy had always been a head taller than everyone else. Leave it to him to stick out like a sore thumb and make his presence known.

Warm fingers cupped my face, turning my head until we were almost nose to nose. "What are you looking at, Daisy-daze? You feel okay?"

"My ex is here. I didn't think he'd be in a place like this."

Miles turned, scanning the crowd. "The guy in the green button-down?"

"I don't know. I didn't get a good look at what he was wearing. Is he with someone?"

It felt like a hundred years passed before he answered.

"Uh, I think so. He's holding hands with a blonde—"

"Fuck," I whispered. "Fuckity, fuck, fuck, fuck. I didn't, I—"

His thumbs stroked my cheeks and the corners of my mouth. "They're going to pass right by us. No way for us to escape."

Reaching up, I clutched his wrists, panic making my heart gallop. I'd thought about this moment many times, but it was always a year or two in the future when I had my shit together, was leading some fabulous life, Andy a distant memory. This was way too soon. Two months wasn't enough time for me to be able to play it cool.

"Hide me, Miles. I'm not ready to see him. *Please.*"

His eyes darted to the side then back, bouncing between mine with indecision.

"Please, Miles."

He exhaled, his thumbs pressing the sides of my mouth. "All right. Fuck it. I'm going to kiss you now."

He only gave me a second to inhale before his warm lips were on mine. I froze, my brain and limbs offline, then his lips moved over mine, gently slotting between them, and I awoke. My body moved into his on instinct, grasping his shoulders to bring us closer.

Firm, leisurely presses of his lips made my toes curl in my booties. I leaned in for more. It was easy to forget the reason we were doing this and fall into the sweetest kiss I'd ever experienced.

My lips parted ever so slightly, and our tongues met, tip to tip. We both tasted like lemonade, like summer and home. Miles groaned, his fingers slipping into my hair. I chased his lips and tongue, nipping and sucking before he came back with a firm press, taking my breath away.

Glass shattering somewhere in the distance brought me back to the present, and I jerked away. Miles pulled back a little more slowly, touching his lips to my forehead as he straightened. The kiss was over, but not our connection. He wrapped his arms around me and brought me straight into his chest for a hug.

"I don't think that worked," he murmured.

"What?" My thoughts were still in soft focus. "What didn't work?"

"The kiss. Your ex is now glaring at me from the bar like he's going to stab me with one of those cocktail swords."

I gripped the back of his shirt, dread replacing the pool of warmth in my belly. "Bea wouldn't let him. She'd stab him first."

He nudged my chin with his knuckle to tilt my face back. "We need to make a decision right now. Go, or stay and face the douche?"

I puffed my cheeks and blew out a heavy breath. We were here for a reason—and it had nothing to do with Andy. Besides, we were bound to run into each other again, and I couldn't run away every time.

"I'm not going to let Andy mess anything up for me. I was here first, so I'm staying."

Something rumbled in Miles' chest. "That's a brave, good girl. Proud of you." He kissed the top of my head, and my toes curled in pleasure again. "Come on. Let's look at some art. Maybe Bea will poison him, and this will all be moot."

⚜

An hour later, we still hadn't run across Andy. He must've been sticking to the other side of the gallery. I excused myself to use the restroom while Miles chatted with a few men his father knew from their country club.

When I stepped out of the bathroom into the short hallway, I realized my mistake in letting my guard down. Andy was leaning against the opposite wall, clearly waiting for me.

I nodded, intent on breezing past him. I did not wait to listen to anything he had to say. Of course, he couldn't let things lie and caught me by the bicep.

I yanked my arm away, but stopped to face him, not uttering a word until he did.

"You cut your hair."

"I did."

His eyes scraped over me. "It'll grow back. I'm surprised you would succumb to a breakup haircut."

I touched the bottom of it, which was still inches above my shoulders. "I like it short."

He looked like he was biting his tongue, which pleased me. He wasn't allowed to have an opinion on anything I did anymore.

"You never said."

I shrugged. "I mentioned cutting it once. You told me my long hair was one of your favorite parts of me."

He had the decency to wince. "Now, it doesn't matter."

"No. What you think doesn't matter anymore. Have a good night."

I started past him again, but he touched my elbow, slowing me. "You're seeing someone."

A scream was lodged in my throat. We should have been looking forward to our engagement, but we were little more than strangers making uncomfortable small talk.

"Yes."

He nodded quickly. "Good. That's good. I am too."

"Good luck to you, Andy. If we see each other at another one of these things, we don't have to do this, all right? It's better if we don't."

Right then, I was happy to be wearing boots instead of heels to hasten my exit.

I found Miles alone, looking for me with a pinched brow. Worried. He'd been worried for me. When he spotted me, it was like a cloud lifted from his expression, brightening all at once. I walked straight up to him and leaned into his chest.

"Would it be all right if we left?"

"You took the words from my mouth. I was going to suggest that." Wrapping his arm around my shoulders, he plastered me to his side and guided me outside.

The beginning of the ride was somewhat quiet. Miles fiddled with the radio until he found a song he liked then drummed to the beat on his steering wheel.

"I saw him follow you into the hallway." Miles glanced over at me. "My first instinct was to drag him out, but I thought you might want to talk to him. Did he say something? Did he upset you?"

"He's seeing someone." I spread my hands on my thighs. I couldn't really pinpoint how I felt. Not great, but not like I wanted to hole up in my bed and endure another month of grief bacon.

"You are too."

I huffed. "Yeah. Guess I am. I wonder if his girlfriend's fake too."

"Doubt it." He reached across to toy with my fingertips. "No one's got as good of ideas as I do."

That made me snicker. "That is definitely true."

Before I knew it, Miles had pulled into the drive-thru of a local burger joint. He didn't ask me what I wanted. He just ordered most of the menu then pulled into a parking spot to wait for our food.

"I don't personally know the guy, but I can say with confidence he's a dick."

Tucking one foot under my leg, I turned in my seat to face him. "Why so confident?"

He snarled with disgust. "He dumped you then had the audacity to corner you at an event. He should've—"

"Why do you assume he dumped me?"

The momentum of Miles' rant came to an abrupt halt, knocking him back against his seat. "Are you saying you broke up with him? Did he cheat?"

"Yes. And no, he didn't cheat."

He flicked his fingers in the direction of my face. "Then what's this about? You broke up with him but look like a sad little kitten. If you miss him that badly, you should be with him."

A girl holding three paper bags of food and a drink tray knocked on Miles' window. He rolled it down and grabbed the food, passing it to me. I dug into the fries in the first bag before he even tipped her. Then he passed me a strawberry shake without asking and set the other drinks on the console between us.

Like we'd done this a hundred times, we worked to spread all the food out on our laps and the dashboard. His car smelled like a greasy fast-food joint—the exact antithesis to the rarified air of the gallery. It relaxed me. I slurped my shake and munched on a chicken tender while Miles started in on a cheeseburger.

"We were together for seven years, since college. When we were young, dumb, and madly in love, we talked about marriage and kids.

All our future plans were with each other. He was *it* for me. So, at first, I didn't notice when he'd started to avoid future talk. He'd always say 'soon' or tell me he loved me, but never 'when.' That he was the one who got to make that decision never struck me as fair. It should have been an open discussion, but he'd closed it."

Miles was silent and still, watching me with an intensity I wasn't used to from him. No, he was *listening* to me, shutting everything else out around us.

"Two months ago, we were coming home from a friend's wedding, and I made a remark about what ours would be like. He *hummed*." I took a slurp of my milkshake to get his hum out of my head. "That hum made me snap. I asked him, point blank, if he ever intended to marry me, and he was finally honest."

"He didn't want to marry you?" he asked gently.

I shook my head. "He said he wasn't sure if he wanted to be married at all. Ever."

His exhale was jagged. "You left?"

"The next day. He didn't think we needed to break up over this, but I couldn't stay. All I could hear was that hum and remember all the times he'd given me a non-answer. He'd known for years he didn't want to marry me, just like he knew I wanted a family like the one I grew up in. I thought I'd have it with him while he knew for a fact it wasn't going to happen."

Miles took my hand in his and gave my knuckles a soft kiss. "I'm sorry, Cupcake. I knew that guy was a dick, but for your sake, I'm sorry to be so right."

"Thanks, but he's not a dick in general, we just wanted different things." I let my head loll on the rest. "You don't think I'm crazy for leaving a perfectly nice relationship for that?"

He chuffed. "I'd think you were crazy staying in something *perfectly nice*. Why would you settle for nice when you could have mind-blowing?"

"I don't know. It was my only relationship. Ever. Seven years is a long time to spend with someone and just walk away."

"He hummed at the thing you wanted most." Miles scoffed, incredulous. "He's a dick. You'll see that when you find someone who won't make you wait. He'll leap into action when you give even a hint of wanting to be locked down. That's the kind of guy you should be with—who recognizes what he has."

Another slurp of my milkshake, cold replacing the dread in my belly. "Since I don't plan to date anytime soon, I won't hold my breath, but I appreciate you saying that."

He kissed my knuckle once more before giving me my hand back. "Feel any better?" He positioned his head like mine, sweeping his gaze over me.

"Yeah." I smiled at him, and when he smiled back, my stomach did a strange sort of dance. "Now you know the sordid truth. Do with it what you will. I'm going to eat some chicken tenders."

He held up a little container. "You need to dip them in ranch. It's illegal not to."

I snatched the dip from him. "I would never break the law, officer."

His gaze stayed on me a minute longer, warm and wary. I found it comforting, so I allowed it, happily eating my chicken and drinking my milkshake, until he finally dug back into his food.

We ate and listened to music until our stomachs couldn't fit anything else. Miles drove me home with a bag of leftovers for Reed in my lap and a lightness in my chest.

I'd seen Andy again and hadn't fallen apart.

It had been strange, a little bit sad, but it'd also reaffirmed my decision to go. Two months hadn't been long enough to fully heal from almost a decade of loving that man, but I was moving on.

I knew for sure I was going to be fine.

And having Miles with me tonight to sort it all out hadn't hurt at all.

Chapter Eighteen

Miles

From a very young age, my father had drilled into me my last name would open any door I wanted it to.

He'd had no idea what he was talking about.

When I was a kid, the one place I wanted to go was where my brother was—and more often than not, that had been Levy's house. Elliot Levy had been his best friend for as long as I could remember. Their friendship had been a twosome. On the rare occasions I'd been allowed to third-wheel it, both had made it known I was unwanted. And it hadn't been because I was younger since they'd let Elliot's sister Elise tag along whenever she asked.

It took me a while to recognize the reason: they didn't like me.

Looking back, I had been annoying as fuck. My doctor hadn't found the right meds for me, and I'd had a bad habit of skipping them anyway. I had the zoomies on speed. Talking a mile a minute, loud and obnoxious. Making impulsive decisions, stealing, destroying, saying awful, hurtful things.

Once it sunk in that I wasn't wanted, I stopped trying to be around West and Elliot and got into trouble on my own.

Back then, I never would have pictured myself being invited to their bi-weekly Sunday brunches, yet here I was, sitting in my favorite spot between Elise and Saoirse.

Saoirse was married to Luca, Elliot and Weston's college bestie. I wasn't even salty anymore they'd added a third to their group when I'd been *right there* for years. Luca was slick as hell, rode a motorcycle in his off time, and ran a Fortune-500 company without letting them see him sweat.

I bounced my knees, giving my favorite toddler a pony ride. "Say 'Miles is the best.'"

Joey furrowed her brow and scrunched her button nose at me. "Bah!" she yelped.

I tapped her little wrinkly nose. "Yep, that's right. I'm the bah."

Her mother, Kit, beamed at the two of us from the other side of the table. "Did Saoirse tell you Joey said 'cat' when I took her to see Clementine last week?"

I frowned at Saoirse, who I worked with every single day. "No, she didn't. Did you not think Uncle Miles would have wanted that update?"

Elliot, Kit's husband, sighed, but he didn't deny my title. I'd been working on getting his kid to call me Uncle for the last year. At some point, he'd accepted it was going to happen. Maybe it was one of the times I'd volunteered to babysit when he'd wanted to take his wife out.

Saoirse folded her arms in her lap. "I apologize. I did get her on video, though. If I send it to you, would that make up for it?"

Joey slapped my leg to tell me to move before I could get too pissed about this video existing and being withheld from me. So, I got the pony going, keeping my niece happy. It didn't take a lot. She was a cool kid. Took after her mom.

Elliot eyeballed me like he could hear my thoughts. We both knew he had a stick up his ass ninety percent of the time, so he shouldn't have been surprised I was thinking it.

He and I weren't ever going to be best friends, but I didn't need that from him. I had his respect, and he had mine. Me taking a bullet protecting his wife had probably made the biggest inroads for me in his esteem. For me, him having a wife like Kit and a sweet baby like Joey had shifted him from "fuck that guy" to mostly tolerable.

Luca put down his coffee cup to toy with the ring on Saoirse's finger. "I always hear about Saoirse's half of the business. What have you been working on lately, Miles?"

I raised a brow at Saoirse. "I'm disappointed you don't talk about me to your husband."

"Oh, I talk about you." She smirked. "But not about your clients."

"I'm intrigued. All I do is work and sleep. Unless you're the one who put the hidden camera in my bedroom, you won't have anything to say about how I sleep."

Weston choked on his water. "What was that? A hidden camera?"

I waved him off while Elise patted his back. "That was a joke, Westie." Then I cocked my head. "Or was it? I have seen a little green light in the corner..."

Elise knocked against my arm. "Don't tease Weston. He'll have his security team sweeping your house for bugs before we even leave the restaurant."

I huffed a laugh. "Don't worry. I don't know any secrets about Andes, so I can't spill them."

My brother gave me a hard look. I braced for the admonishment to come, but he took a breath and switched gears. "I'm surprised you didn't invite Daisy today. She would have been welcome."

Luca lifted his coffee cup. "That's what we've talked about."

I swiveled back to Saoirse. "You're discussing my dating life with Luca? Is married life that boring?"

"There's nothing boring about being married to Luca," Saoirse replied. "I didn't think you had a dating life until Elise told me she'd met your girlfriend—who is our client."

Elliot hissed air through his teeth. "Dating a client?"

I lowered my chin. "You married your assistant."

Kit snickered. "Miles has a point. Don't throw stones."

The look he gave her transformed him from Elliot Levy, powerful CEO, to Kit's adoring husband. They'd been together a year and a half, and it still startled me to see Elliot openly displaying his heart.

Just like it had startled me the first time I'd realized he'd actually had one.

"We met before she became a client," I explained.

When I came up with the fake dating scheme, I hadn't considered having to defend our faux relationship to these guys. That was on brand for me, though. When it came to others, I could see every angle of a situation. I was myopic around my own issues.

"I didn't think it would bother you," I told Saoirse.

"It doesn't, really." She shook her head. "We're supposed to discuss everything that might affect Peak. A conversation would have been nice."

"You're right," I conceded. "I apologize."

Baby Joey smacked my leg again, crying, "Mah!" I interpreted that as her saying my name. The kid was going to get all the bouncies she wanted.

"I *really* liked her," Elise chimed in. "And I could tell Miles is smitten."

Saoirse's brow winged. "Smitten? Now I need to see you together."

"I do too," Kit agreed. "I didn't know Miles could be smitten."

"She's coming to our wedding." Elise reached for Weston's hand. "Under a month now. I can't believe it."

"Not soon enough," Weston murmured.

"The wedding? Really?" Elliot shot them a dubious look. "You approved of this?"

Elise nodded. "I was the one to invite her. Just wait until you meet her, El. She reminds me a little of you."

I gaped at her and her filthy accusations. "Take that back." If I started associating Daisy with Elliot, I wouldn't even be able to *fake* get it up for her.

She giggled. "I mean, she was wary at first, but once I started to get to know her, I found her warm and familiar." She placed a hand on my shoulder. "As someone who's a big fan of my brother, me comparing Daisy to him is a compliment."

Kit leaned forward, her chin on her fist. "Well, damn. Now I'm dying to meet this girl."

Elise gasped. "Bring her to the cabin next weekend. It'll be perfect."

"Really?" I flicked my gaze to Weston.

Next weekend, our group was sharing a house in Breckenridge for Elise and Weston's bachelor and bachelorette celebration. Calling it a cabin was a stretch since it was ten thousand square feet with six bedrooms, a huge game room, a ten-person jacuzzi, and all the amenities anyone could need.

I was the only one going solo, which I tried not to think about too hard. Bringing Daisy would certainly be a lot more fun than playing the seventh wheel yet again, but it would also be outside the confines of our agreement.

Weston nodded. "If you think she's going to be around, I'd like to get to know her better."

Yeah, this was where my guilt should have made me step out of the way of the speeding locomotive. Entwining Daisy with my real-life blurred lines that shouldn't have been blurred. But she'd get why I wanted her there, and with my track record, none of my friends nor my brother would be surprised when, at the end of the summer, I announced things hadn't worked out for us.

"I'll ask her and let you know."

Joey reached back and gave me a smack on the stomach.

I hear you, kid. None of this is a good idea, but the brakes are fried and there's no stopping it.

Me: *Can I come over?*

Daisy: *I'm hanging with Reed.*

Me: *Perfect. Your place?*

Daisy: *Perfect? How is that perfect? I'm busy.*

Me: *Nah, Reed likes me. I'll be there in 15.*

Daisy: *You can't always have your way. You know that, right?*

Me: *Oh, I know it. But I'm going to have my way with you today, Cupcake.*

Daisy: *Sullen teen brother present. No ways will be had.*

Me: *You filthy little minx. That isn't what I meant, but I'm glad to know where your mind is. See you in 15!*

⫷◦⫸

Daisy opened the door to me before I could knock and stepped out onto the landing, which was crowded with the two of us on it.

I looked her up and down, a grin sliding across my face. "You look cute."

Her cheeks instantly flushed. I was so pleased to have been the one to do it, I had to stop myself from rocking back on my heels or I might've gone tumbling down the steps. But damn, Daisy in her fitted Andes vest and cropped black joggers was the perfect mix of emo meets outdoorsy. She also had a small braid running from one side of her head to the other, acting as a headband.

Too cute.

"Thanks." She put her hands on her hips. "Did you want something specific?"

I held up the Korean fried chicken I'd gotten on the way. "I brought food. I hear Reed likes to eat a lot of it."

Her brows lowered, and a hip cocked to one side. "You're really here to hang out with me and my brother?"

"Yeah. Why not? I just got done hanging with mine, why not hang with yours now?" Unable to resist anymore, I reached out to touch her braid, running my finger from behind one ear to the other. "I also have to ask you a favor."

"Here we go," she muttered.

"Don't be such a pessimist. I don't think you'll mind this favor."

"Okay, lay it on me. What's the favor?" She sounded as enthusiastic as someone about to eat a bowl of glass.

"Need you to come with me to Breck next weekend for Weston and Elise's bachelor-slash-bachelorette celebration."

A shallow line formed between her eyebrows. "Next weekend? What? Do they know you're inviting me?"

I took her by the shoulders and dipped down to whisper in her ear, like this was a big secret. "Cupcake, they issued the invitation."

Her eyes rounded like she was astonished they'd want her there. It was so adorable, I booped her nose like I'd done to Joey's earlier.

"Come on, say yes."

She tilted her head. "Do *you* want me there?"

"Uh, yeah. Everything's more fun with you around."

Those cheeks pinkened again. "Literally no one has ever said that about me."

Her door swung open, and Reed poked his head out, looking as put-upon as ever. He barely glanced at me, focusing on his sister. "Are you going to come back inside, or should I go home?"

I held up the chicken and wrapped my other arm around Daisy's waist. "We're coming in. I brought Korean chicken."

After a beat of hesitation, he moved away from the door. He didn't open it wider, but I took him not slamming it in my face as all the sign I needed.

Reed was standing by the kitchen island, using his phone, uninterested in me and what I'd brought. I could respect his need to play it cool, which was why I wasn't going to point out how much I loved him and Daisy wearing matching vests. He'd paired his with cargo pants that were barely hanging on his scrawny hips.

I put the food on the island, opening all the containers, then walked away so Reed could pick what he wanted without me seeing he wanted anything at all.

Daisy bumped my shoulder as I looked out the window overlooking the funeral home.

"We're going to watch a movie," she said.

"All right. I'm assuming it's Reed's choice."

She grinned. "You know it."

I hooked my thumb into the armhole of her vest. "I like your matching outfits."

"Thanks for not mentioning it in front of Reed. I don't think a day has gone by he hasn't worn his vest since he got it. I think it makes him feel kind of good about himself, which has been...tough."

"He looks good in it, so I get it." I glanced back at the couch. He was getting settled with a plate of chicken in his lap. "You look good in it too, Daisy-daze. Make sure you bring it with you next weekend. Weston and Elise will be pleased as punch to see you wearing their gift."

"Did I agree to that?"

I gave her zipper a tug. "Yep, you did. Now, shut up. It's movie time."

"You shut up," she muttered.

I grinned like an idiot. Everything really was more fun when she was around.

———◆———

Me: *How's your week going, Daisy-daze?*

Lydia-Daisy-Cupcake: *I only saw you two days ago.*

Me: *I'm still recovering from those movies.*

Reed had some intense taste. He'd picked *Requiem for a Dream* followed by *Oldboy*. I'd left Daisy's somewhat shell-shocked, but Reed had had a good time.

Lydia-Daisy-Cupcake: *Poor you. I've seen them both before, so I was prepared. Should I send you my therapist's number?*

Me: *No thanks, have my own. How is your week looking?*

Lydia-Daisy-Cupcake: *I have deadlines I have to meet before next weekend. In other words, NO SLEEP 'TIL BRECKINRIDGE.*

Me: *Did you just Beastie Boys me?*

Lydia-Daisy-Cupcake: *Maybe. BTW, does anyone in the group, besides you, have allergies?*

Me: *Not that I'm aware of. Are you gonna make us cupcakes?*

Lydia-Daisy-Cupcake: *I can't show up empty-handed. Whitney Mae would faint.*

Me: *I have a busy week too. Thanks for asking.*

Lydia-Daisy-Cupcake: *What are you up to this week, Miles?*

Me: *One of my clients is launching their T-shirt business. Would you wear a shirt with an irreverent saying on it?*

Lydia-Daisy-Cupcake: *I would not. But good luck to them, and congrats to you. Proud of you.*

Me: *Thanks, Cupcake. That means a lot. See you this weekend.*

Lydia-Daisy-Cupcake: *Looking forward to it. xx*

My chest was warm and fuzzy from her unexpected praise, so I decided to try my luck with the other Dunham sibling. He'd given me his number, albeit grudgingly, but I hadn't needed to twist his arm either. I'd sensed a kid who needed to form all the connections he could right now. If he got too untethered, he might just...go. I knew what that felt like. Remembered it all too well. So, I reached out.

Me: *Hey, Reed. I'm here for the movie recs. Preferably something that won't make me cry in the bathroom while everyone else is eating cold Korean fried chicken.*

Five minutes passed. I didn't think I'd hooked him. Then the dots on my screen started to move, and finally, a text appeared.

Reed: *That's an incredibly specific reference. I'll have to look over my lists to find movies for emotionally sensitive people.*

Me: *That would be ideal. Send me some music too. Need to know what's good.*

Reed: *You won't be into my kind of music.*

Me: *Why don't I be the judge of that? Try me. I'm open-minded.*

Reed: *You don't have to act interested in me to get with my sister, you know.*

Me: *One has nothing to do with the other. If you don't have any good music recs, you can just say that...*

Reed: *Manipulation 101. I respect that. Hold on, I'm gonna make a playlist for you.*

An hour later, he came back with a custom playlist for me. Ten songs, all weird as hell, transient electronic music. I listened to every track.

Me: *Gonna take some time to let it all sink in.*

Reed: *You actually listened?*

Me: *Yeah, I did. Not my style, but I'm flexible. Thanks for the tunes.*

Reed: *Welcome.*

I needed to make this kid a playlist that didn't suck. My brain wouldn't let me do anything else until I did. So, I spent the rest of my evening creating the perfect playlist for Daisy's younger brother.

Hoping he liked it.

And if I was honest, hoping he might casually mention to Daisy I'd done it for him.

Chapter Nineteen

Daisy

THE MOST INCREDIBLE THING happened this week: a woman I'd met at the gallery opening had booked a grazing table for her daughter's baby shower in late June. It wasn't a lot, but to me, it was huge. The start of a dream I'd put off, deeming it too hard to make real.

Yet, here it was, happening.

I'd think, plan, obsess over my layout for her table soon enough, but not until after this weekend in Breckenridge. I planned to soak up the mountain air and relax as much as possible. I hadn't been out of town, not even for a weekend, in ages.

Miles reached across the console to grip my knee. "Nervous?"

"No. Why?"

"You haven't stopped moving since you got in the car."

I released a heavy breath. "Okay, maybe. Slightly. Meeting new people isn't my favorite."

"You know half of them already. Kit's cool as hell. You're gonna love her. Same with Luca. Elliot...well, he'll be there."

I snorted. "Is there something I need to know about Elliot? I seem to recall you referring to him as a friend when you were showing me your ass."

"Yeah, but that was back when you and I were just getting to know each other. Now that we've shed our formalities—"

"You were *showing* me your *ass*."

He cleared his throat and went on like I hadn't interrupted him. "—I can be real. Elliot Levy and I would not exist on the same planet if not for the people who connect us. And that's cool. I'm good with that."

"All right. I don't know if I'm any less nervous now."

"Want me to play you a new song?"

I scrunched my nose. "Will that help?"

"Just listen."

Rolling beats started playing, something familiar but not quite. Then Noah Kahan started singing about Vermont in a trippy, sped-up version of the song. It was his voice, but with electronic dance music backing it. I...didn't know what to think.

I turned to Miles. He was beaming, moving his head with the beat. It felt like I was missing something. Surely, this strange remix wasn't the thing making him that happy.

He glanced at me, catching me watching. "It's Reed's."

I flicked my eyes to the screen on the console then back to Miles. "My brother's?"

"Yeah. He sent it to me last night. Amazing, right?"

Head swimming, I let it fall against the rest. The two of them had exchanged numbers last Sunday when Miles had crashed our brother-sister bonding time, but I hadn't believed they'd text each other.

Apparently, I didn't know anything.

"He hasn't let me hear any of his stuff," I admitted.

"He told me. He asked me to play this for you."

My heart leaped into my throat. "Really?"

"Mmmhmm. I get the impression he was too nervous to ask you to listen directly."

I stared at the side of his face, trying to wrap my head around all this. Reed didn't talk to strangers. He barely talked to his family. Miles had wormed his way in on Sunday, badgering Reed in his signature way, teasing him and bombarding him with questions until he cracked. Not a lot, but more than I'd gotten out of him in ages.

And now, this song.

"Thank you," I squeezed out. "I love it so much. Don't tell him I got choked up or he'll never let me hear another one."

He shot me a crinkly-eyed grin. "No worries. I'll play it cool for you."

I clutched his forearm. "I was twelve when he was born. He's my brother, but a little bit my baby too."

He nodded. "I got it, Cupcake. I'll be careful with whatever he gives me, and I'll share it if it needs to be shared, all right?"

"I trust you, Spreadsheet."

It was surprising to admit it, since for me, trust had always been hard won. Miles had wormed his way under my defenses too, and I hadn't even noticed it happening.

⋯⋯◆⋯⋯

The house was far beyond any place I'd stayed before. It blended with the mountains and Evergreen trees of Breckenridge, with its rustic, log-cabin-esque interior, but the inside was pure luxury. In the living room, there was a two-story, gas-powered stone fireplace. With the flick of a switch, it ignited.

Miles and I got the house ready for everyone to arrive. He put welcome packages in each of the bedrooms, claiming this was one of his duties as Weston's best man. I peeked in one, spotting fuzzy socks with this weekend's date and location embroidered on the ankle. There was nothing dutiful about that, but if he wanted to pretend it wasn't a big deal, I'd let him have it.

Coming from Miles Aldrich, it was more endearing than I'd been prepared for.

For my part, I brought a charcuterie board fit for a big party and a couple dozen cupcakes. I might've gone overboard, but when it came to feeding people, that was me. "Too much" was just right. I *definitely* inherited that philosophy from my mama.

Miles came up behind me as I was tweaking the prosciutto roses. His chest grazed my back, and he gripped the edge of the counter on either side of me, arms paralleling mine.

"Are you ready to be my girlfriend all weekend?" he asked.

I turned my head, looking up at him. "I think I can handle it. It's not like we're going to be expected to fuck in front of everyone to prove we're real."

He went still at my back, his breath catching on an inhale. Then, the weight of his head fell on my shoulder, and a rumbling groan from his chest rattled my spine.

"That's a relief since I'm not into sharing," he uttered, sending goosebumps down my limbs.

"You don't have to share me. I'm all yours until this is done."

He let go of the counter to brush my hair behind my ear. "You didn't say anything about our bedroom."

My tongue was stuck to the roof of my dry mouth. I had to swallow a few times to get it working again. "What would I have said?"

"There's only one bed."

The corners of my mouth twitched, matching the twinges in my belly. "I expected that. It's a big bed."

"As long as you're comfortable."

I leaned my shoulders against his chest. "I think we both know we're playing a role in front of the others. When we close the door of our room, we'll go back to being just us. It won't be a problem."

He trailed his knuckle along my jaw. "Nope. No problem for me either. I'll build a pillow wall so you won't be tempted to venture to my side of the bed."

"Don't worry. I'm not snuggly."

"What? I don't believe that." He wrapped his arms around me, lifting me right off my feet in a tight squeeze. "Look at you being snuggled."

Then his face was in my hair, sniffing and growling, all while swinging me back and forth, my legs flopping like a rag doll. I...giggled. He had me giggling as he manhandled me.

"Is this not snuggly?" he teased. "I don't feel any prickles coming from you. It's all softness and light."

"This is you snuggling me," I wheezed, slapping his arm without any real intention of breaking free. "If you try to do this when I'm sleeping, you'll feel a lot more than prickles."

"Oooh." He paused, his teeth scraping my neck. "I'm intrigued. Like what, Cupcake? Are you going to...nuzzle me? Like this?"

His nose pressed behind my ear, hot air blowing against my skin. I squirmed in his hold, and he used my movement to rotate me in his arms, bringing us chest to chest.

"Now you can properly cuddle me," he whispered along my throat.

"Or get my knee to your balls," I whispered back. "Watch out, Aldrich."

"Your knee's so tiny, it would probably feel like a gentle breeze."

"Oh, you asked for it now, my guy."

I brought my knee up, but since I didn't really want to hurt him, there was no force behind the movement, and Miles easily caught me.

"You can't have my leg," I squealed.

He waggled his brows. "Too late." Then he had my leg draped over his arm and went back to gobbling on my neck and shoulders while I screeched and bucked. His body shook with laughter, even when I hit him. In fact, it shook even harder when I threatened to put shrimp in his cupcakes and shave off his eyebrows while he was sleeping.

A throat cleared. And since we were being so loud, it had to have been even louder.

Miles and I froze, our heads turning to the side in unison. There stood Saoirse, her hand over her mouth, the apples of her cheeks pink. The man next to her, who had to be her husband, Luca, had his head cocked and brow furrowed as he studied the scene they'd walked in on.

"How's it going, Rossis?" Miles asked as though he hadn't a care in the world. "Good drive?"

Saoirse snorted. "Great drive, but I think we should have taken the scenic route. We *definitely* interrupted something."

Miles gave me a jiggle. "This is nothing. Just me showing Daisy-daze how snuggly she is."

I let myself go limp in his arms so I was just hanging there and gave him a flat look. "Do I seem convinced?"

He flashed me a wide, pleased grin. "You seem cute."

Then he set me on my feet, making sure I was steady and my clothes were straightened. After that, I greeted Saoirse properly and met Luca. A few minutes later, Elise, Weston, Elliot, and Kit arrived.

I felt like the odd man out. They all knew each other and were clearly very close. And the women, dear god were they beautiful. Kit was the only one I hadn't met, and with her long, thick auburn hair and dangerous curves, she fit right in with Elise's girl next door plump sexiness and Saoirse's lithe, outdoor beauty. The three of them together were like an eclipse. Looking at them straight on was so tempting but too powerful for the human eye.

I didn't think I was ugly or anything, but in the face of the three of them, I felt like someone's twiggy, plain kid sister.

I'd have to get over that really quickly. This wasn't high school, and they were welcoming me with open arms. Beautiful and kind. It was almost too much.

The guys took the bags upstairs while the women drifted into the kitchen. Elise stopped in front of the island and pressed her hands together beneath her chin, peering at the board I'd created with wide, alight eyes.

"Wow, Daisy. This is a work of art. The roses...how did you even do that?"

I bit back the urge to dismiss her compliment and tell her it was no big deal. "I used a wine glass. If we have time later, I'll show you. I promise it isn't hard."

She waved her hand over the board. "Maybe not, but this whole thing all together—" she sighed, "—you have quite the eye. I almost don't want to eat anything and ruin it."

Saoirse leaned over her and plucked an olive off the twigs of rosemary I'd placed around the board. "I have no such problems. I can admire while I dig in."

"Please, eat. That's why I made it."

Elise sucked in a breath like she was going to say something then shook her head.

I touched her forearm. "What is it?

"Well, I was going to say it would be amazing to have something like this at our rehearsal dinner, but then I realized how last minute it is, *plus* you'll be there as a guest, so I decided to keep my mouth shut," she rushed out.

My heart fluttered in my chest. "You know I'm just getting started with this business of mine. I'm not booked. Even if I were, I'd find a way since you've been so welcoming to me. I'd be honored to create a grazing table for you."

"Really?" She glanced at Saoirse. "I shouldn't have said anything, huh?"

Saoirse went in for a piece of cheese. "Sure you should have. Daisy's building her business. Every job counts. And you *will* be paying her regular fee, even if she tries to give you a discount."

Elise shook her head. "I would never ask that."

Saoirse pinned me with an accusing stare. "I'm one-hun-dred-and-ten-percent certain you wouldn't have had to ask. Daisy would have insisted. Luckily, I'm here to knock sense into her before she makes a mistake." She held up a finger. "Take it from the girl who did far too much free labor before I decided to take myself seriously and charge what I'm worth."

I nodded, my eyes bugging. "Okay. I'll take myself seriously."

Kit leaned her elbows on the counter, giggling as she picked up a piece of Manchego and a breadstick. "As someone who joined this group last year, a word of advice: let yourself be swept up, Daisy. It's going to happen no matter what."

I glanced from one gorgeous face to the next. "You guys are so fucking nice."

Saoirse snorted a laugh, and the others chuckled with her. "Why wouldn't we be?" she asked, as if it were that simple.

To her, it probably was. The three of them weren't suspicious of intentions. They were warm and open-armed without needing me to jump through any hoops. I wondered if they had always been like that. Maybe I could get to that place one day too.

If I hung around them for a while.

I corrected myself before letting that thought get too far. There was a time limit to my relationship with Miles.

All this loveliness would disappear from my life right along with him.

CHAPTER TWENTY

Miles

THE TEMPERATURE DROPPED ALONG with the sun. We built a roaring fire in the outdoor pit and all eight of us were sitting around it, blankets covering us. Everyone was drinking but no one was wasted.

A year ago, in this same position, I would've been blitzed and acting stupid. The next day, I wouldn't have remembered anything, but the shame would have been there.

Now, I got to spend a cozy evening in the mountains, Daisy by my side, curled into me to steal my warmth, talking to my brother and his friends. *My* friends. Even Elliot was tolerable without a few shots to soften the effect of his existence.

I trailed my fingers along Daisy's side, tracing the curve of her waist and hip, down to her upper thigh, and back again. She must not have been aware of it, but every time I started my ascent, she let out a high-pitched sigh I felt in my gut. It was so sweet and content—and *I* was the one making her feel it.

Weston unfolded from his seat, holding up his empty beer bottle. "I'm going to grab another drink. Anyone want a refill?"

Answers were murmured as he grabbed a couple empties on his way, pausing by Daisy and me. "Daisy? Beer? Wine?"

She smiled up at him and lifted her pink lemonade in a tumbler. "I don't drink. I'm happy with my pink lemonade."

"All right. I'll make a mental note." He winged a brow at me. "You, Miles? I'm surprised you haven't cracked the Macallan."

My stomach twisted into ugly knots. "I'm not drinking."

"Ah..." He nodded like something had dawned on him. "Solidarity with your girl. Nice of you."

He walked off, and I felt Saoirse's glare from one side, Daisy's curious stare from the other. Neither would say anything around everyone else—which was good. I didn't particularly want to delve into the topic of my brother never seeing me, even now.

"You don't drink, Daisy?" Saoirse asked.

"No. I did the whole college experimenting thing, but getting wasted has never really held any appeal."

Elise tuned into their conversation. "You don't ever want to curl up with a glass of wine after a long day?"

Daisy huffed a laugh. "I work from home designing websites. By the end of the day, I'm so scrunched up, the last thing I want to do is sit more."

"She lies," I told them. "She has one of those walking pads under her desk so she can work and walk."

"It helps me focus and be more productive," she defended even though she didn't need to. I liked that she had a body that needed to move, just like me.

"I've heard that," Kit chimed in. "I've been thinking about getting one, but my desk chair is so comfy..."

"You don't need to be more productive," Elliot murmured. "You do enough."

"Thank you for noticing." Leaning over, she kissed his jaw. "And for the desk chair."

"I could use a new chair, Levy," I called across the fire.

He lowered his chin, giving me a long stare. "You have money, Aldrich. Use it."

"I do have money, it's just that sometimes I get these random pains in my ass. My doctors said that might happen after getting shot. Remember that? When I jumped in front of a bullet for you?"

Elliot exhaled. "You didn't so much as jump, just happened to be in the same place the bullet was going."

I scratched the side of my head. "I guess we remember it differently. Trauma does affect memory. That's what my surgeon told me."

Kit pressed her hand on Elliot's chest before he could tell me to fuck off. He was too much fun to goad, and there was no possible way I wasn't going to milk the scar on my ass until my last breath.

"If Miles wants a chair, he can have a chair, right, love?" She had this Elliot-taming voice that instantly melted his spine of ice. He leaned into her like he couldn't help it and nuzzled the side of her face.

"Whatever you want."

Kit's gaze flicked back to me, a grin curving her lips. She knew what I was doing, and though she might've found me amusing, she was firmly on Elliot's side.

As she should be.

"Want a chair, Miles?" she asked.

I waved her off. "Nah, that's okay. Thanks for asking."

The night went on. We hung by the fire, telling stories and talking until, couple by couple, everyone drifted back to their rooms. Daisy stuck around to help me shut everything down and clean up.

By the time we got to our room, I was ready to face-plant on the mattress—and looking even more forward to it since she'd be there with me.

She went into the bathroom to change while I put on my pajamas in our room. When she was dressed, she cracked the door open, inviting me in. She was bent over the sink, scrubbing her face. I stopped right beside her to take a good long look at the body that had been attached to mine the last few hours.

Since she was wearing a cami and shorts, more of her skin was on display than I'd ever had the pleasure of seeing. I was surprised to find she didn't have tattoos. With her combat boots and general "fuck off" attitude, I'd assumed they were par for the course. Daisy wasn't like anything I'd expected. It made sense she was all pale, smooth skin.

"I feel you staring." She was holding a steaming washcloth over her face. "Why are you staring?"

"Looking at your jams." I ran my finger along the spaghetti strap of her top. "I didn't know what kind you wore."

She tossed the cloth in the sink and patted her face dry while sweeping me with her gaze. For her sake, I wore black sleep pants and a white T-shirt. Normally, it was boxers or nothing, but that wasn't in the cards this weekend.

Even though I would have loved nothing more than to strip both our clothes off, get in bed, pull the covers over us, and hold her bare skin against mine.

"I thought for sure you slept naked," she said.

"You thought right." I plucked at my shirt. "This is me protecting your modesty."

The sputter that burst out bent her in half. "Don't worry about me. My modesty's a-okay without you protecting it." She started for the door, throwing a quick glance over her shoulder. "Wear, or don't wear, what you want. It won't bother me."

By the time I'd brushed my teeth and lost the shirt, Daisy was tucked in bed, lying on her side, facing my spot. I slid in, rolling to face her. We both smelled a little like smoke from the fire, but it was comforting rather than bothersome.

She was chewing on her bottom lip, her eyes dancing over me. Forcing a half-smile, I exhaled.

"Ask it, Daisy-daze. I can see you're dying to."

She let go of her lip, and a line appeared between her furrowed brow. "Doesn't Weston know you're sober?"

"I told him after I made the decision to stop drinking. I'd been a month sober, completed three weeks in rehab, and felt ready to tell him I was really doing it."

Her eyes flared. "And he just...forgot?"

"No." My lids lowered, the memories of all the times I'd vowed sobriety flooding back. "He just didn't believe me. I can't even tell you how many times I've told him I wasn't drinking anymore only to get plastered that same night. I don't blame Weston for taking what I'd said with a giant grain of salt."

"But you've almost got a year, Miles." She scooted closer and poked my chest. "That's a huge deal. Are you're just...never going to tell him? Let him figure it out himself in a decade?"

"I don't know, Cupcake. I haven't planned that far." I scooped her up and rolled so she was on top of me. "You wanna lie on me for a while and maybe fall asleep on my chest? It'll be cute."

She wiggled around until she was propped on her forearms. No way she couldn't feel me hard beneath her, but neither of us were acknowledging it.

"I think you should tell him. It's important to have support around you."

"Saoirse knows, which I figure means Luca does too." I cuffed her chin with my knuckle. "Now, you do too. That's all the support I need."

Her nostrils flared. "I disagree."

"Message received. Now, lay your big head on my chest and go to sleep."

"My head isn't big. Shut up."

"Prove it by putting it right here." I patted the center of my sternum. "Come on, Cupcake. I'm tired and need my prickly little snuggler to put me to sleep."

Her head slowly lowered right where I wanted it to be, and I exhaled in pure contentment. The weight of her pressing on me combined with her fingers sliding around my neck to toy with the hair at my nape and her soft breaths on my skin relaxed me like nothing else had.

We shouldn't have been doing this. Holding her in this bed had nothing to do with starting her business and everything to do with a craving I was choosing not to deny.

It was one night. That was all. A few blurred lines wouldn't bring everything crumbling down.

We'd get back on track tomorrow.

No problem.

She let out a happy sigh, and I clutched her to me like she'd blow away if I didn't.

Yeah. No problem at all, asshole.

Chapter Twenty-One

Daisy

I woke up hot, but not confused about what was making me that way. Miles' legs were pretzeled with mine, and his heavy body was half burying me into the mattress. Sometime in the night, we'd gone from me lying on top of him to him taking up every inch of my personal space.

Wide awake, I remained in that position for a few minutes before carefully extricating myself from under him. My full bladder wouldn't allow me to stay any longer, and Miles looked like he needed a lot more rest.

Once I took care of my business, including brushing my teeth and hair, I threw on a hoodie and thick pair of socks and ventured downstairs. The smell of coffee reached me before I hit the first floor. Soft murmurs next. I almost turned back. These weren't my friends, they were Miles'. The last thing I wanted to do was intrude.

I forced my feet forward. I'd grab a coffee, then get out of their hair...whoever was in the kitchen.

Turning the corner, I regretted my decision. Weston had Elise's back against the fridge, his hands planted on either side of her head. Her arms were looped around his waist, and her head was tipped back, giving him her full attention as he spoke to her in a low tone. I couldn't make out what he was saying, but from the hearts in her eyes and flush in her cheeks, it was something good.

I backed away, getting three steps in before I hit my hip against a console table, knocking over a small, wooden block statue.

"Shit, shit, shit," I hissed, righting the statue, hoping they were too wrapped up in each other to hear the cacophony.

"Are you okay?"

No such luck. By the time I lifted my head to reassure Elise I was fine, the two had switched positions. Weston was now beside her, casually holding her shoulders, as if he hadn't just been in an intensely intimate moment with his fiancée. Maybe they were always like that.

"I'm fine," I assured her. "I should probably start looking where I'm going."

She beckoned me forward. "See yourself into the kitchen. I'm not a chef, but I *can* make a mean cup of coffee. I'm assuming that's what has you down here this early."

I shuffled into the kitchen, giving them space by settling on a stool at the far side of the island. "There must be something about the mountains. I slept so well, I woke up ready to go."

Elise slid a mug filled with coffee in front of me, and Weston placed milk, creamer, and sweetener on the island. They went about doctoring up their own drinks, and I relaxed while the attention was off me.

It wasn't that I was shy, I just wasn't used to being accepted into a group this way. To me, it said a lot about their affection for Miles. He might not have seen it, and perhaps they did a piss-poor job of showing it at times, but they cared for him. Even I could see that.

Elise launched into the plans for the day. We were going to ride a gondola to the top of a mountain where there was an alpine coaster and other rides. I'd been skiing in Breckenridge with Andy's family, but we'd never come during the off-season. This was all new to me.

"I hope you like wild rides," Elise finished.

Weston huffed as he brought his mug to his mouth. "She must, being with Miles."

Elise grinned. "This is true. There's no predicting what he'll do next."

"He's fun," I agreed, because it was true. "I've known him a fraction of the time you have, but I also find him to be dependable and steady. It's one of my favorite things about him."

I would never break Miles' trust and talk about his sobriety, but I had no problem hinting at it. I just hoped his brother picked up on it. Miles needed support, and Weston should've been proud of how hard he'd worked to turn his life around.

"I hope he stays that way." Weston set his mug down on the counter and gave me a considering look. "Do you know if he's been in touch with our parents?"

"He hasn't mentioned them."

Elise sighed, rubbing Weston's shoulder. "No news is good news, right?"

His jaw rippled with sudden tension. "We didn't invite them to the wedding," he explained. "I wouldn't be surprised if my mother tried to manipulate Miles into giving her information on the date and location. She knows how to incite his pity."

I shook my head. "I haven't noticed him speaking to your parents, and like I said, he hasn't mentioned them. Are you sure they even know about the wedding?"

"Oh, they know," he intoned.

Elise laid her head on his arm. "If they show up, they show up. All that matters is we're married by the end of the day."

A deep line carved between his eyebrows. "I want it to be perfect."

"It will be," she promised.

"I'll keep my ears open," I said.

Weston nodded. "Thank you."

I sucked in a breath. I might not have another chance like this, talking to them with no one else around.

"You should keep a look out too."

His brows shot up. "What?"

"Yeah. You should pay attention to what Miles is doing...and isn't doing. What he hasn't done for quite a long time."

It was cryptic but heavy-handed at the same time. If Weston was any kind of brother, he'd pick up on what I'd laid down pretty quickly.

I slid off my stool. "I'm going to go check on Miles."

I found him right where I'd left him, sprawled on his belly, his arms and legs at odd angles. He looked cozy, half under the thick duvet. Padding across the room, I left my three-quarters full coffee mug on the bedside table and climbed in beside him. As soon as I hit the mattress, his arms banded around my middle, dragging me into him.

His eyes were still closed as he rubbed his nose along my temple and cheek. "You smell like coffee," he murmured.

"I have some, if you want."

"I'm not ready to wake up." He flopped on top of me, trapping me against him, and bunched the fabric of my sweatshirt in his fist. "What is this? Too many clothes." Then he slipped his hand under my hoodie and cami to splay his fingers wide on my stomach. That elicited a contented sigh from him. He settled even more, the loose weight of his limbs trapping me. Not that I had any intention of leaving. I liked being wrapped up in his strong limbs too much to try.

"Miles?" I whispered.

"Mmm?"

"Have you spoken to your parents lately?"

One eyelid cracked halfway. "I allow my mom two texts a week and one twenty-minute phone call."

I'd started to laugh but cut it off when I realized he was being serious. "How did you choose that number?"

"Therapist helped me. Never knew what boundaries were before."

"Weston's worried she's going to manipulate you into telling her about their wedding."

The thing about me was I was loyal. I wasn't going to have conversations about Miles without telling him. I might've been not-so-truly his, but while we were doing this, I would be on his side.

His other eyelid cracked. "She's asked. I shut her down every time."

"That easy?"

He rolled onto his back, taking me with him. "You really want to hear what a mama's boy I was?"

"If we were really dating?" I scrunched my nose. "Major red flag. But since we're faking this thing, I'm all ears."

"I've been overlooked a whole hell of a lot, but my mother doted on me like I was her favorite person in the world. When my dad was shit to her, she came to me—her kid. I'm talking being nine or ten and her crying to me when he cheated or another of his companies failed or he sold her jewelry. It took some serious introspection and guidance from a professional for me to understand how absolutely fucked up it all was. She knows her crying is a trigger for me and uses it to her advantage."

"Miles..."

I shook my head. How could anyone not see this man? Sure, Weston was a super-genius, which was great and all, but Miles was no slouch. Ridiculously handsome, he could charm the pants off a chilly nun. He wouldn't, though, because he was a good guy. I would *never* excuse bullying, but at least I understood why he might've been so angry back then.

"You limit contact with her so she doesn't have a chance to do the crying thing?" I guessed.

"Mmmhmm. It's been working well, but she never fails to let me know how utterly devastated she is at not being invited to the wedding. I don't know why she wants to be somewhere she isn't wanted."

I thought I did. "There will be talk if your parents aren't there. It'll get around. Aldrich is too big a name for it to stay secret."

He tapped my nose. "Exactly. She's panicking. I'm not sure my dad even remembers he has sons, much less that one is getting married."

"Just a couple more weeks and she'll have to find something else to complain about." I slid my hand up his chest to cup his cheek. The scar on his eyebrow caught my eye. "The scar...that was a truth, wasn't it?"

His eyes darted between mine before he nodded once. "I'm far too strong and buff to be a wrestler. They'd never let me on the team for fear I'd destroy them all."

I smiled but melancholy lodged in my chest. "Anyone who doesn't see you is really missing out."

He was quiet for a long beat, then he wrapped me in a bone-shattering hug. "Aw, Cupcake, if you have a crush on me, just say that."

⚬

After a long day playing on the mountain, our group was hanging out by the fire in the expansive yet somehow cozy living room. Elise had the remote, searching for a movie to watch, while we ate pizza and the remaining cupcakes and charcuterie.

Weston groaned when she paused on *Beetlejuice*. "Not this one. We watched it enough when you were a kid."

Kit perked up from her spot beside Elliot. "Oh my god, I love *Beetlejuice*. I always wanted Lydia's wardrobe."

Weston smirked. "Talk to Miles about Lydia. He could write a dissertation."

"I completely forgot about that." Elliot tapped his chin, amusement playing at the corners of his mouth. "The posters all over his walls."

Luca scrubbed his scruff. "Who didn't have a thing for Winona Ryder?"

"No." Elliot shook his head. "I once asked for clarification on that. It was all Lydia. Winona Ryder as herself did nothing for him."

Saoirse arched a brow at me. "I think he still might have a thing for her."

Luca's gaze swept over my black T-shirt and skinny cargos, and he grinned. "I think you're right, Pretty Girl. Good for Miles."

I shrunk against Miles, who had gone stock-still and hadn't uttered a single word to defend himself. Who hadn't had posters on their walls as kids? My obsession had been Adam Driver, circa his Kylo Ren days. And, to be fair, if he walked into this cabin right now, I would have let him toss me around with his oversized baseball mitts.

Miles finally moved, handing the remote to Weston. "You pick something. I'm going to grab a drink."

He was up and gone before anyone could say anything, leaving me flailing to remain upright as the couch cushions jostled in his absence.

Saoirse cleared her throat. "Sorry, Daisy. I went too far. I shouldn't have implied he likes you because...you know..."

I stared at her, surprised she was apologizing to me. They'd embarrassed Miles, although I didn't see what was so—

Realization exploded in my brain.

"The all-black clothes, prickly temperament, bangs—Lydia suits you."

I reminded Miles of the character he'd had a childhood crush on. Everyone in this room had seen it the moment they'd met me. I'd been the only dumb bunny who'd had no idea.

I shook my head. "Don't worry about it. I know why Miles likes me." Channeling my mama, I threw in a wink to put her at ease. "My cupcakes, of course."

The topic swiftly changed, getting rid of the lingering awkwardness, and I went to find Miles. He was in the kitchen, his butt propped against the counter, a tumbler of pink lemonade in his hand, a crumpled cupcake wrapper beside him.

I paused at the entry, giving him a devious little grin. "So...Lydia, huh?"

He squeezed his eyes shut. "Don't you think I'm sufficiently embarrassed?"

I closed the distance between us, leaning my chest against him. "Do you want to fulfill all your adolescent fantasies with me? Should I call you Beetlejuice?"

He covered my mouth with his hand. "You're the worst. Couldn't you have let this slide? Pretend it hadn't happened?"

I licked his palm, but he didn't pull his hand away. Not until I bit a chunk of it. Yanking it back, he cradled it to his chest like I'd injured him gravely.

"I do have this dress I wore one Halloween. I was going for the whole goth bride thing." I bit my bottom lip, and his chest expanded as he heaved a breath. "If I wore that for you, fancied up my bangs a little, I could—"

He cut me off again. This time, with his mouth on mine. He crushed my lips, kissing me roughly. In a split second, I decided to go along with it. I'd never been kissed roughly in my life.

Hands in my hair, he tugged my head back, taking my breath away. I clutched his shirt, my mind in such a whirling spiral, he was the only thing keeping me upright.

Then his tongue delved between my parted lips, and my knees gave out. Miles was there to stop me from falling with his hand on my ass, kneading and lifting me. Spinning, he placed me on the counter and shoved himself between my legs.

"Shut up," he gritted out.

That was my only chance to take a full breath before he devoured my mouth with such force, I might not ever recover. Not that I was thinking about recovering. I was barely thinking about anything other than his soft, sweet mouth doing demanding, naughty things to mine.

A peel of laughter split the air, and reality slowly returned. Miles pulled back slightly, but he didn't jump away or apologize.

A man who kissed the way he did had *nothing* to apologize for, except ruining every single woman who fell apart under his lips.

"We're not going to talk about this again," he uttered.

"So, no dress?"

Before I knew what he was doing, he leaned in and tugged my bottom lip between his teeth, nipping to the very edge of pain before releasing me.

I liked the results of teasing him, so I went on. "You could dress up as Kylo Ren, I'll be Lydia. It'll be a whole kinky thing."

His forehead rolled against mine as he exhaled through his nose. "I expected you to be weirded out, not doing...whatever it is you're doing."

I circled my arms around his neck. "I'm taunting you. Maybe if I'm bad enough, I'll get another one of those kisses."

His groan was pained. "Jesus, Cupcake. You need to stop or I'm going to bend you over this counter and spank you until you can't walk straight."

He had me panting with one threat. "Out here, where anyone could see?"

"Mmmhmm." Sucking in a breath, he raised his head and took half a step back. "Are you okay?"

I touched my lips, which were tingling now that he wasn't ravaging them. "I'm fine. You?"

"Good." Twisting to the side, he adjusted himself in his joggers. "I didn't make it weird by kissing you?"

My eyes flared. "You think the kissing was the weird part?"

One second passed, then he was bent in half, laughing so hard, he barely made a sound. His laughter drew mine out. My body contracted, falling to the side as I giggled until my eyes were watering and my abs gave out. Then I slid off the counter. Miles caught me, hugging me against him until the last tremors of laughter disappeared, and we were left smiling at each other.

"We should go join the others," I said.

"Yeah. We should do that."

We stood there a minute or two longer, smiling at each other like two people who'd uncovered the very best secret. And we had. We now knew the taste and feel of one another, and that our wilds just might match. What we did with that knowledge was yet to be seen, but there was no going back to how things were before.

Chapter Twenty-Two

Miles

I HAD A RECKLESS streak a mile wide. That was a facet of my personality abstaining from alcohol made no dent in. It was brain chemistry. My ADHD and the general makeup of who I was urged me to test boundaries, to balance on narrow ledges and tease hungry lions.

Or, in this case, the woman who'd entrusted me with her business and herself in a lot of ways. Kissing Daisy had been the start of my recklessness, but it hadn't ended there.

We were supposed to check out of the house this morning. The others had already packed up and were headed home. But I took one look at the hot tub I'd barely dunked my toes in, arched a brow at Daisy, and she'd nodded.

It was broad daylight, cleaners would be descending on the house any minute, but we were sitting in the hot tub like we had all the time and privacy in the world.

"You should put a hot tub on your deck," she said.

"Probably." I spread my arms out on the sides and let my head fall back. "But then it wouldn't be special anymore. I like hot tubs because I only get to use them when I take trips."

"That's a good point. When we took road trips, we'd always stay at hotels with continental breakfast. I was obsessed with the cheese danishes inevitably on the buffet. One time, after we got home, I convinced my mom to buy me a package of them for breakfast."

I groaned, knowing where this was going. "Ruined it for you?"

"Yeah. I was so sad. On vacation, I lived on those danishes, but at home, it was like eating cardboard with curdled cream in the center. They were never the same for me."

I found her foot under the water and hooked it with mine, drawing it into my lap. "I like your stories, Daisy-daze. Hearing that kind of normalcy is like a balm."

She pressed her toes into my abdomen. "You might not have had it when you were a kid, but there's nothing stopping you from having it now."

I caught her foot in both hands and dug my thumb into her arch. She immediately went lax, her head falling against the cushion, lips parting.

I wanted to kiss her again. Then I wondered if the churning in my gut and lightness in my chest was due to the magic of vacation. When we got back to the drudgery of real life, would kissing her lose its spark?

If it did, I didn't want to know.

I lifted her foot out of the water. Her nails were painted navy blue, the soles soft and taken care of. I leaned in and pressed my lips to the ball of her foot. Gasping, her head popped up.

"What was that?"

Looking her straight in the eye, I kissed her foot again. Another gasp, and her foot jerked, but she made no effort to steal it away.

"Your feet are cute." I dragged my fingers over the delicate bones in her ankle. "Sexy."

"Really?" She pointed her toes like a little dancer. "What's your favorite polish color?"

I ran my thumb over the nail of her big toe. "Right now, I'm partial to navy blue."

"What else?"

I kissed the tip of her toe. "I can't deny classic red does it for me."

"Hmmm. No one's ever paid attention to my feet before. I don't know if I like it or not."

Scooting closer, I dipped my head to trail my lips over the top of her foot. "You don't know if you like this?" Her skin was smooth and warm against my tongue as I licked her from heel to the tip of her toe.

Her breath caught. "That isn't so bad. What else would you do if you were really doing this to someone?"

I hooked her other foot and brought it to my lap. She had to cling to the side of the tub so she didn't go under. "I would rub the hell out of both your feet until you were boneless. Then I might lay you down in front of me and bring your foot up to my mouth so I could suck each of your pretty little toes."

Turning my head, I closed my lips over the tip of her big toe, which was a misnomer since it wasn't very big at all. I swirled my tongue around it until Daisy's breathing stuttered and her fingers dug into the padding along the side of the tub.

She'd taken her other foot from me, using it to massage high on my inner thigh. Her movements were unpracticed, but dear god, did it feel good. If she was going to keep teasing me, I would do the same.

I licked the arch of her foot and circled my tongue around her ankle bones. Then I kissed a line up the top of her foot, ankle, and shin. Once I was as far as I could reach without pulling her underwater, I nuzzled my cheek against her smooth calf.

"I might have a foot thing too," she breathed.

"Yeah?" I raised my eyes from her leg. "You like that, Daisy-daze?"

Her lids were at half-mast, and the rest of her was so relaxed, she'd slid low, the water lapping at her chin.

"Think so," she replied. "You made me feel a little drunk."

Despite how turned on I was, I laughed. She really was adorable.

"I've found the key to making you chill out, huh? I bet I could talk you into anything right now."

Her eyes locked on mine. "Probably. And you wouldn't even have to be very persuasive."

A surge of need had me grabbing her around the waist and placing her on the side of the tub so only her calves and feet were in the water. I hooked my fingers on her bikini bottoms, grazing bare skin beneath.

"And if I wanted to pull these aside?"

"I wouldn't stop you." Her voice had dropped an octave, husky and sexy, luring me to follow my impulse and pull the gusset of her bikini to the side, revealing her slick, pink pussy.

"Fuck," I gritted out. "If you don't stop me right now, I'm going to put my mouth on you."

I counted to five. She didn't move, and my forebrain didn't stop me. Her thighs fell open at the same time I moved forward. Lowering, I hooked her legs on my shoulders, spreading her even wider, and dragged my nose up her length. When I hit her clit, I replaced my nose with my lips, kissing the hard little bead beneath silky slick skin.

"Miles," she breathed. "*Please.*"

This might've been my one and only shot at having her like this. I was going to make it count. Nothing could get me to hurry my perusal of her sweet lips, making a path with my tongue along the way. Underneath the taste of water was pure Daisy. Euphorically sweet and spicy, exactly how I thought she'd be when I allowed myself to think about her in this way.

"This is crazy." It was no objection. Her fingers dug into my hair, pulling me deeper into her pussy. "God, Miles, that feels so amazing. You're so good at that."

Her praise sung to my soul, spurring me on to make this the best time she'd ever had with a man between her legs. It was easy for me to delve deeper, to suck her flesh and lick her cream. The more time she was out of the water, the more her real flavor and scent revealed themselves. Fucking intoxicating. If I had this on tap, I'd never be tempted by alcohol again.

"Miles, Miles, Miles," she panted. "Oh god, what—"

I slipped a finger into her pulsing channel and closed my lips around her clit. The moan that broke free cracked in the open air, echoing off the mountains.

Her hips rose and fell with the steady, gentle rhythm I finger-fucked her. She might've been chasing something, but I was more than content to stay right here. On the precipice, alive with anticipation.

More awake than I'd been in years. So present. Sights, smells, sounds as sharp as the edge of a blade, my senses were overwhelmed.

"*Miles.*"

She panted my name, so much desperation poured into that one syllable, she might as well have been pleading for more. I gave her what she needed, adding another finger inside her, curving them to drag along her inner wall.

Hips rocketing off the edge of the tub, her fingers tightened in my hair. I repeated the motion, and Daisy cried like she'd been stabbed. Ragged and pained, needing something, anything, to fill her emptiness.

I thrust my fingers and curled, hitting the spot she was begging me to find, and laved her clit with the flat of my tongue. That was what she needed, what I'd known by instinct to give her. She gripped my ears, holding my mouth against her as she rode my lips through her climax.

Before she could come down and return to her senses, I lowered her into the hot tub, her legs on either side of mine. My bathing suit was paper thin, plastered to my skin, letting me feel her lower lips spread   around   my dick.

I only had a split second to try to come to terms with her pussy being on me before she dove for my mouth, then every one of my thoughts bailed. Mouths, tongues, teeth. Clashing, nipping, sucking, her tongue tangling with mine. She took my face in her hands and tipped my head back. Her lips covered mine, dominating our kiss.

It was cute, so I let her have it before taking back control. Yanking the sides of her hair, I ripped her mouth off mine.

"No," she rasped.

"Yes."

I held her eyes as I lowered my face to hers, brushing my lips over her waiting mouth. She chased my lips, whimpering when she couldn't quite catch them. Not until I wanted her to.

Her hips rocked against mine, and I was seconds away from being even more fucking reckless than I already had been. Draping her over the side of the hot tub, belly down, I'd tasted her little pussy again then sink—

We were saved from my impulsiveness by three maids swinging open the deck door and informing us through giggles over what they'd obviously interrupted that we had to leave so they could clean for the next guests.

Like last night, instead of being mortified, Daisy took it in stride, laughing at the ridiculous situation. Climbing off me and out of the tub, she wrapped herself in a towel and shook mine at me.

"Come on, you. Before we get banned from this town."

I got out of the hot tub, pressing the heel of my palm against my erection. She stepped into me and circled the towel around my waist.

"Thank you, Cupcake."

What a good girl. Truly the best girl. The highest quality. Her ex was an idiot for not locking her down years ago. Even more so for letting her walk away.

We were dressed, dry, and on the road before I got another chance to look at her. She was wearing her oversized black hoodie and jeans with the knees ripped out. The screen of her phone held something interesting, since she hadn't even glanced my way.

"Still good?" I asked, taking my eyes off the road for a moment to meet hers.

"Of course. We were having fun, right?" She tucked her phone in her hoodie pocket, giving me her full attention.

"I definitely had fun."

She sniffed, her lips tipping upward. "It seems we always do when we're together."

"No doubt. Just wanted to make sure we're both on the same page."

"We are. Don't worry, Miles. I don't plan out my future wedding with every guy who shows the slightest interest in me. It'll take me a solid seven years to ask you why you won't marry me, so you're free and clear."

"I'd be the lucky one in that situation, and anyone who'd make you wait that long would be too stupid to have you anyway." I reached over and squeezed her hand. "Thanks for making this weekend so easy on me."

"You don't have to thank me. I loved being there with you. If circumstances were different, I'd be demanding you take me on all future group trips."

She smiled. My stomach sank.

There were no future group trips for her. This was a one-and-done kind of thing. She seemed to get it, but my insides snarled in protest. We wanted Daisy with us for all the fun and difficult things. In the relatively short time I'd known her, she'd started to make the hard things bearable, the uncomfortable things a breeze.

I could get used to this.

I already was.

Next time I went somewhere with the group and she wasn't with me, I'd feel it in a significant way. But if I kept letting her in, relying on her to be content, I'd go searching for something to take her place without her.

My reckless nature would have me reaching for a bottle. Alcohol had a history of filling more of my hollow parts than anything else.

I exhaled, twisting my grip on my steering wheel.

Therapy, friendships, work, Clementine, Westie, Lisie, baby Joey, my house.

Alcohol wasn't all I had. I had lists of things and people who filled me up. I just had to be careful not to add Daisy to it. She wouldn't be around long. Once she got over that ex-boyfriend and her hang-ups with her last name, she'd see she didn't need me at all.

I couldn't be reckless here. Daisy was too special and far too fragile from the destruction of the last guy for me to be anything less than meticulous with how I handled her.

I would not be another person to hurt her.

I'd do my best not to hurt myself either.

Chapter Twenty-three

Daisy

My mother kissed my cheek. "Thanks for comin' over to help. Unfortunately, it's been nonstop busy the last two weeks."

I squeezed her around her shoulders. "Make sure you're taking breaks, Mama. And ask me for help *before* you're run so ragged."

She waved me off and bustled around her desk to collapse into her chair. Her sigh was heavy with exhaustion. If I'd gone downstairs to check on my dad, he would've sounded the same. Landry and Tom worked here full-time too, but my parents were the worst martyrs, claiming they should do all the overtime since my sister's family was young.

They had a point and should have hired outside help, but they were too stubborn to admit it. They'd rather work until they collapsed and drove their children out of their minds with worry.

"Tomorrow's Reed's last day of school, isn't it?" I asked.

"Yes, it is. Finally. Seems like the school year really dragged on."

"Should we take him out to dinner? Or do you want to celebrate at home?"

My mother stared at me with a blank expression. "I...hadn't thought of it. We should celebrate him makin' it through his freshman year, shouldn't we?" She flipped open her notebook, her pen poised between her fingers. "I'll make a list of what we need for a little party. Oh, it'll have to be after seven. We have a late viewing tomorrow. But that's okay, we can tell Reed we're being European—"

"Mama," I laid my hand over hers, "you can do that, *or* I'll take him out. He's mentioned an arcade he wants to go to. It's filled with vintage games. I can see if he wants to do that."

Her eyes fluttered closed. "That would be wonderful, my love. You take such great care of all of us—especially Reed. I'll make his favorite dinner this weekend when it's not rushed."

"Sunday please?" If I knew my brother, he'd want barbecue, and I didn't want to miss that. "I have a thing with Miles on Saturday."

Her brow arched. "Miles? I haven't heard you mention him in a while."

"Yeah. We've both been busy with work lately." I folded my arms over my stomach, which hadn't stopped aching since I'd realized Miles had pulled away from me.

Two weeks of twisting organs was a lot to bear, but here I was, still alive and kicking.

Kicking myself, mainly. Wondering what I'd done wrong, where I'd misstepped. We'd become friends. I hadn't imagined that. The other stuff...the kissing, touching, we could have put that away if he'd wanted to. After our conversation in the car on the way home, I'd assumed as much. Disappointing, but probably wise. By no means did I consider Miles might've no longer wanted *anything* from me.

It stung.

Badly.

Almost knocked me off my feet. I expected the worst from most people, but not him. Never Miles.

The things keeping me afloat? Booking four more Grazing jobs for late summer and early fall with several more inquiries on top of those, cursing men with Bea, Miles continuing to text with Reed even after he went radio silent with me, family dinners, and spite.

Spite was a powerful thing. It kept me from returning to my bed to rot and working hard on my marketing for Grazing.

"I heard Reed laughin' the other day," Mama said quietly as she shuffled papers.

"You did?" Reed's laughter was such a rarity these days, it was like a special occasion when he did. "What was so funny?"

"He had the door cracked. I shouldn't have eavesdropped, but I was so shocked his door wasn't sealed shut, I couldn't help myself and stood outside it." Her mouth curved, and her eyes shone. "He was on a video call with Miles, playing his music for him. They were makin' fun of some DJ. No one I've ever heard of. My beautiful boy was grinning ear to ear, and he looked so much like Quinny, I had to walk away."

My heart lodged in my throat. *Quinny.* We didn't talk about her a lot. Not when we had one more Dunham kid to get past the hurdles she hadn't been able to surmount. She would have been twenty now, and probably reminding us she was *Quinn*, not Quinny anymore, but she was forever frozen at sixteen.

"They always looked so much alike," I squeezed out.

She nodded. "Lately, he's been sad like she was."

"I know. I see it too. I've been keeping a close eye on him." I pressed my lips together, waiting out the stinging in my nose. "He won't be the same."

Mama dabbed under her eyes with a tissue. "He came out of his room and told me he wants to go to this summer class for making music on the computer. I think Miles found it for him, but he didn't tell me."

"Did you sign him up?"

She laughed. "Before he even finished explaining what it was. Anything's better than him being holed up in his room."

I couldn't quite gather my thoughts about Miles staying involved with Reed when he'd ditched me like a bad habit.

"I'll thank Miles when I see him."

When I sat down at my desk, I decided to send Miles an email. Things needed to be said before we were headed to an event where we had to pretend to be a happy couple. As we stood now, if he tried to put his arm around me, I'd bite it off.

To: <u>milesaldrich@peakstrategies.com</u>

From: <u>daisy@grazingbydaisy.com</u>

Miles,

It has become apparent, from your two-week withdrawal from my life, you are putting in place boundaries after everything that happened in Breckenridge. While it is understandable and completely fine with me to cut off our physical interactions, I'm not okay with the sudden end of our friendship.

If you no longer wanted to have any sort of relationship with me outside of our professional agreement, I wished you'd have respected me enough to say that instead of ghosting me. I never would have treated you this way, especially after all we've shared.

This is all I have to say on the matter. When we see each other on Saturday, we can go back to professional acquaintances.

Not So Truly Yours,

Daisy

Miles arrived to pick me up right on time. After my unanswered email, I'd half expected him to cancel, but I was ready to go when he knocked on my door just in case. This time, I stepped onto the landing and locked the door, not allowing him in.

"You're ready," he remarked.

"Yep. Let's go."

I had my heels in my hand so I could go down the steps without breaking my neck. At the bottom, I bent to slip on my platform pumps and buckled the strap that looped my ankle.

Straightening, I smoothed my dress and sucked in a breath. I wasn't confident in how this night would go, but I knew for certain I looked good. Black was my power color, and though this was a daytime event, I'd made it work. The lacy skirt was flowy and hit mid-calf. The bodice fit like a glove, hiking up what little boobs I had. My arms were bare, but I'd draped a charcoal gray shawl around my shoulders, providing just enough warmth.

"Nice shoes," Miles remarked. "Pretty dress."

"Thanks."

I tried for breezy and unaffected, but I hadn't mastered those emotions yet. My "thank you" had come out as more of an admonishment. His compliments weren't wanted—not when he was so capable of withholding them and himself.

Miles tried to help me into his car, but I was already feeling bite-y. I jerked my hand away and helped myself. He huffed, but didn't argue, and carefully closed the door once I was in.

A moment later, he climbed in on the other side and pressed the button to start the engine. When we didn't move after a minute, I turned to look at him, finding his eyes already locked on me.

"I saw your email late last night. My assistant had placed it in a folder I never check." Chuffing, he shook his head. "Not that it matters since I'd already spent two weeks putting you out of my mind by ignoring you."

I stayed silent. He'd established boundaries, and so had I. After two weeks of being set aside by him, I'd decided I wouldn't pretend to be okay with crappy treatment just to keep the peace. I'd done that with Andy far too many times. I wouldn't be starting *any* new relationships—friendships or otherwise—that required me to bite my tongue or bend over backward.

Miles continued. "I'm sorry for being a shitty friend, Daisy-daze. To be honest, I'm surprised you see...or saw me as one."

"Why would that surprise you?"

He exhaled, heavy and ragged. "It doesn't matter. What matters is I thought I was doing us both a favor by pulling back, but I did it in a hurtful, burn-it-all-down way that wasn't necessary."

I blinked at him. "Look, I just recovered from a broken heart. I'm not looking to do that all over again anytime soon. I told you we were on the same page. I guess I was wrong, though. I thought you meant what the things that happened in the kitchen and hot tub meant—*not* the rest of it. You didn't break my heart, but you definitely kicked me in the gut."

His head fell forward, eyes fluttering shut. "I hear you. I went about it wrong, but I didn't think you'd care. Honest to god, I didn't. I thought I'd show up today and we'd get back on the right track."

I flicked him on the arm, sending him shooting back against his door with wide eyes. I held up my fingers in flicking position as a threat.

"Two older siblings. I can flick you straight through your window if you don't get off that self-pity horse right now. You can't carry around the '*my older brother rejected me as a kid so I expect everyone to reject me*' yoke for the rest of your life."

His brow dropped. "You don't get it, Daisy."

"Don't I? Didn't I just get dropped before *I* could drop *you*? You liked hanging with me so much, you decided to ditch me."

"You're thinking highly of yourself."

"I don't think highly of myself at all. I do know you like me. The same way I like you—well, before you turned out to be the jackhole I'd originally expected you to be."

"Guess we're two messed up humans living a self-fulfilling prophecy, aren't we? I expect to be rejected, you expect people to screw you over, and here we are."

I went to flick him again, but he caught my hand, holding it in his. "Shut up, Miles. I'm not messed up. I gave you a chance when my instincts told me not to, and you kicked me in the freaking gut." I narrowed my eyes at him. "If you were going to do that, why'd you bother to keep talking to my brother? Are you going to ditch him too? If you do, I'll eviscerate you. He *can't* handle that."

"I'm not going to ditch him," he said softly. "I promise you I won't."

Without another word, he got out of the car and circled the front, his eyes on me. Next thing I knew, he yanked my door open and leaned in, his face a breath away.

"I don't deserve it, but I want another chance to know you." He brushed his nose back and forth along mine. "I'm sorry I stopped talking to you. I was protecting myself…and I thought I was protecting you. If I'd believed for a second I was hurting you, I would have been here, asking how to make it right. That's the opposite of my intention."

I leaned against the headrest to gain a tiny bit of distance. "How have you been the past two weeks?"

"Feeling stupid. Working a lot to stop feeling anything. Talking to your brother on the off-chance I might hear something about you. In other words, not great."

"Did you drink?"

"No. Hate that you have to ask."

"Proud that you didn't."

He rolled his forehead on mine, then pulled me out of my seat and hugged me like he'd been waiting to do so for weeks. It took me longer to curl my arms around him, but I told myself this was it. I'd forgive him this once, but we were not at the start of a pattern. This was one-and-done.

"Put me down. We'll be late."

He picked his head up from my shoulder, a half-grin pulling at his mouth. "Enough feelings for one night?"

I rolled my eyes. "More than enough. Come on, I have to get in business mode."

He sat me back in my seat, but not before delivering a kiss to the top of my head. "Missed you, Cupcake."

I grumbled, and he waited, staying in my door and space before I relented. "Fine. I missed you too. Can we go now?"

I heard him cackling even after he closed my door, but I didn't mind the sound. If Miles was laughing, things couldn't be so bad.

Right now, they were pretty damn okay.

CHAPTER TWENTY-FOUR

Miles

I was stupid.

I made reckless decisions.

I regularly blew up my life.

All of that had been established.

What I came to face today? I was one lucky motherfucker. I'd been offered forgiveness more than I was certain I'd deserved.

I had not foreseen Daisy being as angry with me as she was. Nor as hurt. She'd been right, though. I had baggage, and I let that affect my relationships—including with her.

Stupid.

I had her forgiveness, and it went without saying it was a one-time thing. If we parted again, it would be for good. The idea of not seeing her ever again made my gut sink like a stone.

I just had to get my shit together and stop making out with her whenever I felt the whim. She wasn't exactly making it easy in her pretty, black, Lydia-coded dress. Smelling like flowers and sugar, working the room like a boss.

We were at a fundraiser luncheon for the local Boys and Girls Club. Peak Strategies donated to them, which meant when their fundraising chair—who didn't know the meaning of personal space or mouthwash—set his sights on me, he waylaid me into a prolonged conversation. Daisy, wisely, had gotten out of dodge as fast as she could, murmuring something about seeing someone she recognized. We both damn well knew she'd been lying. Finally extricating myself from Garlic Breath, I went in search of her. In another setting, I might have given her bratty ass a smack for leaving me on my own like that.

She wasn't easy to spot. Even in her heels, she was shorter than most of the mingling crowd. A few more people tried to stop me, but every minute that passed I couldn't see her made my stomach knot.

My searching gaze landed on the well-preserved woman she was speaking to before I found her, and my guts dropped in horror.

Hell no. This isn't happening.

I crossed the room as quickly as I could, hoping against hope not too much damage had been done. Those hopes were dashed as soon as I picked up on their conversation.

"It's grazing-by-Daisy-dot-com? Is that where all your pictures are?"

"Some pictures are on my site," Daisy kindly explained. "The majority are on Instagram, though. I add more with each job."

"Oh, how clever. I'm not the greatest with social media, but I'd love to see more of your work. By chance, are you doing any weddings soon?"

I placed a none-too-gentle hand on my mother's shoulder. "Hello, Mom."

She stiffened for a split second before shifting into acting mode. She turned to me with wide, innocent eyes. "Oh, Miles! I had no idea you were here, my love. What a coincidence. I was just talking to this sweet woman about—"

"I heard. You were trying to pry information about Weston's wedding out of Daisy."

The color drained from Daisy's face as she looked back and forth between us. Probably searching for the resemblance. I had inherited her hazel eyes, but I was the spitting image of my father. A nice face was the one thing he'd given me, as much good as it'd done me.

"Oh my, do you two know each other?" My mother chirped like this was some grand coincidence. "What a small world."

"I didn't know," Daisy whispered.

I shook my head and mouthed, "You're fine." Then I gave my attention to my mother. "You want me to believe you just happened to come across my girlfriend—?"

"Girlfriend?" She sniffed. "You didn't tell me you were seeing anyone."

I held up a finger. "I don't remember the last time you asked about my personal life. That isn't the point, though. You were trying to manipulate Daisy, and I won't have it."

"I wasn't," she protested. "We were talking about her very interesting new business. I thought if she did weddings, I might tell Weston about her services."

I stared down my nose at her. "He doesn't take your calls, Mom. How would you have told him?"

She waved this minor detail off. "Oh, that isn't true. He's just busy, which is understandable. Your brother is a very important man. Sometimes he forgets things, but he always makes it right."

She meant he'd *forgotten* to invite her to his wedding. As if he could have accidentally overlooked inviting his own mother. This was what she did. She carefully constructed a narrative that had little to do with reality. It had taken me almost thirty years to see her as clearly as Weston always had.

"You know that isn't going to happen," I stated.

She gasped softly. "Why are you speaking to me so harshly? In front of your new girlfriend, no less?" She swiveled to Daisy. "What did you say your last name was?"

Daisy shook her head. "I didn't."

My mother lifted the business card in her hand and read it as if it were the first time. "Dunham. Hmmm. You don't happen to be related to the *funeral home* Dunhams? What a ghastly way to make a living."

"I am related to them." Daisy straightened her spine, one brow arching. "In fact, I finished embalming a corpse before coming here."

While my mother sputtered, Daisy tapped her temple. "Did I remember to wash my hands...?"

My mother stumbled back, clutching at her chest. Her panicked eyes landed on me. Like I was supposed to save her. There was nothing to save her from except my naughty little Cupcake. I hooked my arm around Daisy's shoulders, guiding her to my side.

"Miles, you can't possibly think it's a good idea to be seen in public with someone like...this. Have you no shame?"

"Plenty of it, thanks. I'm not interested in any more. I'm full up," I quipped. "Excuse us, we have other people we need to talk to."

She slid in our path, bringing us to a halt. "But, darling, I haven't seen you in months. It would be lovely to sit together and catch up."

"We speak every week," I reminded her.

"You should come over for dinner. Bring Daisy, of course. Your father would love to meet her. Best not to bring up her last name, though. We've been for too many—" she dropped her voice to a mock-whisper, "—Aldrich funeral services at Dunhams' for him to be comfortable with someone from that family in our home. But you know your father. Names don't matter as long as she has a pretty face."

"All right. That's enough." I gently pushed Daisy behind me, and she went without a fight. "Consider this our twenty minutes for the week. I'll call you next week. You ever say anything remotely like you did now, twenty minutes will drop to zero in a flash. My girlfriend will never be a topic of conversation for you to bring up."

Without a goodbye, I took Daisy's hand in mine, and we walked away from my mother. Daisy was stiff, staring straight ahead. I was just sorry I hadn't gotten her out of there sooner.

It wasn't until we were in the car that she spoke again.

"I don't like your mother."

I groaned in frustration. It took a lot of effort to stop myself from slamming my head into the steering wheel. I'd just gotten back on Daisy's good side. Of course we had to run into my mother, and naturally, she'd be on her worst fucking behavior.

"I'm so sorry, Daisy."

She shrugged. "It isn't like I haven't heard similar all my life. No one likes to be reminded of their mortality. Being in the presence of someone whose family business *is* death can be uncomfortable for a lot of people."

"To small-minded peons." Reaching across the space between us, I slid my fingers into the back of her short hair. "There's no one who reminds me more of all the sweet things about living than you do."

A small puff of air escaped from between her lips, warming my arm. "That was really nice," she whispered.

"It's true." I stroked her nape with my fingertips then cupped her neck. "I can guarantee you my mother came up to you knowing who you were. She'd probably heard about you through the gossip channels and came prepared to be a bitch if things didn't go her way."

She tilted her face toward me. "Will she take it out on you?"

"I don't care."

And for the first time, I meant it. Thinking about my mother crying pissed me off instead of sending me into a panic.

"She tried to hurt you to get her way. This is why Weston cut her off for good. He knew she'd try to go through Elise to affect him, and he wasn't going to give her a chance. Now, she sees you're important to me—"

"You're pretending I'm important to you," she corrected. She was wrong.

"No, Daisy. Even though the girlfriend-boyfriend thing is fake, you're important to me. I'm not going to allow you to be caught in the crossfires of my toxic family."

She raised her stubborn chin and met my gaze. "I'm sorry that's the person who's supposed to love you the most. You got the short end of the stick."

I chuckled at her bluntness. "Appreciate it."

She smacked my knee. "It's amazing you came out as well as you did."

"Only half fucked up?"

"Nah." The corners of her eyes crinkled. "Just a quarter."

"Shut up, Cupcake." I loosened my grip on her neck and trailed my fingers down before letting my hand fall away. "I promised you lunch, and I'm going to make good on it. Sorry it's not going to be the overcooked chicken and watery carrots you might've been expecting to be served in there."

She snorted a laugh. "I think I'll be able to get over it."

———◆———

I was still laughing when we pulled up to Daisy's place. We'd stopped for Chinese on the way home. When the server had brought the food to my car, he'd been wearing gloves, reminding me what Daisy had said to my mother about coming to the event from an embalming.

"I can't believe you said that." I shook my head. "You have the most wondrous, creepy mind, and I fucking love it."

She wiggled her fingers at me. "Do you love these creepy, dead people hands too?"

I spluttered, letting my head fall against the steering wheel. "I think I do."

Her giggle was light and airy. "You know, I made that remark nearly an hour ago."

I turned my head to look at her. "It didn't get the proper attention then. I'm righting my mistake."

"It wasn't even that funny," she muttered as she climbed out of the car, leaving me there, laughing by myself.

As she sauntered toward her stairs, I sobered, watching her soft curves sway with each step in her high, high heels. Her skirt swished around her legs, and when she got to the steps, she shot me a coquettish look over her shoulder that I felt all the way to my core.

I wasn't going to be stupid and reckless when I walked into her place. No kissing the living hell out of her or falling to my knees to unbuckle her sexy shoes.

Actually...

Taking out my phone, I sent a text to Reed.

Me: *Daisy and I got way too much Chinese takeout. Come next door and help us out with it.*

A couple minutes later, Reed stalked out of his house. I jumped out of the car, the plastic bag loaded with food in hand, and met him at the steps.

There was something off about his appearance, but I couldn't quite put my finger on it.

"Hey, man."

"Hey," he grunted. "Did you get eggrolls?"

"Yep. Four of them. You can have two, if you want."

He grunted again. I'd take that as a "yes."

He went ahead of me up the stairs, and Daisy's surprise at his appearance was tinged with happiness. I wasn't sure if Reed got how much his sister loved him, but dear god, it affected me almost as much as watching her walk away had. Viscerally. A deep-down knowledge I'd never be the same.

"Did you smell the food?" Daisy asked her brother.

"Nah." He walked into the kitchen where she was taking down a third plate for him. "Miles texted me. He said you have extra. Is it okay I'm here?" He glanced back at me. "You're all dressed up."

"Yep. You're always welcome." She spun, her dress moving with her. "Don't I look nice?"

"You always do," he mumbled, tucking his hands in his pockets. "I'm just gonna take my food and go, if that's all right. I was in the middle of something."

Daisy's mouth opened, probably to deny him, and I shook my head. Not because I didn't want him here, but because I thought it was better not to force our company on him. I also got the vibe he was trying to give us alone time. It was the opposite of what I needed right now, but I'd let him do what he felt was right.

I placed the heavy bag on the counter. "Have at it. Just leave a few scraps behind for us."

As he loaded up one of Daisy's Tupperware containers, she told him about the luncheon and how many cards she'd passed out. She even told him about meeting my mom. The descriptor "bitch" was not used, but it was heavily implied.

I watched them both, so at ease with one another, and envied the hell out of them. This was what I'd always wanted with Weston, but we'd been set up to fail by having toxic, emotionally unstable parents.

I clicked my fingers, realizing what was different about Reed. "Where's your vest, Reed? I thought it was part of your uniform."

In the middle of packing his eggrolls, he stilled. Instead of answering, he continued, quickly stuffing what he could in the container and cramming the lid on top.

Daisy went on alert, her attention jerking from me to her brother. "Reed? Is your ve—"

He backed away from the counter, his head down. "I just didn't feel like wearing it, all right? Don't call the fashion police or whatever."

Little fucker.

He ditched us like his feet were on fire, leaving Daisy staring after him, and me looking at her.

"He didn't have it on the other day either," she murmured. "I didn't think anything of it until now."

I stood in front of her, cupping her tense shoulders. "Maybe he spilled something on it or lost it and doesn't want to tell you. He's a teenage boy. My former people are gross and messy."

Her exhale was slow and shaky. "I hope that's all it is. At least school's out. He'll get a break from the shit he gets there but doesn't tell us about."

Alarm bells rang in my head. "He's being bullied?"

"I suspect, but he won't talk to me about it." She humphed. "Even though I know exactly what it's like."

I pointed at her, anger weakening my knees. "You were bullied, Cupcake?" She nodded, and my chest hurt.

"Beau and Landry made it through school without being picked on too badly. Beau because he never gave a shit, and kids could tell. And Landry...well, you met her. She was the quintessential, all-American cheerleader. Then came me, Quinn, and Reed. Our feelings were too big, and we couldn't fit in to save our lives—" She broke off, swallowing hard.

"Quinn?"

"My sister." She studied the remnants of our Chinese food. "She had it really rough and got mixed up with a crowd who didn't care about her."

"What happened to Quinn?"

"She died four years ago."

Aw, hell. As hard as Weston and I fought, if I lost him, I didn't think I would be whole again. Yet, here was Daisy, carrying on and following dreams. Whitney Mae was still kind and welcoming. Landry had her cute kids and nice husband. The Dunhams were resilient. I didn't know how they did it, but Jesus, I ached for them.

"How old was she?" I asked, wanting to know more about this sister I'd never meet.

"Sixteen. She was being reckless and had an accident." Her jaw tightened, and I wondered if there was more to it than what she was saying. "It was an indescribably dark time for our family. We didn't have her funeral here. My mama insisted she wouldn't have been able to stand living here anymore if we had. My dad stayed with her...body while his colleague prepared her. He didn't leave her until she was in the ground. None of us were the same after. If we lost Reed—" She brought her fist to her mouth, shiny eyes finally meeting mine.

"You're not going to lose Reed, Daisy." I took her hand in mine. "Give me the names of the kids who are bullying him. I'll end them."

She gave me a long look I couldn't decipher. "You can't just end kids."

"I know, but—"

"If anyone's going to do it, it'll be me."

I closed my eyes, laughing. "You little vicious devil. Why do I believe that?"

"Because it's true." She sucked in a breath. "Enough of this. I'm too hungry to be this sad."

"Then let's get you fed."

I'd drop it for now, but if she thought I was going to forget people had hurt her and her family, she was wrong. Hyperfocused Miles was a thing to be reckoned with, and since I'd met her, she'd had all my attention. I didn't see that changing any time soon.

CHAPTER TWENTY-FIVE

Daisy

ELISE AND WESTON'S REHEARSAL dinner was my first official Grazing job.

It would have been a gift, but when I tried to offer it as such—ignoring Saoirse's previous advice—Elise put her foot down and insisted on supporting my business. She allowed the friends and family discount, though, since we were "basically family."

When she'd said that, I'd had to swallow several times to stop the bile from surging from my stomach. Guilt, but also regret over something that would never be true.

Me: *How is the rehearsal going?*

Miles: *Chaos! Would you believe Elise and I are now married?*

I grinned at my phone. Miles and I had gotten back into a good place. We didn't hang out every day, but we saw each other most days. He'd roped me into renovating his house with him in the evenings, but he always fed me and talked Grazing business, so it was a fair trade-off.

There had been no more kissing.

And definitely no more...anything else.

I couldn't say I didn't miss the *anything else*—what had happened in that hot tub had set a new bar for future partners—but I liked being with Miles more than a handful of orgasms. If I had to give up one, it would be the orgasms, hands down.

As long as I got to keep Miles.

Me: *Did the officiant come from clown school or something?*

Miles: *Something like that. Luckily, Luca looked up how to get out of a wrongful marriage. All we have to do is circle the real groom seven times backward and that'll undo it.*

Me: *Makes total sense. Be sure to write a scathing review for that officiant, though. Not everyone has a friend like Luca who thinks so fast on his feet.*

Miles: *Absolutely. I'll see you soon, Cupcake. Can't wait to eat your table.*

"Um, excuse me. When you asked me to help, I didn't realize that meant I'd be doing everything myself."

I tucked my phone away and looked at Bea, who was tapping her foot and scowling at me.

I smiled.

"Sorry, just checking on the rehearsal progress."

She rolled her eyes. "While you were flirting with your boyfriend, I opened four packages of crackers and made ten meat roses."

I snorted a laugh. "I see your point. My phone's away. The table has my full attention. Let's get going."

Over the past few weeks, my calendar had begun to fill. As exciting as it was to see my business blossoming, panic had set in, and I wondered how in the world I thought I could do all the labor on my own.

Miles had suggested hiring Bea. She was familiar with my products from my time at High Bar, and no one worked more diligently. This was our first job together, and since Elise had asked for a six-foot table, I was more than happy Bea was assisting me.

We worked well together, arranging the varieties of cheeses and meat, nuts, slices of fresh fruit and vegetables, olives and pickles, to look like they had a pattern and weren't just haphazardly dumped on the table. We added fresh flowers for color and height. Overall, it took us a little more than an hour to complete—slightly less than I'd budgeted.

Now, I had to scramble to make myself presentable as Miles' date for the dinner. Bea forced me into the bathroom to change while she cleaned up on her own. She did this with a frown, but we both knew she was being nice, which gave me a warm feeling in my chest.

I changed into a black sheath dress, leather harness cinching my waist, with straps over my shoulders, and black platform heels. I added a red headband with a silk flower with feather leaves on the side. To match, I swiped on red gloss. I'd done the rest of my makeup earlier, and I was pleased to see it had held up through making the table.

Checking myself out from all angles in the mirror, I nodded. I would do Miles proud as his date.

When I returned to the private room where the rehearsal dinner would soon be taking place, Bea was in a conversation with a stately blonde woman. She caught my eyes, beckoning me over to them.

"There she is. Daisy is the one you want to talk to about all this," Bea informed her in her best customer service voice.

The woman turned, and her familiarity struck me so hard, my steps faltered for a moment. I was certain I hadn't met her before, but at the same time, I *knew* that face.

"I'm out of here," Bea called. "See you later, D."

She swiped past the blonde woman before either of us could say a word.

I quickly put on my professional hat and strode toward her with my hand out. "Nice to meet you. I'm Daisy. Are you here for the rehearsal dinner?"

She slipped her hand in mine, giving it a firm shake her fine-china features belied.

"Lily Smythe-Kelly."

I grinned. "The two of us would make half a garden."

Her laugh was deep and resonant. Practiced too, like she was told jokes often and knew exactly how to modulate her response to them.

"That is true. We must seek out a Rose and Violet to complete our quartet." The corners of her eyes crinkled. I'd guess she was in her fifties, but it was hard to tell, since she'd probably had some very-skilled work done. "I see how you're looking at me, Daisy. You recognize me because you know my daughter, Saoirse. I had the pleasure of giving her my whole face."

My eyes widened, taking her in. The resemblance truly was uncanny. "Wow, you absolutely did. Lucky Saoirse."

"She has her father's kindness, which is even more valuable in my opinion." There was something wistful and sad about the way she said this, but she moved on quickly enough for me not to be able to spend too much time on it. "I'm terribly embarrassed to be here so early. I was killing time in the bar, but some old fool kept hitting on me so I thought I could hide out in here until everyone arrived."

"Of course." I checked the time on my phone. "It should be any minute now."

Lily gestured toward the grazing table. "I was speaking to your employee about your business. I've never seen anything so marvelous. It's too bad you don't live in California. I'm at several events a week, and they would be much more interesting with a setup like this." She waggled her perfect brows. "I'm a cheese and crackers girl. Give me a choice between filet mignon or a lovely Camembert on a cracker, and I'll snatch the Camembert before you're finished asking."

I clutched my hands in front of me, wondering what advice Miles would give in this situation. I could almost hear him saying, *"All contacts are good contacts."* I didn't want to turn Lily's interest away just because of a little geography problem.

"I'm always up for traveling if the job's big enough. I can also ship smaller charcuterie boards."

Her eyes lit. "Can you? That would be delightful." She pressed her fingers to her mouth. "Actually, are you free next month? I'm throwing a retirement party for one of my colleagues in the Senate. It'll be casual, around two hundred people. The catering is taken care of, but one of these tables would be the cherry on top."

I nodded. If I wasn't free, I would make myself free. "I'll give you my card, and you can send me the details, but I don't see why I can't make that work."

As soon as I handed over the card, Miles burst through the door, his head swiveling left and right. "Where is she? Where's my girl?"

When he found me, I waved, and a grin split his face. He stalked to me, sweeping me off my feet. His face went to my neck like it was pulled by a magnetic force, nuzzling me roughly.

Squealing, I batted his shoulder. Before Miles, I had never squealed. Before Miles, I would have kicked a man in the shin if he'd dared pick me up without my explicit permission. What had this man done to me?

"Dammit, Miles. I'm supposed to be professional."

He spun me so my back was toward the wall, his big body blocking me from view, and gave my butt a swat. "You're not working anymore, Cupcake. Now, you're my plus one. As my date, I demand you let me carry you everywhere since I haven't seen you in two days and missed you."

"I missed you too, you goon, but I was in the middle of talking to Lily Smythe-Kelly about doing a very big job—"

He pulled back, his brows raised. "Really? That's awesome. But Saoirse's mom lives in California."

"I'm aware. I would fly out there to do it."

"A plane ticket would eat your profit." He placed his forehead on mine. "We'll take my father's plane. It's decided."

"Is flying private magically free?"

He swatted my butt again. "For you it is."

"Stop hitting my butt in public."

"Private is okay?"

"Only if you want to be hit back."

He tilted his head, not denying it. *Actually, that could be fun...*

I cleared my throat. "Is Saoirse's mom a big deal? I was getting that vibe."

"Yeah. Her family has been in the state senate for a couple generations. Lily had been in office for years. It's funny because Saoirse's dad is a rancher in Wyoming. I can't picture Lily ever stepping foot on a ranch. Guess that's why they're not married anymore."

He slowly put me on my feet, looking me up and down. "God-damn, Daisy." He hooked a finger under the waistband of my leather harness. "This thing is sexy. It feels like a kink thing, but I don't think you're the kind of girl to wear a kink thing in public."

I snorted a laugh. The room had begun to fill in with guests. Too many people were milling around to talk about kink. Well...not for Miles. He probably had no such limit, but not too many people were like him. None I had ever met anyway.

"It just cinches in my waist and spices up my simple outfits," I explained. "Andy hated when I wore them."

"Andy is dumb as a box of rocks," he snapped, hands settling on my hips, just below the harness. "If he was too insecure to have a hot girlfriend, he didn't deserve one."

I pressed my hands to his chest. "By the time you're done with me, you'll have repaired all I thought was too broken to get back." I pecked his chin. "Thank you for being sweet to me, Miles. That wasn't part of the agreement, but it is a welcome bonus."

His humor dropped. "Do we have to talk about the agreement?"

I lifted a shoulder. "Not always, but we do when I'm in the midst of playing my role for you. Everyone here thinks we're a couple. We're the only ones who know we aren't. Remembering the agreement while we're here is important."

For me. So I didn't let the feelings I'd begun to catch grow beyond what they were. I really couldn't afford to get hurt again. There was only so much grief bacon a body could take.

"Message received." He backed away, taking my hand in his. "From here on out, you and I are a wholesome, loving couple."

The rest of the night went quickly. Elise loved the grazing table, and for once, I got to be around to watch people go to town on my creation.

There were speeches and lots of love all around. Anticipation for the big day tomorrow sent a buzz through everyone in the room. Weston and Elise were lucky to have so many people excited for them.

At the end of the evening, I went home, wishing it was all really mine. The friend group, the love, the way Miles made sure I was comfortable, having fun, never cold, never alone. He'd held my hand or grazed my back. When he'd laugh, he'd checked in with me so we could laugh together. He'd been especially amused by the slideshow Elliot had prepared with pictures of Elise and Weston through the years. She was always looking at him, and he was smiling at the camera, completely oblivious.

And tomorrow, they were getting married.

It made my stomach warm, and my heart feel like it was wrapped in a cozy scarf. They were going to have a lovely life together, I could tell. I wished I'd be around to see it.

While that wasn't meant to be, I now knew I wouldn't settle for anything less than what I'd seen and felt tonight.

Chapter Twenty-Six

THE LAST PERSON I expected to show up at my door was Andy.

But there he was, neatly combed and finely dressed, taking up my doorway.

"You look nice," was his greeting.

"I'm going to a wedding," I intoned.

I had a half hour before I needed to leave, but I wouldn't be telling him that. If I did, he'd take it all for whatever this ill-timed visit was about.

"Can I come in for a minute? There's something I need to talk to you about." He shuffled forward, like he was so sure I was going to let him in.

With a huff, I stepped to the side and allowed him. I guessed he did know me well.

I shut the door but didn't lock it. He wouldn't be staying long, and I wanted it to be as easy as possible for him to leave.

He was in my living room, scanning the place. When my heels clicked on the floor behind him, he spun, giving me a half smile.

"You've made it nice in here," he remarked. "Your style."

"That's the best part of living alone. No one to veto my decorating decisions."

My jaw was so tight, I felt a headache coming. Why in the hell was he here?

He sat down on my couch, resting his ankle on the opposite knee, and nodded to the cushion beside him. I took the armchair, gingerly sitting on the edge so I could spring up if I wanted or needed to.

"What are you doing here, Andy?"

He cupped his hands on his knee, fingers locked. "You're doing well? Still dating?"

"Yes, and yes. You?"

"I'm well, and I'm still with Samantha. You're seeing...Miles Aldrich?"

"I am."

He expelled a long breath. "You left me, you know. I don't know why it seems like you're angry at me. You made the decision to go."

My chin dropped, and I pinned him with a hard glare. "Do we need to go over everything? Is that why you're here? Because I will."

He nodded, as if to tell me to rant at him. I didn't need his permission in my own home.

"Andy, you led me on and lied to me. You lied to my parents. You looked them and me right in the eye and told me an engagement was coming. At some point, you changed your mind about me, about marriage, and never said. Since we're here, since we're being honest, when was it? What changed your mind?"

He looked at me for a prolonged moment, his jaw rippling, then shook his head sadly.

"You were right. We don't need to do this."

"Why? Is telling the truth uncomfortable to you? Just tell me when you changed your mind so I can grasp how long you deceived me. I don't know why—"

"After Quinny died," he uttered, and the world stood still.

I blinked at him many times, but he stayed. This wasn't some sort of strange nightmare. "You decided not to marry me when my little sister died?"

He scrubbed at his face, groaning behind his hands. "I think I always knew, Daisy, but the way your sister died...the *reasons*...it clarified things for me. I still loved you and wanted to be with you, but I didn't see us having kids and a life with this...this *cloud* over our heads."

Oh, that smarted. The cloud was my family name and our reputation in this city. The way he'd always winced when introducing me to people. My parents had treated him like their own son, despite his shortcomings. He'd watched ball games with my dad and had traded books with Tom. My mama had always baked him a birthday cake, and they'd invited him on family vacations with us. To call *that* a cloud was beyond the pale. The only cloud in this town was the small minds who had driven my sister to...and he'd *been* there. He'd held me through losing her all while making an exit plan.

"I can't believe you." I stared at this stranger who'd once been my world. "You should have left me."

"When?" He threw his arms out. "When you spent a year barely functioning from grief? The next three when you were building yourself and your family back up? When I loved you and couldn't see myself without you? When, Daisy? In those four years after she died, when would have been a good time to leave you?"

My eyes narrowed on him. Sure, I'd been a mess for a long time after we'd lost Quinn, but not so long he couldn't have let me down gently.

"A conversation, Andy. If you'd told me you'd changed your mind about marriage and kids, we could have ended things amicably. You denied me that chance by lying and lying and *lying*." Tears pricked the backs of my eyes, but I refused to cry. I'd spent too much time perfecting my makeup before he'd gotten here. The inside of my mouth might've been chewed to hell, but on the outside, I was unaffected.

He sighed, his hands falling to his lap in heavy defeat. "I didn't come here to argue or dredge up things we've gotten over."

"I haven't gotten over my sister's death."

His shoulders rolled forward. He was shrinking by the second, right in front of my eyes. "I know. I didn't mean that."

"Why'd you come here if not to dredge things up?"

"I need to tell you something before you hear it from someone else."

It was incredible. To love someone for seven years then three months later, having them feel and look like a stranger. The eyes that had greeted me every morning weren't the color I remembered. The voice that had whispered "goodnight" in my ear no longer sounded smooth and comforting. What had once been an easy companionship was now like falling into a prickle bush. I wanted out of this situation as quickly as possible.

"Tell me," I said.

Andy's face had gotten pale, and the breath he sucked in didn't bring back any color.

"Last weekend, I proposed to Samantha, and she said yes. We're engaged."

It wasn't pity I saw in Andy's eyes, it was imploring. For what? For understanding? For me not to freak out and call him an asshole? He could implore all he wanted. I didn't answer to him.

Rising to my feet, I marched to the door, yanking it open. "Get out, Andy." Later, when I didn't feel like I'd had acid sprayed on every one of my surfaces, I'd praise myself for keeping my shoulders and words steady.

Andy crossed the room, bracing his hand on the doorframe. "I know it's fast. I know I said—"

"Get. Out," I gritted through clenched teeth. "I want nothing to do with you. You're a stranger to me."

"Daisy," he crooned. "I wish it could have been you. It was supposed to be."

I met his foreign eyes. "I think you've proven it was never supposed to be me. Three months ago, you said you loved me and begged me to stay. Now, you're marrying someone else. That says a whole fuck of a lot about what we meant. Get. Out."

"I'll always love you, you know," he whispered. "I wish it could have—"

He reached for my hair, and I batted his hand away. "All that talk of 'it's not you, it's me' was a complete lie, huh? I was always the problem for you." I raised my chin. "Go away, Andy. I have somewhere to be."

He chuffed, his face coming slightly closer to mine. "You know, the short hair is growing on me." His knuckle grazed the side of my face before I could push him away. "I'm sorry, Daisy. I wish things were different."

I narrowed my eyes on him. "I wish you were swallowed by a black hole. We don't always get what we want, now do we?"

He huffed a laugh, looking me over for a long beat. Patting the doorframe, he walked out. I slammed the door behind him and threw the lock in place before he could make it down one step.

———◆———

Everyone looked dashing in a tux, but Miles took the top prize.

My eyes should have been glued to the bride. Or even the groom, whose stoicism had broken the moment she'd come into view, a few tears escaping before he could swipe them away. Those things were beautiful, but Miles had captured my attention.

He bounced on his toes as he watched his brother marry Elise. When Weston and Elise cried, he did right along with them, all while looking like Pierce Brosnan's James Bond.

After the ceremony, he winked at me as he strode by me down the aisle, and Lily patted my hand.

"Keep him. He's one of the good ones."

"Yeah," I whispered.

Maybe I could. Not the way she meant, but the truth in her observation rang clearly. Miles was absolutely one of the good ones.

This day was one of the most beautiful.

The ceremony and reception were on the lawn of a gorgeous, stately old mansion. The guests were quivering with excitement. The bride and groom were wholly, madly in love. The friends and family surrounding them couldn't have been happier for them.

Watching them was nothing like the last wedding I'd attended. Surely that couple had been just as in love, but I hadn't felt it. I'd let my envy and desperation cloud how I saw them.

I understood what I hadn't then.

Andy and I should have been over for years, but I clung to the idea of him. To the hope that one day we'd be this bright and shining couple too, surrounded by this same kind of excitement. I had grasped at the straws of our dwindling relationship because it was all I'd known.

Without him, the clouds disappeared, and at *this* wedding, I was able to see Weston and Elise's love clearly. I'd never had this. No one had ever looked at me the way Weston did Elise.

That realization sunk into my bones and filled me with regret tinged with sadness.

Seven years, and I'd never been loved right, all because of my name. Who my family was. Andy had loved me as well as he could have, but it had been in spite of who I was, not because of it.

Miles' attention landed on me from across the lawn as he posed for pictures. The grin he shot me was unabashed and wide. He held nothing back, not a single care for who saw his connection to me.

My heart panged, but I tried to wipe away my melancholy. This was Weston and Elise's day, and the last thing they needed was some sad sop bringing down the mood.

With a crooked smile on my face, I watched the happy couple begin their life together. Though I still longed for something exactly like this—the love, the friend group, the acceptance—none of it was truly mine. Getting too attached to these people and this kind of love would make it hurt worse when the summer ended.

CHAPTER TWENTY-SEVEN

Miles

I figured I'd gotten asked to be Weston's best man over Elliot and Luca for optics. Knowing that, I'd thrown myself into the role, making sure my brother never once regretted his choice.

Plus, I figured one day he might return the favor and wanted him to have a lot to live up to.

So far, the day had gone smooth as silk. Weston had been chomping at the bit to get to Elise. Once he'd slid his ring on her finger, he'd mellowed in a way I'd never seen.

Now, we were at the reception, watching them dance their first dance as a married couple. My heart was pitter-pattering a mile a minute as they rocked and smiled at each other. This was true love. No denying it. And being in the face of it was a powerful thing.

I looked behind me for Daisy but couldn't spot her in the crowd. No surprise since she was a foot shorter than everyone else. Fuck, I wanted her next to me, swaying to the music with me. Why couldn't she read my mind and know that?

That was the last of the traditional activities. No father-daughter or mother-son dances. No awkward slow dancing with a random bridesmaid I just met. We got to sit down and dig into the food.

Since we didn't have assigned seats, I went in search of Daisy. So far, she was doing a lousy job as my plus one. She hadn't been in my presence for even a minute today. If I hadn't seen her tearing up when I'd walked down the aisle, I wouldn't have known she was even here.

After a minute or two of weaving through tables, I found my girl chatting up Lily Smythe-Kelly.

My breath got stuck in my throat. This girl...she was a vision. For once, she'd replaced her ubiquitous black with pale gray lace. The bodice was strapless, pushing her breasts up into creamy little mounds. Her dark hair was curled and swept away from her face by a crystal-covered headband. A delicate silver daisy rested in the hollow of her throat.

I pulled out the chair beside her and slung my arm around her shoulders.

"Hello, Cupcake. You're stunning."

She turned to me slowly. The instant her eyes hit mine, I knew something was wrong. They weren't puffy or red from crying, but there was something haunted in the brown depths.

"Hey." Her violet-painted mouth lifted, but I wouldn't have called it a smile since that was the only part of her into it. "You were the best, man."

"Thanks. I gave it my all." I trailed my fingers along her bare shoulder and arm. Leaning forward, I found my manners and greeted Saoirse's mom. "How are you, Lily?"

"Wonderful. Beautiful wedding." Her gaze caught on something over my shoulder. "Oh, I see someone I know. I must go speak to him. It's been ages."

As soon as she was up, waiters began coming around with the first course. My stomach growled, but I didn't dig in, too concerned over Daisy.

"What's up, Daze?"

She picked up the roll on her plate, ripping it with her bare hands. "Nothing. I'm just enjoying the wedding. Are you ready to give your speech?"

"Not really." I patted my jacket pocket. "I have it, though, so that's something."

She swiveled in her chair, her knees slotting between mine. "You look so handsome in your tux." Her flattened palms smoothed my lapels before she straightened my tie. "They're going to love your speech, Miles."

"Thanks." I pressed a kiss to her warm cheek, and the unmistakable stiffening of her jaw put me on alert. "What's going on? You're not your usual self."

She turned, our faces a breath apart. "It must be being at the wedding. The last time I went to one...you know."

"Ah, that's what these blues are? Ol' Andy showing up when he's not wanted?"

She nodded. "I think so. I'm going to shake it off. West and Elise don't deserve my bad vibes bringing down their day."

"Eat your soup so I can spin you on the dancefloor until you're too dizzy to remember why you were ever sad."

Her nose scrunched. "I don't know if that sounds fun."

"It will be. Trust."

A little food so my stomach didn't eat itself, a little dancing to cheer up my cupcake, then I was in the spotlight, given a microphone and told to make a speech in front of one hundred of Elise and Weston's closest friends.

The truth was, I really could have used a drink. It would have been a hell of a lot easier.

I also heard my therapist asking me why everything had to be easy in my head, and I was out of my chair, my note cards in hand, standing next to where Elise and Weston were wrapped in each other, waiting with bated breath and probably a whole lot of worry over what I had to say.

"Good evening, everyone. If you don't know me, I'm Miles, Weston's favorite little brother."

Chuckles were good. I kept going.

"To tell the truth, Weston and I weren't close growing up. Four years older and a million times smarter, he got out of our house as quickly as he could. I was the little brother always nipping at his heels. I didn't want much from him, just all his attention, love, and devotion."

I glanced at Weston. He was watching me intently, his face void of expression.

"When I couldn't get it from Weston, I tried my hand with Elise. I was the proverbial kid on the playground, yanking her ponytail for attention. All wrong. She couldn't wait to get away from me either."

I shook my head to emphasize how stupid I'd been, in case it wasn't already obvious.

"Then, one day, we grew up, and magic happened for all three of us. Elise came to work for Andes, and I tried a different tactic of annoying her into compliance, parking myself on her desk every day until her face didn't fill with dread when she saw me. And while I was winning her over as one of my very best and dearest friends, Weston was getting her to fall in love with him."

The rest, I knew by heart. I tucked my cards away and lifted my glass of water.

"My favorite part about Elise is her capacity to love and forgive. For Weston and me, it's a really good thing. Otherwise, we wouldn't be here. The thing about us Aldrich brothers? We learn from our mistakes, and you can count on us never repeating them."

Laughing, Elise mouthed, "Thank goodness."

"Elise, Lisie, Lise—you are the glue in our family. You have softened my brother and opened him up to an entire world outside his office. You've brought West and me closer than we ever would have been without you. I couldn't have designed a better wife for my brother or sister for me. Weston, Westie, West—I know you count your blessings every damn day. You found a woman who likes you in all your serious, grumpy, ambitious glory, who inspired you to let your heart grow, who allows you to be her protector even though we all know you need her far more than she needs you. If you screw up, I'll be on Elise's side."

Weston mouthed, "As you should be," and Elise swiped at the underside of her eyes.

"To Elise and Weston, the walking definition of true love. May all your days be as sweet as this one. Cheers."

I tipped my water back, swallowing the knot in my throat, then turned to give the next person the spotlight. Weston caught me before I got far, pulling me into a tight hug.

"You're drinking water," he said beside my ear.

I nodded.

"How long?"

"Eleven months."

Exhaling, he pulled back, gripping my shoulders. His jaw rippled. His nostrils flared. His eyes shone.

"Love you, kid," he gritted out. "We'll be having a conversation."

He passed me to Elise, who gave the warmest, softest hugs. Weston was possessive over them—he was possessive over everything about her—and I understood.

"I'm glad you forced yourself back into my life, Miles," she said.

I raised my brows. "Am I your favorite brother now?"

That made her laugh. A grunt followed by a chair scraping the floor behind me told me Elliot didn't find me as amusing.

"One of my favorites," Elise replied before rising on her toes and murmuring in my ear, "Proud of you, Miles."

Sniffing, I gave the top of her head a kiss. "Thanks, Lisie. Means a lot."

I found Daisy waiting for me on the other side of the dancefloor. As soon as she was within reach, I swept her up, letting her toes dangle off the ground.

She patted my back. "Good job, Miles. You made everyone cry."

"Including you?"

"A little."

"Good."

She snickered next to my ear. "Sadist."

"Let's dance."

Her sigh was hot but not too pained. "Oh, all right."

After the speeches, Daisy and I danced all night. A few times, I passed her off to the girls and let them do their thing, but we only left the dancefloor to eat cake or gulp down water.

I may have been biased, but I was pretty sure Weston and Lisie's wedding was the best I'd ever been to. Never had more fun, that was for sure.

A second after that thought, the realization struck. This was the first time I'd been to a wedding stone-cold sober. Maybe that contributed to how much fun I'd had—not wasting time in line at the bar or pissing every ten minutes.

I dipped my head down beside Daisy's ear. "I'm sober."

"Yeah, you are."

That was all I had to say. She understood how monumental this was for me. To have experiences with a clear head. To know I'd remember the tiny details of the day and be able to look back without any shame over shit I might have said and done while I was too loose and uncaring of the consequences to hold back.

She rubbed her cheek against mine. "You're incredible, Miles."

I pulled her closer, tucking our joined hands between us. I felt pretty fucking incredible.

◆

After it was all over, I twirled Daisy down the hall into the elevator. We were staying in the mansion tonight. I'd convinced her she couldn't drive home at midnight and had to stay with me.

"Good night, Daisy-daze?"

"Mmmhmm." She looked down at her feet. "I'm ready to get out of these heels, though. They've never seen so much action."

"You *were* a dancing queen tonight."

The melancholy I'd seen in her earlier was still there, underneath her smiles and living in the moment. I wanted to question it, to ask if it really was just being at a wedding or if something else had happened.

I didn't.

We were having such a good time, I selfishly didn't want it to end. Big conversations could wait until tomorrow. I had stolen cake and pink lemonade filled the mini fridge—the party was just getting started.

As soon as we were in the room, Daisy kicked off her heels and marched to the two side-by-side queen beds.

"Two beds this time?" she asked, hands on her hips.

I came to stand beside her, brushing my knuckles along her shoulder blade. "I figured no one would report if we didn't sleep in the same bed. Our secret is safe."

She nodded and swiveled on her toes, presenting her back to me. "Can you unzip me?"

"Sure."

My fingers were almost too big for her delicate zipper, but I managed to drag it down her back without ripping the fabric.

"Want to borrow a T-shirt, Daze?"

Her dress parted, revealing the line of her back, only interrupted by a black satin bra. Her skin was so pretty, smooth and unblemished. I remembered what it felt like after she'd been in the hot tub, but I didn't know how it would feel now. If things were different, I'd follow the bare line of her spine with my lips. I'd get down on my knees and ease her dress off her until it pooled on the ground. I'd take her by the waist and—

She pulled away from me, holding her dress to her chest. "I'd love a shirt, thanks. I'm going to wash all this makeup off. Be right back."

The bathroom door clicked, and I sat down on the corner of the bed, sucking in a deep, steadying breath. *Jesus.* My head fell forward into my hands. If Daisy could read my mind, she'd never share a room with me.

I pressed on my half-hard dick, willing it to calm. That wasn't what tonight was about. We were going to eat cake and maybe watch a movie until we fell asleep. In separate beds.

The bathroom door swung open a minute or two later, and I realized I'd forgotten to get her a shirt.

"Shit. Sorry, Daze." I looked around for my bag. "I'll grab you something to wear—"

"Not necessary."

She walked out of the bathroom in nothing but her bra and a matching pair of silky black panties. As she approached me, she reached behind her, unclasped her bra, and let it drop. She didn't stop when she got to me. Climbing onto my lap, she straddled me. I caught her on instinct, holding her ass in my hands.

"What—?"

"I didn't have a chance to tell you how good you look in this tux. You made me wet the second I saw you." She tugged on my bowtie until it unraveled, me right along with it. "Can I take it off you, Miles?"

"You sure?"

She nodded hard. "I need this."

"You need it from me?"

"Yes, you."

I trailed my fingers up the line of her spine to grip her nape. "You're so gorgeous, Daisy. I'm going to eat you up."

She unbuttoned my collar. "Do it. Show me."

I jerked my hold on her, grabbing her attention. "If this is only happening one time, I won't be rushed."

Her breath rushed out, thready and bare. "As long as it starts happening now, you can set the pace."

In the back of my mind, there was a reason this shouldn't have been happening.

Would one time really hurt anything, though?

It was hard to see how this could possibly be wrong.

Taking another breath, Daisy leaned forward, stopping just before she kissed me. Her eyes darted to mine, pleading, and I gave her what she wanted:

Permission.

Chapter Twenty-Eight

Miles had me naked, my chest pinned to the headboard, my knees under my belly. He was behind me, devouring every inch of soaked flesh between my thighs. He took my thoughts away. Closed off my doubts with thick layers of pleasure. The way he touched me made me forget, if only for now, that I was untouchable outside these walls.

When I'd come out of the bathroom and offered him this night with me, I'd thought he'd take it hard and fast. I hadn't expected hesitation. Nor for him to want to take his time once he gave in.

He had.

Slipping my panties off in slow motion.

Kissing me with the leisure of a man who had all the time in the world.

Studying my breasts like topographical maps. Licking and sucking them with the same enthusiasm he had for my cupcakes.

I couldn't even remember how I'd ended up on my front, only that Miles had taken complete control of my body, moving it into the position he wanted. I'd allowed it to happen because he made letting go the easiest thing in the world.

"I'm going to come," I panted. "Please, let me come."

He moaned against my skin and pulled my clit between his lips. I had no idea why I thought he'd tease me, but he didn't. He encouraged me, practically shoving me over the edge until I was clawing at the headboard and bucking against his mouth. It was so much, the tightness in my abdomen, his constant licking and humming. He wouldn't let up. I saw stars from the overwhelming power of it.

That was when he flipped me over, flat on my back. My legs went over his shoulders, and two of his thick fingers filled my fluttering channel. He curved them inside me, and my hips flew off the bed.

"Miles!" I yelled, the world turning to blinking stars. "Oh my god, Miles."

He'd found a raw spot inside me, and he wasn't letting it go. "There you go," he rasped from between my thighs. "That's a good girl. Keep coming for me, Daisy. Gonna wring you out."

I shuddered and writhed, fighting it because it was new and strange. The heaviness in my belly, the liquid heat flowing from within me to where his fingers laid waste to everything I thought I knew about my own pleasure.

He pressed and rubbed, licked and sucked. Pressure built inside me. I moaned for relief, wiggled my hips to escape or maybe to take more. Nothing helped. It had to happen. I had to let him do this to me. Resistance was only prolonging this sweet torture.

"Miles, I can't—" I raised my arm above my head to push on the headboard, bringing me closer, him deeper. He growled at me, and that did it—unpinned the grenade and pulled the plug. An explosion and a release at the same time.

I rocked sideways, screaming into the pillow beside my head as lava flowed from within me and my hips flopped on the mattress, out of my control. Slick arousal slid down my thighs and ass, and Miles' waiting mouth drank it like the finest honey.

"More," he demanded, his lips grazing my inner thigh.

"I really can't."

He'd wrung me out as promised. There was nothing left. Even if I'd wanted to come again—it was questionable—I didn't have anything to give. Two orgasms in a row was a record for me—and two orgasms like *that*? I'd never experienced anything like it.

"You can, Daisy-daze."

Gripping my thighs, he rolled and shifted us higher on the mattress. I barely knew where I was before he was yanking me down on his tongue and lapping at me again. My hands shot out to hold onto the headboard.

"No. This isn't—" I forgot what my complaint was about.

It might've been that he didn't want me sitting on his face, but he very obviously did. He had me pinned there, an iron-clad hold on my legs making movement impossible. The sounds coming from him as he buried his face in my folds were nothing short of euphoric. He wanted me here. He was having fun doing this. If he'd told me it was his favorite thing on earth, I would have believed him.

Miles deriving pleasure from pleasuring me made me lightheaded. Nails digging into the headboard, I ground myself against his tongue, trusting he would adjust me if he needed to. The way he groaned and lapped harder, I didn't think I was going anywhere anytime soon.

One orgasm rolled into another. Then another. Time lost meaning. The air was thick with my arousal. He explored me from beneath, touching me as he drove me mad with his mouth.

I'd thought I'd had nothing left, but Miles kept finding more. The world tilted, and he had me on my back again, kneeling at my knees. He shrugged his dress shirt off, discarding it behind him. Saliva pooled in my mouth as I watched his powerful form revealed little by little. Knowing I'd been sitting on his face while he had been fully dressed turned me on beyond reason. *All* of this was beyond reason.

"Come here," I rasped, my throat raw from screaming for him. "I want you."

"I'm not going to keep you waiting. Not after you were a good girl, painting my lips with your cream."

With heavy-lidded eyes, he dragged his fingertip beneath his lips and sucked on it. As if he were sucking *me* off his skin. Dear god, the way I'd come, he probably was.

His gaze never left me. Once his pants were off, his hands didn't either.

Lowering himself between my legs, the thick ridge of his cock wedged between my puffy lips, hitting my sensitive clit. He did this once, twice. On the third time, he pulled back and pushed in at a slightly different angle, the head of his cock breaching my entrance.

My mouth fell open, and Miles stared. This was it. We'd crossed so many lines, but this was the last one. The biggest one. If he tried to go back now, I'd chase him down. I couldn't think of anything more I wanted than for him to push the rest of the way inside me.

"Give me all of it, *please*," I begged.

"You're gonna get it," he promised, rearing back until he almost fell out of me.

His eyes on mine, he paused.

"Daisy," he whispered.

"Miles," I whispered back.

My heart jumped into my throat. I reached for him, clasping my fingers behind his neck. Our mouths met in a hot, wet kiss. I followed his lips, needing him to keep kissing me more than I needed breath.

He took my hips in his hands, giving me a brief second of warning before he plunged into me, splitting me in half. My mouth fell from his in a gasp, neck arching from the unimaginable fullness.

"Miles," I cried. "You—"

"Hold onto the headboard, Daisy. Gonna fuck you hard now."

He waited for me to reach up and wrap my fingers around the slats. It was all the consideration he gave before he let loose, our bodies colliding in a violent, carnal clash—movements of desperation and too-long ignored need.

He had control of me, pushing me onto his length as he drove into me, reaching depths that had never been explored. If I hadn't been soaked and softened from countless orgasms, he would have hurt me. As it was, he was already reshaping my insides, custom for him.

One hand came loose from the headboard, grabbing his rippling bicep. Nails digging into his taut skin, they made pinkened trails. He grunted, tossing his head to the side toward my raking hand. I brought it to his mouth, and his teeth caught the pad of my palm, digging in.

Not hurting me. Never hurting me.

Capturing my attention. Bringing my eyes to his mouth, his face.

He let me go, and I cupped his jaw. He leaned into my touch, watching my expression.

It wasn't just his cock carving me up, it was the feelings growing roots in my chest, spreading wide and wild. My nails were gentle in the scruff on his jaw, affection for this man like live wires beneath my skin, crackling hot and freely the longer his eyes stayed locked on mine.

He caught my palm again, placing sweet, firm kisses that made my eyes roll back and my breathing shudder.

"Miles, Miles, don't be sweet to me."

"Can't help it." He moved my hand down to touch where we were joined with him. Our fingers spread around his cock, painted with my arousal, spearing into me in long, powerful thrusts. "Never had better, Daisy. Never felt anything like your pussy sucking me in, begging me to stay. Need more of it. I'm never going to have enough of this."

It was just talk, but I let myself believe it. I let myself get dizzy from the headiness of it all. My eyes slammed closed, and I let myself immerse in the moment, as fleeting as it was.

He hooked my leg over his arm, lifting my hips off the bed, drilling deep into my core, finding that same raw spot as before, unleashing pure heat from within me. My stomach spasmed. My muscles seized. His name was on my lips when I came for the thousandth time.

He released my hand to roll my clit under his thumb, and I wrapped my fingers around the base of him, feeling him enter me again and again. He swelled in my hand, and his thrusts quickened.

"Come inside me," I slurred, drunk on this night, this man, the pleasure he was pouring into me. "Fill me up, Miles."

The noise emanating from his chest sounded like nothing short of torture. Ragged and pained, his grunt vibrated his bones and mine.

Then he was pulsing in my hand and deep within me, filling me, relieving the echoing hollow inside me.

He took my face in his hands and planted his mouth on mine, kissing me slow and deep, his tongue winding around mine. Our kiss didn't break even when he rolled us, plastering me on top of him, his cock slowly slipping free from me as it softened.

Finally, we took a breath, his head falling back on a pillow, my chin resting on my arms. He leisurely stroked my lips and chin with his thumbs, peering at me through glassy, half-opened eyes.

"Did I just knock you up?" he asked.

A tired laugh broke free. "I hope so." He went still, and I laughed harder. "I'm kidding. I'm on the shot. There won't be any Miles juniors running around in nine months."

He expelled a long breath. "I like that you think my newborn sons would be so athletic like me, they'd be born running."

I shoved his face with my hand as affection for him bloomed thick gardens in my chest.

"Shut up, Miles."

He grew quiet, stroking my face and neck. I let my eyes flutter closed. It made accepting his intimate perusal of my face easier.

I couldn't quite lasso my feelings, but at least I was no longer numb.

Miles broke the thick silence. "You okay, Daisy?"

I cracked an eye open to look at him. "I'm good. You?"

He released my face to circle his arms around me. "Feeling like I won something."

This man...

I let my head fall on his chest, a smile tugging the corners of my mouth. "You did. First prize in the cunnilingus contest."

"Yes!" I felt him pump his fist. "I always wanted to win that."

"Proud of you," I murmured, my fingers sliding into the hair at his nape. "I'm going to take a little nap now."

His lips touched my forehead right before I slipped into sleep.

———◆O◆———

I woke to Miles behind me, his arms around me, one hand on my breast, the other working my clit. The clock on my bedside table said three a.m. The middle of the night.

I raised my knee, giving him room and permission. Another minute of rolling my clit, and he pushed into me. I was somewhere between dreamland and fully awake, and he kept me there, holding me, rocking me, his lips warm butterflies on the back of my neck.

Our fingers curled together over my breasts, over the thumping of my heart. His mouth slid to my ear, whispering how he hadn't been able to wait until morning to have me, that his cock had missed me, his skin had itched to be touching mine. I nodded, agreeing, because it felt right.

His body surrounded mine, almost fully on top of me now. Safe. So safe. He buried me into the soft, cloudy mattress, and I let him. Helpless to stop, hungry for more.

I came with barely more than a whimper, our hands joined beneath my chin. His pace quickened, thrusts became longer, deeper. He twisted my head, and his mouth touched mine. Soft at first, becoming swirls of easy passion when he had me in position.

Once he emptied himself in me and drank his fill from my mouth, he pulled the covers over our shoulders, carefully tucking us in.

"Goodnight, Cupcake."

"'Night, Miles."

I fell asleep with my hand in his, safe and sound.

CHAPTER TWENTY-NINE

Miles

THE BED FELT WRONG. Cold. That was what drew me out of the deepest, most satisfying sleep I'd had in ages. When I realized I was alone, I shot up with a start, my head whipping right and left, searching for Daisy.

She was nowhere in sight.

Gone?

Even if she'd needed to get home, she would have told me good-bye...right?

The bathroom door swung open, and Daisy stepped out in her dress from last night. Her head jerked back when she saw me up and awake.

"I thought you'd snuck out."

"Not yet. I do need to go soon, though." She pinched the sides of her dress. "I haven't done the walk of shame since college."

I raised a brow. "Are you ashamed?"

She chewed on her bottom lip, eyes sliding to the side then back to me. "No. I wasn't ashamed back then either. I just don't like anyone knowing my business."

"That you've been fucking all night?" I filled in.

She snorted a little laugh. "Indeed. And what a night it was."

"Worth it?"

A nod, then she crossed the room to my bed. Placing her knee on the mattress, she leaned over me.

"In a different world, under favorable circumstances, I'd say we need to do that again," she murmured. "Since we only had the one night, I'm glad it was that one."

She pecked my nose. As she pulled back, I caught the back of her thigh, tipping her over onto me. Her shriek pierced my eardrums, and her flailing limbs smacked me in the face and shoulders. I circled my arms around her and yanked her up my chest, bringing us face to face.

"Tell me what's going on with you, Cupcake. You were sad yesterday, and I'm feeling those blues radiating off you again. Talk to me."

Propping herself on her forearms, she sighed. "I didn't mean to bring my bad mood with me to the wedding."

"Don't worry. I'm the only one who noticed, and that's because I know you so well. Is it Reed? Something happened with him?"

"No." She shook her head. "Andy stopped by before the wedding."

"Dick," I muttered.

"He came to tell me he's engaged to Samantha."

"What?" That was the last thing I'd expected her to say. It should've been more like he'd come to plead with her to take him back, to grovel on his knees, beg for her hand. "He's engaged? But...?"

"Yeah. Turns out, he doesn't mind getting married, it was getting married to me he didn't want." She blinked hard, turning her head. "I shouldn't have been surprised."

"Why shouldn't you have been? I can guarantee Samantha is boring as hell compared to you."

She gave me the Dunham squint and pinched my chest.

"Maybe he wants boring. Maybe he wants a girl whose name doesn't come with a reputation. Complicated is fine when you're dating. When you settle down for life, easy is what everyone wants. He never would have gotten that with me."

"Yeah, I'm not into you making excuses for him. What he did to you was messed up, and coming to your place yesterday was even worse. He made you feel unworthy?"

After a beat of hesitation, she nodded. "I guess he confirmed it."

"All he confirmed was that's what he thinks. As far as I can tell, his opinion doesn't mean shit since he's obviously a dolt."

"A dolt I spent seven years with. What does that say about me?"

She wiggled off me, and I let her go. Something hit me square in the chest. Something ugly I wanted to deny. But goddamn if the truth wasn't blaring me in the face.

"Daisy?"

She stood next to the bed, smoothing her dress. "Yes?"

"Did you sleep with me last night to forget?"

After a beat, she nodded, and my chest cracked in two. I felt like I'd lost something, but I couldn't name it.

"Did it work?" I shoved out of my tightened throat.

"For a little while," she whispered. "Thank you for being there for me. Always."

When she was gone, I got up and showered off her scent like I was getting rid of evidence of a crime. Last night had been...unwise, but also inevitable. I hadn't had time to consider what I'd thought it was, but Daisy losing herself in me to take her mind off the man she loved marrying someone else had never crossed my mind.

Not when every second we'd spent in bed together had been all about her. Nothing beyond these walls had existed. That was my problem. Hyperfocusing on the wrong thing. Not seeing the forest for the trees. If I'd paid attention, I would have seen she wasn't with me for me, but the distraction I could provide—the ability to make her feel good after the man she really wanted had crushed her to pieces.

With anyone else, I wouldn't have minded being used in such a way, but this was Daisy. For her, in a different world, we'd have more than one night together. For me, if conditions favored us, I'd have all my nights with her.

<hr>

The next time I saw Daisy, she greeted me with a smile that was unnatural on her. Lopsided. Not meeting her eyes. Like it was only there because it was held up by a string.

I'd taken her to a social event at my parents' club—after ensuring they were off-continent on a wine tour in Italy with close friends. The way I was feeling, if I had a run-in with either of my parents, none of us would come away unscathed.

Daisy wore a navy blue sundress with one side of her hair pinned behind her ear. I swallowed the urge to stroke her bare skin with my fingers, my tongue, my lips, my cheeks. The only concession I gave myself was one light touch no sooner than ten minutes apart. My boundaries were the center of her back and the length of her bicep.

Daisy laughed at something the man we were speaking to said. Her arm brushed against mine, and she shared her crinkly smile with me. When she didn't move away, keeping her arm aligned with and pressed against mine, I had to step to the side. We'd had several of those incidents already, and each time, I became more sure she was doing it on purpose.

She looked up at me, her crooked smile fading. "Should we go for a walk? I'm told there's a lovely lake outside."

"Man-made," I replied.

"I think I'll check it out. I could use some fresh air."

She turned, heading for the doors leading outside. I gave myself a few minutes to decide: stay or follow. It was safer to remain where I was, but night had fallen, and now, Daisy was on her own out there, so it wasn't safer for her.

I followed a path I'd taken a few times before. The gardens were ostentatious in their verdancy. Red rocks and sagebrush would have been more appropriate for the area, but I wasn't a member shelling out the big bucks for the water bill so my opinion didn't matter.

Daisy was standing on a short ledge, her elbows propped on a wooden railing overlooking the lake. Fountains shot water up in several spots, and colored spotlights made it somewhat of a show.

I stepped up behind her, bracing my hands on either side of her arms, allowing myself to do this on a technicality. We weren't touching, but I was close to her, almost embracing her.

Her breathing shuddered, and her eyes fluttered closed.

That was all it took for me to be reckless once again.

Her breathing.

Something her body did automatically, without any effort or conscious thought.

Dear god, was I easy when it came to Daisy Dunham.

She leaned her head on my shoulder, and I gathered the back of her skirt until it was at her waist. Smoothing my palm down her lower back, I cupped her ass, hooking one finger around the barely-there floss between her cheeks.

"Miles," she whispered, arching into me. The softness of her backside met my rigid cock, grinding against me.

We weren't alone. People were outside, their voices carrying from the balcony of the room we'd just left. Anyone could walk the same path we'd taken and stumble across us, finding a couple wrapped in each other. A man in a suit, his jacket open, flanking a woman in an A-line dress, her skirt fluttering around her shins. They would not see her bare backside or her thong shoved to the side. Nor would they see me sliding my fingers through her folds to roll her swollen clit.

If they took one look at her face, tilted upward in the beginnings of rapture, they'd know. As it was, I was the only one being tortured by Daisy's parted lips and huffing breaths as I toyed with her clit and ground my cock against her.

"Do it, Miles," she breathed. "Fill me up."

Rotating my wrist, I stuffed two fingers inside her. She bit down on a moan, her insides squeezing me.

She shook her head against my shoulder. "No, you. I want you in me."

I stopped moving my fingers and lowered my mouth to her ear. "If I do this, you have to be completely quiet or I'll stop."

Her nod was near frantic. "I can be quiet."

The sound of my zipper coming down made her gasp, but she swallowed her moan and held still for me. With her in heels standing on a ledge, we were perfectly aligned. I flattened my palm on her lower stomach, tipping her to an angle that brought the head of my cock to her entrance. She wriggled, trying to pull me in, but I waited, gathering patience from a fount far deeper than I'd ever realized.

Finally, she exhaled, giving in, and only then did I sink into her, inch by inch, until my pelvis met her plush, round ass. There, I stayed in the torture of her tight heat for as long as I could without moving.

It was lucky I did.

"Lovely night," a man called as another couple strolled by on the path behind us.

"Absolutely beautiful," I answered.

He walked on with his woman, leaving us with the sounds of our mingling breaths and nearby grasshoppers. Once they were out of sight, I pulled almost all the way out of Daisy and slid back in, bottoming out again. Her hands covered mine where I held her at her stomach and the curve of her hip.

"Miles," she whispered.

"Daisy," I grunted beside her ear.

I pushed into her, flesh hitting flesh. It sounded so loud, out here in the still of the night, but there was no one around to hear it. I kept going, intoxicated by her.

Lips on her shoulder, the side of her neck, I took in her scent—cupcakes, sugar, and undeniably her.

Trapped between me and the railing, she had no choice but to let me have complete control. Reaching up, she hooked her hand on my nape, holding on as I moved inside her with forceful thrusts. Going as deep as I could, pulling out as far as I could bear before needing her heat to cover me all over again.

Now that I knew what this was—scratching an itch and nothing more—it was easier to get lost in the feel of her—the pleasure her body wrought from mine. It's why we were both here. Not the closeness—the worship and caring—slow kisses and long looks.

None of what I'd mistakenly given inside our hotel room.

"I'm close," she whispered.

I didn't know what I was. Tuned in and disconnected at the same time. Wires crossed and frayed. I wanted her, and I was pissed at us both for that. I longed for her, and here she was, right in front of me, but I wouldn't take any more than was offered—a tight pussy and inevitable release.

Holding both her hips, I bent her forward to drive into her, not caring about our public position. Now, I was chasing my own release as well as hers.

I felt her fingers moving between her legs, desperately rubbing her clit to get herself there before I came. She didn't need to worry. I never would have left her behind.

Covering her hand with mine, I rolled my fingers over hers. She moaned into her arm, her teeth digging into her flesh. It wasn't enough to muffle it from me, though. Her sounds spurred me on, making me want to tip her head back and devour her lips, swallow her noises, but dear god, I was trying not to be self-destructive. Kissing her that way, pretending this was more than the meeting of basic needs, would only lead somewhere I didn't want to be.

We rode each other to our own climaxes, quietly, and for me, entirely fucking unfulfilling. When I unloaded all I had, I fell forward, my nose buried in her hair. Her sweet sighs echoed in my hollow chest. She reached for one of my hands, pulling it beneath her chin so I was half-embracing her, and nuzzled my wrist and knuckles.

For one minute, I let it happen. I wanted it. Telling myself I felt nothing for her was a lie I couldn't sell—not even to myself. I did not take anything other than her face rubbing against my hand. I did not pull her into my arms and kiss the top of her head, nor did I get down on my knees and clean the mess I'd made between her thighs.

Once I'd counted to sixty, I pulled out. "We should get back inside before we're caught."

Silence, then a heavy sigh. "You're right. We're supposed to be here to make contacts and look at us. This was irresponsible."

That was exactly what it was.

She let out a giggle. "No one else I'd ever be this irresponsible with."

I froze in the process of rearranging her dress. If she thought for a second doing something like this with someone else was a good idea...*no.*

"No, Daisy. You should only be with someone who's careful with you."

She spun to face me, and for once, we were nearly at eye level. "I can't imagine anyone being as careful with me as you are, Miles."

"One day, Daisy, someone will be."

And I wouldn't be around to see it.

CHAPTER THIRTY

Daisy

My mama tapped on my door as I was getting ready to head out. Tonight was my last shift at High Bar, and I was running late. I hated being late.

"Look." She held up a handful of black material.

"What am I looking at?" I asked.

She shook the material out and pinched it between her fingers. "It's Reed's Andes vest."

I gasped, shocked at the state of it. Dirty and ripped in a couple spots, I couldn't believe what I was seeing. Reed had loved his vest. How could he have let it get like this?

"He hasn't been wearing it lately but wouldn't tell me why. You think he might've torn it up riding his bike?"

She shook her head. "He hid this. Dad found it this morning when he ran something out to the garbage at the curb. Reed must've snuck it in there last night after Dad put the can out. I was hoping he'd said something to you about it."

"No," I whispered. "He hasn't said anything. In fact, when Miles asked him where his vest was, he made excuses."

"Something's not right. I don't like him being secretive."

She didn't need to say it reminded her too much of Quinn.

"I don't like it either, but he also has a right to privacy. Let's just keep an ear out, and I'll ask Miles to be vigilant too. All right?"

She sighed, her shoulders slumping. "I suppose that's all we can do." Then she looked me over. "You look gorgeous. Are you goin' to work?"

"Yep. I told Nick I'm done. I've picked up too much web work, and I see Grazing taking off in the coming months. I don't need three jobs."

She held up her hand, and I slapped my palm against hers. "Good goin', babe. I'm so proud of you for taking a chance and going after what you've always wanted. Do you know how few people do that? How many live stagnant because it feels safe?"

Why did my mind conjure Miles' smiling face? I might as well have kicked myself in the shin.

"I don't know, Mama. I just know it feels good to be moving forward."

I just had to swallow down the bad and concentrate on what I had.

⋯⋯⋯◆⋯⋯⋯

Duke and Lloyd were making me wistful. Nick's foul mood, on the other hand, was making my decision to leave High Bar a lot easier.

Nick had no reason to snark at me. I wasn't even really his employee. Me arriving ten minutes late barely affected him. He gave me attitude anyway and had been ever since.

About an hour into my shift, a group of women sitting in Bea's section waved me down. When I recognized them, my mood lifted. Saoirse, Elise, Clara, and Shira were here.

I walked over to their table with a big smile. "Cupcakes, charc cups?" I offered.

"Oh my god, how cute are you?" Saoirse exclaimed.

Elise pressed her hands to her cheeks, her diamond-encrusted wedding band glinting in the light. "I love this whole thing. You look like you stepped out of a movie from the fifties."

"Thank you." I did a little curtsy. "You're lucky you came in tonight. It's my last one. I'm retiring from being a cupcake girl."

"Oh, I know. Miles told us, so we planned an impromptu girl's night," Elise explained. "We couldn't miss this."

Again, thoughts of Miles left me with a sharp pain. Since Elise and Weston's wedding two weeks ago, we'd had a couple dinners, worked on his house, and had gone to two events, but it hadn't been the same. We'd kept a respectful distance. No hugging, no flirting, nothing. Even faking it in public together, at most, he'd graze my back or brush my arm. Except once.

We had sex last weekend, and it had been nothing like the first time. As impersonal as possible, Miles managed to be inside me while barely touching me. Never kissing me. Not looking at me. He hadn't been mean, nor had he made me feel used. It had just been another brick in the wall he'd mounted between us, and it made me heavy with sadness.

Goodness didn't come free. Filling myself with everything lovely and bright and wonderful that was Miles had left me feeling ugly and dark and awful when I'd left that hotel two weekends ago, and it hadn't waned.

Forlorn I now knew what I wanted and couldn't have it.

Miles had made it clear he wasn't interested in dating or anything more. I hadn't thought I would be so soon, but that was before I'd known someone like Miles Aldrich was a possibility.

Except...I didn't want someone *like* him. For me, it was Miles or no one at all.

Taking in a deep breath, I turned to Clara and Shira, whom I'd only met once in far different circumstances. Both looked beautiful, Clara with her sleek bob and clear, perfect skin, and Shira with her long, dark waves and elfin features—though, Shira seemed slightly shrunken in on herself.

It was hard to believe it had been nearly three months since they'd overheard my conversation with my mama in the funeral home. I felt like I was a different person than I'd been back then.

"It's so nice to see you again," I said to them. "I've been wanting to properly thank you, but my go-to gift is cupcakes, and that won't cut it this time."

Clara waved me off. "Please don't think I'm ever above accepting cupcakes."

I cast my hand over my tray. "Well, take your pick for a sneak peek."

Clara plucked a couple off my tray, and I turned to Shira, forcing her to as well. She was far more reticent, reaching in slowly and only taking one.

I wanted to ask her how she was. If the ache of losing her husband was still just as bad. Was she lonely? Did she wake up and have to remember her husband was dead all over again?

Of course, I kept my mouth shut.

"You should join us," Saoirse suggested.

"Yes." Elise perked up. "Can you come hang out? Or will your boss get pissed?"

"Considering I'm my own boss and I'd love to hang out, chances are low I'm going to get pissed." I placed a couple charc cups and several cupcakes on the table. "I'm going to drop off my tray. I'll be right back."

Ducking behind the bar, I hustled into the back room and deposited my tray on the little table reserved for me. I took off my hat and threw a hoodie over my skimpy outfit, then turned to rejoin my friends when Nick appeared in the doorway.

"It's barely ten," he gruffed.

"I'm not leaving. Just a break."

His brow pinched. "You don't take breaks."

"I do when I need one. I have friends here I'd like to spend time with." I put my hands on my hips. "What's up with you tonight?"

He folded his arms across his chest. "I think it's obvious, D. I'm not happy about you leaving, and I worry your little business venture will blow up and you'll be without an income."

"Your worry is unwarranted, Nick. I have a big brother for that." I wasn't about to discuss the intricacies of my income. That was none of his business.

"Beau's not around. I am. I'm going to step up—"

"Nope." I raised my hand. "I appreciate all you've done by letting me work here, but this isn't necessary. I'm doing really well, and if I happen to struggle, I have my family to back me up. Now, if you'd let me pass, I'd like to go see my friends."

He hesitated for a drawn-out moment, and I became nervous he wouldn't let me by. Finally, he did, and I shot past him with an edge of panic. I really didn't like the way Nick had been behaving, like he had some hold over me. He was my brother's old friend. After tonight, that was all he'd ever be. If he wanted more than that, he needed to get over it.

I passed Bea on my way to our table. We'd done two Grazing jobs together recently, and I felt like we'd been bonding. She was certainly a quick learner, grasping my vision right away, and to tell the truth, working with her was more fun than by myself—especially with the unabating loneliness I couldn't seem to shake lately.

"Hey, love. Can you grab me a pink lemonade, please?" I asked.

"Sure. I'll add it to my long, long list," she deadpanned. "Was Nick bothering you back there?"

"He's doing the whole big brother routine."

Her brow winged. "Big brothers don't want to fuck you."

I scrunched my nose. "Gross. Never say anything like that to me again."

She went on her way to the bar, and I wove between tables back to *ladies' night.*

Elise pulled out the chair beside hers, welcoming me back. "You're back to normal and still cute as a button."

I snorted a laugh. "Thanks. I don't think anyone's called me that since I was a child."

She balanced her chin on her fists. "Oh yeah, I get that. You give off a whole tough girl vibe. But I've seen you being lovey with my brother-in-law. It's kind of impossible for me to be intimidated by you anymore."

I gaped at her. "*You* intimidated by *me*? You're all, like...fucking gorgeous—and you're married to Weston freaking Aldrich. I don't get it."

"First, thanks for saying I'm hot. I appreciate it." She flashed me a dimpled grin. "Second, yes, my husband is who he is, but I'm just a girl who fell in love with a boy I've known since we were kids."

I bumped her shoulder. "A boy who turned into a very hot man."

"Damn right," she agreed.

From across the table, Clara lifted her glass. "I was already devastated at having to miss Elise and Weston's wedding, and when I heard you and Miles are a couple, I nearly wept. I feel like a matchmaker."

I forced a smile, hoping it wasn't as off-kilter as it felt. "I guess you are. Though, technically, Miles and I had already met and exchanged numbers before I went to Peak—"

Clara held up her hand. "Please. I'm a single mom of a toddler. I have so few victories. Let me have this one."

Bea dropped my lemonade off just in time for me to raise it in cheers. "Thanks for introducing me to Miles. He's the most wonderful surprise." And I meant that completely. Even if he wasn't truly mine, I would never regret knowing him.

Saoirse blinked rapidly, using her hands to fan her eyes. Shira patted her arm, and I frowned, confused at her reaction.

"Sorry." She laughed. "It's just...Miles isn't only my business partner, he's one of my best friends. I've seen how hard he's worked to get his shit together over the last year, all quietly and in the background so he wouldn't let anyone down in case he failed. I'm proud of him, and I'm happy he's found someone who sees how wonderful he is."

Tears pricked the backs of my eyes. If only this were real and finding Miles meant happiness, not this aching heart.

Elise sighed. "Weston is beside himself for not realizing Miles was sober. He sat and recounted each time he'd offered Miles a drink over the last year. It was...too many. I'm certain I did too. Fortunately, he hadn't kept track of that."

"Miles doesn't blame him...or you." I sipped my drink. "I don't want to speak for him, of course, but I do know he's very self-aware and sees your and his brother's mistrust as a byproduct for his past behavior."

Clara lifted her drink. "Here's to growing and learning. May the past not cast a shadow on the future."

She gave Shira a pointed look and clinked her glass.

"Cheers," Shira murmured. "Let's hope that can be true for all of us."

"Speaking of celebrating Miles..." All eyes around the table ended up on me. "He'll be one-year sober on Thursday. I want to throw him a small surprise party to celebrate. We can do it at my place. It's tight, but so long as the weather cooperates, we can use the back patio. That is...if you all are interested in coming."

Elise, Saoirse, and Clara spoke at once, while Shira gave me a sad, polite almost-smile. For a moment, just looking at her gave me an unbearable sense of melancholy. There was something exquisitely sad about her. She was lovely and tragic. I wondered if she missed her husband every second of every day, or if minutes passed in which she didn't think of him. I wondered if it had gotten better in the three months since we met, or if the pain had only become more acute. She probably could have used a Whitney Mae hug. I knew my mother would have loved to squeeze some of the sadness out of her. She was an expert at that.

We discussed party plans for Miles, and it was decided he needed all the cupcakes his heart could desire. Luca would grill, Weston would supervise. Saoirse would bake, and I had already roped my mama into making sides. Pink lemonade for all. Lots and lots of love and support for Miles.

Elise suddenly stopped speaking, frowning at something over my shoulder. I turned to check for monsters, but the only person I noticed was Nick, stopping by each table as he headed in our direction.

"Is that Nick Garcia?" Elise asked.

"Yes. Nick owns this place," I replied.

"Do we know him?" Saoirse chirped. "Do we hate him?"

"I used to know him. I'm happy to say I don't anymore." Elise had soft features, and her eyes and smile were welcoming without trying. She wasn't made to give hardened, vicious looks, but that was exactly what she shot Nick. "I went to high school with him. Barely survived him."

Shira looked over her shoulder, worried. Saoirse sucked in air through her teeth.

"That doofus is the guy who—" Saoirse cut herself off when Elise nodded.

"He bullied you?" I asked.

"He was cruel to everyone who wasn't part of his group. I don't even blame Miles for being his friend. If you weren't, you were a target, and my ass made a *sizable* target." Elise shook her head. "I'm over high school, but damn, seeing that man brings me back."

I touched her hand lightly. "People were cruel little shits to me, so I get it. It shapes who you are. I just...I guess I knew Nick and Miles were friends, and I'm aware Miles had been a bully in his own right, but I didn't suspect Nick...I didn't know..."

"When my mom died, everyone else backed off. Especially Miles," Elise explained. "But Nick took them going easy as his signal to dig deeper. He started a rumor that my mother had killed herself to get away from me. For a year, he whispered, 'mother killer,' every time he passed me in the hall. He was an absolute demon."

That was all I needed to hear. Pushing back from the table, I told them I would take care of this, and headed Nick off at the pass. His eyes lit up when I grabbed his shirt sleeve.

"Hey, I was just coming to say hello to your friends." He chuckled as I yanked him in the opposite direction. "If you need to talk in private, I'm game for that too."

If I said something now, I'd end up screaming in his face, and I had enough respect for the customers and my coworkers not to ruin their night. Biting my tongue, I dragged him with me to the back room. Once the door closed behind him, I spun around to face him head on.

"You know, Nick, it's interesting how you warned me away from Miles Aldrich—"

He groaned. "Wait. You're not still hanging around him, are you? If you are, I'm going to have to talk to Beau about this. He won't approve."

"Isn't Miles your *friend*, Nick?"

"He's an acquaintance more than anything." He folded his arms over his chest. "Why are we talking about him anyway?"

"Because one of my friends is his sister-in-law. Her last name was Levy back in high school. Remember her?"

If I hadn't watched his face pale, I might have believed his "aw shucks" gestures: scratching his head, shrugging his shoulders, a lopsided smile.

"High school was a long time ago," he stated.

"But you remembered what Miles had been up to without any trouble."

"Why are we talking about Miles?" He snatched my arm and pulled me toward him. "Why are you hanging out with his sister-in-law?"

"I told you, Elise is my friend, you jackass." I yanked my arm free from his light grasp. "Are you actually going to pretend you don't remember what you did to her?"

He tried the innocent shrug again. "Everyone did shit they regret when they were young. If you want me to apologize to her right now, I will."

"What would you apologize to her for? Specifically?"

"Uh…" He rubbed his jaw until it was red. "I probably shouldn't have said shit about her being an orphan."

My stomach sank to the floor. Nick was just another disappointing man. Fortunately, I'd never been particularly attached to him, but he'd been on the periphery of my life since I was a kid. It was painful to realize he wasn't who I thought he was.

"So, you do remember her and were playing dumb." I put my hands on my hips. "Warning me away from Miles when you were ten times worse is rich."

His eyes narrowed. "You keep bringing him up. Don't tell me you're fucking him."

"None of your business."

"Goddammit, Daisy." He shoved his fingers into his hair. "You finally got rid of the asshole who rode your coattails all those years, and now you're going after another one? What about dating someone who cares about you for you? Who knows you like no one else does?"

"Who I date is none of your business."

"What if I want it to be?" He tried one of his trademark meaningful looks, all soft eyes and crinkled brow. It was too much. *Way* too much.

I barked a laugh. "No. Are you kidding? Absolutely not."

His dark brows angled into thunderbolts. "No, I'm not kidding. Beau approves, and I—"

"Oh my god, *Beau* approves? You talked to my brother about dating me even though I've never shown a drop of interest in being anything more than what we are? Come on, Nick." I shook my head, spotting my tray and silly little hat sitting on the table he always kept empty for me. There was no way I could bear putting my costume back on tonight. Not after this.

"Just calm down." He laid his hands on my shoulders and lowered his voice like he was talking to a child or hysterical woman.

I wasn't hysterical.

I was pissed off.

"You tried to ruin my friend's life for absolutely no reason." I narrowed my eyes at him. "You trash-talking Miles, your friend, should have been my first clue about the type of man you are. Now, I know for sure. I'm going to get my things and take my friends somewhere else. Their drinks are on the house, by the way."

"Daisy," he bit out, his hold on me tightening, "there's no way I'm letting you—"

The door swung open behind him, and Bea sauntered in, her tray tucked under her arm.

"How's tricks, kittens?" she asked, her eyes sliding back and forth between us.

I shrugged out from under Nick's hands and backed up a couple steps. "I was just telling Nick I'm taking off early. He's not too pleased."

"Hmmm." Bea popped a hip, considering the two of us. "Your friends asked me to check on you. Looks like I showed up just in time to help you pack your things, huh?"

"Daisy..." Nick tried, "please. Let's have a conversation."

"We just did," I said flatly. "Thanks for everything. I'm going to head out as soon as I get packed up."

He waited another few seconds, then stomped to his office, slamming the door behind him. I was relieved he hadn't gone into the bar. At least Elise wouldn't have to see him again.

Bea helped me gather my things in silence, then she spoke, a tentative edge to her words.

"I want to say Nick's an asshole."

I grinned at her. "True. You called that one."

"Yeah. I have a good spotter." She tucked her blue hair behind one ear. "I'm thinking, if you don't mind, I'd like to keep assisting you."

My head jerked up to look at her. "Of course you're going to keep assisting me."

"Okay, good." She exhaled, pressing a hand to her stomach. "So, I have a sister. She does monthly book clubs. I told her about your business, and she wants to buy a board for her club. Like, a monthly thing."

I nodded. "That's awesome. Get her on the books."

"I will. But I was thinking, maybe you're missing a demographic by going after all the rich people. What about Millennial wine moms? They're always doing book clubs or crafting parties or fundraiser shit. My sister is on the PTA at her kids' school. I think it's an untapped resource."

"Bea!" I never exclaimed, but I did this time. From the way she jumped, I'd alarmed her with my sudden display of enthusiasm. When I threw my arms around her, she actually yelped. "You're brilliant, woman. Millennial wine moms. I love it so much."

She wiggled out of my arms, eyes wide. "Yeah, so, I could probably get us a lot of bookings for boards."

My toes wiggled in my boots with happiness.

"Let's do it."

She shot me a full-wattage smile for probably the first time in our acquaintance. "Let's do it."

After that, I walked out of High Bar for the final time, my girls helping me carry my boxes and bags, cautiously optimistic about what was to come.

Professionally.

That was what I'd hang onto for now.

Because personally, I was still as lost as ever.

CHAPTER THIRTY-ONE

Miles

SAOIRSE WAS BEING WEIRD.

First, she'd roped me into going to look at a litter of kittens with her after work, claiming Clementine needed a companion. We all knew Princess Clem would obliterate her enemies with a single swipe of her paw. And Luca and Saoirse were too busy worshiping her to even think of sharing their hearts with another.

Even though I didn't buy she was genuinely looking for another cat, I'd agreed to go along. Because kittens. Maybe I'd adopt one for myself.

My house was kind of a hell hole at the moment, though. It'd probably be better to wait until I had floors and my electrical wires were no longer exposed.

That could be a while—especially since I'd taken a sledgehammer to almost every single wall. While cathartic, the physical manifestation of my frustration had only created a big fucking mess for me to clean up.

Saoirse had been driving around a neighborhood I recognized as being near Daisy's. Up and down streets, she kept checking her phone and muttering.

"Why did I ride with you again?" I asked.

"We're saving the environment by carpooling. Weston would be proud of us."

"I don't think you know where you're going."

"I'm following the directions, but they're unclear. Oh, look. Daisy just texted. She has something I need to borrow. Let's go there, then we'll come back for the kittens."

I stared at the side of her blonde head. "What do you need to borrow from Daisy?"

She lifted a shoulder. "Oh, you know, girl things. It's private, Miles."

"Do women loan out their vibrators?"

She burst out laughing. "I don't think so. If they do, I don't want to know about it."

A minute later, she pulled up in front of Daisy's place. Strangely, Saoirse seemed to know exactly how to get here. Then again, I didn't know every move Daisy made. Maybe she and Saoirse hung out regularly.

Saoirse patted my knee. "Come on. It's around back. I need your help."

"So, your secret girl thing is heavy?"

Her nostrils flared. "What are you today, the question man?"

I followed behind her, noticing Reed's light on next door. I hadn't talked to him in a few days. I made a mental note to text him. He was starting his music class soon, but he was probably bored at home. Kid might've wanted to make some money by cleaning up drywall some idiot had scattered all over my house.

We rounded the corner to the back of the house, and I was about to ask if Daisy knew we were coming when everyone I knew and loved sprung out of nowhere screaming, "Surprise!"

I stumbled backward from the force of my shock. My first thought was we'd messed up someone else's surprise. Then I scanned the crowd and decorations and landed on a banner strung between trees that very much had my name and "congratulations" on it.

Finally, there was Daisy, walking straight toward me, a "1" balloon in her hand.

She'd remembered.

This beautiful, confusing, fantastic fucking woman had remembered I'd been one year sober today.

"Daisy, what did you do?"

She was giggling as she fell into my arms, squeezing me tighter than her diminutive muscles should have been capable.

"Did you honestly think I would let this day go by without celebrating the shit out of you, Spreadsheet?"

Squeezing my eyes shut, I buried my face in the top of her head, inhaling her cupcake and Daisy scent. I hadn't let myself be close to her like this since that night by the lake. I'd missed the feel of her on a bone-deep level.

"Thank you, Cupcake."

She rubbed slow circles in the center of my back. "Don't worry, I told my family it's your one-year anniversary of going to the gym. I don't know if they bought it, but they wanted to celebrate you anyway."

I held her tighter for keeping my privacy, and for having a family who thought enough of me, they wanted to celebrate my accomplishments.

"I don't have words."

She pulled back from my embrace, still grinning. "You don't have to have words. Have a balloon." She shoved the ribbon attached to the "1" into my hand. "Now, let me take a picture."

Humoring her, I stood with my balloon, smiling at the camera. She got one in before Saoirse and Luca crowded around me. Then little Hazel threw herself in front of us, cheesing like we were all here for her. Landry tried to drag her away, but we told her to stay, so then Edie needed to be in it too.

By the time Daisy took the final picture, everyone she'd invited was surrounding me. Even Reed had shuffled into the frame. Flipping the camera around, she held it in front of her and took a selfie with all of us.

The whole thing was so damn wholesome and sweet, it felt like watching someone else's life. Then Kit handed me Joey, who screeched and slapped my cheeks, Luca threw his arm around me, telling me the cat ruse had been his idea, and Edie started rubbing her tummy and patting her head.

I looked up, my eyes landing on Weston. He was watching it all, a bemused expression taking over his face.

"You still manage to be the life of the party," he quipped.

"Can't help it. They're moths to my flame."

Elliot breezed by, plucking his daughter from my arms. "Congratulations, Miles. Doing *anything* for a year straight is difficult. Changing a lifetime of habit isn't for the weak."

I blinked at him. "I—thanks."

He nodded once, then went to find his wife, who he was even more protective of now that she had another bun baking in her oven.

I swiveled to Weston. "Did you see that? Elliot said something nice to me."

He chuckled. "He's capable. I'm pretty sure he's been playing into the same nemesis schtick you have for the last decade. Is it time to give it a rest?"

I scratched the side of my head. No way Weston believed all the tension between Elliot and me had been a schtick. Maybe it was now. Maybe we were all right.

"Nah. Why start now?"

"Good. I would have been alarmed if you and Elliot had started being nice to each other."

I pretended to gag. "Don't say it."

Weston put his hand on my shoulder and sighed. "I get I failed you."

"You didn't."

"I did. I saw you at least once a week over the last year and didn't notice you were sober." He scrunched his eyes...his whole face. "I always have this *idea* of you. My wild, crazy kid brother. The creative, the irresponsible. But that idea isn't you. You're not a series of adjectives. It's my fault for being focused on what is right in front of me and not what's always been beside me. I'm sorry for that, Miles. I see you now."

What I'd always wanted. Why I'd acted out, had made a spectacle of myself, misbehaved, ruined dinners and furniture, just so Weston would see me. It had only taken me completely turning my life around and no longer begging him for a crumb of attention to finally have it.

It was as good as I'd always thought it would be.

"Shit, West. Don't make me cry. I'm not going to be a public crier." I scrubbed my face with my hand. "I get I haven't given you a reason to believe I'd follow through on my promises. But the stakes are higher for me now. I've got Peak Strategies, my house—"

"Daisy," he added. "Me and Elise. I wasn't there for you like I should've been growing up, but I'm here now. You get that, Miles? I'm here, even if there are times you're not at your best. I'm still going to be here."

Oh hell. That had done it. I hung my head, nodding. "I get it," I replied thickly. "Thank you."

He pulled me into a tight hug. This was only one of a handful he'd given me since I was a kid, and it was one for the ages. Made me feel cared for and secure that my big brother had my back.

After that, I was passed from person to person. Food was shoved into my hands, and Whitney Mae made sure my plate was never empty. Everyone sat around me, sharing stories and tall tales. There was barely a minute without laughter. Even Reed had managed a smirk or two.

I ended up beside him when I went to toss my plate in the garbage. "Is that track ready to send me?"

He looked at me with a pinched expression. "Why were you an alcoholic?"

"I, uh...I thought the story was I'm a gym bro."

He clucked his tongue. "That might work with the little kids, but I'm not stupid. I hear things."

"Right." I nodded, suddenly queasy. I'd gotten this kid to admire me, to think I was sort of cool. The last thing I wanted was for him to know how boringly fallible I was. "I can't say for sure why I'm an alcoholic. Genetics has something to do with it. Growing up in an environment where alcohol was constantly flowing contributed. When I got older, I felt like I had to be trashed to be interesting. I used my alcoholism as a reason for my failures instead of facing the real problem: me. A lot of reasons, none stronger than the rest."

His mouth had fallen open sometime around my second reason. "Whoa. I didn't expect you to be that honest."

"I don't have a reason to lie to you, kid. If you ask me a straight question, I'm going to give you as straight an answer as I can."

He rubbed the back of his neck, kicking some rocks by his feet. "I guess all those reasons made it hard to get sober."

"Yeah," I sighed. "Didn't think I'd be standing here. Never thought anyone would throw me a one-year party."

"That's Daisy." He looked up at me, the confusion fleeing his expression. "She knows what's important. That's why she's always after me. Showing me I'm not alone. Guess she's doing that for you too."

"Guess she is. Aren't we the lucky ones?"

I glanced at Daisy on the other side of the patio, bouncing baby Joey on her hip. She looked stunning and happy. My gut twisted with what I now recognized as longing for her. She had to stop being so goddamn wonderful or I would never get over her.

⸺◆⸺

A couple hours later, the party was winding down. Daisy was bustling around, throwing things away and stopping to chat with anyone who grabbed her.

I finally had my chance to speak to her and stepped into her path. "Daze."

Her momentum had her stumbling into my chest, a giggle bursting out of her. "Some warning might've been nice." She patted me right over my tumbling heart. "After all, you're all buff from your year at the gym. This is like granite."

"Daze," I said softer now, catching her big brown eyes. "Thank you for this. All of it. Bringing everyone together, your support. I can't—I've never had someone like you in my life."

Her breath hitched. "I can say for sure I've never had someone like you in my life either. I feel lucky to know you. It's my privilege to be here for your one-year anniversary and help you celebrate it."

My throat tightened. "Good party," I gritted out.

"Yeah," she sighed. "Great party."

Before I could say anything else, Saoirse called my name. Daisy backed up a step, until we were no longer touching. I turned to Saoirse, cocking a brow.

"Luca and I are heading out. Want a ride back to your car?"

"Oh, uh…" I checked back with Daisy. "You need help cleaning up?"

She shook her head. "Not at all. It's almost done. Besides, it's your party—you don't clean."

"All right." I rocked back on my heels. "I think I'm gonna head out with them. Thank you again, Daisy-daze. I'll always remember this."

"I hope you remember all the people who showed up for you, Miles. You don't have to go it alone anymore." She pushed up on her toes and kissed my jaw, and it took all my willpower not to grab her and bring that kiss where I really wanted it.

Instead, I backed away from her, just as I'd been doing for weeks. "Goodnight."

Her eyes searched mine then settled. "Goodnight, Miles."

Chapter Thirty-Two

Miles

WHY DOES IT HAVE to be easy?

I was in my car, getting ready to drive home, when my therapist's question rang in my skull.

What I was doing was easy. Going home alone without putting myself out there. Keeping my feelings to myself. Not taking a chance they could be, by some miracle, reciprocated. Maintaining a fake relationship with Daisy that was fucking killing me.

I steered my car in the direction of her place. It wasn't too late, and I didn't think I could go another night without saying what I needed to. I had to know where she was. If I was never going to have her, at least my question would be answered and I could figure out how to move on. This...in-between was untenable.

I parked at the curb and jogged up her steps. She must've heard me coming because the door swung open before I could knock.

"Did you forget something?" Her words came out husky, sexy enough to almost bring me to my knees.

"Yeah. I need to say something to you, Daisy."

She stood in her doorway, leaning against the jamb. I was on the landing, outside looking in.

"Okay. Say what you need to, Miles." There was wariness there. Her arms folded around her middle in a protective stance. She was prepared for me to hurt her, but I was almost certain I was about to break myself.

Why does it have to be easy?

Why the hell did this have to be so damn hard?

"The thing is, I can't keep doing this fake dating thing with you. I need to end it tonight."

She flinched like I'd punched her in the face. "Of course. I get it. I—"

"No, I'm not done."

Her mouth flattened into a hard line, and her eyes almost killed me with their shine.

"I can't be fake with you because my feelings are real. They might've always been real, but recently, I seem to have fallen hopefully in love with you."

She gasped a small breath. "Hopelessly?"

I shook my head. "No, I said it right. Being in love with you is all about hope. Hope you might feel a fraction of what I feel for you. Hope you'll be ready to love me back one day. Hope I can keep you when this agreement is over. Hope I am worthy of you. Hope I don't screw things up."

"Miles..."

"You don't have to love me back, Daisy. I'm not expecting that. But I want to know, do I have even a small chance with you? Or is your heart still wrapped up with Andy?" I chuffed. "Or, the third possibility, would I ever be a consideration, even if Andy had never existed? Am I shooting way out of my league here?"

"Stop talking," she ordered, and my heart began to plummet. It didn't get too far before she grabbed the front of my shirt and yanked me into her apartment, kicking the door shut behind her. "Sit down, Miles."

Her tone had gone from confused to demanding, brooking no argument. I sat on her couch in her little living room, clinging to my last vestiges of hope. Turning around and walking away when I'd been on the landing would have been a lot easier. Now, surrounded by everything Daisy? *I might have to crawl.*

She turned to me with flushed cheeks and razor-sharp eyes. "How can you stand on my doorstep and tell me you love me but know nothing about me at all?"

My mouth opened. Closed. I didn't understand. "*What?*"

"Except for when Andy showed up here, I haven't thought about him. Have I brought him up to you?"

"You had sex with me because—"

She held up her finger. "If you say it was because of him, I'll scream." She stalked into the little living area and sat on the coffee table directly in front of me.

"You asked me if I slept with you to forget, and I did, that's true. You didn't ask what I was forgetting, or why you were the one who could wash it all away."

I stared at her, thinking back to that morning. She was right. I'd made assumptions. I hadn't asked the right questions.

"What were you forgetting, Daisy?"

She scooted to the edge of the table and rested her forearms on my knees. "You've never made me feel like my last name was a negative. From the beginning, you've treated me like a regular person."

"I beg to differ. You have never been regular to me."

Her mouth hitched at the corners, and hope soared. "This is what I mean. When I'm with you, you make it all fade. I can just be Daisy. No matter what we're doing, I feel good, sometimes great, other times wonderful. After a lifetime of just 'okay,' you are a breath of fresh air. You're sunshine in beautiful human form."

I heard what she was saying, but it was nearly impossible for me to take it in. "You're over Andy?"

Her fingertips dug into my thighs. "Miles...that relationship was important. I once thought I'd spend my life with him. But I came to a realization months ago: he did me a favor by not wanting to marry me. If we hadn't broken up, I would have settled for him, believing that was as good as it got, and I never would have known you. I never would have experienced what it was like not to have to apologize for who I am or where I come from to the person I'm with, fake or otherwise."

I shook my head. "I haven't been pretending with you for a long time, Daisy."

Her breath hitched, and she slowly raised her hand to my cheek. "I didn't think you wanted this."

Turning my head into her hand, I kissed her palm. "I wasn't ready when we met."

"Neither was I," she admitted.

"I've got a year of sobriety. I feel steady, and I think I could be really good to you." I slammed my eyes closed for a second. Now wasn't the time to lose my confidence or sow any doubt. "No. I *know* I can be really good to you."

Tears welled in her eyes as she nodded. "You've been nothing but good, great, and wonderful to me."

"It's impossible not to be." I kissed her palm again. "We can go slow. You've been the only thing I've been able to think about for a long time, which has put me several steps ahead of you. I can be patient and wait for you to catch up. I don't need you to love me today, so long as I know there's a possibility you might in the future."

"Oh, Miles," she whispered. "How could I not be in love with you? Like you said, it's impossible not to be. I want to be your real girlfriend."

Taking her other hand, I dragged her into my lap and cradled her beautiful fucking face in my palms.

"The second you handed me the bill for the cupcakes I stole, there wasn't a chance on this green earth I wouldn't fall stupidly in love with you, Daisy Ethel Dunham." I placed her palm on my chest, over my pounding heart. "Do you feel that? You did that. You can call yourself my girlfriend, but I'm calling you the commander of my heart. You own me, through and through."

She dove headfirst into my neck, her arms closing around me. We'd hugged, held hands, kissed, had done things that would've made me blush if I'd paused to think too hard. But this...this was the first time I'd had her in my arms with nothing but honesty between us.

"Tell me you love me, Daisy," I murmured into her hair. "I need to hear it so it feels real."

Her soft lips pressed against my throat twice before she raised her head. Her cheeks were flushed, eyes wet, lips swollen. *Beautiful girl. My girl.*

"I love you, Miles Aldrich." Clear as day, she said the words I never thought I'd hear from her. "I'm going to be good for you."

I dug my fingers into the sides of her hair, holding her head a hairsbreadth from mine. "*Not a chance on this green earth*, Cupcake. I'm stupidly in love with you, and I'm going to keep you."

High and soft, she uttered one word that was absolutely everything.

"Okay."

My mouth met hers in a slow, thorough binding. Sealed together, our breath and tongues mingled. Daisy might not have known it, but this kiss was a contract. She'd have to sue me to get out of it. I wasn't worried about that. What good was my money if I couldn't use it to tie her up in court for the rest of her life?

I wasn't going to fuck this up, though. She'd have no reason to check the fine print of what she'd agreed to when her lips moved over mine.

She shifted in my lap to straddle me and plastered herself to my chest. Her elbows were on my shoulders, fingers in my hair, mouth melded to mine.

We kissed until crickets ruled the night. Kissed away our lingering doubts, until there was no question this was real. Our cores were pressed together, hot and aroused, but kissing was the point. We made out like time was endless, and I loved every second of it.

"I love you," she breathed against my lips.

"I love you," I returned.

"I'll love you more if you touch me."

I slipped my hands beneath the hem of her dress and palmed her ass. "Like this?"

"That's a good start."

"You can touch me too."

Given permission, she scrambled to unbutton my shirt. When she had it open, her hands splayed on my chest, she released a sigh of pleasure into my mouth.

I dragged my finger along the valley of her ass, nudging her thong aside to get to her slick skin. God, how long had it been since I'd touched her there?

Years or weeks, it'd been far, *far* too long.

She must've felt the same way. She went for my belt, yanking the buckle open and making fast work of the zipper. Freeing me from my boxers, her fingers wrapped around my length, and she released another sigh of relief.

"Missed that?" I asked, half-amused.

"I really did. I want you inside me, Miles. I need you there, to confirm you're really mine and it isn't going away."

"It's not going away. I'm yours."

She nodded. "And I'm truly yours."

I helped her rise on her knees and align the head of my cock with her entrance. She took me slowly, struggling slightly as she lowered herself little by little until her backside hit my thighs.

"God, Miles. I forgot." She shuddered, goosebumps pricking her arms.

"I'm not going to let you forget what this feels like ever again."

We stayed like that, me fully seated, her inner walls clenching around me. Raking my hair, she kissed my jaw and forehead, then murmured how good I felt inside her before her lips touched the corner of mine.

The straps of her dress slipped from her shoulders, and I hooked my finger through them, bringing them down the rest of the way and tugging her bodice until her breasts were free. She rose, and I dipped, taking her pebbled nipple in my mouth and suckling like the starving man I was. Ravenous for her—her attention, touch, everything.

Daisy moved over me, holding my shoulders to help her work her way up and down. I let her have her way, needing her to want me as badly as I craved her.

"Miles." Her head fell back, revealing the pale column of her neck. "God, Miles."

Her body had gotten used to mine, each slide up and down easier, smoother. I couldn't take my eyes off her or my mouth off her skin. My brain was still catching up that she was mine, but my heart knew. It thrummed in my chest, and a pulse of rightness spread through the rest of me.

Right girl.

Right time.

Right place.

Stars and circumstances had aligned for us. Maybe I was overly confident, but I was almost sure they were going to keep aligning.

As long as we both wanted this as much as we did today.

Daisy's mouth balanced on mine as she rolled her hips in tight circles, moaning from the continuous contact. My gorgeous girl was taking what she needed from me, and I willingly handed it over. Her pleasure was mine. All I needed was for her to get herself off, and I would follow.

"Beautiful, Daisy. Use me." Gripping her hips, I ground her down into my pelvis. Her eyes flashed, and her mouth fell open, hot pants skimming my lips. "Come on, gorgeous girl. Take what you need and let go."

Nails digging into my shoulders, she rode me with purpose and meaning. Her little breaths hit me each time she reached the bottom. I watched her in awe, her beauty, confidence, how she felt around me, on top of me, everything about her claiming every ounce of my attention.

Her eyes fell on mine at the last moment, and her lips curved into an almost-smile I returned. I had to. She made me that fucking happy. Even on the verge of coming, I was blasting her with a loopy smile.

Head falling back again, she moaned my name and yanked on my hair. Her inner walls pulsed around my cock as she rolled and rolled her hips. That was all it took for me to follow her over, growling her name and fastening her to me with my teeth on her neck.

Once we'd rung every drop from one another, I pulled out and flipped her on her back. She whimpered as I buried my face between her legs, tasting the two of us mingled together. That was all it took to get my softening dick back to full mast. Ignoring it, I took my time lapping her sweet cunt.

Between her moans, she asked me why I was doing this, saying she'd already come, reminding me I didn't have to.

As if she thought this was for her.

She didn't understand yet, but her pussy was going to be my main sustenance.

Only when her thighs trembled and she shoved me away did I stop. Raising on my knees, I kissed along her thigh and calf. Reaching her ankle, I licked the delicate bones and nuzzled my nose into the arch of her foot.

I looked down at her, dazed and sweaty. She was blinking up at me with that same half-smile, and for the first time in my life, I knew I was enough. For her, for myself, for what we were going to build.

"You're a monster," she slurred.

I fell over her, growling into her neck. "Monster for you, Cupcake."

Wrapping her limbs around me, she sighed. "For me."

"Only ever you," I agreed.

Chapter Thirty-three

I'd been to Peak Strategies several times, but never unannounced, and never as Miles' real girlfriend. But I had an idea I needed to discuss with him, and…

Well, I just wanted to see him in the middle of the day.

This man had flipped me from an emotional, pining mess to a pile of loved-up goo. I'd never known myself capable of being gooey. I'd certainly loved Andy, but I'd never felt this inner squishiness around him. Since my big conversation with Miles last week, I'd caught myself thinking of him and squealing and kicking my feet multiple times.

I was happy and excited for what was to come.

Rebecca, the receptionist at Peak, showed me to Miles' office, telling me I'd gotten lucky and he had a meeting-free afternoon. When I opened his door and he immediately beamed at me from behind his desk, I certainly felt lucky.

"What? My girlfriend is here for a surprise visit?" He shot out of his seat and bounded straight for me.

Behind me, Rebecca laughed. "Have a nice lunch, you two." She closed the door firmly right before Miles got to me and swept me off my feet.

"Careful, I have sushi," I admonished without any actual force.

He stopped mid-spin and stared at me. "You brought me my girlfriend *and* food? Fuck, Cupcake, I've fallen in love with you all over again."

"You're very easy to please."

"Only you hold the key."

He planted a kiss on my lips and set me on my feet. "Is this going to be a thing now? Are you going to appear out of nowhere and brighten my lonely days?"

I snorted. "I was told it's hard to catch you in your office at this time most days since you're always out for client meetings or grabbing lunch for everyone."

He directed me to the round table where we'd sat the first time I'd come here. "I can stay put if it means you'll show up more often."

"God, you're sweet." I snagged the front of his shirt and dragged him down to me, kissing him hard and fast. "How about if I call first to make sure you're going to be around?"

He took the bag from me, placed it on the table, and yanked me into his arms. One hand slid up my spine into the back of my hair to cradle my head, then he leaned over, dipping me, and covered my mouth with his. It was a movie star kiss, not just in position but the sheer romanticism of it. I clung to him so I didn't tip over and lose contact.

"There," he whispered to my lips. "That's better. And yes, call or text. I'd kick myself if I wasn't here for a visit from you."

He let me go so we could sit down and allowed me to choose my sushi first, acting like he was doing something gentlemanly. We both knew if I didn't pick what I wanted before he started eating, he'd eat both our shares.

"Bea and I had a meeting this morning."

He looked up from his food. "Yeah? Was it productive?"

"Mmm. We made an order with the cheesemonger Saoirse told me about, and one with the supplier I use in France. Since Bea and I spoke about Millennial wine moms, she's brought in ten new bookings plus her sister's monthly order. She's contributing so much—and I would be screwed if she left. I brought up the possibility of becoming partners."

His expression gave nothing away. "Yeah? And what did she say?"

"She's into it. I know I should have talked to you about this first—"

"Why? Grazing is your business, Daisy. I helped you get it off the ground, but you—and Bea—have been the ones to fill your calendar. You charmed people at the events I took you to. Your social media presence has brought you customers. That's all you."

"You definitely did more than you're taking credit for but thank you. Now, tell me the truth: do you think this is a good idea?"

"I think it's a great idea. This way, if you want to take an out-of-town job like you're doing this weekend, Bea can hold down the fort here or vice versa."

"I thought that too. And Bea is incredibly competent."

He winged a brow. "You trust her?"

I nodded. "I do."

"Then let's do it. You're gonna need a new logo, huh?"

"I was thinking you could add a bee next to the daisy."

He cocked his head. "That's awful cutesy for my little emo cupcake."

I shrugged. "I can be cutesy."

"Correction: you can be cute. And you are, often. If you want a bee next to your daisy, I can do that for you."

I beamed at him. "Having you as my boyfriend is going to come in handy."

He wagged his chopsticks at me. "Did you think this was going to be free?"

"I didn't." I leaned into him, hands on his knees. "How many feet pics will this cost me?"

Without warning, Miles plucked me right out of my seat and into his lap. "Do you think I'm that easy? One promise of looking at your feet you flash around for everyone to see, and you think I'm going to be making you logos for free? Next thing you know, you'll be asking me to come up with a business plan for a dear friend who's really someone you met once at camp when you were ten."

I started to defend myself, but he went on. "That being said, two feet pics would be lovely."

I shoved at his chest, glaring. "You almost made me feel bad."

"Come on, Cupcake." He smoothed his palm along my spine. "I want you to lean on me for things. Ask me favors. Make use of my few talents. I'm yours, aren't I?"

I bit my bottom lip and nodded. "I don't want to take advantage."

"You couldn't possibly. First, I know you'd never ask me for more than I have to give. But more importantly, there's nothing I wouldn't do for you. Altering a logo is nothing. I can do it in my sleep."

I wrinkled my nose at him. "Please don't. I'd like it to look good."

He growled. "As if I'd give you a shitty logo." He dragged his finger down my nose, ironing out the wrinkles. "Now that we've got Bea settled, was there something else on your mind?"

I blinked at him. "How could you tell?"

"I can see it in you. You're not relaxed." He stroked my spine, which should have done it. I wanted to melt into him, but he was right. I did have something else on my mind. "Come out with it."

"Okay...well, I know you just finished telling me I can ask for anything, but I want you to know you can say no to this and I won't be mad."

He cocked his head. "Go on."

"I was thinking I would like to take Reed with us to California this weekend. I would love to go away alone with you, but my brother...I think he could use a break. Just a change of scenery, out of his room, away from everything. You know him, he won't be any trouble. There's an extra bedroom at the house we're staying at, so I thought—"

His mouth came down on mine, cutting off my rambling in the only acceptable way. I didn't know if this was a yes or no, but I kissed him back anyway. It wasn't a quick kiss either. Miles split my lips with his tongue and tasted me fully, lapping at me the way he did my pussy—with enthusiasm, taking pleasure from making me feel good.

When he broke apart, he cradled my face, stroking his thumb along my bottom lip.

"Yes."

I sucked in a breath. "Yes, he can come?"

"Of course. I like Reed, and I agree, a change of scenery will do the kid well. Should we stay a day or two longer and show him the sights?"

"That would be really nice, but some of us have to work."

He rolled his eyes. "I know that, sassy-face. But you can work from anywhere, and I can arrange my schedule to take a couple days off. What do you think?"

My stomach got that squishy feeling, and my heart thumped with happiness.

"I think...we're taking a few extra days in California."

He reached down and patted my ass. "Damn right. And we're going to have a hell of a time. Just me and the emo twins."

God, he was cute. And he liked my brother. I hoped I could keep doing whatever I did to land him.

Deep down, I knew what it was. When we'd met, I'd been my unmitigated self, and Miles had liked every bit of my bite and grouch. It stood to reason, all I had to do was keep being me.

So, I said the first thing that popped into my head. "I'll get you in guyliner yet."

He flinched away from me. "That'll take a lot more than two feet pics, Cupcake."

I grinned. "But that wasn't a no."

"I told you I can't say no to you."

⋯◆⋯

Reed had been slack-jawed since we'd boarded the Aldrich private plane. To be fair, I had a feeling I hadn't been much better. I did not know how I'd ever go back to commercial after this experience.

The seats were actually comfortable, and there were no odd smells or annoying passengers. No security lines or cattle calls to board. It was heaven.

The downtown penthouse Miles had rented for us in Sacramento was ridiculously luxurious too, with views of the river, a private roof-top pool, and more space than we needed.

By comparison, Lily Smythe-Kelly's house was modest—but *only* in comparison. Mid-century modern, it had been carefully renovated, keeping with the era it was built. She showed Reed, Miles, and me around while dashing off orders to the caterers preparing the rest of the food for the party.

We were guests tonight, but first, we had to set up a six-foot grazing table. Miles vaguely knew how I did things, and Reed was pretty good at following directions, so I hoped we'd get this done in no time.

Lily stood next to the table as we worked, her hands clasped under her chin. "How's that daughter of mine?" she asked Miles.

"She brings me fresh fruit and honey every Monday from the farmer's market."

Lily laughed. "Her favorite time of year. I take that to mean she's doing well."

"Well, and busy," he said. "She's training our Rebecca to assist her."

Her eyebrows rose. "Oh? Does that mean you'll need a new receptionist?"

"I think so. Rebecca and Sersh make a good team and clients like her. I have a feeling she'll get the official promotion pretty soon."

Lily sighed happily. "My girl. For a while, I wondered if she'd find her place, and look at her—expanding her business and still taking time to go to the farmer's market each weekend."

He chuckled. "She's living the dream."

"Her dream. That's all I ever wanted for her. Well, I would have liked her living a little closer, but beggars can't be choosers."

"The flight was only two and a half hours," Reed supplied, bringing all eyes to him. Before now, he'd been quiet as a mouse, as usual.

Lily lowered her hands to smooth the front of her dress. "You're right, you're right. It's not as bad as I like to think it is, and I suppose I'll eventually move closer to her since I can't convince her to come to me. My son lives in southern Wyoming. There's really no point for me to live here once I retire at the end of my term."

"My brother lives in Laramie, Wyoming," Reed supplied.

"Not too far from my boy. He lives on his father's family ranch in Sugar Brush Creek. It's all very...rugged."

Reed shuddered. "Open spaces give me the creeps."

Miles clapped a hand on his shoulder. "Oh, kid. Tell me you're a city boy without telling me you're a city boy."

Lily waved them off. "No, I quite understand. When you're used to being snug in one spot, going to a place where the possibilities are endless can be petrifying and intimidating."

"See?" Reed turned to Miles, a crooked smile on his face. "Lily understands me."

That made her laugh lightly. "I like you, Reed. And don't worry, there will be a whole contingent of kids your age at the party. You won't have to hang with the old folks."

He tensed, his body locking. "Thank you," he intoned, barely moving his jaw.

Miles leaned over and murmured something only Reed could hear. As I watched my brother relax, I did too. I didn't need to know what Miles had said. With him, we were in good hands. That much I knew without a single doubt.

CHAPTER THIRTY-FOUR

Daisy

I WASN'T ONE TO throw the word "perfect" around. That might have been due to circumstance. There hadn't been many things in my life or experience that had even verged on perfection. But tonight...

I was tempted to use it.

Reed was happy, and that was everything to me. The teens Lily had told us about had converged in her pool house. There were six or seven, a mix of boys and girls. I'd sort of forced Reed to go with them, but when I checked a little while later, they had accepted him as one of them.

The next time I went back to peek, they were eating junk and remixing a song together on someone's laptop. Reed didn't even glance up at me.

Miles had to stop me from checking on them a third time. Though, it wasn't exactly checking, more like spying. Reed was a loner. To see him getting along—no, to see everyone gathered around him digging one of the songs he'd made—was a sight that made my heart swell.

I snuck a picture to send to our parents. That was when Miles had put his foot down and barred me from going back.

That was okay. Once I knew he was having fun, I relaxed and enjoyed myself too. Lily introduced us to everyone like we were celebrities. Miles was her beloved daughter's business partner, and I was the genius who'd created the masterpiece everyone had been pecking from all night.

It was over the top, but Miles and I kept looking at each other and grinning.

A man in his thirties wearing a crisp business suit approached as we were piling our plates with canapes.

"I've been checking out your website," he said without preamble.

"Oh, have you?"

Miles slipped my plate from my hand, giving me space to talk.

"I have. It's clean and to the point. Give your web designer props."

I raised my hand. "That would be me. Thank you for the compliment."

"Multi-talented."

"I do a few things well, sure. Were you looking for something specific on my site?"

"Actually, yes. My name is Brad Hamilton. I'm the state senate building events manager. My job has many dimensions. One is arranging catering for meetings. Your charcuterie cups would work perfectly, but according to your website, you're based out of Colorado. Is that right?"

Disappointment lodged in my chest. "That's right. I'm able to travel for some jobs, but it sounds like this is something you'd need on a regular basis."

"You're correct." He glanced at his phone then back at me. "It's too bad. I was really hoping I'd found something good." Whipping out a business card, he handed it to me. "If anything changes, get in touch."

"I will. Thank you." It felt wrong, wrong, *wrong* turning down an offer like that, but I couldn't see any way around it. As fun as it had been to fly out here for Lily's party, regularly commuting to California wasn't feasible.

Once he left us, I took my plate from Miles and stuffed a piece of cream cheese and salmon toast in my mouth. He cupped my nape, bringing me closer, and kissed the top of my head.

"Sucks, Daze, but let's take it as a learning opportunity. When we get back to Denver, I'll see what kind of contacts I have in local politics. Maybe we can make the same kind of arrangement back home."

I nodded and pressed my hand to his chest. "This is why I love you, Miles. You have a way of flipping things around to show me the bright side I never would have seen without you."

"It's easy with you because I only want the best for you."

"And I want the best for you." I held up a cream cheese and salmon toast, bringing it to his lips. "Which is why you're going to eat this."

He took it from my hand, nibbling on my fingertips for good measure.

Later, after the party ended and we brought a talkative Reed back to our rented penthouse, he retreated to his bedroom, and Miles and I went up to the rooftop, not ready for the night to be over.

We found a cozy lounger, and Miles nestled me in his lap, my back to his front. His arms banded around me, and he tucked his hands beneath the tank I'd changed into.

"Can I put my cock inside you?" he murmured against my ear.

I turned my head, frowning. "Is that foreplay now that you've got me?"

"No." He brushed my hair away from my face and kissed my jaw. "I don't want to fuck you right now. I want to sit here, enjoying the night, with my cock warming inside you."

"I've never...well, okay. I can't think of a reason to say no."

He shifted us around, pulling his boxers off and sliding my panties to the side. Draping my legs on either side of his, he raised me by my cheeks and slowly lowered me into his thick length. I wiggled until I had him all the way in, then he pulled me back against his chest and resumed stroking my belly and tracing circles around my navel.

"How's that?" he asked.

"Strange not to be moving. Full." I bit down on my lip. "I always like when you're inside me."

"I do too. I'll be able to stay here for a while longer this way. Close to you like no other way."

He was right. The night was warm, with a slight breeze. City noises drifted up to us, while our view of the river and lights reflecting off the flowing surface was unencumbered. We talked about the night, about us, and he held me tight as I did the same to him.

"Remember the country club?" he asked.

"Yeah. You were distant. I kept bumping my arm into you to get your attention."

"Hmph. I knew you were doing it on purpose." He cupped my pussy with his big palm. "You've always had my attention. That's why I followed you to the lake that night. It's why I tried to keep my distance and ended up fucking you in view of anyone passing."

"I liked that part," I admitted. "I didn't like how you barely touched me and didn't kiss me."

"We won't do that again." His lips touched the hinge of my jaw. "The not kissing and touching part. I'll fuck you in public any time I please."

I breathed a laugh and squeezed around his cock, which had grown thicker. "Oh? Any time *you* please?"

He swatted my pussy lips. "I feel what you're doing. I'm not ready to fuck you yet. No squeezing."

I wiggled my butt back and forth in his lap. "I can't help it."

"Try a little harder for me, Daisy. Show me how good you can be."

"Okay." I swallowed, willing myself to calm down. It was difficult with this unabating heaviness low in my belly. If I moved, leaned forward and rocked my clit against him, I'd come in no time. But I didn't want this to end—and I definitely wanted to show him I could be good.

"When we get home, I want you to think about moving in with me," he said.

"You do?"

"It's not too soon, so don't say that."

I smiled against the underside of his jaw. It was too soon by most people's standards, but I was kind of feeling sure about Miles

Aldrich. The idea of moving in together wasn't scary. Living with his duck-in-sunglasses wallpaper was.

"I was going to say it's too much of a wreck for me. I'm not sure I can stand living in your brand of renovation."

"Mmm. Then I'll hire someone to finish it and live with you while the work is being done. I only bought it to keep me busy and out of trouble. Now, I have you to occupy my time."

"You don't want to live in my tiny apartment."

He raised his pelvis just enough to remind me where he was. "I would live inside your skin if you'd allow it."

"I'm glad you know there are limits."

"I know *you* have limits, which I'll respect." Another thrust. "Reluctantly."

I rubbed my cheek against his. "Are you going to keep teasing me, or are you finally going to fuck me? I really hope it's the second."

"Hmmm." He moved his hand from cupping me to rolling my clit under a finger. "How are you swollen and wet when I've barely touched you, beautiful?"

"You. It's you."

"Like that answer. I think I *will* fuck you right now after all."

In a feat of strength, Miles stood with me attached to him and turned us around so my knees were on the cushions and he was bent over me, bracing his hands on the back of the lounger.

He stopped teasing and started working, powering into me with low grunts and firm hands. Holding my hip, he helped me rock back on him as he drove into me again and again. I was so swollen and tender from holding him inside me for so long, each stroke made me moan and scrabble for something to hold onto—for some kind of relief.

"Do you know how pretty you look in the moonlight, Daisy?" He caressed the curve of my ass and slid his hand up the slope of my spine. "I'm going to get you naked outside in every light—golden hour, sunset, sunrise, midnight—and see which I like best."

Bending over me, he kissed my cheek and lips. "I might have to do it over and over. I have a feeling it'll be difficult to choose just one."

I moaned in response. Really, what could I say? No one had spoken to me that way. My body and mind had not been shaped to receive such reverence. It took time to sink in and hold onto. To know it was mine and true.

Truly mine.

Rolling my hips and spine, I made waves for him to ride. He followed me like he knew what I was going to do before I did it, matching my moves with his own, until we were one undulating form, floating and falling.

His fingers between my thighs tipped the scales for me. I quivered all over, barely able to stay on my knees. His arm banded around my belly, holding me up as he followed me over in several sharp thrusts accompanied by a guttural groan. Heat filled me and touched my back where his mouth had latched.

A laugh burst out of me, quickly sparking out when my inner walls clenched around him and he gave my ass a light tap.

"What's so funny, Cupcake?"

"Not funny. That was ridiculously good. I hope no one was out on their balcony down below. Otherwise, they definitely heard us."

He nuzzled the side of my head. "Does that bother you?"

"Someone hearing us?" I thought it over, but not for long. "No. Well...strangers. I'd die if my brother or yours heard us."

He chuckled and pulled me closer. "Don't worry. We're on the same page there."

⸺⟡⸺

Later, after we'd cleaned up and were lying in bed, on the verge of sleep, Miles took my hand in his.

"I like it here."

"I do too," I agreed. "We'll have to come back."

I closed my eyes and let myself sink into him, my favorite day coming to an end.

CHAPTER THIRTY-FIVE

Miles

SOMETHING ABOUT THIS PLACE, combined with the three of us, just...clicked. Sunday, we'd spent hiking. Daisy had complained the trails were too flat, and Reed had muttered about wide open spaces, but once we'd reached our lookout destination and taken in the views, they'd both shut their complaining little mouths. Reed had even screwed up his face when we'd taken a silly selfie.

Then we'd parked our asses on the patio of a tap house and had spent the rest of the day there. Not the usual spot for a fourteen-year-old, a non-drinker, and a sober person, but they had good pretzels, outdoor games, and the vibe was relaxed.

Nothing like spending the day in the sun with people you loved.

On Monday, Daisy had to get work done, so Reed and I left her in the penthouse to explore a paved trail by the river.

I pulled into a parking spot, and Reed frowned. "This isn't the trailhead."

"Nope. We're stopping here first."

"The Humane Society? You're adopting a dog?"

"I'm not, unfortunately. Maybe one day. Today, we're going to borrow a dog."

"Wha—it's not a library."

"True. But this Humane Society has a program where you can borrow a dog for the day. Take them on walks and give them freedom. What do you say?"

"What makes you think I like dogs?"

I patted his shoulder. "You're a cool guy. No way you don't."

Actually, I had no idea. I'd read about this program while I'd been checking out what Sacramento had to offer. I was here for me. I wanted to play with a dog or two. Reed also enjoying it had been an afterthought—not that I would ever tell him that.

In the end, Reed was the one to select Solomon, the somber, snow-white greyhound who hadn't even gotten up to sniff us through the glass when we'd put our fingers through the holes. He'd only started to perk up when we'd gotten him to the trail and let him explore. Since he'd started sniffing every surface and cranny, his tail hadn't stopped wagging.

We ventured off the trail on a dirt path to the river, and Solomon splashed around, yipping and bounding like a puppy. I'd never heard Reed laugh like he did when the damn dog rolled his long body in the dirt then stood up, looking like he'd bathed in mud.

"The shelter didn't mention having to return him clean, did they?"

Reed huffed a laugh. "If they did, I didn't hear anything about it."

I pointed to the river. "Solomon, go clean yourself off!"

The big, goofy dog seemed to understand me, trotting back to the water and stomping around. He was having the time of his life.

"I already feel like shit giving him back," Reed said.

"Same, kid. Maybe he'll hang onto the happiness he's feeling for a while and some lucky family will come in, see a smiley good boy, and want him."

He kicked a rock, sending it skittering off the paved path. "Sucks he has to be cheerful for someone to like him. Can't just be himself."

"Nah. We liked him, didn't we? It just took the right people seeing the potential in him." I thought we might've been talking about more than the dog. "We took one look at him and knew we wanted to hang out with him, right?"

"Why'd you want to hang out with him? Was it pity?"

Definitely not talking about the dog.

"Look, Reed. You and I get along because we're straight with each other, right?"

He nodded once.

"I'm thinking you want to know why I'm hanging out with you, yeah?"

Averting his eyes, he nodded again.

"Right. I get that. You might be surprised, but you remind me a *lot* of me when I was your age. Different outside vibes, but very similar on the inside. I had a lot of friends, but I never felt like any of them knew me. My older brother couldn't stand being around me, and my parents were too caught up in hating each other to give me the attention I'd been begging for."

His eyes slid my way. "Did people give you shit at school?"

I shook my head. I really hated to admit this to him, but since we were doing the whole honesty thing, I went all in.

"I went the opposite direction and lashed out before anyone could come at me."

His brow furrowed deeply. "You were a bully?"

"I didn't think of myself as that back then, but yeah. For the most part, I did it to make people laugh. If they were laughing with me, they weren't laughing *at* me, you know? I didn't think about what I was doing or who I was hurting. I just didn't want to be hurt anymore, and that was all I could do to protect myself."

"That's stupid," he bit out.

"No kidding. You know who I was the worst to?"

He shook his head, his jaw rippling. He was pissed at me, and I deserved it.

"My sister-in-law—the woman my brother married. I was a little shit to her and got other people in on it. They took what I'd started and ran with it."

His frown was deep and thoughtful. Like he was trying to figure it all out. "Weren't you in their wedding? The best man or something?"

"I was. Elise forgave me. Weston too. I'll never think I deserve it, but I'm glad they're better people than me."

He kicked another rock. "You think I should forgive the people who mess with me?"

"Are they sorry? Have they done anything to earn your forgiveness?"

"No," he uttered.

"Then hell no." Taking a chance, I reached out and squeezed his shoulder. "But don't let those little shits change you. I see you, Reed. You're cool, creative, and your family loves the hell out of you. High school is a blip—"

"My sister, Quinn, didn't make it out of high school. People don't think I hear things, but I do. Her accident, as they call it, wasn't so accidental. The kids she hung out with, they kept daring her to do dangerous things, and she'd wanted to fit in so badly, she did them. The last one? They dared her to dive off this bridge. People jump off it sometimes, but only when the water's high enough. It was too low when Quinny went over. I heard my parents talking. They don't know if she jumped or was pushed. They'll never know because those kids all had the same story—that it was Quinn's idea."

He scoffed, but it was thick, bitterness giving way to a wave of grief.

"Either way, high school killed her, right? All the pressure to fit in, the shitty people, false friends, it all came down on her and broke my sister's neck."

He fell down on his ass before I could grab him to stop it from happening. I flopped down in the dirt next to him and rested my hand on his back as he gulped heaving breaths.

"Breathe, Reed. Slow and steady, in and out."

His anguish had knocked me sideways. I'd known about Quinn, but not the details. Not how she'd died. No wonder Daisy didn't like talking about it, and given my history, why she'd been so wary of me. My guts churned with remorse for the careless way I'd tromped through my adolescence. My heart lurched for Reed, living in the shadow of his sister's death, struggling to get through the same years she hadn't.

And my Daisy...she loved her family fiercely. Losing Quinn must've broken parts of her.

Solomon edged closer to us. When he was in front of Reed, he dropped to his belly and rested his narrow head on Reed's legs. Reed responded immediately, digging his fingers into Sol's short fur and scratching him behind his ears. The dog's tail was a metronome, ticking back and forth at a steady, even pace. Eventually, Reed's rapid breathing slowed to line up with it.

"Good boy," I murmured. "What a good dog you are, Sol."

"I don't know why I just dumped all that out," Reed rasped.

"You needed to get it out. I'm glad you did."

He slid a glance my way. "Would you have dared your sister-in-law to jump off a bridge?"

"I can honestly say I wouldn't have. I made fun of her in what I thought was a funny way because I was an idiot. No way in hell I ever wanted to see any harm come to her. Or anyone."

"But you hurt her."

"Yeah, I did. If I could have looked past my own inner turmoil, I would have seen that back then. Daring someone to jump into shallow water, though? That's insidious. I can't tell you how sorry I am you lost Quinn that way."

"I'm sorry too. I wish I'd been older so I could have known her better. We all thought we had time. Even though our family deals with death every day, it was a surprise when it touched us."

There wasn't much more to say after that. We sat with Solomon for a while, watching the water stream by and patting our borrowed dog.

On the way back to the car, I knocked into Reed with my shoulder. "What happened to your Andes vest?"

His breath hitched and he swallowed hard. "I, uh—can you not tell Daisy?"

"I can't make that promise until I know what happened."

"I just don't want her to worry. She worries enough." He sighed, his hand tightening around Sol's leash. "A couple idiots from school noticed me wearing it all the time and just took it—slipped it right off me and trashed it. They poured milk on it, ripped it, stomped on it, spit on it, then they gave it back."

Anger boiled in my gut. I'd been afraid something like this had happened, but to hear him casually describe these kids taking an item of clothing off him and maliciously ruining it made me want to do violence. I'd been a prick in school, but nothing I'd done had ever come close to that.

"Give me names, Reed. I'll take care of it."

He shrugged. "They left me alone after that. Guess they didn't like me having something I was proud of. I don't know."

"I'll get you a new one. If you don't want them to see you in it, you can wear it on the weekends."

His head was bowed, but I saw the smile hinting at the corners of his mouth. "That might be all right..."

"It's done."

⸻ ◆ ⸻

Daisy rarely squealed, but a napping, dirty Sol curled up in the backseat of my rental got her going.

"Miles! I love him. What did you do?" She couldn't tear her eyes off him.

"We borrowed him for adventures." I draped my arm over her shoulders and looked at the muddy dog like a proud dad. "Reed and I hadn't been counting on Sol becoming our bestie today, though."

"How could you have looked at that weirdly shaped body and pretty face and not known you'd get attached?" She shook her head. "He's perfect asleep. I'm sure he's even better awake."

"Now, we have to take him back." Reed peered down at him through the open door, filled with regret. "He'll hang on to the happiness."

He turned back to me, and I nodded in confirmation. We loaded Sol and ourselves up. Reed had *un*loaded a lot of what he'd been holding in, trusting me to take it, and despite how tragic his revelations and been, he was lighter now. I could almost see his spine straightening and his shoulders leveling out.

Made me feel really good to have done that for him.

From the brow she raised, Daisy must've noticed too.

"He's good," I mouthed.

She mimed wiping her forehead with the back of her hand and mouthed back, "Phew."

When Solomon woke a minute later, raring to go, Reed took him for one last walk, giving me a chance to fill her in.

I leaned against the SUV, and Daisy leaned against me. "You guys had a good day, huh?"

"Something about this place." I gave her a soft kiss. "He told me about Quinny."

Her mouth formed a little *O*. "What did he tell you?"

"About the bridge. That your parents don't know if she was pushed or jumped."

"Oh." Her teeth clamped on her bottom lip. "I didn't know he knew that."

"Yeah." I rolled my forehead along hers. Seeing her sad was akin to having my skin stripped from my bones. "I'm so sorry, Daisy."

"I miss her a lot."

"I think Reed does too."

She exhaled. "Of course he does. We don't talk about her enough. I have so many Quinny stories. He's going to be sick of me talking about her by the time I run out."

A stretch of silence lingered, the knowledge that eventually, no matter how many stories she had, she *would* run out sitting heavily between us.

"Thank you for listening to him."

"You don't have to thank me. That's what family does, right?"

She tipped her head back, and the corners of her mouth curved. "Yeah, Miles. That's what family does."

CHAPTER THIRTY-SIX

Daisy

Reed and I spent our last morning exploring an art museum and buying souvenirs for our parents and nieces. Miles had some work to do, so we'd left him. It was nice to do the tourist thing, just my brother and me, even if he was humoring me through most of it.

I brought up Quinn, and he didn't immediately shut me down, so I told him about the time she'd crunched up white Tic-Tacs in her mouth, ran to our mom, and told her she'd broken her teeth. Mama had almost fainted when she saw all those white chips, but when my sister started laughing, it only took about twenty seconds for Mama to join in.

Our sweet Quinny had had that way about her. At least...until she'd gotten her personality squeezed out of her by purported friends who'd never given a damn about her.

We didn't talk about that. We stuck to the good times. Where we should've been sticking all along. Instead, we'd let the end dim the memories of sixteen years of pranks, laughs, music, love, and just...our sister.

We had planned to meet Miles on the plane for our flight home, but Reed and I boarded an empty airplane. Now, we were twiddling our thumbs, wondering where the hell Miles was.

He finally texted he was on his way without explanation.

Ten minutes later, the explanation burst through the door ahead of him.

Reed tore off his buckle and leaped to his feet. "Solomon!"

I jumped up right behind him. "What's Solomon doing here?"

Miles appeared in the aisle behind the gangly, bouncing dog, patting his backside. "That's my son, Solomon Aldrich. Isn't the resemblance uncanny?"

He panted with his tongue out, and I must've really loved him because I found it cute.

"You adopted him?" Reed asked. "He's coming back to Denver?"

"Yeah, the big lug is mine," Miles said proudly.

Reed took his phone out to snap pictures. I happened to know he now had a text group with the friends he'd met at Lily's party and was willing to bet he was sending the pictures to them.

One trip, and my brother had a *text group.*

Sol returned to us and put his head right beneath Miles' hand. My brother not only had a text group, but he smiled freely down at the dog then took a selfie with him. A *s   e   l   f   -   ie.*

When things were too good to be true, I couldn't help but question them. "Isn't there a waiting period? Home inspection?"

Miles flashed me an enigmatic smile. "For *some* people. I'm sorry to tell you, Daisy, but having money means not all rules apply."

"And that sucks the soul right out of me." Solomon trotted over, butted his head against my leg, and looked up at me with soulful eyes. "But I can't find it in me to be angry this time. I can't believe he's yours."

We took our seats, and Sol stuck by Reed, settling at his feet.

"I think I'm going to have to share him." Miles sighed, like it was a big hassle, but I saw right through him.

He'd adopted that dog as much for my brother as he had for himself.

⊰•◦○◦•⊱

When we got home, the first thing my mother did was invite Miles over for family dinner. She wanted to hear everything about our trip and meet Miles' new son. We'd managed to hold her off a couple days so we could settle in, but then she'd rounded us up, insisting she missed her kids.

Landry showed up without her daughters and husband, much to Mama's dismay. Her explanation that they were with her in-laws and Tom was finishing up work didn't pass muster, but there wasn't anything Mama could do about it besides kidnapping. I was almost certain she wouldn't resort to that.

"It's flat there." Reed was back to being a man of few words. All the fun we'd had and exploring we'd done had been chalked up to "it's flat there." For some reason, I really loved his answer.

"Really? Isn't there a mountain range in the area?" Landry asked before popping an olive into her mouth.

"Nearby is relative," Miles replied. "The Sierra Nevadas take several hours to get to. Reed and I went on a hike, and it was not only flat, but paved."

Dad shuddered. "That doesn't sound like a hike."

"It was a walk. I wore my Vans," Reed supplied. "Sol managed to get dirty, so it was worth it."

Solomon's ears moved but his body remained prone on the nest Mama had made him from a pile of blankets and pillows. After knowing this dog for two whole days, I'd learned he had two modes: zoomies or lazy as hell.

"A dirty dog is always a good sign." Dad turned to Miles. "How in the world did you choose this boy to adopt?"

"He chose us," Reed answered. "We—"

Someone bellowed my name outside, loud enough to penetrate my parents' walls. Then the pounding began. *Bang, bang, bang.* All of us abandoned our dinner and ran for the windows, peering out to see what the commotion was all about.

There, standing under the porch light on my landing, was my former boss, Nick. Crowded next to him was another man, much broader and taller. I had to squint to make him out, and even then, my mind couldn't make sense of it.

"Is that Beau?" Mama screeched.

I guess I *had* been seeing things correctly. My oldest brother truly was standing beside Nick, pummeling my door and yelling my name.

What. The. Fuck?

"Beau?" Miles stood behind me, his hands squeezing my hips. "That's the elusive Beau Dunham?"

Mama opened our back door and yelled across the courtyard. "Beau David Dunham. Quit waking up the neighborhood and get your behind in here."

His head swiveled sharply. "Sorry, Mama, but I have to find Daisy."

"You're in luck. Your sister's here. Now, come on. Dinner's almost ready."

She left the door open for them and bustled to the table to put out two more place settings. I didn't particularly want to break bread with Nick after the last time I saw him, but it'd been a while since I'd seen Beau, so I couldn't be disappointed he'd shown up out of the blue.

Beau stepped into the house, eyes widening when he caught sight of Landry, Reed, Solomon, and finally Miles. Dad approached him, giving him a hug and pat on the back.

"What brings you to town, son?" Dad asked.

"I need to talk to Daisy." Beau zeroed in on me standing in Miles' orbit. "I've been hearing some disturbing things, but it looks like I'm too late."

Nick walked in then, his expression serious. He greeted my father and mother while barely taking his eyes off Miles and me.

"Disturbing things?" Mama laughed. "What could you have possibly heard?"

Beau was a mountain man. He'd grown taller than our dad by several inches, and his breadth always took my breath away. His beard was thick and bushy, and the only time he didn't wear flannel were the dog days of summer. And when he crossed his arms over his barrel chest, it was like two tree trunks twining.

Miles lowered his mouth to my ear. "You guys look a lot alike."

I snorted a laugh, which only deepened Nick's scowl. Nick could go step on a Lego. He had no business being here.

"I heard Daisy's caught up with an Aldrich. Not the environmentalist CEO either. The drunk, pussy-chasing loser. Nick's known him since they were teenagers. He's not the kind of man we want Daisy mixed up with."

Beau lowered his bearded chin to stare down his nose at Miles. And even though I knew my brother would never hurt a fly, I found him intimidating as hell right then.

"Beau, you're out of line," I started.

Mama stormed right up to him, yanked on the end of his beard to bring his attention to her, and pointed straight at him.

"I'm always happy to see my boy, but you can march your behind right out of my house if you think you can show up here talkin' like that. I'd think you, most of all, would know not to judge someone based on their last name. You disappoint me."

Beau softened from our mom's admonishment, but only a fraction. I wondered what Nick had been poisoning his ear with. It had to have been pretty damn bad for my brother to make the drive here from Wyoming.

"I'm sorry if you don't like my delivery, Mama, but I've been hearing some alarming things. I'm here to make sure Daisy doesn't get hurt." Beau frowned at Miles' hold on me. "I can only guess this is Aldrich. You know what kind of hurt he caused back in school? You know he's an alcoholic? Goes through women like water?"

"Shut up, Beau," Reed gritted out. "You're talking about my friend, and I'm not gonna stand for it."

Beau's eyes rounded, and he swung a glance to Nick then back to Reed. "You're...friends with this guy?"

"Yeah, I am, and you can fuck off, Beau. Go back to your mountain. It's not like you care enough to visit anyway." He copied Beau's stance, arms folded over his chest. Except Reed was half the width of Beau, so it was cute rather than intimidating.

Miles placed his hand on Reed's shoulder. "Thanks, kid, but you don't need to defend me. You and I both know Beau's information is outdated, given to him by a guy with a huge ulterior motive."

Beau's nostrils flared. "What ulterior motive could Nick possibly have?"

"That's simple," Miles stated. "He wants to get with your sister. He thinks he has a rightful claim on her since he waited out the last guy. When he couldn't sabotage my relationship with Daisy, he went to you to make you do the dirty work."

"No." Beau laughed darkly. "Nick would never—"

He turned to Nick, who only raised his chin instead of denying what Miles had to say. "I would look out for her."

I rolled my eyes. "I can't believe you took my lack of interest in dating you as a sign to go tattle to Beau. It's really clear how little you know about me, Nick, since as much as I love my brother, he's literally never had a say in my life."

Beau raked his fingers through his hair. "What the hell is going on here?"

Our dad clapped him on the back. "It seems you've been taken for a ride, son. Your buddy, Nick, played on your trauma from growing up with an alcoholic dad to use you to bludgeon a path for him straight to Daisy."

"Dad..." Beau shook his head. "I don't have trauma. It's been a long time. I barely remember you like that."

Miles kissed the top of my head. "I'm going to get Reed out of here. We'll take Sol for a walk. All right?"

I nodded, relieved to have fallen for a man who was thoughtful and sensitive. Reed didn't need to hear any of this. He had enough on his plate. I didn't want Miles to hear it either. He didn't deserve any of the vitriol Beau and Nick had locked and loaded for him.

As soon as Reed and Miles were gone, Mama pointed to Nick. "You need to hit the road, Nicholas. You're not welcome in my home anymore, and if I see you lurking around Daisy's place, I won't think twice about gettin' my shotgun." She stepped into him. "I grew up in the dirt in Alabama. Don't let the nice hair and clothes fool you. I'm not afraid of gettin' messy."

"I'm sorry, Mrs. Dunham. I was just—" Nick cut himself off when Mama kept pointing to the door. Hope sprung eternal—except when a southern mama put her foot down in front of her babies. All hope was lost for Nick in this house. "I'm sorry," he repeated, this time to the room at large, before he made a swift exit.

Landry finally made herself known, clucking her tongue. "I never liked that kid. He used to go through my dirty laundry, and I swear I had more than one pair of panties disappear after he'd visit."

We all looked at her in various stages of stupefaction.

She examined her nails. "What? I took care of it. Last time I caught him in my room, I told him if he did it again, I'd knock him out and put him in a coffin with a dead body. He never bothered me again."

Beau threw his arms out. "You should've told me. We wouldn't be in this position now."

Mama gave him a pointed look. "If you picked up the phone, we could have told you all about the wonderful man in Daisy's life. You chose to believe the worst for no good reason."

"Well, the last guy wasn't anything great," Beau muttered.

"This guy is," I informed him. "I'm hoping he'll stick around for a long time. You're going to have to figure out how to get over his last name and past that's more than a year in his rearview and get to know Miles for who he is. That is, if you want anything to do with me."

"Daisy," he croaked. "I was worried about you."

I put my hands on my hips, trying to keep my defenses up. "Funny way of showing it."

"Flowerpot." He came at me with his arms wide, and I let him envelop me in them.

"Beau-ses," I mumbled into his chest. "Nick's an asshole."

His rumbling laugh vibrated my cheek. "I'm getting that now. And your boyfriend's...not an asshole?"

"Not even a little bit."

"Good." He took me by the shoulders and peered down at me. "You look happy. And Reed looked...happy too?"

Landry squeezed in between us to get a Beau hug. "That's because Miles adopted a dog to share with him."

Mama thumped Beau on his big arm. "We like Miles. How about you be on your best behavior so he still wants to come around every once in a while."

Beau's gaze traveled around the room, to most of his family who was still sort of angry at him, and he exhaled a long breath.

"I'm sorry for the reason I came, but I'm glad to be here."

Dad spoke for all of us. "You're always welcome, Beau. We'd like to see you a lot more."

"Yeah." He rubbed the back of his thick neck. "Me too."

Calm settled over the Dunham house once more. Until Solomon returned, dragging Miles and Reed with him. He immediately went to sniff Beau, giving him a thorough check.

Miles pulled me into his side. "You okay, Cupcake?"

I let myself melt into him, thinking of the way my family had defended him. The night hadn't gone as planned, but I couldn't be mad knowing my family sincerely approved of the man I absolutely adored.

I smiled up at him. "I am now that you're here."

CHAPTER THIRTY-SEVEN

Miles

I pulled Daisy to the side of her bed I'd claimed as mine. Eventually, I'd have to go back to my place, but I wasn't interested in being where she wasn't. "Your brother's big as hell. A literal mountain."

She snickered. "Did I not mention that?"

"You didn't. It's a good thing I treat you right. He could crack my head like a walnut with one hand."

Things could have gone either way tonight. What Nick had told Beau hadn't been factually wrong. I'd been a drunken womanizer, I wouldn't deny it. But the Dunhams knew me now and gave me a lot of grace for my past. They were good people who understood what it meant to screw up, and they actually liked me. Whitney Mae had even threatened to give me Beau's portion of pie for being a dick to me.

For a guy who'd grown up in a freezer, getting used to hanging out by the hearth wasn't easy, but I craved the warmth.

"I'm sorry that happened." Her head banged on my chest. "I love my family, but there are times I wish we had a little distance."

"You know...you could move in with me. Then you wouldn't be living in their backyard."

She raised her head, squinting. "Is your house still a wreck?"

"You know damn well it is."

"I'll pass. Besides, they'd just show up there unannounced too."

I cocked my head on my pillow. "Are you…do you want to move?"

"I've always thought I would eventually. I don't want to die in the same place I grew up." She sighed and dropped her head to my shoulder. "I say that a lot. It's been my motto for years."

"I wouldn't mind moving either."

I felt her smile against my skin. "Yeah? Then maybe we will."

"No maybes, Cupcake. If you have dreams, I'm going to help you make them come true."

"As long as they line up with your dreams, Spreadsheet."

"They do. They will."

A minute had passed when her head popped up. "Your truth. You don't want to live in Denver forever."

"That's right." I closed my eyes, remembering that day on my deck, the beginning of *us*, when we'd played Two Truths and a Lie. "We'll figure it out."

❖

Clementine walked into my office seconds before Saoirse. Clem climbed into my lap, and Saoirse made herself at home in the chair opposite my desk.

"As long as you're on board, I'm going to offer Rebecca the promotion to junior strategist."

"I'm on board," I replied. "That'll free us both up to take jobs that require travel."

Her blonde brow arched. "Are you looking to get out of here?"

I dug my fingers into Clem's fur, considering how to answer. Since we'd gotten back from our California trip, I'd been restless. Not unusual for me with my ADHD, but the feeling hadn't abated.

"Not looking, per se, but I wouldn't mind a change of scenery."

Her eyes flicked over my face. "You're not...you're not thinking of leaving the business, are you?"

"No."

That, I could say unequivocally. Saoirse and I had started this together. Peak Strategies was the first thing I'd truly committed to. This business and the woman across from me had been the main inspiration for me getting sober. I hadn't wanted to let her down then, and that hadn't changed.

"I'm not leaving, but I'm feeling the need to plan."

Saoirse leaned forward, her elbows on her knees. "Anything you'd like to share with the class?"

"Not yet. I don't have any concrete thoughts yet. You can count on me, Sersh. I would never leave you high and dry."

Her mouth slowly spread into a grin. "I know you wouldn't, Miles. And my cat likes you better than me, so how could I not trust you?"

⸻◆⸻

The next day, my commitment to stay was put to the test when my mother walked through my office door. Rebecca trailed after her, trying to politely keep her from bursting into my private space, but there was no stopping her.

"It's fine, Beck. I'll take care of this," I assured her.

My mother glared at Rebecca archly. "Yes. My *son* will take care of me. You can toddle off now."

Rebecca scrunched her nose and mouthed, "Toddle?"

I shrugged, no explanation for the words that left my mother's mouth. Given the early hour and knowing her habits, she was most likely blitzed on mimosas from brunch.

Rebecca left us alone, closing the door behind her. I folded my arms across my chest and faced my mother. She was sweeping her gaze over my office, her mouth puckered in distaste.

"You should have called in my designer, Frederick. He would have gone in a different direction. Something more cohesive and luxurious. Surely your clients—"

I interrupted her. I really didn't have the will or time to listen to her opinions on my decorating skills.

"Is there a reason for you popping into my office for the first time in the two years I've had it?"

Her gaze landed on me. "Of course there is." She stomped forward and collapsed in the chair in front of my desk. "You haven't taken my calls. I had to make sure you're okay."

"I've texted you. You know I'm fine."

Her upper lip curled. "Oh, but anyone could have your phone, pretending to be you. The only way I could be sure was to see you in person."

I sat down behind my desk, giving myself plenty of room from her. "We're not in a spy movie. The simplest answer is the right one. I warned you if you said anything bad about Daisy again, I would cut you off, and you didn't listen. *That's* why I haven't taken your calls, as you already know, since I texted you as much."

When I brought up to my therapist that completely cutting off my mom felt like the easy way out, he'd nodded and replied, *"Sometimes, when it's too easy, we try to make it harder on ourselves. But why does it have to be hard?"*

"But you're always asking me why things have to be easy. Which is it?"

He'd given me one of his enigmatic smiles. *"Why can't things just be what they are?"*

I'd been mulling that over for a week now.

My mother sniffed. "I can't believe you're still miffed about that. I merely made an observation. Is there something so wrong with that?"

Daisy hadn't heard my mother's useless criticism. I could have let it slide, but I hadn't. I'd set a boundary, she'd trampled it, so I'd cut her off like I'd said I would. Since then, I'd lost some of the dread I'd carried with me on a regular basis. Just because this woman gave birth to me did not mean I had to allow her a first-row seat to my life when all she did was wreak havoc when she wasn't the star.

"You see me alive. Is there anything else I can do for you?"

She reached into her oversized purse and produced a *Denver Life* magazine. "Imagine my surprise when Barbara Curtman showed up to brunch with this. Did you know there's a ten-page spread about Weston's wedding? Barbara had the nerve to ask me why I wasn't in the pictures, as if she didn't know my oldest son had abandoned me." She jabbed at the magazine with her sharp fingernail. "Try to fathom my dismay when I finally looked at the pictures and saw your little girlfriend. I've never been so humiliated in my life. Weston wouldn't invite his mother to his wedding, but your little girlfriend who looks like she should be hanging out with Ozzy Osborne—"

"Timely reference."

She cleared her throat pointedly. "This was obviously done to hurt me. I don't think I'll be able to get over this."

That last part was said as a threat—and not toward me. Panic lurched in my gut. My father was the one most known for punching holes in walls and destroying mom and pop businesses, but my mother had her own destructive streak.

"You'll get over it if you ever want a chance at having a relationship with me. Daisy was in the pictures because she was my guest. If you have a problem with that, take it up with me."

She chuffed. "As if it's as easy as that. You and your brother have made me a laughingstock among my friends."

She dropped her head, and I braced myself. I knew what was coming next. Her most effective weapon.

When she raised her head again, her eyes were locked and loaded with tears.

"Miles, baby," she choked out. A sob tore loose from her chest, and the tears spilled over, streaming down her cheeks. "How could you and Weston do this to me? All I've ever wanted was to love and take care of my boys."

Those tears had always given me a visceral reaction. This time, though, I thought of Whitney Mae bragging to Beau about what a good guy I was. I thought of Seth patting me on the back, telling me not to let my past get me down in the present. I thought of Reed giving me his trust, and Daisy, sweet fucking Daisy, calling me Spreadsheet and sharing her dreams with me.

Fortified by the people who saw me and loved me, my mother's crocodile tears did nothing for me. I stared at her as she wept. And funnily enough, when I didn't rush to comfort her or ask how I could make her feel better, those tears dried up pretty damn quickly.

She swiped at her damp cheeks and huffed as she stuffed the magazine back in her purse.

"You're so ungrateful, just like your brother and father. Don't think I'm going to let this go." Rising to her feet, she slung her bag over her shoulder.

"This is not how you get back into my good graces," I told her.

Her eyes narrowed. "It's you who should be working to get back into *my* good graces, Miles." She jutted her chin. "We'll see who comes begging in the end. We'll see."

After her big show of storming out, I cradled my head in my hands. I was tired of being accessible to her. Exhausted by her toxic moods. Weary of being leaned on. Fucking through with being her whipping boy.

I was *done*.

Chapter Thirty-eight

Daisy

Bea, Shira, Clara, and I sat in a line of pedicure chairs, passing my phone down from person to person, each of us frowning at my inbox. In the past forty-eight hours, Grazing had gotten ten cancellations. All the bookings Bea had secured were still on our calendar, along with the ones who had contacted us through our website, but at least half of the bookings made by women I'd met at events this summer had been deleted right off our calendar like they'd never existed.

Clara stated what we were all thinking. "This isn't a coincidence."

"No. There are too many of them. It can't be," I agreed.

My heart lodged in my throat, panicked over what to do. Nothing like this had ever happened to me before. My web design clients occasionally canceled, but never in droves. And our Grazing clients had been incredibly happy with our services. I really couldn't fathom what had gone wrong. And now, I had Bea counting on the income from Grazing since she'd quit High Bar. If we didn't rebook those empty slots, we were screwed—Bea more than me.

"Make any enemies lately?" Clara asked.

"I don't think so. Bea's the one more likely to make enemies."

Bea snickered. "I'd be insulted if it weren't true." She flicked the mini butcher knife earring in her earlobe. "However, I don't think it's me. My enemies are drunk guys who try to grab my tits and this rich guy I keep running into everywhere."

Clara leaned forward to look at Bea. "Rich guy? Is he stalking you?"

"Maybe. Does it even count as stalking if they're rich and hand-some?"

"Yes," Shira said softly. "Do you need help?"

Bea waved her off. "I don't think he's the murder-y type. And to be fair, our run-ins *could* be a coincidence. They just happen often and tend to end in violence."

Shira's mouth dropped open in an *O*. "I'm intrigued by you."

Clara waved a hand in front of her. "Can we get back to the matter at hand? I'm due at a board meeting in forty minutes." She bent forward to talk to her nail lady. "I want creamy pink. Sheer as possible."

"No fun colors on your toes?" I asked.

Sighing, she leaned back in her massage chair. "Should I? I always get pink, and I have no one to show them to anyway."

"Nellie would get a kick out of a bright color," Shira said.

"Who's Nellie?" Bea asked.

"My two-year-old." Clara tapped her bottom lip with her finger. "Oh, all right. Nellie's into purple lately. Let's go bright purple."

"Yeah, girl," Bea drawled in her deadpan way. "Get it."

I wiggled my toes in the pedicure tub. "Maybe I'll skip black and go red this time."

Miles would be into it.

Bea twirled her finger. "It's like *Girls Gone Wild, Spring Break in Cancun edition.*"

I shushed her. "Now that our colors are settled, can we talk about our business that's quickly slipping away?"

"I think you need to reexamine who might not be your biggest fan," Clara suggested.

"Nick the asshole," came from Bea.

I scrunched my nose. "Nick's scared of Whitney Mae. Besides, how would he know who had booked with us?"

"What about your ex?" Shira asked. "Is he angry?"

"I don't know. I haven't heard from Andy in a long time. His family mingles in the same crowd as a lot of our clients, but I think it being him is a longshot." I turned to Bea. "Are you sure we don't have a deluge of terrible Yelp reviews?"

"Nope. Plus, if we did, we'd have widespread cancellations." Bea arched a brow. "I think some rich bitch hates you."

"Why would anyone hate Daisy?" Shira asked.

I didn't know her well yet, but I already liked her. "Thanks, Shir, but rich bitches are notoriously not a fan of me."

"So, the field is wide," Clara quipped.

I slapped my throbbing forehead. "I don't know. Maybe it's a lot less wide than I want it to be."

⋅◆⋅

With my shiny red toenails, I mulled over Bea's words. There was only one rich bitch who'd taken an instant dislike to me, and I hated to even think she was behind this. If I told Miles I suspected his mother was screwing with my business, would he believe me?

Dread pooled in my gut as I blindly clicked around on my computer with one hand and scratched behind Solomon's ears with the other. He was such a good, lazy boy. I'd never been a dog person, but I'd grown accustomed to Sol leaning on me, as if his own weight was too much effort for him to bear. He had spurts of hyperactivity, but for the most part, he liked to chill and nap, and he *really* liked taking leisurely walks with Reed.

My door swung open, and Miles strolled in like he owned the place. He'd all but moved in, so I didn't mind. I liked it very much actually. Eventually, my little bungalow wouldn't cut it, but since we could barely pry ourselves apart during the hours we spent together, we didn't need more space.

"Hello, Cupcake." He kicked off his shoes, raking his eyes over me.

"Hey, Spreadsheet."

He immediately frowned and strode over to me, gently shoving Sol out of the way so he could turn me in my chair and kneel between my knees. "What's wrong?"

I combed my fingers through his hair, sighing. "I have to ask your opinion on something, and I'm not sure how you're going to take it."

"Just ask. My mind is already going to the worst-case scenario. You don't want to know the ugliness I've conjured in the last thirty seconds."

I tried to smile, but it was one of my lopsided ones that didn't feel right. I had to get this over with so Miles didn't spiral and I didn't burst.

"We had more cancellations today."

He exhaled. "Shit, really? A lot?"

"Yes. And while I was getting a pedicure with the girls, Bea suggested—"

Miles lifted my foot and growled. "You're wearing socks."

I tugged my foot out of his grip. "Those are a treat for after this hard talk."

The scowl I received would have burned me to the ground if I hadn't known this big, beautiful man was pissed I wouldn't show him my newly pedicured feet. As it was, I struggled not to giggle.

"Listen!" I tugged his hair. "Bea suggested, and I quote, 'some rich bitch hates me' and is sabotaging Grazing. The only people canceling are other...um, rich bitches, and I couldn't help where my mind went—"

"My mother." His jaw rippled as he ground his molars. "My mother did this. She's pissed at me and taking it out on you."

Standing, he backed away. "Fuck, Daisy. I'm sorry. I don't—" He twisted left and right, looking around blindly. "I'll take care of it. I'm so fucking sorry."

I went to him, leaning my weight on his front the way Sol liked to do. "How will you take care of it?"

His arm banded around me, though he was still staring at nothing. "I'll have a talk with her. See what she wants to make it stop."

"No," I said with a firmness that surprised even me. Miles finally snapped out of his daze and stared down at me. I took his face in my hands. "That's exactly what she wants, isn't it? I'm not allowing you to continue that cycle with her."

"She can't fuck with you to get to me." He exhaled sharply. "I'm sorry, Cupcake."

"You keep saying that, but you have nothing to be sorry for. This isn't you, Miles. You're not responsible for what she does. And we don't know for sure it's her..."

"Nah, it's her. This is very much in her wheelhouse. I'm sure she's at the club, dripping poison in susceptible ears." He let go of me and took a few backward steps, threading his fingers behind his head. "Goddammit. I knew she was going to do something, but if I thought for a second she'd go after you—"

"If you even think about saying you wouldn't have been with me, I'll never make you another cupcake again."

He scowled at me. "I'm just trying to think of what's best for you. Do you think I want to be apart from you?"

"Yeah, I do, if you consider leaving me a solution." I walked right up to him and flicked the center of his forehead. "There, that stupid thought is now banished from your mind."

His mouth opened and closed, opened and closed, then he rubbed his forehead. "That hurt. I didn't know you were so violent."

"Remember that the next time leaving me becomes a possibility."

"I never said I was going to leave you."

I wagged my finger at him. "I saw where your mind was going. Don't deny it."

His arm darted out to gather me against him. I kept going, climbing him like a tree until we were face to face, my legs locked around his waist.

"It wasn't a real thought, Daze. I fucking panicked for a second." He dropped his face to the crook of my neck, inhaling my scent. "I don't know what to do. For once, I can't think of how to plan my way out of this."

"I love you, Miles. Your mother isn't you, okay? You aren't re-sponsible for her behavior." I squeezed him hard with all four limbs and stroked the back of his hair. "I've been thinking about this, and I've decided it's okay. Bea brought in her Millennial wine moms, and we've gotten a lot of attention through social media. It's just...I'd booked so many jobs so quickly, when they went away, it felt like I was losing everything. But the thing is, I don't need those rich bitches. I had to reframe how I saw this business growing, and that took me a minute, but I'm there. We just got started, and we're making a name for ourselves. It's happening."

His lips touched the curve of my neck, my jaw, my chin, then my mouth. "So, this summer, all the events, the whole fake dating thing, it was all pointless?"

"No, it wasn't pointless." I took his face in my hands. "The point was you and me. We never would have happened if we hadn't tricked ourselves into it."

His huff was hot against my lips. "My little storm cloud is looking on the bright side, huh?"

"You're wearing off on me, sunshine."

He closed his eyes, his head shaking slightly. "I can't believe she's doing this to you. I should be able to believe it, but I really can't."

His voice cracked with emotion, and my heart panged for him. Nothing about this was right, but I'd resolved to make the best of it for Miles' sake. I would never ask him to stop his mother's path of destruction. We just had to get out of the way so we didn't get trampled further.

"I'm sorry she let you down in such a massive way." I pecked the tip of his nose. "You have to know you're more important to me than any business, and that's an always thing."

"God, I love you, Daisy." He strode into the bedroom with me in his arms and sat on the edge of the bed. For a long moment, he studied my face, neck, chest, shoulders—all the places he could see with me plastered to him.

I stroked his hair, letting him look all he needed to. I wasn't going anywhere.

CHAPTER THIRTY-NINE

Long seconds of silence ticked by where we held each other and merely breathed.

Then Miles looked me directly in the eye and said, "I'm ready for my treat now, Daisy-daze."

My toes curled as I smiled. "What treat? I don't know what you mean."

"You do." He moved fast, spinning and tossing me flat on my back. "If you won't give it to me, I'll take it."

Squealing, I scooted away from him, up the mattress until I hit the headboard. All the while, he prowled, taking his time crawling after me.

"No, no," I cried, giggling and kicked at him. My stomach was a tilt-a-whirl from the thrill of him hunting me down and taking what he wanted. "Not my feet. Anything but my feet."

He caught my ankle and lifted my leg so my socked foot was right in front of him. I kicked him with my free leg, but he caught that too. His hands were so big, fingers so long, they wrapped around both my ankles. He worked my socks off with the other hand and tossed them aside. Then he kissed the soles of my feet, which were smooth as silk from my afternoon treatment.

"So soft," he uttered.

Lowering my legs, he pointed my toes down so he could see them too, breath hitching when he caught sight of the polish.

"Fuck, Daze. Red? For me?"

When his eyes found mine, they were already glazed. I nodded. "For you. I hoped you'd like it."

"I love it." He softly kissed each of my toes while telling me how pretty I was, from the bottom to the top. All over. Everything about me was lovely, sweet, perfect. I'd never been happier about a nail polish choice than I was then.

We came together from a place of hope. *Hopefully in love.* There was no anger or desperation when removing each other's clothes, only hope for what the future would bring us as fingers explored and mouths devoured.

Miles settled between my thighs, where he'd told me more than once he hoped he'd die. And though I'd let him live there, lavishing me with his tongue, bringing me wave after wave of pleasure, that wasn't how I envisioned our end. I saw us old, holding wrinkled hands, watching a final sunset together. He might call me Lydia because he forgot, and I might let him because it reminded me of when we were young.

And just before the end, he'd wink and smile, and I'd close my eyes for the final time, knowing no matter what came after, I'd already had heaven.

"I love you," I whispered, my heart hammering in my ears.

He answered me with his tongue rolling over my clit and the brush of his fingers along my inner thighs. In my mindless haze of pleasure, I realized the brushes were done with intent, spelling out "love" over and over.

"Love you, love you, love you, love you." There weren't enough times I could say it to convey how much I meant it, but I would try.

Miles rode my waves until he drew nothing but whimpers and pleas from me. Kneeling at my feet, he brought one to his mouth and cherished it with his lips and tongue. Once satisfied, he did the same with the other.

There was something about him worshiping a part often forgotten that made me feel like the most special woman in the world. His lips and tongue could have touched any part of me, and I would have reacted, but him kissing the arch of my foot had me scraping at the sheets for an anchor so I didn't float away.

"Love you, love you, love you, love you."

He moved over me, rolling us to our sides to curl around me. My shelter.

I opened for him, and he slid into me easily. We took time staying joined but not moving much, staring at each other, saying pretty things, confessing our love again and again. His lips pressed on the crook of my neck, then his teeth joined, a contrast to his soft, gentle affection. If we'd been supernatural, the bite he'd left on me would have tethered us for life.

But we were mere mortals.

And this was the real world.

Even better than I could have imagined.

Our lovemaking was slow and sweet. Whispers and kisses, caresses and kneads. Miles held my face to tell me he loved me. I kissed his lips and breathed his air.

Seven years couldn't touch what had been created in this handful of months. To be seen, known, accepted, loved so dearly, was not something that came along more than once in a lifetime. We had it. We shared it. And I would protect it like a flame in the wind.

I touched my lips over his thrumming heart and sighed.

He brought my gaze back to his, and between breaths, he smiled at me. I traced the curve of his happiness and applied it to my own mouth. It tasted sweet and distinctly like Miles.

"I love you," I repeated for the thousandth time.

"I love you," he said with the same hopeful smile.

He was truly mine.

And I am truly yours.

CHAPTER FORTY

Miles

"We should take Reed on another trip before school starts." I glanced over at Daisy curled up in my passenger seat, looking at me like she loved me.

Because she did.

If I'd had any doubts, they'd been laid to rest. After realizing my mother was trying to sabotage Grazing, Daisy had had every reason to throw her hands up and tell me it was too much for her—that I wasn't worth the baggage of a toxic mother. Instead, she'd held me closer. Reminded me at every turn I wasn't responsible for my mother's actions and we would figure out our next steps together.

In the days after, I'd been tempted to take action. To call a lawyer, a reporter, to call my fuckwit father. It had taken a call with Weston to calm me. He'd reminded me he hadn't heard a single word from our mother after the *Denver Life* article because she was well aware he wouldn't give her the drama she craved.

So, taking a note from my big brother's playbook, I remained quiet. It wasn't easy for a man like me. Luckily, I had the most distracting woman who liked to keep me on my toes.

"I'd love that. I think the vibes from our last trip are wearing off. Mama said she had to drag him to class this morning and he's been looking forward to it all summer."

"Hmmm." I drummed my thumbs on the steering wheel. "Wonder what that's about. I talked to him Sunday night, and he was practically vibrating with excitement."

"Maybe he'll tell us when we ply him with junk food."

Whitney Mae hadn't been able to leave the funeral home, so we'd been tapped in to grab Reed from day two of his summer music class.

I parked the car, and Daisy and I got out. We'd been hoping he might've been able to let us listen to what he'd been creating, but when we walked into the classroom he was supposed to be in, only a couple kids remained, and none were Reed.

A man with a goatee and shaggy, salt-and-pepper hair approached us. "Hey, are you picking someone up?"

"Yes. My brother, Reed Dunham. Our mom put my name on the list of approved—"

"Some wires must've gotten crossed. Reed isn't here today." The man clucked his tongue. "It's a shame. I recovered his beats that got deleted yesterday. I was looking forward to seeing what else he could do. Hopefully he'll be back tomorrow."

"Excuse me, what?" Daisy frowned. "My mother dropped him off here this morning. You're telling me he hasn't been here at all today?"

The man's brow dropped, and he rubbed the patch of hair under his lip. "No, he didn't show at all. I haven't seen him since yesterday afternoon."

"Why were his beats deleted?" I asked.

He shook his head. "A couple guys thought it would be funny to mess with Reed's computer when he got up. Let's just say, Reed didn't see the humor in it, and neither did I. In my class, we respect each other's creative efforts—"

Daisy and I got on the phone as soon as we were out of the building. She called her mom, and I dialed Reed. Whitney Mae picked up, but Reed's went straight to voicemail.

Me: *Hey, kid. Where are you? Daisy and I were at class to pick you up.*

Me: *You're not going to be in trouble for bailing. We'll come get you, wherever you are.*

Me: *Let me know if you're safe. If you need some time, just tell me you're not in danger, and I'll give you the time you need.*

"I'm worried," Daisy whispered.

"I know." I kissed her head. "What'd your mom say?"

"She's checking the house, his room. She'll check my place if he's not there."

"Good. Let's drive around here. Maybe he's hanging out somewhere and lost track of time."

We cruised up and down the road near the class, peering in windows of restaurants and fast-food joints. Tension filled the car. I wanted to tell Daisy I was sure Reed was fine, but I couldn't bring myself to when I didn't believe it.

He wasn't at home.

Not at Daisy's place either.

All of us had called him, but he wasn't picking up.

Daisy and I drove while Landry called his friends. We stopped in his favorite restaurants, a comic book store, the public library. We even swung by my house on the off chance he was hiding out there.

Nothing.

I sat in the driveway, helpless, while Daisy quietly spoke to her panicked mother. Dropping my head to the steering wheel, I tried to think like Reed.

Had he felt helpless like this when those kids deleted the beats he'd created? Had he been defeated when the one thing he'd looked forward to all summer was just a repeat of the bullying bullshit he'd been dished out at school?

Probably, yeah.

Where would he want to go, feeling like that?

Reed was a sensitive kid. Artistic. He wouldn't go sit in a greasy burger bar when his world was crumbling and he felt like he had no way to stop it.

He'd go somewhere meaningful. Somewhere—

"Daisy."

She lowered the phone from her ear. "Yes?"

"Where's the bridge?"

"Bridge?"

"Where Quinny died. Where is it?"

Her eyes rounded. "You think he's there?"

"I don't know, but I'm thinking we need to check."

⋯◆⋯

It took a half hour to drive out to the bridge Quinn had died jumping from. I hated bringing Daisy here, but she'd insisted on coming with me. If Reed was here, even if the worst had happened, she wanted to see—to know.

I wasn't thinking too hard about that. If I did, I wouldn't be able to be steady for Daisy, and I'd promised I'd be that for her.

I parked in gravel and jumped out of the car. No one used this bridge anymore. I hadn't known it was here.

Weeds grew from cracks in the pavement, and trash huddled in corners. Our footsteps echoed on the cement as we started across.

I spotted him first, squeezing Daisy's hand hard. When she gasped, I knew she'd seen him too.

"Reed. Baby," she croaked thickly, not nearly loud enough for him to hear. It was a lament. A cry for the pain he must've been in to lead him here.

Reed was sitting on the ground in the middle of the bridge, his legs dangling over the side. He had to have heard us coming, but he was focused on the water below.

As we grew closer, the scene around him almost brought me to my knees. His backpack. A dog-eared paperback. A crumpled sack of fast food. A few empty, crushed soda cans. He had to have been here a while. All day, probably. And he was just a kid, not even fifteen years on this earth. He'd been here, suffering all alone, not knowing for certain he had at least two people he could've leaned on without question.

It killed me.

"What time is it?" he asked when we were next to him.

"Almost six," I replied.

"Huh. I didn't think it was so late."

I crouched down beside him, careful not to touch him. "Did you mean to come back before the end of camp?"

He shrugged. "I've been thinking about getting up for a while now, but I can't make myself do it."

"You don't have to get up," Daisy said softly. "We'll sit with you."

She scooted in beside him, her legs dangling half the length of his, and I took his other side.

"I'm not going back to that class."

"You don't have to," Daisy assured him. "We know what happened. You never have to go back there."

"I tried to tell Mama. She told me she'd paid a lot of money and I had to give it another chance."

"She didn't understand. I'm sure she does now." She hooked his pinkie with hers. "If there's a problem, I'll explain. I'll tell her about the kids who deleted the song you were working on."

He sucked in a jagged breath. "They're from my school, you know. They're not gonna forget how much they hate me. Even if I don't go back to class, I'll still have to face them."

I wanted to tell him if he gave us names, we'd go to the principal. I'd contact their parents. And if that didn't work, I would set about destroying their families piece by piece. But his shoulders were overburdened enough. He couldn't bear my anger, righteous or not.

"We'll find a way where that doesn't happen," Daisy said.

Reed lifted his head, his glazed eyes distant and unfocused. "I wanted to think about Quinn today. I wondered if she felt this...exhaustion from life that day. I wanted to look down at the shallow water and contemplate why that had been a better choice than staying and facing another day, another week—hell, two years of more of the same."

He turned to Daisy. "I got it. The consequences of making that jump had looked better than whatever had waited for her if she hadn't."

"Reed," Daisy choked out, devastation blooming from her like funeral flowers.

"I don't wanna die, but I don't wanna be here anymore either." Reed crammed the heel of his palm against his forehead. "Mama says to ride it out, and I tried, I really did, but I can't do it. I can't get up from here knowing I've got three more years of people hating me for nothing I've done."

"She doesn't get it, baby," Daisy murmured. "Neither of them do. That doesn't mean they don't love you. They just don't understand how bad it is."

He drew in a shaky breath. "I know. Dad has been in his own world his whole life. And Mama didn't grow up a Dunham. If she had, she never would have given you the initials 'DED.' It's like she put a 'kick me' sign on you."

Daisy put her head on her brother's shoulder. "I understand. Trust me, I do."

Reed grew quiet. I barely breathed while I waited for him to speak. I wished I knew what to do, how to handle this. My mind was stuck on committing violence. That wouldn't help Reed, though, and it would only make me feel better temporarily.

Reed inhaled sharply. "Do you think Quinn was scared?"

"Yeah. I think she was probably scared way before she stepped foot on this bridge," Daisy replied.

They were breaking my heart, these two. All I could do was be here, steady for them, while they faced down their sister's tragedy, and count my lucky stars Reed hadn't gone the same way. But he was on the edge. If today hadn't proven that, I didn't know what would. Something big had to be done. A change had to be made. This...misery was un-fucking-tenable.

"I'm scared," he admitted.

She nodded. "I am too."

He exhaled a long, exhausted breath and let his head fall on top of hers. "I don't know what to do, Daze."

"Listen to me, Reed." She took his hand and held it against her cheek. "I promise you the solution will not be to ride it out. If you figure out a way to get up, we'll take you home and talk until we have a plan."

I squeezed Reed's shoulder. "If you let me, I'll be there to help. Plans are my thing."

"Okay." He picked his head up and turned to me. "How much trouble do you think I'm going to be in?"

I gave his cheek a pat. "None. This is probably the one time you'll get off scot-free for scaring the shit out of your family. Everyone's going to be too relieved you're in one piece to be angry."

"I didn't mean to scare them."

"I know you didn't," I told him. "You're a good guy. We all know that."

"I needed to think about Quinny. About her last day. That's all."

"Did you get enough thinking done? Are you ready to go home? I'm sure Sol's bladder's about to burst. You're gonna have to take him for a walk as soon as we get there."

A concrete task lit him up and gave him a reason to move his body. His climb was slow, but he got to his feet with Daisy bracing him. I grabbed his backpack and bag of trash, then I threw my arm around his shoulders.

"You're important to a lot of people, kid." I didn't recognize the gruffness of my voice, thick with fear and myriad emotions I couldn't name. "Including me. Next time you need to think about Quinny, or anything, let me know."

He nodded. "I will."

Daisy squeezed him from the other side. "Let's go home."

CHAPTER FORTY-ONE

Daisy

I'D NEVER DOUBTED MILES loved me.

But I became certain he was my person for life when he didn't hesitate to sit down with my family to find a solution for how we could do what was best for Reed.

It had taken planning. A lot of heavy discussions with the people in our lives. More planning and phone calls and spreadsheets and contracts. Miles had been in his element, no doubt, and watching him put every ounce of his knowledge and attention into our project had made me fall even more hopefully in love with him.

I should never have questioned whether he'd do absolutely anything for someone he loved. After all, he had a sexy scar on his ass that proved he'd take a bullet for his friends.

Two weeks had passed since that dreaded day on the bridge, and we'd finally gotten all our ducks in a row. In another week, we'd start our new adventure.

Today, we were informing the last of the important people in our lives about our next moves.

When we arrived at the restaurant, Weston, Elise, Elliot, Kit, Saoirse, and Luca were already waiting for us to join them for brunch. By necessity, Saoirse knew what was up, but we hadn't had a chance to tell anyone else. And maybe it was easier to get it all out of the way in one fell swoop.

"What a surprise, you're late," Elliot deadpanned before rising to kiss my cheek and pat Miles' shoulder.

"How would we make an entrance if we were on time?" Not one to settle for a friendly pat, Miles went around kissing the tops of everyone's head. "Where's my baby Josephine?"

Kit picked up her iced coffee. "Baby Josephine is actually a toddler who doesn't like to sit still for long periods of time. Her mother wanted to have a relaxing meal, so she's with one of her favorite uncles."

We exchanged a glance, and I squeezed Miles' hand. We'd have to make time to go love on Joey in the next week.

Miles sighed. "Fine. That's fair, I guess."

Miles pulled out my chair for me, and I took my seat next to Saoirse while he sat on my other side, next to Weston. He was nervous, and so was I. Mostly for him. He really wanted to be supported and for everyone to understand our decision.

Conversation picked up normally after that. Kit and Elliot told us about her pregnancy—they were having a boy—and the mischief Joey had been up to lately. We weren't quite ready to start our revelation. We'd already decided to wait until after we'd ordered.

Our server was particularly efficient today. Drinks were served, orders were taken before we wanted them to be, and it was now or never.

Miles took my hand in his and rested them on the table. "We have some things we would like to share with everyone."

All eyes were on us.

I imagined they were guessing we were about to announce we were moving in together or getting engaged. Even pregnancy.

"I'm all ears," Luca said.

Saoirse gave us a nod of encouragement, and Weston watched his brother intensely.

Miles took a breath. "Daisy, her brother Reed, and I are moving to Sacramento next week."

"What?" Elise gasped. "Next week?"

"What about Peak?" Luca swiveled to Saoirse. "What about Peak?" he repeated.

She patted his arm. "It's okay, love. Just listen."

Miles was most worried how Weston would react. Despite everything, he still looked up to his big brother and didn't want to disappoint him.

"I'm not leaving Peak," Miles explained. "Saoirse and I have always talked about expanding to work with businesses in other states, and this is part of that. I'll be able to take meetings online and commute when I need to. The timing works well, since we've promoted Rebecca to junior strategist. She can pick up the day-to-day slack while I'm in California."

"You knew about this?" Elise asked Saoirse.

"I did. I'm pretty heartbroken Miles won't be in the office with me every day, but as far as the business goes, I think we have a solid plan on how it will work."

Miles winked at her. "It's kind of our job."

She laughed. "That it is."

Weston cleared his throat. "And Grazing by Daisy? How about that?"

I let Miles take this one.

"Mom decided to take it upon herself to sabotage Daisy's business. She's gotten all her friends to spread the word not to use Grazing for events. All the contacts we made, the work we did schmoozing with people I wouldn't be caught dead with otherwise, was wasted."

Weston tensed, gripping the edge of the table. "What was her goal in doing this?"

"I can only assume she did it to get me to call her," Miles explained.

Weston leaned forward, intent on his brother. "What did she have to say for herself?"

He shrugged. "I wouldn't know. Didn't call her. My girl pointed out I'd be playing right into her hands if I did, so we just let it go."

"You let it go?" Weston repeated, perplexed.

I squeezed Miles' hand. "Bea and I don't need those jobs. They would have been nice, but we're going to be fine without them. And once I remove the Dunham name from the Denver side of Grazing, she's not going to have any trouble filling up those empty spots."

Weston blinked. "I'm—you're letting our mother get away with this?"

Miles stared down his nose at his brother. "We're changing courses so I don't have to get wrapped up in that never-ending toxic cycle." He lifted our joined hands and kissed my knuckles. "Again, I got that from Daisy-daze."

"That must've been hard," Elise said. "To stand by and not do anything."

"It was hard to see my girl hurt by my own mother. But I stood by in awe as she dusted herself off and moved on, never once blaming me," Miles replied.

"You're not responsible for your mother," I reminded him. "Neither of you are."

"Hmm." Weston's hum came from deep within his chest. "I don't know about that."

"I do," Elise said softly. "I'm relieved you've finally cut ties, Miles."

He nodded. "It's been interesting to get used to. I didn't know how heavy the weight of keeping her happy was until it was gone—mostly gone," he corrected. "I know she won't stop if I'm accessible to her."

Weston's brow pinched. "You felt moving was your only option?"

Miles looked at me, and I nodded before taking over.

"One of the first things Miles told me was he didn't want to live in Denver forever, and I've always known I didn't want to die in the same place I grew up."

Weston shifted. "I remember you saying that on our hike."

"Yeah." I gave him a crooked smile, pleased he'd paid such close attention. "We took a trip to Sacramento and loved it. Our names didn't carry the burden they do here. My brother made friends with some kids he's still talking to in a chat group. It was nice to just...feel new. So, when we decided we needed to leave Denver, it was obvious to all of us Sacramento was where we'd start fresh."

Miles kissed my knuckles again. "Daisy's too modest to mention she's already landed a lucrative contract with the state senate building manager. And Lily has been spreading the word about her services."

"I think my mother loves Daisy more than me," Saoirse confirmed with a grin.

Luca tossed his hands out. "Even Lily knew about this? Next, you'll tell me Clementine knows."

"Of course she does, my love." Saoirse leaned into her husband. "Clem knows all."

"Josephine's going to miss you," Elliot said flatly, like he was pissed on his daughter's behalf. "I think you're making the right decision. I would do the same in your position."

Miles stared at him for a long moment before nodding. "Thank you, Elliot. That means a lot coming from you." He said this with all the sincerity in the world.

Elliot dropped his chin. "As long as you intend on Facetiming and visiting my daughter frequently."

That made him cackle. "Yep. I'm going to be coming back here at least once a month, and Joey is welcome to call me any time she demands it."

There were a few nods of approval around the table. I hoped it was obvious we'd put a lot of thought into our plans.

"How old is your brother?" Kit asked me.

"Reed is fourteen. He'll be fifteen at the end of August, right before he starts tenth grade. He's the reason our move is happening so quickly. I want to keep his privacy, but I can tell you two weeks ago, he was in crisis, and my family came to realize how bad his situation had become. We've decided, as a family, he'll have a better shot at happiness living with Miles and me in Sacramento the next three years."

"He can stay with us after he graduates too," Miles added.

"Of course." I smiled at him, a surge of love hitting me in the face. "He'll probably be sick of us by then."

"I can't imagine he'd be sick of *me*," he teased.

"Shut up, Spreadsheet," I murmured.

With a low sob, Elise got up from her seat, circled behind Weston, and threw her arms around Miles then me. Her breaths were shuddery as she gave us a watery smile.

"My brother dropped everything for me when I needed him when I was in high school," she whispered. "Sorry, I just—I love that you're doing this for him. He'll never forget the way you're going to the mat for him."

Miles stood and pulled her into his arms, giving her an all-encompassing hug. My eyes fell on Weston, who was watching his brother and wife with an expression I couldn't decipher.

Then his gaze flicked to mine. "Thank you," he murmured. "For standing with him."

"He's taking on me and my teenage brother," I replied. "I'm sort of madly in love with the guy."

That got a smile from Weston and an "aww" from Saoirse and Kit.

And just like that, the hard part was out of the way. We were peppered with questions for the rest of brunch, but the tone had switched from challenging to genuine curiosity. They seemed to understand we weren't moving on a whim. We were going to save my brother's life and carve out a new one for ourselves.

In the end, we hugged and kissed everyone, promising to stop by Elliot and Kit's to squeeze baby Joey before we left. Weston and Elise lingered until it was the four of us outside the restaurant.

"I never pictured you leaving," Weston said.

Miles slipped his arm around my waist. "I never had the right reason to."

"I think you're making the right decision," he added.

Miles nodded. "I know we are, but it's really fucking great to have your support."

Elise looked up at her husband then back at us. "I hope you know you can always come back."

"We know." I bumped my head against Miles' arm. "Luckily for us, the flight isn't very long."

Weston's eyes narrowed on Miles. "You better not be planning on flying private on your monthly trips back. Do you have any idea the CO2 emissions—"

Miles' cackle cut off Weston's rant. "There's my brother. I'm gonna miss you and Lisie something fierce."

Weston frowned. "That's not an answer."

Miles laughed harder. "I guess you'll have to wait and see."

After a few more hugs, we walked away, melting into each other from laughter.

"His face," Miles chuckled. "I bet he waited as long as he could to bring up CO2 emissions."

"He loves you. They all do."

"I know," he said with an assuredness I hadn't heard from him regarding the affections of his friends. "And I love you, Daisy-daze. I'm so fucking excited for what comes next."

Packing. Cleaning. Driving for two days. Repeating the process in reverse. I honestly couldn't wait either. With Miles and Reed, we were bound to make it fun.

"Me too, Miles. Me too."

We wove our hands together and walked toward our next adventure.

Hopefully   in love.

EPILOGUE

Miles

Three Years Later

I RIGHTED THE CAP on Reed's head and straightened the dangling tassel, trying my damnedest not to weep. But god*damn* was it a losing game.

"You look good, kid," I choked out.

He laughed at me right to my face. "I knew you were going to cry."

"Yeah, well, crying is just a physical release of emotion. Am I not allowed to be emotional about my boy graduating high school?"

Looking away, he scrubbed his mouth with his hand and shrugged. "It's all right I guess." The thickness of his voice hadn't gotten past me. There was a time, not too long ago, he didn't think he'd get to this day. "I'm the one who has to go out there and walk across the stage. Don't try to make me cry with you."

"Then I suggest you not look at your sister," I murmured.

Of course, we both did at the same time.

Daisy had just come down the steps and caught sight of us. One hand cupped her bowling ball belly, the other was pressed to her cheek—a sure sign of imminent tears.

Reed shielded his eyes. "No. Not you too."

She waved her hand in front of her face. "I'm trying, but you just look so cute in your cap and gown, and this creature inside me is pressing directly on my heart bones. I have no control over myself at the moment."

"There's no such thing as heart bones," Reed chided.

She put her fists on her hips. "Then explain what I'm feeling inside right now." She paused, waiting for either of us to say anything. We did not. We knew better by now.

"That's what I thought." She padded across the living room of the house we bought soon after moving to Sacramento, barreling directly into Reed. He caught her easily and took all her weight, wrapping his arms around her gingerly. Since she'd gotten pregnant, he'd basically tiptoed around her, nervous to jostle or startle her.

It was cute as hell, and I loved seeing him care so deeply for his sister and future nephew.

She was seven months pregnant, and with her small stature and delicate frame, she truly looked like she'd swallowed a watermelon. I found it hard to believe her belly could get any bigger, but I never doubted Daisy could do anything she set her mind to, including carry my massive son to term.

"I love you, Reed. I couldn't be prouder of you," she said against his chest.

He gently patted his sister's back, looking at me with a slight panic. Not because of the hug. Hugs were commonplace around here. But because Daisy had let loose a sob to end all sobs.

"Love you too, Daze."

He passed my crying wife to me and skedaddled out of the living room. Probably to text his girlfriend about his guardians traumatizing him with their great big love for him.

I took Daisy to the couch and let her cry against me, splaying my hand on her belly. We had time before the ceremony and the descent of the Dunhams and Aldrichs to get some tears out.

The last three years had been the easiest of my life. Not at first, of course. We'd all been off-kilter when we'd arrived, and Daisy and I had been watching Reed like a hawk. We'd gotten him in therapy right away, but the thing that made the biggest difference had been starting school and getting to be a regular kid. Still quirky, but he'd found his people who'd enjoyed what he did, sat with him at lunch, and invited him out on the weekends.

Once he was settled, Daisy and I had been able to breathe and fall in love all over again. We hadn't had to wait for the next shoe to drop or look over our shoulders. No exes or crazy mothers showing up on our doorsteps. No one gasped when we said our last names. We could just be Daisy and Miles with our boy Reed. Because that was what he became. Not our son, but something more than a brother. Our boy.

He'd helped me plan my proposal when we'd been here for three months, and when Daisy and I had gotten married on the one-year anniversary of our first meeting, he'd stood up for me along with Weston.

Funny thing was, somewhere along the way, West and Elise had taken to Reed too. We'd hosted them at our place just as often as we'd been back to visit them. At least, until their son, Elias, had been born last year. Now, we'd been crashing with them much more frequently to get that baby fix.

Solomon climbed up on the couch and rested his narrow head on Daisy's belly—his favorite spot since she'd conceived.

"He's going to be such a good big brother," Daisy said as she stroked his fur.

"Thank god we're having a baby for him. He's going to go into mourning when Reed leaves for college."

"We all are." She sniffed. "But it's good. Berkeley isn't that far."

"Not far at all." I rubbed the underside of her belly, feeling Baby Boy rolling around. She placed her hand over mine and gave me a lopsided smile.

"We'll be happy too, and we'll hold onto it."

"That's what we do, Cupcake. Hold onto happiness for all its worth."

We'd had a lot of that over the years. Grazing by Daisy and Bea was steadily growing. Daisy still held the state senate contract, and through the contacts she'd made, she'd booked enough jobs to keep her busy and the business flush. My girl was proud of what she'd built, along with Bea, who was killing it in Denver. More than anything, I loved seeing her take pride in her accomplishments.

She inspired me not to slack off, which used to be a bad habit of mine. I kept striving so I'd be a partner she could be proud of too.

She was good about telling me she was. Always baking me cupcakes to celebrate my small and big wins. Never failing to remind me I was as important to her and this family as she was to me.

Even on the bad days—and there were some, like when my mother had managed to call from a number that wasn't blocked—I held tight to the happiness Daisy and I had created. There was enough of it, it never faded.

Reed tromped down the stairs, making as much noise as a herd of buffalo in his size thirteen shoes. The kid had surpassed my height at six and a half feet tall and had finally filled out. Since last year, he'd had girls calling and texting at all hours, but he seemed pretty stuck on the one he'd started dating the beginning of his senior year. We'd see how college went.

Oh shit.

There I went, getting choked up again.

"Are all eyes dry?" Reed called warily.

"I don't know what you want from us," Daisy lamented. "If you think we're bad, just wait a half-hour for Mama. She's going to be bawling."

He slapped his forehead. "Can you keep her away from me until after the ceremony? I don't want everyone's last memory of me to be crying like a baby walking across the stage. I'd like to leave high school with a little cred."

"Don't worry, Reed. No one's cooler than you," I assured him.

He stomped back up the stairs, leaving us in a fit of quiet laughter. Solomon *ruffed* at Daisy for his bouncing pillow, but he put up with it like the Velcro he was.

"Do you have any idea how much I love you, Miles?" She threaded her fingers through mine. "Not many men would have stayed after sitting on the bridge three years ago. But you, you never faltered. You took on a teenage boy and his grumpy sister and loved us so well without ever asking for a single thing in return."

I shook my head. "I didn't have to ask, Daisy. You've given me everything. And anyone who would've walked away after the bridge wouldn't have been worthy of you and Reed."

"I love you so much, Spreadsheet." She smiled up at me like she always did when she called me that. "Tell me you love me so I don't cry right now."

I took her face in my hands and rubbed the jut of her lower lip. My own personal storm cloud. The kind welcome after a blistering day in the sun. That brought life and relief. My Daisy.

"I love you, Daisy Ethel Aldrich. There is not a chance on this green earth I'll ever stop."

<hr>

We're not leaving Denver yet!

The Mile High Billions series is coming and Clara, Shira, and Bea are going to find their own happy endings.

Clara's book, In The Details, is coming Fall 2024! Preorder now: https://mybook.to/InTheDetails

The Traveling Roses

Want to meet Daisy's distant rock star cousin, Callum Rose? https://mybook.to/StoneColdNotes

They called him Stone Cold.

Once upon a time, I called him my pen pal.

When I wrote to Callum Rose five years ago, I never expected a response. He was an up and coming rock star, afterall, and I was just a shy seventeen-year-old. He did write back though, and through **hundreds of emails**, we became best friends.

Until the day we unknowingly broke each other's heart.

It's been three years since our last email. I'm all grown up with a new job at Good Music, and finally have my act together. But then Callum Rose walks in the door, and I'm instantly thrown back to the days when he meant everything to me.

The thing is…he doesn't know who I am. He's never seen my face. And this Callum Rose lives up to his stone cold reputation.

That is, until one night, he sees me in another man's arms, and decides to claim me. Then there is *nothing* cold about him.

Callum becomes a man on fire for *me*, introverted, awkward, chubby Wren Anderson. He's **obsessive, possessive, and kind of stalker-y**—and I like it…a little too much. The problem is, he still doesn't know I'm the girl who walked away from him *or* the reason behind it, and I'm afraid when he finds out, I'll be right back in the cold again.

PLAYLIST

"I Wanna Be Yours" Arctic Monkeys

"Sex, Drugs, Etc." Beach Weather

"Beautiful Things" Benson Boone

"Big Love Ahead" Mon Rovia

"Daylight" David Kushner

"4runner" Brenn!

"Beggar's Song" Matt Maeson

"Go Easy" Matt Maeson

"Stick Season-Stutter" Stutter Techno, dreamy

"Miserable Man" David Kushner

"Bad idea" Girl in Red

"Ceilings" Lizzy McAlpine

"Half a Man" Dean Lewis

"I am not who I was" Chance Pena

"Reckless" Madison Beer

"Heart Like Yours" Williamette Stone

"Love in the Dark" Adele

https://open.spotify.com/playlist/2ilLwEUJ6uDP5uX22jpwkq?si=fc6c3b7df07946d9

THANK YOU TO...

You know Miles wasn't supposed to get a book, right? Westie, Luca, and Elliot were my main men and Miles was just a goofy side character. But no, you guys loved him at first sight. After Dear Grumpy Boss came out, I can't tell you how many people checked to make sure Miles was getting his own book. As the series went on, and his character grew in depth and richness, I knew there was no way I couldn't give him a story. So this book, my dear readers, exists because of YOU. You asked, emailed, begged, and I was very easily convinced.

Thank you for loving Miles. He's now one of my very favorites!

Thank you to Kate Farlow, my cover designer, for absolutely killing this series. She came up with the series name and helped brainstorm the title for this book, not to mention looking through hundreds of pictures to help me choose the handsome fellas on the covers!

A big shout out to Jenn for beta reading this book and answering my myriad questions.

Thank you to Monica for your editing genius and Laura for stepping in at the last minute to proofread.

I would be remiss if I didn't thank the countless bookstagrammers and TikTokers who blasted their love of P.S. You're Intolerable to the world. You guys really shined a light on the whole series when you fell in love with Elliot, and that has meant everything to me. I hope you love Miles and Daisy just as much!

www.ingramcontent.com/pod-product-compliance
Lightning Source LLC
Chambersburg PA
CBHW070405310726
48977CB00003B/569